Praise for
Vienna Secrets

"Outstanding . . . Tallis's darkest and most compelling novel to date."
—*Sunday Times* (London)

"Tallis is exploring serious themes here—among them, the political and religious climate that made the rise of fascism possible, and the conflict between secular and religious ethical systems."
—*The Spectator* (London)

"[*Vienna Secrets*] has a strong, intelligent plot and a terrific atmosphere of fin-de-siècle Vienna."
—*The Times* (London)

Praise for
Fatal Lies

"Tallis's singular achievement is to bring vividly to life many of the glories and dangers of a great city at a crucial moment in its history. . . . Immensely satisfying. . . . The author delights us with rich, often gorgeous prose. . . . [He] has an exceptional ability to move seamlessly among varied plot elements, characters and emotions. . . . If you're looking for the best in popular fiction, it's well worth seeking out."

—*The Washington Post*

"Frank Tallis has surged to the front of the field riding his dark horse, Vienna in the last days of the Austro-Hungarian Empire. . . . While it's always a delight to visit the ballrooms where Strauss is played and the opera house where Mahler is rehearsing and the coffeehouses where ideas are devoured *mit Schlag*, this smart series has far more to offer than decorative charm."

—*The New York Times Book Review*

"Another immensely satisfying novel in Frank Tallis's intelligent and subtle Dr. Liebermann/Inspector Rheinhardt series . . . dense, engrossing . . . a fine adventure."

—*The Boston Globe*

"St. Florian's Military Academy outside Vienna serves as the forbidding backdrop for Tallis's stellar third historical to feature Insp. Oskar Rheinhardt and Dr. Max Liebermann. . . . Several late twists lead to a startling resolution of this compelling tale."

—*Publishers Weekly* (starred review)

"What is basically a murder mystery becomes something quite extraordinary as Tallis skillfully weaves in the politics, history, music, and social customs of turn-of-the-century Vienna. Another outstanding entry in an erudite and mesmerizing series; a must for historical-mystery devotees."

—*Booklist* (starred review)

"Elegant . . . Tallis has come up with a particularly ingenious method of murder. . . . His novels show the modern world coming into existence in one of Europe's great cities, and are all the more poignant for the knowledge that the first world war will soon cast its shadow over his deeply human characters."

—*The Sunday Times* (London)

"[Tallis's] handling of the psychoanalysis and criminal pathology are fantastic . . . a romping tale."   —*Scotland on Sunday*

Praise for
Vienna Blood

"A dazzling tour de force."   —*The Washington Post*

"[Tallis] cunningly folds psychoanalysis, early forensics, eugenics, music, and literature into a captivating suspense novel."   —*The Boston Globe*

"A murder mystery of great intelligence . . . a fascinating portrait of one of the most vibrant yet sinister cities of fin-de-siècle Europe."   —*The Times* (London)

"Tallis uses his knowledge of medicine, music, psychology and history to create an endlessly fascinating portrait of 1902 Vienna."   —*Kirkus Reviews* (starred review)

"Brilliant . . . Tallis can ratchet up the suspense."   —*The Globe and Mail*

"Gripping . . . The clever plotting and quality writing elevate this above most other historicals."   —*Publishers Weekly* (starred review)

"Excellent . . . Tallis handles his themes adroitly."   —*The Sunday Times* (London)

"Exhilarating . . . expertly crafted . . . The layers of Viennese society are peeled away as delicately as the layers of each mouth-watering Viennese pastry that the portly Rheinhardt makes it his business to devour."   —*The Daily Telegraph* (London)

Praise for
A Death in Vienna

"[An] elegant historical mystery . . . stylishly presented and intelligently resolved."
—*The New York Times Book Review*

"[*A Death in Vienna* is] a winner for its smart and fin-de-siècle portrait of the seat of the Austro-Hungarian empire, and for introducing Max Liebermann, a young physician who is feverish with the possibilities of the new science of psychoanalysis."
—*The Washington Post*

"Frank Tallis knows what he's writing about in this excellent mystery. . . . His writing and feel for the period are top class."
—*The Times* (London)

"An engrossing portrait of a legendary period as well as a brain teaser of startling perplexity . . . In Tallis's sure hands, the story evolves with grace and excitement. . . . A perfect combination of the hysterical past and the cooler—but probably more dangerous—present."
—*Chicago Tribune*

"Holmes meets Freud in this enjoyable . . . whodunit."
—*The Guardian* (London)

Vienna Secrets

Vienna Secrets

A Max Liebermann Mystery

FRANK TALLIS

VOLUME FOUR OF THE
LIEBERMANN PAPERS

RANDOM HOUSE TRADE PAPERBACKS

NEW YORK

A Random House Trade Paperback Original

Copyright © 2009 by Frank Tallis
Dossier copyright © 2010 by Random House, Inc.

Published in the United States by Random House Trade Paperbacks,
an imprint of The Random House Publishing Group,
a division of Random House, Inc., New York.

RANDOM HOUSE TRADE PAPERBACKS and colophon
are trademarks of Random House, Inc.
MORTALIS and colophon are trademarks of Random House, Inc.

Originally published in the United Kingdom by Arrow Books,
an imprint of The Random House Group, Ltd., in 2009.

LIBRARY OF CONGRESS CATALOGING-IN-PUBLICATION DATA
Tallis, Frank.
Vienna Secrets : a Max Liebermann mystery / Frank Tallis.
p.   cm.
ISBN 978-0-8129-8099-8
eBook ISBN 978-1-58836-944-4
1. Liebermann, Max (Fictitious character)—Fiction.   2. Psychoanalysts—Fiction.
3. Police—Austria—Vienna—Fiction.   4. Vienna (Austria)—Fiction.   I. Title.
PR6120.A44F38 2009
823'.92—dc22   2008023474

Printed in the United States of America

www.mortalis-books.com

2 4 6 8 9 7 5 3 1

To Paul Samet
For a gift I will treasure

Part One

The Breaking of the Vessels

I

LIEBERMANN STEPPED DOWN FROM the cab.

Two constables wearing long coats and spiked helmets were standing in the middle of the street, ready to block the passage of traffic. One of them came forward.

"Herr Dr. Liebermann?"

"Yes."

"This way, please."

The sun had barely risen, and the morning air was cold and dank. Ahead, four black lacquered carriages were parked: one of them was a windowless mortuary van. A flash of bright light unsettled the horses, signaling the presence of a police photographer. As Liebermann and his companion advanced, a cobbled concourse came into view, dominated by a white church with a convex baroque façade.

"Maria Treue Kirche," said the constable.

Liebermann had often passed the church on his way to the Josefstadt theatre, but he had never paused to appreciate its size. He had to tilt his head back to see it all. Two spires, each decorated with a girdle of globes, flanked a classical columned pediment. A gilt inscription declared *Virgo Fidelis Ave Coelestis Mater Amoris*, and below this was a clock face showing the early hour: six o'clock. Winged figures peered over the gable. They were disporting themselves beneath a gold crucifix, enhanced with radial spokes to represent rays of divine light.

On both sides of the concourse were identical three-story buildings. They were plain, functional structures, with roughcast walls.

Liebermann saw the word "gymnasium" carved beneath a stone escutcheon.

In front of the church were two gas lamps, and around one of these a loose group of men had assembled. The photographer and his assistant were preparing to take another photograph. Again, there was a brilliant flash, which exposed something dark and shapeless on the ground. The smoke from the magnesium ribbon hung motionless in the air. Liebermann was dimly aware of clopping hooves and a nervous whinnying.

One of the men turned round, a portly gentleman with a well-waxed upturned mustache.

"Max!"

Detective Inspector Oskar Rheinhardt marched over to greet his friend. "Thank you for coming, Max."

The constable clicked his heels and hurried back to his post.

"When did you receive Haussmann's call?"

"About five," Liebermann replied, stifling a yawn.

"I'm sorry," said Rheinhardt, his eyes luminous with compunction. "I thought, as you do not live so very far away . . ."

"Of course," said Liebermann, unable to disguise a note of reproach.

"What time must you be at the hospital?"

"Seven-thirty."

Rheinhardt nodded and invited him to follow.

"Did Haussmann explain?"

"Yes, he did."

"You know what to expect, then. Good."

Grasping the photographer's arm, Rheinhardt said, "A moment, please." He then ushered his friend forward.

Within the circle of light around the gas lamp was what appeared at first to be a heap of clothes. It was situated within a large area of reflective blackness, the edges of which were irregular—like the borders of a country on a map. The air smelled faintly of rusting iron.

"Brother Stanislav," said Rheinhardt.

The monk's body appeared shapeless on account of the habit worn by the Piarist order. It was similar to that of the Jesuits—closed at the front, with three leather buttons. The corpse was supine, its feet hidden beneath the hem. A hand with curled fingers stuck out on one side. This pallid bony claw was the only visible part of Brother Stanislav. The cowl was sodden, flat, and unmistakably empty.

Liebermann looked beyond the body and located the monk's head. He had been forewarned, but this did little to mitigate the shock.

"He was discovered at about half past three," said Rheinhardt. "One of the Piarists—Brother Wendelin—could not sleep, and came out for some fresh air."

"Where is Brother Wendelin now?" asked Liebermann.

"In the church, praying."

"Did he see or hear anything?"

"Nothing at all."

Liebermann advanced, and made his way—somewhat warily—around the expanse of congealed blood. He squatted, and looked directly into the truncated stump of the monk's neck. The dawn sky provided him with just enough light to identify the remains of the key cervical structures; however, what he observed was nothing like the cross sections that he remembered from his anatomy classes, which had resembled the fatty marbled meat of a freshly sliced joint. The aperture of the trachea was displaced, as were the hardened remnants of cartilage. The vertebrae were fractured, and the muscles ripped and twisted. A rubbery length of artery hung out over the trapezius, still dripping. Something purple, veined, and lobulated was lying on the ground close to the monk's right shoulder. Liebermann guessed that it might be a piece of the thyroid gland.

A memory of his old anatomy professor's voice invaded Liebermann's mind: *scalenus medius, sternocleidomastoid, omohyoid.* The young doctor was perplexed. He was not a pathologist, but he knew enough anatomy to be deeply troubled by what he saw.

"What is it, Max?"

Liebermann waved his hand, indicating that he was not ready to comment. He stood up and moved toward the severed head. It seemed to take him an inordinate amount of time to travel the relatively short distance—and all the while the horrific object exercised a curious fascination. He could hear Rheinhardt following behind him and the sound of muted voices. The world seemed to recede.

Again, Liebermann bent down.

The dead monk's face was pressed against the cobbles, eyes closed, lips parted: hair and beard flecked with silver, pale skin maculated with spots of blood. His large aquiline nose was bent to one side. Even though Liebermann was all too aware that the object of his attention was insensate, he was suddenly seized by a powerful urge to reach out and rotate the head so that the monk would experience less discomfort. Years of adjusting the position of patients in their beds had made his concern instinctive, even, as now, in circumstances of unquestionable redundancy.

Liebermann scrutinized the monk's neck and noted once more the same anatomical havoc: stretched and contorted musculature, identical displacements and splintering. The macabre skirt of papery skin was particularly disturbing.

"Well?" said Rheinhardt.

Liebermann stood up.

"It looks as if the head has been . . . *torn* from the body."

"That's what I thought. Perhaps I should go to the Prater this afternoon."

"I'm sorry?"

"To interview the strongmen."

*The sound of a barrel organ: gentlemen in white body stockings and black
trunks, tensing their arms to make their biceps bulge.*

Liebermann couldn't imagine one of those vain, posturing clowns
grasping the monk's head and ripping it from his shoulders.

"Oskar," said Liebermann. "Do you realize how much force is required to pull someone's head off?"

"Considerable force, obviously."

"Even with a horse—and some means of holding the body still—
it would still be difficult."

"Then it was several men?"

"Perhaps . . ."

"How many?"

"Two or three heavy fellows sitting on the body, and a third and
fourth to turn the head . . . but it would still have taken a while."

"How long?"

"It's difficult to say. But however long it might have taken, they
don't seem to have been terribly concerned about being caught! They
performed their heinous act under the gas lamp! Observe the pattern
created by the flow of blood." The young doctor re-created the out-
pouring in the air with his hands. "Look at those splashes, which
show us how the head rolled away from the body. Brother Stanislav
was almost certainly decapitated as he lay on the ground in the very
position we currently find him; however, he might not have been
conscious when he was killed. His eyes are closed. . . . A man struggling against four or five assailants would almost certainly have had
his eyes wide open when the spinal cord was severed."

"Couldn't the murderers have closed his eyes after the head was
removed?"

"Well, they could. But it would be a strange thing to do, don't you
think? Closing the eyes of the dead is usually a sign of respect."

The door of the church was unlatched, and an elderly monk appeared. He saw Rheinhardt and made his way over.

"Father?" said Rheinhardt.

"My son, the children..." He looked exasperated. "Brother Stanislav's remains must be removed before the school opens. I'm afraid I cannot allow—"

"Our work is almost done," Rheinhardt interrupted. "It won't be long now, I promise you." He turned to Liebermann. "Excuse us." He then signed for the photographer to continue and steered the old monk back toward the church.

In spite of the presence of so many men it was remarkably quiet. The police team spoke in hushed, reverential tones.

On the other side of the road, facing the church, were some mansion blocks. Liebermann's view was partially obscured by a monument—a pillar of stone rising out of the concourse and surmounted by a statue of the Virgin Mary. It was as high as an Egyptian obelisk. He went to take a closer look.

At the base of the column were three large figures. The first of these held an open book and possessed an unusually compassionate face: head tilted forward, melancholy eyes, and creases suggesting depth of feeling. The figure wore robes of stone that had been masterfully sculpted into sensuous layers and folds. He or she—for the gender was ambiguous—wore a generous hood, beneath which hair flowed back in delicate waves. Liebermann admired the artistry that had gone into the figure's hands, which were delicate and beautifully poised. He noticed—with some regret—that one of the fingers had been broken.

Liebermann walked around the column and paused to consider the second figure. It too was hooded, but the hood enveloped a face invested with less sentiment: a long curly beard, staring eyes, and a somewhat vacant expression. Two birds, possibly doves, sat on a featureless slab held in the saint's left hand.

The third figure, a bearded man with no hood, was more interesting than the second. His gown billowed out, as if caught in a breeze.

One of his arms was extended, and his posture suggested that he intended the passerby to look toward something from which he had averted his gaze. He rested a hand on his heart, an attitude that evoked sympathy.

This holy triumvirate was arranged around the pedestal of the column, on which a number of other figures of varying sizes (angels, cherubs, and knights) were mounted. The column itself rose to a great height and was decorated with a spiral motif of disembodied putti; however, their chubby little faces did not look happy. Indeed, the effect was quite sinister. It was as if the stone were sucking them in like quicksand.

On top of the column was a golden globe out of which projected two sharp horns, and on this ball of metal stood the Virgin. A ring of stars circled her head, and her hands were pressed together in prayer.

Liebermann took a step backward to get a better view and trod in what he thought at first was horse manure. He grimaced as he felt his foot sink into it; however, when he looked down, he saw that the cobbles were covered with scattered earth. He had to pick his way through the clods to avoid getting more on his shoes.

Rheinhardt had finished talking to the old monk and was now issuing instructions to the men standing beneath the gas lamp. The photographer lifted the camera off its tripod and placed it on the ground. There then followed a general dispersal. The inspector's assistant—Haussmann—ran over to the mortuary van and spoke to the driver. The van then turned a full circle in the street before mounting the pavement and rumbling onto the concourse. Some of the constables had to look lively to get out of its way.

"Well," Rheinhardt called as he approached, "what do you think?"

Liebermann grasped his chin, and tapped his pursed lips with his index finger.

"An anticlerical group?"

"Who?"

Liebermann shrugged.

"Or some former pupils, originally educated by Brother Stanislav, who returned to settle a score? A payback for some cruelty, some violation, perpetrated when they were powerless to retaliate."

"He was a priest!" said Rheinhardt, balking a little.

Liebermann threw his friend a look of wry amusement. He did not believe that an outward show of piety automatically merited respect.

"One should never underestimate the murderous rage of children. It is fierce, and unfettered by civilizing influences. I can well imagine some cherished infantile fantasy of revenge, shared by a close group of friends, festering, incubating in the unconscious, generating tension over many years—the release of which could then only ever be achieved by the performance of a brutal, cathartic murder. Ritualistic acts often focus and channel the energies of a community. They provide a means of safe discharge. Think, for example, of our funeral services and ceremonies. Appalling and otherwise unmanageable grief is contained by the time-honored practice of vigils, processing, and rites. There is certainly something ritualistic about decapitation. I wonder whether it served some similar purpose." Liebermann turned and faced the column. "What is this?"

"A plague monument, like the one on the Graben."

"And who are these figures?"

They began to walk around the pedestal.

"This, I believe, is Saint Anna," said Rheinhardt, pointing to the androgynous figure with the compassionate face. "Mother of the Virgin. I don't know who the fellow with the two birds is supposed to be, but this one here"—Rheinhardt nodded at the final statue—"is almost certainly Saint Joseph, husband of the Virgin. Do you want me to find out who the fellow with the birds is?"

Before Liebermann could answer, he slipped on the cobbles. Rheinhardt caught his arm.

"Have you noticed all this mud?" exclaimed the young doctor. "It couldn't have been carried on people's shoes. There's too much of it. Is there a garden close by?"

"Not that I know of." Rheinhardt squatted down. "*They* might have arrived in a carriage ..." The inspector squeezed some of the mud between his thumb and forefinger. "It could have been stuck to the wheels."

"In which case there should be wheel tracks. Can you see any?"

Rheinhardt studied the ground.

"Then perhaps it is inconsequential. Someone was carrying pots here earlier—and dropped them."

Liebermann scraped his feet on the iron railings surrounding the pedestal. The mud was sticky and not easily displaced.

"I can't attend a ward round with dirty shoes."

"No," said Rheinhardt. "That would be a catastrophe, I'm sure."

Liebermann ignored the inspector's pointed remark. Dirty shoes might not seem very important to Rheinhardt, especially when set against murder; however, in Vienna, a doctor indifferent to sartorial etiquette might just as well give up medicine. Liebermann took out a handkerchief, bent over, and started to polish.

Rheinhardt raised his gaze to the sky.

"What are you doing? There's a shoeblack who sets up a stall just outside the theatre. He'll be there in a few minutes!"

Liebermann was not prepared to wait.

2

MENDEL LIEBERMANN HAD NOT been very attentive during Professor Freud's lecture. The first part—a history of the scientific study of dreams—had been quite interesting, but the second part, which had dealt mainly with the professor's recent discoveries, seemed impenetrable. It wasn't the first time that Mendel had heard Freud talk at the B'nai B'rith lodge. Freud had addressed the brethren many times before, and when he wasn't talking about his psychological theories, Mendel found him perfectly intelligible, even entertaining. His talks on "The Goals and Purposes of the B'nai B'rith Order" and "The Role of Women in Our Union" were perceptive and thought-provoking; however, when Freud spoke about psychoanalysis, Mendel became utterly lost.

The audience was still clapping when Mendel turned to his son and said, "I'm not sure I understood very much of that."

"What didn't you understand?"

"He said that dreams are about events that happen the previous day—but on the other hand, he said that dreams are to do with forbidden wishes. So what are they? Memories of the previous day—or wishes? . . . I don't understand."

"They're both, Father," said Liebermann.

Mendel stroked his beard and glowered at his son.

"What does that mean? Both? In life, things are usually either one thing or another. Can't you doctors explain things in a straightforward way . . . a way that someone like me, a simple businessman, can understand? As a rule, if something can't be communicated in plain German, then it's probably not worth knowing. That's what I believe, anyway."

"Very well," Liebermann said. "Think of it like this: in every business undertaking there is a capitalist—who covers the required outlay—and an entrepreneur, who has the idea and knows how to carry it out. In the construction of dreams, the part of the capitalist is played by the *unconscious wish*: it provides the energy for the dream to be made. The entrepreneur is the *day's residues*. It is the *day's residues* that determine how the outlay is to be spent. There! Is that plain enough for you?"

"Yes, that's plain enough. If Professor Freud had put it in those terms, I'd have had no trouble following him."

"He did, Father. You just weren't listening."

Mendel waved his hand in the air, as if to say that the subject was closed.

"Come," Mendel said curtly. "Let's go."

Liebermann and his father made their way toward the door. They passed Professor Freud, who was being detained at the rostrum by a few men asking questions. One of them had raised his voice. He didn't sound very friendly. In an adjacent room, drinks were being served. Father and son positioned themselves by a window overlooking Universitätsstrasse. Outside, it had started to rain.

"See him over there. Do you know who that man is?"

"What?" said Liebermann, pulling his head out from behind the curtains.

Mendel tutted.

"Nathaniel Rothenstein. The banker. As rich as . . . What's the expression?"

"Croesus."

"Yes, as rich as Croesus."

Rothenstein was a tall, handsome man in his mid-fifties with an impressive head of hair, brushed back like a poet's.

"I don't know who the other fellow is," Mendel added pensively.

The banker was talking to an older gentleman whose bald, perspiring head was gleaming beneath a gaslight. His grizzled beard was thick, long, and rather unkempt. A pair of pince-nez balanced on his long, straight nose. He was evidently talking with some passion, as his hands repeatedly chopped the air.

"I think he's an academic," said Liebermann.

"Is he?"

"Yes, I'm sure I've seen him at the university. I think he's a professor, a member of the philosophy faculty."

"A friend of Professor Freud's, perhaps?"

"No, I don't think so."

Mendel's interest in the identity of Rothenstein's companion was short-lived. "Banking," he sighed, his thoughts returning to Rothenstein. "If I had my time again, that's what I'd do. The textile business is all well and good, but it's only one step removed from the market stall. Banking is something else entirely, a different world. A man like Rothenstein doesn't have to concern himself with factory managers like Doubek, or suppliers like Zedlacher and Krakowski. He doesn't have to go to Prague to check up on incompetent accountants! Which reminds me—another trip is well overdue. No, a man like Rothenstein is invited to the Hofburg. A man like Rothenstein dines with emperors. When Rothenstein speaks, people listen."

"His friend from the university isn't listening," said Liebermann.

Mendel turned sharply.

"Why have you always got to say something *clever*?"

Liebermann did not respond. There wasn't any point. He already knew that if he tried to defend or justify himself it would make matters worse. Mendel's rebuke was simply a venting from a reservoir of suppressed anger (the depth of which the young doctor did not care to contemplate). He had disappointed his father in two ways. First, he had shown no interest in taking over the family business, and second, only five months earlier he had broken off his engagement with Clara Weiss, the daughter of one of Mendel's closest friends. The first of these "disappointments" had placed a considerable strain on their relationship; the second had almost destroyed it. Liebermann's mother had worked a small miracle in getting father and son to talk again; however, the truce that she had brokered was fragile.

Mendel's remark had created an uncomfortable atmosphere that effectively killed further conversation. Subsequently, it was a great relief to father and son when a dapper fellow wearing a spotted bow tie and a floral vest emerged from the crowd and came straight toward them.

"Liebermann," cried the new arrival, taking Mendel's hand and shaking it vigorously.

"Blomberg."

"What did you think of the talk, eh?"

Mendel shook his head. "I didn't really understand it."

"Nor me . . ." Blomberg turned slightly, extending his hand again. "This must be your son—the doctor?"

"Yes, this is Maxim. Maxim—Herr Blomberg. You remember me mentioning Herr Blomberg, don't you? He's the gentleman who owns the department store."

Liebermann bowed. "A pleasure to meet you, Herr Blomberg."

"And you too, dear boy. . . . Dreams, eh? Well, we all have our dreams, don't we? I'm not sure what Professor Freud would make of mine, but I suspect that all my dreams have the same meaning. I have only one wish, and it's certainly not unconscious. Another department store . . . on Kärntnerstrasse!" Blomberg's eyes glinted a little too brightly. "That's what I dream about."

"Have you seen who's here?" asked Mendel, his gaze flicking across the room.

"Rothenstein? Yes, of course. I might try to have a word with him later. You never know, eh?" Blomberg tapped the side of his nose.

Mendel pulled a face.

"Ach! Always the pessimist!" Blomberg raised his hands.

"Pessimist?" said Mendel. "A pessimist is just a well-informed optimist!"

People were still streaming out of the lecture hall and dispersing around the room. They were joined by two more of Mendel's friends, and the conversation turned from business to politics. Liebermann was expecting these men to express views similar to those held by his father. He expected to hear them criticize the mayor and lambast the traditional enemies of Austrian Jewry: the clerics, the aristocracy, and conservative Slavs. They were, however, far less preoccupied and troubled than Mendel. In fact, they were—on the whole—extremely positive about the condition of Jews in Vienna.

Liebermann had declined previous invitations to B'nai B'rith because he had assumed that everyone there would be much the same as his father. Even though he knew that Professor Freud was an active member—and Freud was *certainly* very different from his father—this did little to change his mind. Indeed, he was only attending that evening because his mentor had promised him a particularly lucid account of the dream theory. Now that he was there, standing in the lodge house, he had to admit that B'nai B'rith—which translated solemnly from the Hebrew as *Sons of the Covenant*—was nothing like the organization he had imagined. It was much more like a club for progressive thinkers than a "Jewish society," which made Liebermann wonder why his father was such a regular attendee. He could only conclude—as he frequently did when trying to understand aspects of his father's behavior—that it was *good for business*.

Professor Freud finally emerged from the lecture hall and was now standing on the other side of the room. He was engaged in conversation with a short, spindly youth with closely cropped black hair. Liebermann immediately excused himself from his father's group.

"Professor."

Freud shook Liebermann's hand.

"Delighted you could come." He gestured toward his companion. "Are you acquainted? No. Then allow me to introduce Dr. Gabriel Kusevitsky, a recent convert to our cause. Dr. Kusevitsky—Dr. Max Liebermann."

The youth smiled and inclined his head. He looked far too young to be a doctor.

Liebermann congratulated Freud on his talk, but the professor was dissatisfied. "I should have said more about infant sexuality—but to do so invariably arouses resistances, hostility. Even the scant allusions I made this evening managed to offend some of our little congregation. Had I been addressing a professional body, I would have been more courageous. Still, the audience may yet have derived some benefit."

Liebermann and Kusevitsky were quick to protest.

"The audience will almost certainly have benefited!"

"The dream theory could not have been explained more clearly!"

"Nobody in the audience—at least no thinking person—will ever be able to wake from a dream again without pondering its significance!"

Yes, he might have said more about infant sexuality, but he had surely said enough—given that the audience was mostly laymen.

Freud was gratified by their response but maintained a show of glum indifference. The imposture, however, could not be sustained, and his sober attitude was subverted by the appearance of a sly, almost coy smile.

Their subsequent conversation did not last long. Almost immediately, a plump gentleman with an officious manner approached and said that Freud was needed elsewhere. The second lodge committee (of which Freud was an important member) was having an impromptu meeting by the punch bowl. Freud apologized to his acolytes and allowed the official to whisk him away.

Liebermann and Kusevitsky exchanged pleasantries, praised Freud's genius, and in due course spoke of their respective situations.

It transpired that Kusevitsky had only just completed his medical training and had been awarded a prestigious research scholarship at a private teaching hospital. The post was funded by the Rothenstein foundation.

Kusevitsky nodded discreetly toward the banker. "I have *that* gentleman to thank. It is a great opportunity."

"And what area have you chosen to study?" asked Liebermann.

"Symbolism in dreams," said Kusevitsky. "Professor Freud has suggested that, when interpreting dreams, we must discover what a certain object represents to the dreamer by examining where it stands with respect to his or her unique cluster of experiences and associations. Thus, a horse may represent different things to different people." Kusevitsky had dark, intelligent eyes that floated behind thick spectacle lenses. A tapering wispy beard covered his receding chin. "At the same time," Kusevitsky continued, "Professor Freud has also noted some intriguing regularities, elements that appear and reappear in the dreams of many of his patients and that psychoanalysis has shown us have the exact same meaning. For example, an emperor and empress are often found to represent the dreamer's parents; a prince or princess, the dreamer him- or herself; and so on. . . . I find these common symbols extremely interesting, and believe that they arise from a deeper level of mind."

Liebermann tilted his head quizzically.

"Perhaps," said Kusevitsky, "we possess not only a personal unconscious, in which all our idiosyncratic memories are stored, but in addition a *cultural* unconscious, in which we find the inherited distillations of ancestral experience. We encounter these distillations in the form of symbols, which sometimes emerge in our dreams; however, they can also be identified in other contexts—for example, in our storytelling. Emperors and empresses, princes and princesses frequently appear in myths, legends, and fairy tales."

"You are already familiar, no doubt, with the work of the romantic philosophers," said Liebermann. "Didn't von Schubert propose something very similar almost a hundred years ago?"

"Indeed he did. But von Schubert could only speculate. We are in a different position today. We have psychoanalysis, which equips us with new tools. I believe that Professor Freud's methods can be used to probe and explore the cultural unconscious."

"That is very ambitious. In effect, you are aiming to analyze not just one man but all mankind."

"Well, let us say one race to begin with. The psychiatric patients at the private hospital are mostly Jews. They will be my first subjects."

"What does Professor Freud think of your proposal?"

"He is very enthusiastic. Apparently he was intrigued by what he called *endopsychic myths* many years ago, and I understand he discussed the possible existence of ancestral memories with a colleague . . ."

"Fleiss, probably."

"He was writing *The Interpretation of Dreams* at the time and never gave the topic his full attention. He assures me, however, that one day he intends to revisit the area. Until then, he gave me his blessing and said that he was looking forward to reading the results of my investigation."

"Yes, I can see how the idea of archaic remnants embedded deep in the psyche would appeal to Professor Freud. He has always loved archaeology. Have you been to his apartment yet?"

"No."

"It's full of ancient artifacts: little statues, stelae, amulets, and urns . . ."

The bald university professor who had been talking so passionately to Rothenstein earlier raised his hand, capturing Kusevitsky's notice.

"I'm sorry," said Kusevitsky. "You will have to excuse me. I am being summoned by Professor Priel. Until we will meet again . . ."

Kusevitsky bowed and joined the animated professor, who welcomed him into his group with an expansive embracing gesture.

Liebermann was not sure what he thought of Kusevitsky. He was a pleasant enough young man, but somewhat overearnest. Liebermann also wasn't convinced of the value of his research—even if Freud did approve of it.

The cultural unconscious, endopsychic myths, archaic remnants.

It was all a little too arcane for Liebermann's tastes.

Could ancient memories really be passed on, from generation to generation?

He was abruptly roused from his meditation by a hand falling heavily on his shoulder.

"Have you had any cake yet?"

It was his father. He was holding a piece of *guglhupf* over a small dish. The sponge was sweetly fragrant and dense with raisins.

"No."

"You should try some." He held the slice up, creating a little shower of icing sugar. "It's from Grodzinksi's shop. He supervised the baking himself."

"In which case . . ."

At least there were some things that he and his father could still agree on.

3

THE ZADDIK—REBBE ELIMELECH ben Solomon Barash—was a thickset man with craggy features, a long black beard, and uncut sideburns that had been styled into springlike coils. He wore a somber frock coat—lined with fur—a white shirt, and slippers without buckles or laces. White tassels hung from his waist (each individual thread knotted five times to represent the five books of Moses). His large head was shaven, but shadowed with enough spiky stubble to keep his velvet skullcap firmly in place. He was enthroned on a quilted armchair with a high back.

In front of the zaddik was gathered a group of young men—about ten in number—sitting cross-legged on the floor. Each wore an ornately embroidered shawl draped around his shoulders. Prayer books were scattered among them on the Persian rug. Like their master, they had shaven heads and their sideburns hung in uncut ringlets or braids.

"*The magid of Safed* tells us that the world in which we live is imperfect. The divine light could not be contained in the sacred vessels—and the sacred vessels were broken. Thus it was that His mighty undertaking failed. What came to be was not correspondent with the divine plan. What came to be was flawed—a universe out of humor, an ailing universe, a universe in which wickedness might thrive."

The zaddik turned his head, making eye contact with each of his disciples. His gaze was particularly intense, and some of the young men had to look away.

"When something is broken, it must be repaired. This is our task: *tikkun*, the mending of the vessels, the healing of the cosmos. When you ask yourselves "What is the purpose of human existence?" you now have an answer: *tikkun*. What is the purpose of the sky, the earth, the stars, and the moon? You now have an answer: *tikkun*. It is the purpose of the holy books, the purpose of scripture, the purpose of prayer. The achievement of *tikkun* is the *only* means of redemption. It brings perfection back to God and so to the universe, to humanity, and to the people of Israel."

Barash paused and gripped the arms of his chair. His hands were large, like the oversize hands on a classical statue—a rough assembly of bulbous knuckles and swollen phalanges.

"And how are we to achieve *tikkun*?"

He paused again, allowing his question to persist in the minds of his disciples.

"My rebbe . . ."

A young man sitting at the front raised his hand.

The zaddik nodded, encouraging him to speak.

"Study of the law, observance of the commandments, and absolute commitment to ethical behavior."

"The unselfish pursuit of religious perfection, Gershom," said the zaddik, endorsing the young man's answer while extracting from it an abstract essence. "The task in hand is so great that *all* must participate, *all* have a role to play—however small. The greatest scholar and the unschooled laborer have this in common. No man is exempt. Without total participation, the *tikkun* will not succeed, and wickedness will remain in the world."

The zaddik suddenly leaned forward. One of the young men started.

"There is no such thing as an inconsequential observance. Every observance is of the greatest importance, because through observances the *tikkun* proceeds and that which is wrong is corrected. If you are negligent, it is not only the fate of your soul that is affected but the whole of creation. The burden of *tikkun* weighs heavily on our shoulders at all times. All deeds and misdeeds have cosmic consequences. Every day the choices you make will either cure the world or hasten the progress of its malignancies. Every day your thoughts will either strengthen or weaken the powers of good and evil."

Barash's voice, which was deep and resonant, had been growing steadily louder. He appeared unnaturally large and powerful, monumental, a mountain of a man, with wide shoulders and a barrel chest, huge feet and marble hands. His zeal created an illusion of expansion, and he seemed to fill the room. His commanding presence made it easier for his followers to believe a fundamental tenet of their faith: that God could be approached only through the mediation of a zaddik. Barash was a divine messenger, like his father, Solomon, and his grandfather—another Elimelech—before him. In their Hasidic sect, Barash was regarded as the single human being who could redeem their souls; bring their prayers before God; and ensure that if they sinned, God would accept their repentance. In return, his followers gave him their faith and material security.

The study group came to an end and the young men collected their coats and departed. Barash stood by the window, watching them cross the yard before spilling out onto Grosse Sperlgasse. The surrounding buildings were rather dilapidated, having once been part of the former ghetto. When the last of his followers had disappeared from view, Barash attended to some correspondence, discussed housekeeping arrangements with his wife, donned a large beaver hat, and set off to visit some of the elderly members of his congregation.

Barash marched down the narrow streets, passing numerous shops on the way: a general store, a bakery, a kosher butcher's—with substantial joints of meat hanging from hooks on the wide-open doors—a cobbler's establishment, a watchmaker, a textile merchant. Some of the shop signs were in Hebrew, but most were in German. Occasionally Barash saw other men dressed like himself, although, relative to the rest of the Jewish population, the Hasidim of Vienna were few in number. Even in Leopoldstadt, caftans and beaver hats were not such a common sight.

Turning off the main thoroughfare, Barash entered a dim alleyway—a gap between buildings that served as a shortcut. The temperature dropped as soon as he ventured between its dank, precipitous walls. He became aware of footsteps—a soft accompaniment shadowing his own tread—and glanced over his shoulder.

"My rebbe . . ." It was Gershom.

Barash halted. "What is the matter?"

"I was in Zucker's and saw you passing."

Zucker's was a small coffeehouse on Tandelmarktgasse.

The young man came forward.

"I was reading this." Gershom offered Barash a folded newspaper indicating a particular news item. The headline read PIARIST MONK MURDERED IN JOSEFSTADT.

Barash grabbed the paper and read down the column of Gothic typeface. His tangled eyebrows came together and his breathing quickened. When he had finished reading, he handed the paper back to the young man, who said tremulously, "How did you know?"

The zaddik, who towered over his acolyte, did not respond.

"You said our enemies would be struck down." The young man was nervous, uncertain whether to proceed. But his need for answers spurred him on. "Is this what you meant? Has it begun already?"

"Yes," said Barash. "It has begun."

"My rebbe, how did you know?"

Barash observed a procession of carts passing at the other end of the alley. A peddler was shouting, trying to sell a trayful of dreidels.

"Be thankful, Gershom. Our troubles will soon be over. As the great Maharal of Prague freed his people from persecution, so we shall be freed. Pray, Gershom, and give thanks."

The young man was not consoled by these words.

"But . . . my rebbe, who did this?" He held up the newspaper. "Was it . . ." Gershom lowered his voice, almost to a whisper. "Was it one of us?"

"Of course not!"

"Then who?"

"Not who, Gershom. What?"

4

Light was streaming through a high window. The abbot raised his chin, and closed his eyes against the sun. Rheinhardt thought he looked tired.

"Brother Stanislav was a good Piarist," said the abbot. "I daresay you will consider me grudging with my praise. It does not sound very generous—'a good Piarist'—but as far as I am concerned there is no higher commendation, no greater accolade." The shaft of yellow light faded, and the abbot opened his eyes. "Stanislav exemplified Piarist virtues. He was humble and pious, hardworking and dutiful. He was respected by his brothers in Christ and loved by the children he taught." As an afterthought he added, "The young are less sullied by the world and are naturally drawn toward goodness—of that I am certain."

"Where did Brother Stanislav come from?"

"Poland."

"Does he still have family there?"

"No. His father was impecunious and abandoned his wife and son when Stanislav was a boy. Stanislav's mother died shortly after—God rest her soul." The abbot made the sign of the cross. "She was, however, a devout woman, and Stanislav attended the Piarist school in Kraków. It became his ambition to dedicate his life to the service of others, and the brothers who instructed him became his inspiration. He was ordained when still a young man, and since then the Piarist order has been his only family. What do you know of us, Inspector?"

"I know only that you provide teaching for the poor."

"We owe our existence to Joseph Calasanz." The abbot gestured toward a portrait that hung behind his table. It was an oil painting, darkened with age, that showed an old monk with gentle eyes. "He pledged to assist the needy, but, being a practical man, he wanted to offer them more than just his prayers. He believed that the provision of a good, free education would give children born into poverty a better start in life. Thus, when our order was recognized by Pope Gregory XV, all Piarist monks were bound to take a fourth vow in addition to the usual three: that of complete devotion to the gratis instruction of youth."

The abbot smiled, quietly satisfied with this compressed history.

"Did Brother Stanislav talk to you very much about the children in his classes?"

"Yes. He was always talking about them: how Johannes had mastered his algebra or Franz Xavier his Latin grammar. He enjoyed their little triumphs as though they were his own."

"And what about children who were difficult . . . problematic?"

"How do you mean, 'problematic'?"

"Children who misbehaved."

"Brother Stanislav was an experienced teacher. He had no difficulty maintaining discipline in his classes."

"But what if a child *did* misbehave? Would he punish such a child?"

"Yes, of course."

"How?"

"Penance—the setting of a repetitive written exercise—or prayers for forgiveness."

"And if the child still misbehaved?"

"Well, the child would have to be disciplined."

"In what way?"

"The birch . . . across the fingers of the left hand." The abbot observed Rheinhardt shifting uncomfortably in his seat. "Inspector, if our pupils are to make the most of what we are trying to offer them, it is imperative that they are well behaved. Moreover, it would not be fair to the other children if we let miscreants run wild."

"How often are children punished in this way?"

"Very infrequently."

"About ten or fifteen years ago . . . was there anyone here—a child—whom Brother Stanislav had to punish repeatedly?"

The abbott leaned back in his chair, brought his hands together, and focused his gaze on his fingertips. His brow cracked like dry parchment.

"No. I cannot remember a child like that, not at that time."

"Then earlier, perhaps?"

"Many years ago—perhaps twenty or so—we had to expel a boy called Richard Kahl."

"What did he do?"

"He was a bully and a thief."

"Did Brother Stanislav punish him?"

"We all did."

"Do you know where he is now, this Kahl?"

"In the Saint Marxer cemetery."

"He's dead?"

"Yes. He became a drunkard and strangled his wife." The abbot made the sign of the cross again. "A tragedy . . . a great tragedy." Looking up, the old man continued, a note of desperation catching in his throat. "Inspector, surely you are not thinking that one of our pupils is responsible for Brother Stanislav's murder?"

"I must consider *all* possibilities, Father."

"God preserve us."

"Perhaps you would be so kind as to ask some of the other monks if they can remember any child whom they think might have harbored ill feelings toward Brother Stanislav?"

The abbott nodded.

"Did Brother Stanislav's ministry bring him into contact with individuals suffering from mental illness?"

"He visited hospitals during the course of his work."

"Was he ever threatened?"

"By a lunatic?"

"Yes."

"I don't know. It is possible."

"If he had been threatened, would he have told anyone—a fellow Piarist in whom he confided?"

The abbot shook his head. "Stanislav treated all his brothers in Christ equally. He did not cultivate *special* friendships." Then, after a lengthy pause, he said, "Inspector? Have you ever encountered anything like this before? What I mean to say is . . . Brother Stanislav's head?" He winced as he recalled the decapitation and blood. "It looked as if his head had been ripped from his body."

"I have seen many terrible things, Father."

"But *this* . . . have you seen anything quite like *this* before?"

"No, Father. I haven't."

"If I didn't know better . . ." The old man clenched his fist and pressed his knuckles to his lips.

"What?" Rheinhardt prompted.

"If I didn't know better," the abbot repeated, "I would say it was the work of the devil."

Rheinhardt rose from his chair. "Thank you for your assistance, Father."

Before closing the door, Rheinhardt paused. The abbot's eyes must have been registering the room in which he was seated, but what he was actually seeing in his mind was clearly something quite different: a hideous force, come from hell to unleash its evil power on the doorstep of his church.

5

Councillor Julius Schmidt; his nephew and assistant, Fabian; Councillor Burke Faust; and Hofrat Holzknecht were seated in one of the upper chambers of the town hall.

The agenda had been dispensed with, and a large pile of documents had now been signed and stamped with official seals. Hofrat Holzknecht was going over the paperwork, while Fabian distributed cognac and cigars.

"All in order," said Holzknecht. The title with which he was distinguished—Hofrat—had been introduced in the eighteenth century for high officials. It had come to represent not only social elevation but the power to dispense favors (or what the Viennese referred to as *protektion*).

Schmidt and Faust—both councillors of the same rank—were political allies, but they were not friends. Faust was, on the whole, indifferent to Schmidt. Faust was a pragmatist, and Schmidt's personal qualities were largely irrelevant as far as he was concerned. The reverse, however, was not true. Schmidt was acutely aware of everything that made up the person of Burke Faust, and each constituent part inspired resentment. He resented Faust's diamond ring, his expensive wristwatch, and his edelweiss tiepin; he resented his spotless frock coat, the smell of his Italian cologne, and his relaxed, superior attitude; he resented his spacious Hietzing villa, his full head of hair, and his family fortune. But most of all, he resented the fact that Faust was almost certainly going to get the job that he, Schmidt, wanted—a key position on Mayor Lueger's special advisory panel.

Faust had recently created a stir by writing an article for *Die Reichspost* on the "social question," an eloquently argued piece of polemical writing that not only found a sympathetic audience among the mayor's inner circle but impressed the "Lord God of Vienna" himself. Mayor Lueger needed the services of a talented propagandist, and, luckily, one had appeared. Faust had started writing his piece as soon as old Horngacher had announced that he was retiring. Schmidt had to admire Faust, albeit grudgingly. He was a consummate opportunist.

Schmidt took a cigar and held a match to its tip. He ensured that the burn was even, and then put the match out by waving his hand violently in the air. He dropped the match into a glass ashtray and stared at Faust, who was conferring with Hofrat Holzknecht.

How Schmidt wanted that job.

The successful candidate would become a confidant of Mayor Lueger, would be introduced to important people and be granted significant powers. An ambitious man might even use this privileged position to cultivate more general support among the party membership. Mayor Lueger would not last forever. His eyesight wasn't so good these days, and there were rumors about his failing health. In the fullness of time a replacement would have to be found.

Schmidt sniffed his cognac. The fragrance seemed to enter his skull and excite his imagination. He thought of Mayor Lueger's theatrical public appearances, his gold chain of office flashing in the sunlight, his entourage of laborers, civil servants, nuns, priests, and altar boys, the members of his inner circle, with their special green tailcoats with black velvet cuffs. Even when the mayor opened a factory, he managed to create a sense of occasion. Spectacle! How Schmidt longed to slip his arms into the silk-lined sleeves of such a tailcoat. But it would not be him going to the tailor's. No—it would be Burke Faust.

Still, Schmidt consoled himself, although he might never get to be mayor, he might still get his villa in Hietzing. He had recently learned that money could be made quite easily—if one was prepared to enter into negotiations with the right people. Mutually provident arrangements could be agreed upon with no initial investment, merely the promise of a little "political" protection, should the need arise. They weren't the kind of business associates he could welcome into an office at the Rathaus, but their views on social justice were not that different from his own—or the mayor's, for that matter.

Faust was leaning back in his chair, voicing his opinions in a languid tenor. Schmidt listened carefully so as to pick up the thread of his argument. He didn't want anyone present to think he had been "dreaming."

"I fear that the mayor is becoming complacent," said Faust. "The issue of their status has become a tool, a means to an end: a device used to get the attention and support of the lower middle class. Of course, he's still willing to denounce glorified moneylenders like Rothenstein, Wittgenstein, and their *kind*—but none of this hot air leads to municipal reform."

"He's even consulting them these days," Schmidt chipped in. "I heard that he actually met with Cohen to discuss one of his new building projects."

"It's no good," said Faust. "We can't denounce them in the morning and invite them for tea in the afternoon. He's playing a dangerous game."

Schmidt rose from his seat and went over to the window. His breath condensed on the glass, and he had to wipe the moisture away to see out. Beyond the Rathaus park stood the Burgtheater. It looked particularly beautiful, its windows glowing from inside with a warm amber light. Rain was falling, and the street lamps were surrounded by haloes of luminescence.

Schmidt recalled one of the mayor's most famous speeches.

If you go to the theatre, nothing but Jews. If you walk on the Ringstrasse, nothing but Jews. If you go to a concert, nothing but Jews. If you attend a ball, nothing but Jews. If you go on campus, again, nothing but Jews. . . .

Schmidt's lips twisted to form an ironic smile. The Burgtheater was showing a play written by a Jew. Faust was absolutely right. Mayor Lueger had lost his early zeal. Yet the public still had an appetite for such fiery rhetoric. Schmidt thought of Faust's article and sighed. The rhythms were reminiscent of Mayor Lueger's old speeches, written when he was still hungry for power: insistent repetition, like a fist banging on a door—brooking no refusal—and metaphors so striking, so just that no one could deny the truth of his vision.

Faust would get the job—and he might even be mayor, one day. Faust was an obstacle. Faust was in Schmidt's way.

"Only ten years ago," Faust continued, "the program for reform was accepted by everyone: removal of the Jews from the civil service, medicine, law, and small business. Only ten years ago, these proposals were taken very seriously indeed. Now look at the state of our most important institutions."

"There have been some successes," said Hofrat Holzknecht. "There aren't that many of them in the civil service, and we've managed to limit admissions to the gymnasia."

"But it's not enough!" said Faust.

"Well," said Hofrat Holzknecht. "Should you ever find yourself in a position to revive the mayor's flagging program for municipal reform"—his expression became arch and knowing—"then you would be assured of support from my bureau."

Schmidt felt his heart beating faster. It was so unfair. Holzknecht was acting as if the decision had already been made.

Holzknecht blew out a cloud of smoke. "It won't be easy," he continued, "to fight this new complacency."

"Of course it won't," said Schmidt. "That is why we need something to capture the public's imagination." He wasn't going to let

Faust have a coronation. Holzknecht should realize that Faust wasn't the only councillor with ideas. Schmidt paused, hoping that his silence would be sufficiently cryptic to elicit a further question. His ruse was successful.

"What do you mean, Schmidt?"

"I mean that there is only so much one can do to persuade the electorate with economic and social arguments. Sometimes you have to engage their emotions. Somebody once suggested to me that what we really need right now is another Hilsner."

Fabian, having already distributed the cognac and cigars, had been sitting quietly reading a newspaper. However, he had been half-listening to the conversation, and now he raised his head quizzically.

"Hilsner, uncle?"

Schmidt smiled at his nephew and then turned to Faust and Holzknecht. "He's only eighteen ... one forgets." He came away from the window and sat down next to his nephew.

"Leopold Hilsner, dear boy. He killed a nineteen-year-old virgin and drained her body of blood. It's what they do. Christian blood for their bread. The scandal started a very healthy debate in the popular press. . . . It got people thinking."

"Is it true, Uncle Julius? They really do this?"

"As far as we're concerned, it's true," said Schmidt, his eyes glinting mischievously.

Fabian looked confused.

"No, Julius," said Faust, "I think you can be more emphatic than that. They are a superstitious and backward people. Whenever a child disappears—particularly in the rural areas of Hungary and Galicia—the local communities are quite right to suspect the tinkers and peddlers passing through from the east. I can assure you, young man, ritual murder is a real phenomenon. And you don't have to take my word for it. Read the Reverend Joseph Decker's *A Ritual Murder* or Father August Rohling's *The Talmudic Jew*. They are chilling works that deserve a place on every right-thinking person's bookshelf."

Schmidt's jaw tightened with irritation. He had read neither of these tracts. Faust always seemed to be able to back up his arguments with scholarly references. It was particularly riling because Schmidt, unlike many of his colleagues, had made a thorough study of Jewish lore and was relatively well informed. *Know thy enemy* was an epigram he lived by.

"That's all very well, Schmidt," said Holzknecht, "saying that we need another Hilsner. But you can't expect something like that to happen just when you want it to."

"No," said Schmidt. "My point exactly! You can't!"

The men exchanged glances.

Holzknecht possessed a very expressive face. At first his lineaments showed doubt. Surely he was mistaken, surely he was investing Schmidt's response with too much meaning; however, the balance of his judgment was tipped by Schmidt's rising eyebrow. Holzknecht's doubt turned to amusement, and his features communicated an amalgam of surprise and approval.

The silence was broken by Fabian.

"Uncle, . . . Brother Stanislav is dead." The young man pushed the paper toward Schmidt. "The Piarist monk, remember? We met with him last month. We had to talk to him about that *incident* in Leopoldstadt."

"Stanislav—dead?" said Faust. "I don't believe it!"

"Murdered," said Schmidt, without inflection.

"Murdered?" cried Faust. "Dear God!"

"It says he was decapitated," said Fabian.

"Schmidt, give me that," said Faust, reaching over and pulling the newspaper out of Schmidt's hands. Faust's eyes moved from side to side as he read the column. "Dear God! I don't believe it. He was a good man . . . a truly good man."

"Yes," said Schmidt, "but he wasn't admired universally." He looked innocently at the ceiling. Then he dropped his gaze and caught Holzknecht's eye. He saw that he had hit his mark. Hofrat's face, expressive to the point of transparency, revealed that he was reassessing Schmidt. Perhaps they had underestimated him and his application should be reconsidered.

6

We had arranged to meet at the natural history museum. It is a favorite haunt of Miss Lydgate's—and mine, of course. She tarried longest in the geological halls and became utterly absorbed by the meteorites, identifying the exhibits by their technical names: "ordinary chondrites," "carbonaceous chondrites," "achondrites," etc., etc. It amused me, the way she gazed at those gray-black rocks with the same covetous, lingering gaze that other women reserve for diamonds. Indeed, she hardly noticed the precious stones when we passed through the gem hall. We both admired the Knyahinya meteorite, which is reckoned to be the largest in the world (or at least, the largest one to be displayed in any of the world's museums). It weighs almost six hundred sixty pounds and fell in Hungary. The fiery arrival of the Knyahinya meteorite is celebrated in a canvas panel by Anton Brioschi above one of the doors.

Miss Lydgate said, "How extraordinary that this object, which has traveled between worlds—through the vast emptiness of space—should, in the fullness of time, find a resting place here, in a cabinet, in Vienna." Needless to say, I was minded to agree. It is an extraordinary thing. From where did this great lump of rock originate, and how far did it travel before crashing into Earth? The mind can scarcely imagine such an epic voyage.

When we arrived at the empress Maria Theresa's mechanical planetarium (an exquisite piece of eighteenth-century craftsmanship), Miss Lydgate fell into a meditative state. She was frowning a little—her lips pressed together—and while she was thus distracted, I positioned myself at a distance, just far enough to steal a few glances (inconspicuous glances, I hope) at her figure and hair. The shame that accompanies such improprieties has now become dulled through repetition: the self-loathing is less acute and is diluted by a vague feeling of tired resignation.

Without turning her head (she was not aware that I had moved away) Miss Lydgate began to speak. I quickly came forward from behind my observation post. Her contemplation of the immense distances traveled by the Knyahinya meteorite had clearly prompted her to reflect on the great size of the cosmos. She was speaking of Bessel, the German astronomer, who had demonstrated that even the nearest stars were unimaginably distant. I asked her how he had achieved such a feat of measurement, and she replied, "By observation of the parallax."

My incomprehension must have been obvious, because she immediately invited me to participate in an instructive scientific exercise. "Hold your finger a few inches away from your nose. Then look at it first with the left eye, closing the right, and then the right eye, closing the left." My finger appeared to jump to the left. "Now repeat the procedure, but this time hold your finger at arm's length. Notice that there is still movement, but not so much. The smaller the parallax, the farther the object.

Apparently, by using this simple principle as applied to the apparent movement of stars, Bessel was able to determine the distance from Earth of 61 Cygni, which proved to be much farther away than anyone had previously expected. "Sixty-four trillion miles," said Miss Lydgate (she has a remarkable memory for numbers). In Miss Lydgate's estimation, Bessel's accomplishment ranked among the greatest in all of science.

. "Against the backdrop of the universe, our great globe is but an insignificant speck." She looked at me with characteristic intensity. Her eyes captured and condensed the blue fire of the gas jets: whereas others might have been disturbed by the size of the universe, and conversely human insignificance, Miss Lydgate seemed—how should I put this?—quietly satisfied. The terrifying enormity of the universe was humbling, and therefore its contemplation was virtuous.

But what am I to make of all this? I can no longer consider our frequent engagement in conversations of this kind entirely innocent. They have become a substitute for natural, physical intimacy. We talk—but dare not touch. Our erotic instincts have become frozen in an arctic waste of cerebration. Do I flatter myself? Does she really desire me, as I desire her? And why has this conversation about the great size of the universe stayed with me? We spoke of many things, but it is this conversation that I now recall most vividly. Was she trying to say something to me? Was there hidden meaning in all this discussion of meteorites and stars? Unconscious encouragement? "Given the vastness of the universe, must we be so respectful of social observances? Does any of it really matter?" Was it a disguised appeal? Or is this just wishful thinking on my part? Am I reading too much into what was nothing more than innocent erudition?

I am reminded of young Oppenheim. We were discussing Freud's dream book in Café Landtmann, and Oppenheim said that he thought it shouldn't have been called "The Interpretation of Dreams," but rather "The Over-Interpretation of

Dreams." Sacrilege, but he has a point, and I had to laugh. What am I to do? It is all so very complicated. Yet there is more to my inaction than a fear of embarrassment or rejection. She is sensitive and fragile. I know that—perhaps better than anybody. Human actions do not have cosmic repercussions. Our pathetic little dramas unfold—great rocks fly through the heavens, and planets wheel around the sun. All true. But disparities of scale—however large—do not justify recklessness. Besides, who is to say that the stately progress of stars is any more

7

THERE WAS A KNOCK on the door. Liebermann stopped writing, closed his journal, and placed it in his desk drawer.

"Come in," he called out.

The door opened slowly, and a nurse stepped into his office. He had seen her before but they had never spoken. She seemed rather agitated.

"Yes?" said Liebermann.

"My name is Magdalena Heuber. I am a nurse on Professor Friedländer's ward." She gestured down the corridor. "Would you please come and examine one of our patients? He is very ill."

"Where is Professor Friedländer?" asked Liebermann.

"He has gone home," said Nurse Heuber.

Liebermann glanced at the clock and saw that it was getting late. He had been so absorbed in his journal that he had lost track of time.

"What about Professor Friedländer's *sekundararzt*—Dr. Platen?"

The nurse, looking distinctly uncomfortable, replied, "Dr. Platen has been unavoidably detained." Liebermann suspected that she wasn't being entirely candid, but he chose not to press her. "We only have an *aspirant*—Herr Edlinger—on the ward," the nurse continued, "and he is not sure what to do. The patient is the young Baron von Kortig."

Liebermann sighed and stood up. Remembering his journal, he took a key from his pocket, locked the desk drawer, and pulled at it a few times to make sure that the bolt had properly engaged.

"Confidential case notes," said Liebermann, catching the nurse's eye. This small falsehood still drew an unwelcome warmth to his cheeks.

They made their way down the corridor to Professor Friedländer's ward and entered an anteroom. It was cramped and dim. The shelves were stacked with folders and formularies, and the wooden table—which nestled under the black square of a small window—was covered in medical journals. A metal cart parked beside the table was loaded with flasks, some of which were filled with opaque peach-colored urine. The claustrophobic and stale atmosphere of the anteroom was exacerbated by the presence of the aspirant, Edlinger, who occupied the central floor space. He was a well-dressed young man with blond hair, an exceedingly thin mustache, and a silver dueling scar on his chin.

Edlinger introduced himself, briefly described the patient's condition, and handed Liebermann a weighty buff file. Liebermann sat down and flicked through the summary: Baron Klemens von Kortig: *mood shifts, delusions of grandeur, irrational rages, gambling, spending sprees, vertigo, headache, digestive problems, vomiting, "lightning pain" in the hands and feet.* It was unusual to see a man quite so young in the advanced stages of tertiary syphilis, but presumably, like many of his peers, on reaching puberty the baron had immediately enjoyed the sexual favors of the peasant girls on his father's estate. He was now paying a heavy price for these plein air romances.

"What did you give him?" asked Liebermann.

"Morphine," Edlinger replied.

"Why?"

"He was agitated. I wanted him to settle down."

"The other patients were being disturbed," interjected Nurse Heuber.

"But the syphilis has spread to his heart," said Liebermann.

The aspirant and the nurse presented a united front: void expressionless faces.

"Never mind," said Liebermann, shaking his head. "I'd better go and see him. Where is he?"

Nurse Heuber led Liebermann out onto the ward. It smelled of carbolic. The other patients watched their progress as they approached the last bed, which was hidden behind a screen.

Baron von Kortig, propped up with pillows, was fast asleep. His hair was lank, sweat glistened on his brow, and his eyelids were red and swollen. The hospital gown he wore was rucked at the shoulders, revealing long pale arms and thin white fingers.

Liebermann stood at the end of the bed. He looked at his patient with an expression unique to clinicians, a combination of devotion and predatory interest: a paradoxical look, compassionate yet calculating.

He noted that the baron's head was nodding with each heartbeat, and positioned himself closer. He bent forward and examined the man's fingernails. Edlinger was standing in the light, and Liebermann gestured that he should take a step back. Liebermann observed the subtle blushing beneath the transparent keratin, the color coming and going. He squeezed von Kortig's bony wrist and felt the flow of blood—its physicality—his fingers being raised by the pressure, and their subsequent fall. He then lifted von Kortig's arm and felt the pulse collapse, the loss of power and only a residual *tap, tap, tap*. It was ominously weak, its actual presence sometimes indistinguishable from an anticipatory tactile illusion.

Liebermann asked Edlinger for his stethoscope.

Pressing the diaphragm against the baron's chest, Liebermann listened.

Lubb-dub, lubb-dub, lubb-dub . . .

There was something very wrong.

He heard a rumbling on the second component of the beat, a rumbling that became more marked when he placed the diaphragm of the stethoscope closer to the left edge of the patient's sternum. When he listened to the patient's lungs, he heard a loud crackling. They were horribly congested.

Liebermann took off the stethoscope and handed it back to Edlinger.

"Aortic regurgitation. The infection has all but destroyed his heart. I'm afraid there's nothing we can do."

"He's dying?" cried the aspirant, the pitch of his voice climbing with surprise.

Liebermann quickly raised his finger to his lips.

"Yes," he whispered, looking once again at von Kortig's blushing fingertips.

Nurse Heuber made the sign of the cross and excused herself. The sound of her brisk step, captured and amplified by the vaulted ceiling, fell silent when she reached the anteroom. Liebermann explained, sotto voce, to the aspirant how he had determined the severity of von Kortig's condition. He then suggested to Edlinger that he should go and make a relevant entry in the patient's notes.

There was no reason for Liebermann to stay on; however, having become involved in the young baron's care, he felt a curious sense of obligation, a compulsion to remain a little longer.

Liebermann found a chair, placed it behind the screen, and sat by the patient. He checked von Kortig's pulse again and plumped up the pillows: maintaining him in an upright position would make it easier for the poor fellow to breathe. The gas lamps were humming, and the steady persistence of their inanimate drone lulled Liebermann into a pensive, melancholy state. His mind produced a loose circle of associations: death, mortality, the importance of seizing opportunities because of the brevity of life, Miss Lydgate, sexual desire, syphilis—and, again, death.

Suddenly Liebermann became aware that something had changed. There was a difference in the acoustics of the ward. Where there had hitherto been a constant rhythmic accompaniment to the humming gas lamps—von Kortig's shallow, stertorous breathing—there was now an absence. Liebermann looked up, expecting the worst, expecting to be confronted with the terrible stillness of the dead; however, what he saw almost made him jump. Von Kortig had opened one eye and was staring at him intently.

"I'm sorry," said the aristocrat in a cracked, wheezy voice. "But you are?"

"Dr. Max Liebermann."

"Liebermann, you say." The other eye opened. "Liebermann . . . Ah yes, of course. Karl's friend. I am sorry. My memory isn't as good as it once was. . . . You were my guest last summer—at the hunting lodge."

It was probably the effect of the morphine. Liebermann did not have the heart to challenge him.

Von Kortig winked. "What a summer, eh?"

"Yes," Liebermann replied softly. "What a summer . . ."

"Those girls from Paris . . . Have you ever encountered a more sporting group of ladies?"

"No . . . I haven't."

The young baron paused for a moment and smiled wistfully.

"Hugo, eh? What a fool he was. His father was furious, you know—when he heard. He's threatened to disinherit him. That land has been in the Meissner family for generations. Although, who am I to criticize. We've all been there, haven't we? Luck seems to be on your side, you're dealt one fantastic hand after another, you get overconfident, and then . . ." Von Kortig paused, lifted his arm, but was too weak to hold it up. When it hit the sheet, he winced.

"Are you coming again this year?"

"If I can."

"Good. Karl will be pleased."

The dying young man looked at the screen, but his eyes were focused on a distant, imaginary horizon.

"I must say, I'm looking forward to it again this year—more so than ever before." He closed his eyes and croaked, "Is there any champagne left? Put a few drops of cognac in mine, there's a good chap." The young man drifted out of consciousness, and when he came to again, he said, "They're not going to keep me in here for very much longer, are they?" A note of anxiety had crept into his voice.

"No," said Liebermann.

"Good. What did you say your name was?"

"Liebermann."

"Ah yes . . . Liebermann." Von Kortig's breath was suddenly labored. "Look, there's nothing wrong, is there?"

"Wrong?"

"Well, to be honest, I'm not feeling too good."

"You need rest, that's all. Close your eyes. Get some sleep."

"That's not a bad idea. I am feeling awfully tired."

Von Kortig's eyelids slowly closed.

Liebermann, moved by the terrible irony of their exchange, looked away. Through a gap in the screen he could see the entrance to the anteroom. Nurse Heuber appeared—and behind her stood a priest. Liebermann got up quietly and walked to the other end of the ward.

"I trust I am not too late, Herr Doctor," said the priest, a man not very much older than Liebermann. "Nurse Heuber did her best." He turned to face the nurse and smiled.

"Thank you for coming. But . . ." Liebermann grimaced. "I am not altogether sure that your ministrations will be in the patient's best interests."

"Oh? Why do you say that?" The question was not interrogative, merely curious.

"He is ignorant of his condition. He is not suffering, and because of the brain disease, the morphine, or both, he is under the impression that he will be discharged shortly . . . and he is looking forward to spending the summer in a hunting lodge with friends."

The priest glanced at the nurse, and then at the aspirant.

"I understood that the young baron is close to death."

"He is," said Liebermann. "That is my point: he is very close to death, but is also blissfully unaware of his predicament. He will pass away within the hour—within minutes, perhaps. I fear that conducting the last rites will rouse him from his dreams. Such a rude awakening might cause him considerable distress."

"You would have him die . . . in ignorance?"

"No. I would have him die happy rather than fearful."

"I have no intention of frightening him. I only wish to offer him the consolation—the balm—of *his own* religion."

The priest had pronounced "his own" with sufficient emphasis to make his point.

"With the greatest respect, I am a doctor. And I must decide what is correct in that capacity alone—and no other. My single concern is for my patient's welfare. It was not my intention to question your religious authority, the sanctity of your beliefs, or your good intentions."

"But that is exactly what you are doing, Herr Doctor. Baron von Kortig is a Catholic. I am a priest. In the same way that you have obligations, so have I! Do you really expect me to let the baron die in a state of sin? Please . . . you have already said that we have little time. Please, Herr Doctor, would you stand aside?"

"I am sorry, but I can't let you go through. I have been charged with certain responsibilities and I must honor them." The priest moved forward, and Liebermann stretched his arm across the doorway. "I'm sorry."

The priest looked from the nurse to the aspirant.

"Please, you must help me. We cannot let this godless—" He stopped himself from using the word "Jew" and began again. "Please, I beg you. The fate of a man's soul is at stake."

Edlinger stood up.

"Father Benedikt has a point, Herr Doctor. What I mean to say is, if the baron were lucid, able to know his own mind, he might actually want absolution. Who are we, as medical men, to deny him a religious sacrament?"

"It was not my impression that the baron led a very spiritual existence."

"All the more reason to let me through!" said the priest angrily.

"Nurse Heuber," said Liebermann calmly, "could you please go and make sure that Baron von Kortig is comfortable?"

He lowered his arm, and the nurse passed through. As he did so, he maintained eye contact with the priest.

"Herr Doctor," said the priest, "how do you think the baron's family will react when they hear that their son was denied absolution at the time of his death?"

Liebermann sighed. "Once again, I must remind you that my responsibilities differ from yours. I am sorry that you have had a wasted journey. Edlinger will escort you to the foyer."

Liebermann could hear the nurse's footsteps returning—and knew immediately that the baron was dead.

The priest was an intelligent man. He too recognized the significance of her swift return. Turning, he took his cape from the stand and said, "I can see myself out, thank you."

For a moment he stopped in the doorway.

"Liebermann . . . That is your name?"

"Yes."

The priest nodded and left, his flapping cape creating a gust of chill air that lifted some of the loose papers on the table.

8

THE GOLDEN HORNED SPHERE on top of the plague column was
struck by sunlight, and a flare of white radiance ignited beneath the
Virgin's feet. Two stone figures, casually perched on the Maria Treue
Kirche façade, legs dangling into space, looked curiously unimpressed
by the spectacle. Their raised hands directed the eye toward the ornate
clock face instead of the Virgin, suggesting that the passage of time was
a matter of much greater significance than divine pyrotechnics.

Rheinhardt circumnavigated the plague column and placed himself just inside one of the two doorways that flanked the central and
much larger entrance to the church.

A woman, with a small child in tow, crossed the concourse and
laid a wreath by the lamppost beneath which the mutilated remains
of Brother Stanislav had been discovered. Others had already paid
their respects. The ground was covered with floral tributes that
formed a makeshift garden, the colors of which blazed in the brilliant
light. The woman urged her son to say a prayer, but he was too young
to understand the purpose of his mother's manipulations—the joining of his hands, the closing of his eyes, and the guiding of his tiny fingers to the four points of the cross. His mother let him go, and he
walked back to the plague column, where he peered through the
railings at the assembly of saints, angels, knights, and cherubs. A carriage came rattling down the road, and the boy turned, emitting a
gurgle of pleasure at the sight of two piebald horses.

His mother bowed her head, closed her eyes, and her lips moved
silently as she recited a Hail Mary. The central door of the church

opened and two monks emerged from the darkness. They were both middle-aged but differed greatly in build: the first was tall, pale, and emaciated, while the second was short, ruddy, and plump.

The woman opened her eyes. They were bright with tears.

The two monks halted.

"Romy, come over here—at once." The little boy ran to his mother, but on arrival hid behind her skirts, clutching the coarse material in his hands. "Don't be shy, Romy. Say good morning to the holy fathers."

The boy peeped out from his hiding place, but said nothing. The short monk rested his hands on the projecting shelf of his stomach and smiled indulgently.

"I brought a wreath," said the woman.

"Thank you," said the short monk.

"He was so kind, so caring. I don't know what I would have done without his help. After my husband died, I had no one." She wiped the tears from her face as soon as they appeared. "He was a saint."

"Pray for him," said the short monk.

"Yes, pray for him," repeated his lean companion. "It is what Brother Stanislav would have wanted, and it is all that we poor sinners can do now."

The woman reached for her son's hand and began walking back to the road. When she was out of earshot, the short monk exclaimed, "A saint!"

"Indeed!" said the tall monk, raising his gaze irreverently to the heavens.

They stepped over the wreath and made their way toward the nearest school entrance.

Rheinhardt emerged from his hiding place.

"One moment, please." The two monks turned around abruptly. Rheinhardt showed his identification. "Security office. Forgive me, but I couldn't help overhearing your conversation."

The two monks looked at each other.

"And you are?" the shorter one inquired.

"Detective Inspector Oskar Rheinhardt."

"I am sorry, Inspector," the short monk continued, "but the children are waiting. We have classes to teach."

"Then perhaps I could arrange to speak with you some other time—when it is more convenient?"

The short monk wiped a bead of sweat from his forehead.

"Brother Stanislav," said the tall monk hesitantly, "had a reputation for saintliness; however, those who knew him well—"

"Lupercus!" the short monk interrupted. Again, the two Piarists looked at each other, saying nothing, but obviously engaged in a silent battle of wills. Eventually the shorter monk conceded defeat. He bit his lower lip, and his shiny cheeks flushed a deeper shade of red. "I must go." Marching briskly toward the school, he departed without bothering to excuse his rudeness.

"Brother Lupercus?" Rheinhardt prompted. "You were saying?"

The tall monk surveyed the empty concourse.

"If you want to know what Brother Stanislav was *really* like, read the articles he wrote for *Das Vaterland*." Rheinhardt detected a slight foreign accent in the monk's speech.

"*Vaterland*? What's that?"

"A Catholic newspaper." The school entrance on the opposite side of the concourse opened, and the monk froze. He held his breath until a small boy emerged. "I can say no more," he added with decisive finality. "Good morning, Inspector." He turned his back on Rheinhardt and loped across the cobbles, his loose sandals slapping against the soles of his feet.

"*Vaterland*," Rheinhardt muttered. He took out his notebook and wrote the name down in a quick but barely legible scrawl.

Two women, each with small children, had left the road and were coming in his direction. Both of them were carrying wreaths.

9

"I CANNOT THANK YOU enough," said Rabbi Seligman to Professor Priel.

"Well, it isn't me you should be thanking."

"Yes, I know that it is Herr Rothenstein's money, and I am indeed grateful for his generosity, but it was you who acted as our advocate."

"Please," said the professor, indicating with a gesture that he would not tolerate another word of praise. "The Alois Gasse Temple has a unique charm of its own, and its ark is a treasure. As soon as I saw it, I knew that it was worth preserving. 'The Rothenstein Judaica Fund,' I said to myself. It is regrettable that such a beautiful piece of craftsmanship had been allowed to fall into disrepair. I think we caught the rot just in time."

"My predecessor, I understand, was not a worldly man. Isn't that so, Kusiel?" The rabbi glanced at the *shammos*—the old caretaker.

"Whenever anything went wrong, Rabbi Tunkel just said '*Leave it.*' He seemed to think that God would intervene and sort things out. Even the roof."

"And as we know only too well," said Professor Priel, "God is distinctly inclined to help those who help themselves." The rabbi laughed—falsely—as, in truth, he did not agree with this facile sentiment. "Which reminds me," said the professor. "You mentioned some damp, Rabbi?"

"Indeed, but really, Professor Priel, you have done quite enough."

"It costs me nothing to ask. And there are other funds that might be appropriate."

"Thank you," said Rabbi Seligman. "You are too kind."

The professor finished his tea and replaced the cup in its saucer. "Well," he said, clapping his hands and rubbing them together vigorously, "shall we go and see the finished product?"

"Of course—if you wish."

"I can't wait to see it."

"You will excuse me a moment," said the rabbi. "I must get my hat and coat."

He rose from his seat and left the room, calling out to his wife.

Professor Priel looked at the caretaker and smiled. This small token of goodwill was not returned. The caretaker looked troubled.

"Is anything the matter?" asked Professor Priel.

"No," said the caretaker. "Nothing is the matter."

"Good," said Professor Priel.

10

Councillor Schmidt and his nephew were sitting in a coffee-house, attacking their *zwiebelrostbraten* as if they had not eaten for more than a week. The slices of beef were piled high with crispy fried onion rings and garnished with cucumber. Schmidt felt his stomach pressing against his vest and reached down to undo one of the buttons. A mound of flesh—covered in the tight whiteness of his shirt—bulged out of the gap. He was a big man, prone to putting on weight easily, and he thought, rather ruefully, that it was preferable for a political leader to look lean and athletic rather than heavy and bovine. Burke Faust had been a sportsman in his youth, and he still looked trim! Schmidt considered forgoing the pleasure of a second course, but his resolve evaporated when he placed a piece of meat into his mouth and it melted like butter, releasing with its disintegration a bouquet of savory flavors.

Fabian had been talking incessantly—a constant, tumbling flow of gossip, tittle-tattle, and trivia. He spoke of his visits to the Knobloch household, where he had made the acquaintance of Fräulein Carla, who was very pretty and an accomplished pianist; of his friend Dreher, who had come into a fortune and was about to embark on a world tour; and of the new beer cellar in the fifth district, where he had seen a man give a rousing speech about workers' rights, which he had agreed with entirely, but which had produced a lot of heckling before a fight broke out and he'd been obliged to punch someone in the face to shut him up.

When Fabian was in full spate, Schmidt was content to listen, and say very little. Occasionally he would grunt or look up from his meal. However, that was usually the extent of his involvement. He wasn't particularly interested. But he didn't object to Fabian's talk. Indeed, he found his nephew's nonsense quite comforting, like familiar music played softly in the background, and once in a while Fabian said things that allowed Schmidt to gauge opinion among his nephew's peers—the all-important youth of Vienna. Many of Fabian's friends were disaffected, and Schmidt could see why. What kind of future could they hope for? Too many people, too few jobs, and an unremitting stream of parasites coming in from the east. As soon as people really grasped the gravity of the situation, they would be moved to take action—of that he was sure. It was just a question of giving them something on which to focus their minds.

Schmidt was suddenly aware of a certain accord between his private thoughts and his nephew's chatter. Fabian was reaching the end of a story, and Schmidt sensed that he had missed something that might be important.

"What did you say?"

"He stopped him . . . stopped him from giving the last rites."

"Did I hear you mention von Kortig?"

"Yes, it was the young Baron von Kortig who was denied."

"And where did this happen?"

"The General Hospital."

Schmidt's mastication slowed. "How do you know about this?"

"Edlinger!" Fabian realized that his uncle had not been listening. He pulled a petulant face and sighed. "My friend Edlinger. We play cards together with Neuner and Fink. He's a character, Edlinger, always getting himself into scrapes. He's the one who insulted Eisler's wife and got challenged to a duel."

"And where did Edlinger hear this?"

"He was there when it happened! He's an *aspirant*. He was covering for one of his colleagues. Platen, I think. He'd gotten some tickets for the opera and wanted to take a friend."

Fabian winked.

"And the priest?" said Schmidt. "Do you know the priest's name?"

Fabian shrugged.

"Could you find out?" Schmidt pressed.

"Why do you want to know the priest's name, Uncle Julius?"

"Never you mind. Could you find out?" he repeated.

"Well, I can ask Edlinger, if you like."

"I would like that very much. When will you be seeing Edlinger again?"

"Tomorrow, actually."

"Good," said Schmidt. "Now, isn't this *zwiebelrostbraten* splendid?"

Schmidt allowed another piece of meat to flake into nothingness. It was like manna, and he permitted himself an inner self-congratulatory smile.

II

"Disgraceful," said Detective Inspector Alfred Hohenwart, tossing the folded copy of *Vaterland* onto his desk. He was a stout man with short gray hair and a square mustache that occupied only the space between the bottom of his nose and his upper lip. He was an experienced officer, and one whom Rheinhardt respected.

"I can only assume," said Rheinhardt, "that the censor does not make a habit of reading through Catholic newspapers—otherwise it would never have been published."

"How did you find it?"

"My informant was one of Stanislav's confrères, another Piarist called Brother Lupercus."

"So it would seem that Brother Stanislav wasn't as popular as the abbot wanted you to believe."

"The abbot was a kindly old man, and, for what it's worth, I judged him to be a decent fellow. He probably wasn't aware of Stanislav's hateful essays."

"Or he was deliberately withholding information to protect the reputation of his community."

Rheinhardt shrugged. "It's possible."

"Stanislav," Hohenwart continued, thinking hard. "Stanislav. I seem to recall . . ." His sentence trailed off before he suddenly said, "Excuse me a moment." Hohenwart rose from his desk and vanished into an adjoining room. Sounds issued from beyond the half-open door—noises of rummaging, papers being flicked through, and a private grumbling commentary. In due course, Hohenwart produced a triumphal "Eureka!" and emerged holding a large cardboard file. A paper label had been gummed to the spine, on which was written *Christian Nationalist Alliance*.

"Do you remember Robak? Koell was the investigating officer."

"Yes," said Rheinhardt. "The Jewish boy . . ."

"Found beaten and stabbed to death on the Prater. He was discovered after a rally. A rally held in Leopoldstadt and organized by the Christian Nationalist Alliance."

"Who are they?"

"A fringe political group. They're an odd coalition of Catholics, pan-German sympathizers, and extreme conservatives. In reality, the various factions of the alliance don't have very much in common. What holds them together is anti-Semitism." Hohenwart opened the file and laid it in front of Rheinhardt. "Stanislav! I thought the name was familiar. Brother Stanislav was one of the speakers at the Leopoldstadt rally. The local Jews were offended by his immoderate views. They protested, a fight broke out, and the constables from Grosse Sperlgasse had to be called. No one was seriously hurt—but Robak's body was found later."

"Did you interview Stanislav?" Rheinhardt asked.

"No. We were too busy helping Koell trace alliance members. I'd already collated this file on them, which contains several names and addresses. Needless to say, the murder investigation took priority. We didn't have time to pursue the lesser infringement of religious agitation, and the troublesome monk was quite forgotten."

12

ANNA KATZER AND OLGA Mandl were seated in the parlor of the Katzer residence in Neutorgasse. It was a pleasant room with landscape paintings on the walls and old-fashioned furniture. Opposite Anna and Olga sat Gabriel Kusevitsky and his older brother, Asher. Although Asher shared his brother's diminutive physique, he was generally judged to be the better-looking of the pair. The prescription for his lenses was not so strong, and his beard had been finely groomed to conceal his receding chin. In Asher, Gabriel's weak, neurasthenic appearance was transformed into something more appealing: artistic sensitivity, the romantic glamour of the consumptive—and the small dueling scar on his right cheek advertised that he was not without courage. He also affected a more bohemian style of dress, which was only fitting for a playwright.

The women had been speaking about the congress they had attended in Frankfurt the previous October, the German National Conference on the Struggle Against the White Slave Trade. In philanthropic circles there were many—mostly matrons with thickening waistlines and jowly, powdered faces—who were deeply suspicious of Anna's and Olga's involvement with good causes. Their fashionable dress and frequent appearance at gala balls made them seem more like dilettantes than fund-raisers. Yet there could be no denying that their coquettish charm had successfully loosened the purse strings of several famous industrialists.

"It is a shameful business," said Anna, pouring the tea. "Jewish girls *are* sold by our own people, a fact that many find hard to accept. They cry '*False accusation, slander!*' "

"And one can see why," said Asher. "The town hall would almost certainly use these reports against us—yet another example of Jewish immorality! Even so, I agree it is far better that the problem should be addressed than denied. There will be trouble when it all comes out, but it'll be just one more unpleasant thing to deal with!"

"Why now?" asked Gabriel. "Jewish brothels have always been relatively rare."

"The pogroms," said Olga. An uneasy silence prevailed, as if the room had been preternaturally chilled by a horde of Russian ghosts. "And they are still arriving, these girls. Ignorant of any language other than their own jargon and bad Polish." By "jargon" she meant Yiddish. "Needless to say, they can't get good jobs, and they find themselves working as waitresses, peddlers, or shop assistants. Such positions allow them to develop irregular habits, and without family connections they soon become prey to profiteers and procurers."

"How very sad," said Gabriel.

"Indeed," said Olga.

"But we intend to do something about it," said Anna. "Which is why we wanted to talk with you."

The two men looked at each other, then back at the women, before saying in perfect unison, "Us?" The comical effect made the women smile.

"I am a recently qualified physician," said Gabriel, "and my brother is a struggling playwright . . ."

Anna waved her hand, dismissing the interruption.

"Our aim is to establish a new refuge," she continued, "for young Jewish women. Naturally, it will be situated in Leopoldstadt, and will provide a safe haven for those who would otherwise be at risk. We will also offer assistance to abandoned mothers and their babies, pregnant girls, and those suffering from moral illnesses."

Olga offered the men a dish of vanilla biscuits, shaped like stars and sprinkled with large granules of decorative sugar. Gabriel took one while Asher declined.

"We envisage a middle-size community," said Olga, returning the plate to its resting place on a circular doily. "Two houses—adjoining—with ten to fifteen beds in each dormitory. Both buildings will be furnished simply; however, the atmosphere will be warm and friendly, like a family home, not like a hostel or hospital. There will be no forced detention. Every resident will be free to leave at any time, if that is her wish. And most important, there will be no punishment. These women have suffered enough already."

Gabriel Kusevitsky bit into his biscuit, which crumbled in his mouth, releasing a flood of buttery flavors. He nodded with approval at both the sentiment expressed and the quality of the baking.

"We intend to provide clothing," said Anna. "Which again should be simple, but not ugly or disfiguring. All women—in whatever circumstance they find themselves—like to look their best." She smiled coyly at Gabriel before continuing. "And there will be a schoolroom, where those residents who do not speak good German will be coached by volunteers from the Women's Association."

Olga interjected, "We would prefer our refuge to be staffed entirely by women. It is our view that men—however well-intentioned—and young girls from the street are not a good combination. Further, the majority of our staff should be married, because they will then know about sexual relations and be neither excessively strict nor permissive."

This bold, direct, and unflinching mention of "sexual relations" signaled that Olga and Anna considered themselves "new women." They had both, no doubt, read Mantegazza's popular book *The Physiology of Love*.

Gabriel stopped chewing his biscuit and waited.

"Hallgarten has already promised five thousand kronen," Olga added, maintaining a steady gaze.

"It is a splendid idea," said Asher, clapping his hands together. "And very modern. I like that."

"Yes," said Gabriel. "Much good could be accomplished. Five thousand, you say?"

"Indeed," said Olga. "A very generous donation, but—as I'm sure you will appreciate—such an ambitious project will require funding from other sources."

Anna offered Gabriel another biscuit.

"Should you happen to meet in the course of your work any potential benefactors," Olga continued, "who might consider our scheme worthy of their patronage, I trust that you will remember us."

Olga straightened her back, which had the effect of pushing her bosom forward.

"Of course," said Asher. "If the opportunity arises, you can be assured of our cooperation."

"Thank you," said Olga. "You are most kind."

Now that the main purpose of inviting the Kusevitsky brothers had been accomplished, Anna and Olga were free to steer the conversation toward lighter topics—mutual acquaintances, some royal gossip, and an operetta that they had both found amusing. Having mentioned the stage, the women were then obliged to ask Asher Kusevitsky about his new play. He took their interest seriously—perhaps too seriously—and spoke for some time about his principal themes of mental illness, creativity, and mysticism. The action of the play concerned a man's decline after possession by a dybbuk (an evil spirit and a staple character of old Jewish folktales).

In due course, Anna and Olga politely turned their attention to Gabriel, who in response to their inquiries explained that he was conducting research into the meaning of dreams. Anna began to recount one of her own dreams, but Gabriel stopped her, saying that he would be unable to interpret it without asking her questions of a personal nature and that she would probably be embarrassed to answer them in the company of guests.

"Then some other time, perhaps," said Anna.

When tea was finished and the Kusevitskys had been shown to the door by one of the servants, Anna and Olga retired to the drawing room, where they sat on a couch, heads together, conferring.

"Are you sure they'll be useful?" asked Anna.

"I hope so," said Olga. "They know Professor Priel, who is Rothenstein's brother-in-law. That's how Gabriel Kusevitsky got his scholarship; the professor put in a good word."

"If Rothenstein took an interest in our project . . ."

"We would be able to do everything—and very soon too."

"Where do the Kusevitsky brothers come from?"

Olga paused and looked off into space. A single straight line transected her forehead.

"I don't know. I was introduced to Gabriel by my cousin Martin. They studied medicine together."

"Do they have family in Vienna?"

"I don't think so. Why do you ask?"

Anna caught sight of herself in a silver decorative plate standing on the sideboard. She patted her hair and positioned her necklace more centrally.

"He's interesting, isn't he?"

"Asher, yes, although he did go on a bit about his play. Didn't you think?"

"No, I meant the other one. Gabriel."

"I didn't really understand what he was saying: symbols, dreams . . ."

"And *very* intelligent."

"Did you"—Olga rested her hand on her friend's arm—"*like* him?"

The question contained a hint of alarm.

Anna shrugged. "I *did* find him interesting. Why? What is it?"

"I don't think they're the right type."

"Right type?"

"They're intellectuals, too preoccupied with their work." Olga assumed a piqued expression. "Did you notice when I sat up straight?" She repeated the movement, lifting the fulsome weight of her breasts. "They didn't even look!"

Anna laughed and squeezed her friend's arm. She *had* noticed, and she too had been surprised by the Kusevitsky brothers' indifference.

13

Have recently been playing through the complete Chopin Studies, but am quite dissatisfied with my overall performance. Especially No. 12 in C minor. The left-hand part is extremely demanding, and I lack the necessary strength and flexibility. I was in Schott's and discovered a book of intriguing five-finger exercises devised by Professor Willibald Klammer, a hand surgeon and amateur pianist from Munich. Apparently he is the world's leading authority on strains and breaks and has been consulted by many virtuosi including Caroline von Gomperz-Bettelheim.

The Klammer Method consists of sixty-two exercises executed at the piano and a supplementary set of twenty-four exercises that can be practiced anywhere (finger stretches, contractions, wrist rotations, and so forth). In his introduction, which is copiously illustrated with finely produced anatomical drawings, he fancifully compares his method to the ascetic disciplines practiced by the fakirs of India.

I asked Goetschl if any of his other customers had found the Klammer Method useful, but he couldn't say. He only had the one copy. Needless to say, I bought it. I plowed through the exercises and then attempted the C minor again. It sounded much the same. Even so, I think I will persevere.

As I was playing through the exercises, I kept on thinking

about the incident on Professor Friedländer's ward: Baron von Kortig and the priest. Did I do the right thing? I think so. Yes, I did do the <u>right</u> thing. The young baron was not a man of strong character, and the appearance of the priest would have filled him with terror. That is no way for anyone to die.

14

Rabbi Seligman did not leave the synagogue after the service. He stood alone at the back of the building, deep in thought.

The Alois Gasse Temple was a modest building. It did not have the vast, overwhelming majesty of the "Central Temple," or the ornamental charm of the "Turkish Temple"; however, its manageable proportions were pleasing to the eye. Late-afternoon sunlight fanned through the arched windows. Through this shimmering haze Rabbi Seligman could see the newly restored ark, the cabinet containing the sacred Torah scrolls. It was a beautiful piece of craftsmanship, a gilded tower decorated with intricate carvings: columns, vines, flowers, and urns. The middle panel showed a crowned eagle with outstretched wings, and at the very top, two rearing lions supported a blue tablet on which the Ten Commandments were written in Hebrew. In front of the ark was a lamp—an eternal light—burning with a steady, resolute flame.

"Rabbi?"

Seligman started, and wheeled around.

The caretaker was entering the temple through the shadowy vestibule.

"Kusiel? Is that you."

"Yes, only me."

The caretaker was in his late sixties. He wore a loose jacket and baggy trousers held up with suspenders. His sky-blue skullcap matched his rumpled collarless shirt.

"What is it, Kusiel?"

"I wanted to speak with you about something."

"The damp? Not again, surely."

"No, not the damp." The caretaker rubbed the silver bristles on his chin. "Noises."

"Noises?"

"I was here last night," Kusiel continued, "repairing the loose board on the stairs, when I heard footsteps. I thought there was someone on the balcony, but when I went up, there was no one there."

The rabbi shrugged. "Then you were mistaken."

"That's not all. There was a banging, a loud banging. I don't know where it was coming from."

"What? Someone was trying to break in?"

"No. I checked everywhere. No one was trying to break in. And then . . . then I heard a moaning sound."

Rabbi Seligman tilted his head quizzically.

"It was terrible," Kusiel added. "Inhuman."

Somewhere in the synagogue a wooden beam creaked.

"Old buildings make noises, Kusiel," said the rabbi.

"Not like these."

"Perhaps you were tired. Perhaps you imagined—"

"I didn't imagine anything," said the caretaker firmly. "With respect, Rabbi, I know what I heard, and what I heard wasn't . . . ." The old man paused before saying, "Natural."

Rabbi Seligman took a deep breath and looked up at the balcony. It followed the walls on three sides, being absent only over the ark.

"I don't understand, Kusiel. Are you suggesting that whatever it was you heard was . . . ." He hesitated. "A spirit?"

"It wasn't right—that's all I'm saying. And something should be done. You know more about these things than I do." The old man attacked his bristly chin with the palms of his hands, producing a rough, abrasive sound. "Something should be done," he repeated.

"Yes," said Rabbi Seligman. "Yes, of course. Thank you, Kusiel."

The old man grunted approvingly and shuffled back into the vestibule.

Rabbi Seligman, somewhat troubled by this exchange, climbed the stairs to the balcony. He looked around and noticed nothing unusual. The caretaker had heard something strange, that much he could accept. But a spirit? No, there would be a perfectly rational alternative explanation.

Something should be done.

The caretaker's refrain came back to him.

Rabbi Seligman had no intention of performing an exorcism! It probably wouldn't happen again. And if it did? Well, he would give Kusiel instructions to fetch him at once. Then he could establish what was *really* going on.

15

Rheinhardt flicked through the volume of Schubert songs and placed *Die Forelle—The Trout*—on the music stand.

"Let's end with this, eh? Something cheerful."

Liebermann pulled back his cuffs, straightened his back, and began to play the jolly introduction. His fingers found a curious repeating figure, ostensibly straightforward yet containing both rhythmic and chromatic oddities. It evoked the burble of a country stream; however, the music was not entirely innocent. The notes were slippery, knowing—the effect ironic. Indeed, there was something about the introduction that reminded Liebermann of an adolescent boy whistling nonchalantly while walking away from an orchard, his pockets bulging with stolen apples. The figure dropped from the right hand to the left, then down another octave before the music came to a halt on an arpeggiated tonic chord.

Rheinhardt was so familiar with the song that he didn't bother to look at the music. Resting his elbow on the piano case, like a rustic leaning on a swing gate, he began to sing:

> *"In einem Bächlein helle*
> *Da Schoß in froher Eil'*
> *Die launische Forelle*
> *Vorüber wie ein Pfeil."*

In a clear stream
In lovely haste

> The capricious trout
> Darted by like an arrow.

What is it about? Liebermann asked himself. It was a strange lyric that didn't really lead anywhere.

> *"Ein Fischer mit der Rute*
> *Wohl an dem Ufer stand*
> *Und sah's mit kalten Blute*
> *Wie sich das Fischlein wand"*

> An angler with his rod
> Stood on the bank
> And cold-bloodedly watched
> The fish twist and turn

Rheinhardt sang the poetry with effortless fluency, his rich lyrical baritone filling the room and rattling the windowpanes.

Again, Liebermann asked himself, *What is it about?*

A narrator, watching an angler, hopes that a trout will not get caught. However, when the writhing fish is lifted from the water, he is sent into an impotent rage.

Did the poet mean to show how human beings encroach upon and disturb the natural world? Or was he suggesting that freedom is so treasured by human beings that even a landed fish can find sympathy in a poet's heart?

After an agitated final verse, the burbling theme reappeared in the piano accompaniment and the music progressed to a tranquil pianissimo ending.

Liebermann looked up and saw that Rheinhardt was pleased with his performance. However, when the inspector noticed Liebermann's troubled expression, he said, "It wasn't *that* bad, was it?"

"Not at all. . . . Your voice was relaxed, expressive, and beautifully resonant."

"Then why do you look so perplexed?"

Liebermann lifted his hands off the keyboard but allowed the final chord to continue indefinitely by keeping his foot on the pedal.

"What's it about?" Liebermann asked.

"*Die Forelle?*"

"Yes."

"A man—watching an angler—watching a fish," said Rheinhardt flatly.

"With respect, Oskar, that isn't a terribly penetrating analysis."

"It's what the poet describes," said Rheinhardt. "It's what the words say."

The young doctor considered his friend's riposte, and conceded, "Yes, I suppose so." He released the pedal, terminating the gentle hum of the fading chord. "Sometimes things are exactly what they seem to be, and nothing else."

"A difficult concept for a psychiatrist to grasp, admittedly," said Rheinhardt.

They retired to the smoking room, lit some cigars, sipped brandy, and stared into the fire. In due course Liebermann broke the silence. "I suspect that your choice of *Die Forelle* represents a form of wish fulfillment."

Rheinhardt roused himself, cleared his throat, and replied, "I chose it because I wanted us to end our music-making with something cheerful."

"Yes, but a song about a man catching a fish? Come now, Oskar, the parallels are blindingly obvious! The very idea of *catching* has positive connotations for you, a detective inspector. Your raison d'être is to catch criminals. That is why you find *Die Forelle* so uplifting. It fulfills—at least symbolically—one of your deepest wishes. When the trout is caught, instead of raging with the poet, you experience nothing but satisfaction. You were beaming with pleasure when the song came to an end."

"I thought we'd agreed that sometimes things are exactly what they seem to be, and nothing else."

Liebermann shrugged. "You have certainly been *fishing* this week, and I must suppose from your good humor that you are pleased with your *catch*."

"All right," said Rheinhardt. "You've made your point! I would be most grateful if we could now continue this conversation without any further reference to fish."

"Of course," said Liebermann. "Perhaps we should begin with the autopsy?"

Rheinhardt nodded, poured himself another brandy, and said, "Decapitation was achieved through clockwise cranial rotation." He traced a circle in the air with his finger. "Professor Mathias said that the last time he'd seen anything like it was when he was in the army doing his national service. An infantryman stumbled across a bear and her cubs. She attacked him and ripped his head off." Rheinhardt swirled his brandy. "The monk had no other injuries. Except some superficial damage to the facial skin, some small cuts and grazes, which could have been caused when the head was rolled away from the body. However, Professor Mathias did find a laceration about here . . ."

Rheinhardt tapped his crown.

"Caused by a blunt weapon, no doubt," Liebermann interrupted, "which is why there was no evidence of a struggle. The monk was unconscious when they set about removing his head. Did Professor Mathias express an opinion regarding the handedness of the perpetrator, based on the direction of cranial rotation?"

"No. He wasn't prepared to say anything conclusive. Given that the phenomenon of manual decapitation is so rare, he advised caution in this respect."

"That is reasonable."

"I went back to the Maria Treue Kirche on Wednesday," Rheinhardt continued, "to question the abbot. He spoke very highly of Brother Stanislav and was completely mystified by the monk's murder. So much so that he was inclined to blame the devil."

"Ha!" Liebermann scoffed.

"I waited outside the school and talked to some of the parents as they arrived to collect their children. Some had brought wreaths—costly for people of their class, and yet it was like a flower market! They described a kind, compassionate man, a teacher with a gentle manner, particularly evident in his dealings with the younger boys and girls. Brother Stanislav's good works were not confined to the classroom. He made it his business to help the most disadvantaged families and frequently arranged alms and housing. He was, as far as they were concerned, nothing less than a saint."

"Then you have discounted my suggestion that he might have been murdered by former pupils seeking vengeance."

"It isn't a conjecture that I currently favor, given what has *since* come to light." Rheinhardt paused to light a cigar. "I returned to the church the following day and overheard two monks saying disparaging things about Brother Stansilav. One of them ran off. The other, a Brother Lupercus, was willing to talk a little, although he was eager not to be seen talking to me. He urged me to read some articles written by Brother Stanislav for *Das Vaterland*, a conservative Catholic newspaper."

"Not a publication I can claim to be overly familiar with."

"Nor I," said Rheinhardt, smiling. "Haussmann dug some back issues out of the library, and we were able to find two articles by Brother Stanislav. They were supposed to be about education, but in fact, they were more like political tracts. Some heinous sentiments were expressed with respect to Jews."

"Clerics are always saying such things."

"They can be outspoken, I agree, but it is not customary for them to express their prejudices in such colorful language. He likened the diaspora after the pogroms to the spread of vermin, a *plague*."

Liebermann turned to face his friend. "You think there is a connection here, with the column?"

"There could be."

The young doctor considered this possibility for a moment before gesturing for Rheinhardt to continue.

"We learned that Brother Stanislav had become associated with a conservative political group, an odd amalgam of anti-Semites. A few months ago they held an unofficial rally in the old ghetto area of Leopoldstadt. Brother Stanislav gave an inflammatory speech, and there was some fighting. By the time the constables arrived, the crowd had dispersed, but later the body of a young man was found on the Prater. Chaim Robak, an orthodox Jew. He had been beaten and stabbed."

"The agitators killed him?"

"We don't know that for certain, but it's very likely. Thus, one could argue that Brother Stanislav was responsible for the young man's death."

"Have you spoken to Robak's family?"

"I see that you are already considering revenge as a motive. Yes, I have spoken to them. Robak senior is in his late sixties and walks with a stick. He married a much younger woman and they have three daughters, all under twenty and still living at home. None of them could have killed Stanislav. They are physically incapable of performing such a violent act."

Liebermann inhaled the sweet, fruity fragrance of his brandy.

"I wonder why Brother Lupercus told you about the *Vaterland* articles."

"Even monks are prey to the usual human frailties—rivalry, envy, spite. He was probably resentful of Brother Stanislav's saintly reputation. Or perhaps Brother Stanislav was always getting prefer-ential treatment from the abbot. Who knows?"

"Do you think the abbot knew about Brother Stanislav's political activities?"

"Perhaps. The sad truth—as I'm sure you're only too well aware—is that, for most devout Christians, Jews are—and will al-ways be—the people who killed Jesus Christ. Deicide is not easily forgiven."

Liebermann tilted his brandy glass and watched a point of light move around the rim. "The Hasidic communities are relatively self-contained, congregating around a hereditary leader, or rebbe. These men have enormous influence, and it is just possible that one of them might have orchestrated Brother Stanislav's murder."

"I thought the Hasidic Jews were a peaceful people."

"They are. But there are always exceptions—fanatics. One can imagine how it might happen. Fiery sermons. The idea of *retribution* planted in the minds of devoted followers and justified with quotes from scripture. The rebbe might even claim to have received a direct communication from God Himself. This is all quite plausible; how-ever, what I don't understand is why they would have set themselves the most inconvenient task of ripping off a man's head! If the purpose was to retaliate, then they could have simply struck Brother Stanislav a little harder—smashing his skull instead of merely knocking him out. This would have been quite enough to achieve their aim: an eye for an eye."

"Does tearing the head off an enemy have any religious signifi-cance?" Rheinhardt asked.

"Not that I know of. The only biblical beheading I can think of is that of John the Baptist." Liebermann pulled at his lower lip. "Which doesn't help us very much."

"Then perhaps it was simply an audacious display, meant to make their enemies fearful."

"But if that was their objective, why did they set about their task in such a peculiar way? Why didn't they use a sabre or an axe? It would have been so much easier. There is something going on here that is most strange and I fear—at present—utterly beyond our powers of comprehension."

16

AFTER THE MORNING WARD round, Liebermann returned to his room. On the floor he found an envelope. He sat at his desk, broke the seal, and read the note inside. It was from the hospital's chancellor, Professor Robert Gandler. Liebermann was to report—no later than one o'clock—to the chancellor's office, in order to discuss a matter of utmost importance. Liebermann looked at his wristwatch and, discovering that it was almost noon, set off, walking briskly through seemingly endless interconnected corridors. He had to ask a porter for directions. Finally he managed to find the chancellor's office on the third floor, in the administrative department. The sound of a typist, tapping at her keyboard, created an illusion of heavy rainfall.

Liebermann knocked and waited for an invitation to enter. None came, so he knocked again, this time louder.

"Ah . . ." He heard a voice, sounding as if it belonged to someone being roused from sleep. "Ah . . . do come in."

Liebermann opened the door. It was a large room, lined with shelves, each of which was crammed with files and official-looking directories. He was facing a desk, piled so high with papers that the person behind them was entirely hidden.

"Yes?"

"Dr. Liebermann, sir. You wished to speak with me?"

A head appeared from behind the barricade of paperwork.

Professor Gandler was in his late sixties, but his abundant black hair was only just beginning to turn silver. It was brushed back from a high, pale forehead, and adamantly refused to acknowledge the sovereignty of gravity. Renegade tufts sprouted at various angles, giving the impression that he had only recently been battered by a strong wind. His dress was traditional and sombre, and a pair of eager eyes peered through oval-shaped spectacles.

"Liebermann," said the professor. "Ah yes, Liebermann. Thank you for coming." He pointed to a wooden chair with a quilted seat. "Please . . ."

The young doctor bowed and came forward, but when he sat down, he found that he was staring once again into the blank wall of piled papers. A tower of documents in the center began to retreat and move off to the side, its displacement creating a defile through which Professor Gandler's head reappeared.

"You wouldn't believe the number of documents I have to read, sign, countersign, approve, reject, and so on. It's quite intolerable." The professor made a steeple with his fingers and hummed loudly. "Liebermann . . ."

"A matter of utmost importance?" Liebermann prompted.

"Indeed," said the professor. "Indeed . . . However, with your cooperation I am sure that the *situation* can be managed. And once all parties are satisfied, the affair can be laid to rest."

"Situation?"

"Yes. The von Kortig business."

"I'm not sure I understand . . ."

"I suppose I should hear your side of the story first, although whatever you say, I doubt whether it will alter things very much. The priest would not have misrepresented events, and there were witnesses, of course."

Liebermann still looked confused.

"It *was* you, wasn't it," the professor continued, "who stopped Father Benedikt from giving von Kortig the last rites? We have only one Dr. Liebermann working in the hospital at the moment. So it *must* have been you. I remember that there used be a cardiologist, Emanuel Liebermann, who worked here many, many years ago. . . . Are you related?"

"No." Liebermann crossed his legs and leaned toward the professor. "I'm sorry, sir, but am I to understand that there has been a complaint concerning my professional conduct?"

"The priest wrote to the old baron explaining what happened, and he in turn wrote to me. I was obliged to raise his grievances at the hospital committee meeting, which was scheduled for the following day. Unfortunately the committee members were very troubled by what they heard."

"With respect, Professor, may I see the old baron's letter?"

"Certainly not. It is confidential."

"Then would you be so kind as to tell me what he wrote?"

"That you stopped the priest from giving his son the consolation of his faith."

"Sir, the young baron had been given morphine and was unaware of his fatal condition. He was making plans for the future and was in good spirits. If the priest had been permitted to administer the last rites, the young baron would have realized that he was about to die. He was not, in my estimation, a courageous or thoughtful man. He was completely unprepared for such a dreadful revelation. It would have caused him considerable distress. Fortunately I was able to stop the priest, and the young baron died peacefully."

"Yes, yes, yes," said the professor, repeatedly batting the air with his hand. "You were acting in the patient's interests. That goes without saying. But that isn't the point."

"Then perhaps you could explain?"

"Bishop Waldheim is on the committee and wants you to apologize. First by writing to the old baron; second by writing to the priest; and third in person to the committee."

There was a lengthy pause, during which the reiterative hammering of the typewriter—perhaps in the next room—became exceptionally loud.

Liebermann said, "I am happy to write to the old baron and to Father Benedikt, and I will attend the next meeting of the committee—"

"Excellent!" cried the professor, clapping his hands together. "I knew you wouldn't be difficult! Good man!"

"With respect, Professor," said Liebermann, "I did not finish. I am happy to explain my actions and to answer any questions concerning the legitimacy of my medical judgment."

"Nobody is doubting your medical judgment," said the professor sharply.

"Then why should I apologize?"

"You have caused offense."

"But I haven't done anything wrong."

"Isn't causing offense wrong?"

"Not so wrong as letting a patient die in distress."

The professor got up from his seat and walked over to the window. He pulled the curtain aside and looked out, a crooked smile twisting his lips.

"Herr Doctor, you are placing me in a very awkward position." He turned abruptly. "I am not sure whether you appreciate the importance of the committee. It not only provides the hospital with a moral compass, it also provides us with resources. The members of the committee assist in the raising of funds, and they wield influence on our behalf so that we can maintain the high standards that have made us preeminent in the whole of Europe. We *all* benefit from their patronage and charity—not only the patients but we doctors too. If the committee wants you to apologize, then I would strongly urge you to comply. For heaven's sake, man, it's a simple matter of dashing off a few lines." The professor returned from the window and, resting both hands on his desktop, leaned forward, peering through the gap in his paperwork. "Look, I'll tell you what . . . I'll see if I can charm the bishop into accepting a letter to the committee instead of an appearance in person. There! That should make it easier, eh? How about that as a compromise?"

"But I didn't do anything wrong."

"Herr Doctor, if you see no purpose for yourself in complying with the bishop's request, then perhaps you might consider the interests of the hospital."

"With respect, Professor Gandler, I very much doubt that the fate of the hospital will be greatly affected by whether or not I apologize."

The professor sat down in his chair and sighed.

"I am an old man, Herr Doctor. But I was young once, and thus have the advantage. *You* were never old. Permit me to give you some advice. Most of the battles fought in youth seem insignificant with the passing of time. When I reflect on my behavior as a young man—the arguments, the duels—I find it incomprehensible, and sometimes just foolish. I very much hope that when you reach my age, you will have fewer regrets than I do."

The noise of the nearby typewriter filled the ensuing silence.

"Well?" said the professor.

"I didn't do anything wrong," said Liebermann again, shaking his head.

"Very well," said the chancellor curtly. "You may leave. I will convey the substance of our interview to the committee and will commend you as a man of principle. I fear, however, that this will not be enough to appease them. Good afternoon, Herr Doctor."

17

"It is said that Enoch, who became the angel Metatron, was once a humble cobbler." Rebbe Barash looked around the room at the studious faces of the young men. "But with every stitch he not only joined the upper leather of the shoe with the sole, he also joined all higher things with all lower things. His awl conjoined heaven and earth and united the rocks and stars." He stroked his long black beard, and his eyes became inquisitorial. "What does this mean? How are we to understand it?"

"My rebbe." One of the young men raised his hand. "Does it mean that he undertook his daily work meditating on the divine?"

Barash's large head rocked backward and forward. His coiled sideburns bounced, extending and contracting with the movement. He did not smile, but his heavy features communicated solemn approval.

"Indeed. Thus, even his profane actions acquired the qualities of a sacred ritual. He transformed the mundane task of repairing shoes into a spiritual exercise. And in the fullness of time, he too was transformed. We have much to learn from Enoch, the humble cobbler. Through patient and persistent application much can be achieved. And if we are to transform the world, we too must cultivate the virtues of patience and persistence."

The zaddik paused and noted the rapt expressions on the faces of his followers.

"In the beginning," Barash continued, "when the vessels were broken, much of the divine essence ascended back to its source. But some remained enclosed in the shards of the vessels, the substances of the material world. It is this entrapped essence that sustains all. Nothing can exist—even for a fleeting moment—without its power. If all the essence is liberated, returning to its proper place in the realm of high things, evil will have nothing on which to feed and will cease to exist. The release of divine essence separates good from evil, a process that, if continued, will lead to the end of all wickedness. Eventually everything will be in its rightful place and our work will be done. Obey the commandments, pray, observe the Sabbath, and perform acts of charity and justice. All of these will release divine essence. God alone cannot ensure the triumph of good over evil. He cannot mend what has been undone. Therefore you must be like Enoch and approach every labor as if it were an act of devotion."

Barash clasped his big hands together and held them against his chest.

"If our enemies succeed, they not only destroy us, they destroy everything. There can be no release of divine essence, no mending, no healing. The powers of evil will grow, and the natural order of things will never be restored. The darkness that comes will be impenetrable—and final. There will be no redemption. Yet we should not despair. Our enemies are ignorant. They know nothing of our ancient wisdom, the hidden power of words and numbers. The *magids* have used this power many times before to protect our people, and it can be used again. So let our enemies provoke us, taunt us, and spit as we pass. Let them! For the time of reckoning has come, and such a force will be unleashed against them that they will quake at the merest mention of its name."

18

Rheinhardt halted in order to admire the architectural peculiarities of the Turkish synagogue. Its doors were housed beneath
onion-shaped arches, and its minimal decoration consisted of repeated abstract patterns. Towering above the synagogue's terraces
was a minaret with a domed roof and cusped windows. It could have
easily been mistaken for a mosque had it not been for the Hebrew
characters embossed over the entrance.

A noisy caravan of carts and barrows, heavily laden with crates,
rattled up Zirkusgasse.

This won't do, thought Rheinhardt. *I have fish to catch.*

He remembered the conversation that he had had with Liebermann about *Die Forelle* and, smiling, hummed a few bars of Schubert's
jaunty melody. He cut across the center of Leopoldstadt, turned right
into Taborstrasse, and eventually arrived at Tandelmarktgasse.

The buildings were tall and unadorned, with raked roofs and
stained plaster. They resembled oversize alpine huts. All the ground-
floor apartments had been converted into shops. Rheinhardt passed
two men standing in a doorway. Some of their goods had been put out
on the pavement: a dented samovar, a rusty accordion, a basket containing a tea service, and a few silver candlesticks. One of the men
raised his hat and called out a price for the samovar. Rheinhardt declined and hurried on.

Before reaching the market square—and only just behind the police station—Rheinhardt came to a stall selling savories. A brazier

was burning, and the air smelled of cooking oil and herbs. On seeing Rheinhardt, the stallholder, a man with a thin mustache and pointed rodent features, extended his hand.

"Ah, my dear friend, good to see you." His voice was accented and slightly nasal. "How's life?"

As Rheinhardt shook Moni Teitel's hand, he let go of the coins he had been holding in his palm. Teitel dropped the inducement into his apron pocket and removed a golden-brown potato latke from the brazier.

"Try this . . . and help yourself to the pickled cucumber. They're very sweet."

"Thank you," said Rheinhardt.

"Family well?"

"Thriving."

"Then why such a long face? You should be a happy man. Health is a blessing, make no mistake."

Rheinhardt bit into the latke and looked off toward the market. "So . . . any news?"

"There's always news, my friend."

"Of interest to me?"

"Possibly." Teitel prodded the coals in the brazier with a poker. "Since that business on the Prater a few months back—you know, the boy who was killed at the rally—there've been rumors. There's this zaddik—"

"This what?" Rheinhardt cut in.

"Zaddik, a preacher among the Hasidim. He's called Barash, and they say he knew what was going to happen. They say he knew the priest was going to die."

"How?"

"Perhaps God told him. They're fanatics, these people."

A woman wearing a spotted scarf and carrying a small child

stopped to buy some oatcakes and some pastry pillows filled with curd cheese. While she was haggling, Rheinhardt found a shop window and pretended to be interested in the display. When the woman had gone, he returned to the stall.

"Where does he live, this Barash?"

"Just round the corner." Teitel jerked his thumb toward the market. "In the old ghetto buildings."

"Where did you hear this?"

"My brother-in-law. He was in Zucker's—do you know Zucker's? One of Barash's people was in there. They were talking about the priest, and this boy pipes up that Barash had known— weeks before it happened."

"Anything else?"

Teitel shook his head. Rheinhardt dropped another two kronen into Teitel's hand and said, "For the latke."

"You're very generous," said Teitel. Then, raising his voice, he added, "Have you heard the one about the priest and the rabbi?"

Rheinhardt shook his head.

"A priest and a rabbi are on a train. The priest turns to the rabbi and says, 'Is it still a requirement of your faith to not eat pork?' And the rabbi replies, 'Yes, that's right.' So the priest then says, 'Have you ever eaten pork?' And the rabbi says, 'On one occasion I did succumb to temptation, and, yes, I did eat pork.' The priest goes back to reading his book. A while later the rabbi speaks again. 'Father,' he says, 'is it still a requirement of your faith to remain celibate?' And the priest replies, 'Yes, very much so.' The rabbi then asks him, 'Father, have you ever succumbed to temptation?' And the priest replies, 'Yes, Rabbi, on one occasion I was weak, and I succumbed.' The rabbi nods, pauses for a moment, and then says, 'It's a lot better than pork, isn't it?'"

Rheinhardt dug another krone out of his vest pocket and flicked

it over the pickle jars. Its flashing trajectory was interrupted by Teitel's fingers as he snatched it out of the air.

"You're a gentleman, sir," said Teitel.

"And you are a scoundrel," said Rheinhardt, laughing to himself
as he turned away.

19

Professor Priel and Asher Kusevitsky had been engaged in a deep conversation about mysticism and metaphor. They were sitting in a corner seat in the Café Eiles, which was situated behind the town hall. It was a relatively new coffeehouse and had not as yet built up a very large clientele. There were some regular customers, mostly civil servants and lawyers, but it was always possible to get a seat.

The gas lamps on the wall had already been turned on, but the opaque globes on the brassy arms of the chandeliers were dull and lifeless. A big station clock hung on chains from an archway that led to the kitchen. Beneath it an alert-looking waiter scanned the empty tables.

"You see, my boy . . . ," said Priel, pausing to accomplish the delicate operation of sipping coffee without moistening his mustache or beard. "Lurianic Kabbalah was never the exclusive property of a small closed group. It became the subject of much popular preaching and influenced many aspects of Jewish life. Why? I'll tell you why. The Lurianic creation myth describes a cosmic catastrophe—the *breaking of the vessels*—after which nothing is in its proper place. . . ." He took another quick sip. "And of course, something that is not in its proper place, is—as it were—also in exile. Needless to say, this idea, which is at the heart of the Lurianic canon, is one that finds deep and complex resonances in the Jewish psyche. Human existence becomes the scene of the soul's exile."

Asher Kusevitsky nodded, and picked up one of the *punschkrapfen* that Professor Priel had ordered before his arrival. The symmetry of the cube appealed to him. His teeth sank into the soft pink icing, which cracked, forming a tessellated surface. At once his mouth was suffused with a mêlée of flavors. The coolness of the shell contrasted with the warmth of the alcoholic sponge inside, and he was overwhelmed by an almost dizzying sweetness. After he had swallowed, his taste buds were still tingling with flavors: marzipan, nuts, and jam.

"Is it good?" asked Priel.

"Excellent," Asher replied.

The professor took a large bite, examined the interior, nodded approvingly, and picked a few particles of icing from his beard.

"How are the rehearsals going?" he said, evidently having finished with the subject of Lurianic Kabbalah.

"Very well. Herzog is a fine actor."

"Yes, I saw him at the Court Theatre last year. A very impressive performance."

"And Baumshlager's shopgirl is perfect. She brings such sympathy to the role."

"Excellent. Let us hope that this play receives the plaudits it so justly deserves."

Asher's mouth twisted to form an ironic smile. "Well, given its subject matter, I have to say that I am not expecting very much praise from certain critics."

"Indeed. But they are not your audience. Providing *our* people come to see *The Dybbuk*, that is all that matters." Priel held up his half-eaten cake as if it possessed totemic potencies. "They must become more aware of who they are and draw inspiration and strength from their traditions. Much has been forgotten, but gradually, little by little, we can reintroduce them to their stories, myths, and legends. I have such faith in the power of narrative—to inspire, revive, and sustain. A people who have been cut off from their folklore are doomed. We define ourselves with our stories. We become who we are—by telling stories. And we are held together—as a people—by our stories. Yes, Asher, my boy, you are doing us all a great service. You are giving them something back, which they have lost. You are giving them back their souls."

"Today, the Volkstheatre. Tomorrow . . . ?"

"The Opera House!" Priel lowered his voice. "Perhaps Director Mahler could be encouraged to try his hand at a dramatic piece. After all, his symphonies are dramatic enough. He must be sick and tired of all those caterwauling Valkyries and brutish muscle-bound heroes. *The Dybbuk* would make a fine libretto . . ."

"It could never happen."

Priel squeezed Asher's arm. "It does no harm to dream. And sometimes dreams come true. Ask your brother. He knows a thing or two about dreams!" Asher smiled and swallowed the remains of his *punschkrapfen*. "And how is he, by the way, the good doctor?" Priel continued. "Enjoying his newfound liberty as a Rothenstein scholar?"

"He's . . . well," said Asher.

The professor detected a slight hesitation. "Is something the matter?"

"No, no." Asher paused, grimaced, and added, "Nothing's the matter, but . . ."

"What?"

"He's seeing someone."

"Seeing someone?"

"A woman. Katzer's daughter—Anna."

"Perhap it is just an infatuation . . . a temporary dalliance."

"No. I don't think so."

"He's in love?"

"He talks about her incessantly."

The professor dabbed his mouth with a napkin and thought for a moment. "I see." He peered over his pince-nez. "Well, providing it doesn't distract him."

Asher's expression became resolute. "Don't worry. I won't let it."

"Good," said the professor. "Then there's nothing to worry about, eh?"

He raised his hand to get the waiter's attention and called, "Two more coffees and some more of these splendid cakes."

"Oh, by the way," said Asher. "The Katzer girl . . . she has a project you might be interested in. She's trying to raise funds for a Jewish women's hostel in Leopoldstadt."

The professor turned and, looking over his pince-nez again, said, "Is she, indeed?"

20

Last night I dreamed of Amelia Lydgate, and what a dream it was: a wild, strange dream. Quite unnerving. As I sit here in my apartment, surrounded by familiar things, it seems, by way of contrast, even stranger. Something of the dream has stayed with me all day. I had fancied that writing it down might be cathartic; however, now that the time has come, I find that I am curiously reluctant. I am experiencing what Professor Freud would call <u>resistance,</u> and therefore I can be certain that the dream contains uncomfortable truths.

Am I embarrassed, I wonder? Ashamed? Professor Freud did not balk at intimate self-disclosure when he was writing his dream book. He was perfectly content to describe a boil the size of an apple rising at the base of his scrotum, merely to illustrate the point that the physical state of the body can influence what appears in dreams. Why should I be so coy? What am I afraid of? Writing this journal is not unlike the process of free association in psychoanalysis. I must suspend the urge to censor.

So: we were in a garden, Miss Lydgate and I. A place of extraordinary lushness and beauty. Tropical. Humid. We were surrounded by brightly colored exotic flowers—orange amaryllises, yellow orchids, and purple lilies. They were all oversize. Long filaments drooped under the weight of anthers, heavy with pollen, and a conspicuously phallic spadix rose up from the center of a bright red anthurium. Pink lotus blossoms floated on a lake, the surface of which shimmered with colonies of emerald algae. The colors were so vivid, the light so strong, everything seemed newly made—primordial. Dew-drops had collected on the petals. They resembled pieces from a chandelier, and each glassy fragment contained a captive miniature sun. The air was warm and perfumed with fra-grances of exquisite, intoxicating sweetness. I could hear bird-song, and something that sounded like glissandi played on many harps.

Miss Lydgate was standing next to me—naked. Her hair cascaded over her shoulders and breasts, but it did not descend far enough to conceal her sex. Her mons veneris was covered with fiery curls, and her skin was an unblemished white. She looked at me and said, with some anger, "I will not lie below. I am also made from the earth and therefore must be considered your equal." I responded with some indignation, and we began to argue. Although I cannot remember exactly what was said, the meaning of our heated exchange was quite clear and con-cerned coital "superiority."

Then, unexpectedly, she pronounced my father's name. I turned and saw that he was sitting close by on a throne. As is so often the way in dreams, his presence in our paradisal gar-den did not strike me as in any way remarkable. My father said, "It is not good for a man to be alone." I protested, "I am not alone." However, when I gestured toward Miss Lydgate, she had vanished.

In this instance I can hardly disagree with Professor Freud with respect to his views on the predominance of sexual con-tent in dreams. That Miss Lydgate should appear naked obvi-ously suggests the fulfillment of a "forbidden" wish. But what of our argument concerning coital superiority? An idea suggests itself: Amelia Lydgate is an extraordinary woman, endowed with remarkable intellectual gifts. Yet, would marriage to such a strong-minded woman eventually lead to feelings of emasculation? Does the dream betray a deep-seated anxiety that I am unwilling to own? I have always been a vigorous advocate of equality between the sexes; however, in reality, perhaps I am still—at least in part—a traditionalist. It is not that men are strong and women weak (or any other such crude and dubious distinction), but rather that the sexes are complementary. They <u>do</u> have different attributes. Moreover, the success of a relationship might well depend on these differences coming together, to make a whole that is greater than the sum of its parts. Is that what my father represented? Traditional values? "It is not good for a man to be alone." Indeed, and although I do not feel alone—preoccupied as I am with Miss Lydgate—the fact of the matter is that <u>I am alone.</u>

My relations with Miss Lydgate have certainly reached a difficult juncture. In the normal course of events, a couple grows more intimate until the erotic nature of their mutual attraction becomes explicit; however, if this period exceeds a certain amount of time, then the relationship is conducted largely as a friendship rather than a burgeoning romance. It becomes increasingly difficult for both parties to see each other as anything more than friends. This is how I have chosen to account for my inaction. My dream, however, suggests an alternative. Perhaps my paralysis with respect to Miss Lydgate has more complex origins. Desire is one of those things that seems ostensibly simple but is always—in truth—very obscure. Answering the question "What do I want?" is far more challenging than most people ever realize.

21

The coffeehouse had little to distinguish it from the other shops. It did not have lettering above the windows or a bright awning, only a board standing on the pavement on which the proprietor's name had been painted in flowing red letters: *Zucker*.

Rheinhardt opened the door and entered. His first impression was of humidity and noise. Condensation had made the windows opaque, and the steamy atmosphere was ripe with the savory smells of frankfurters, mustard, and sauerkraut. Although the coffeehouse had only four circular tables, these were fully occupied and were covered with newspapers, which were being continually consulted in order to support one side or the other of a communal debate involving everyone present. In addition to seated patrons, there were many others who were either standing in a central space or leaning against the walls. The general mayhem was compounded by the presence of a shabby violinist who had situated himself in a corner and was singing along to a merry dance tune. There was much shouting, gesticulating, jeering, and occasional outbursts of raucous laughter.

Squeezing through the crowd, Rheinhardt advanced to the counter, where an attractive young woman was ladling a thick orange soup into rustic bowls.

"I'm looking for Herr Zucker."

"What?"

"I'm looking for Herr Zucker," Rheinhardt repeated, raising his voice.

The young woman wiped some perspiration off her brow with

the back of her hand and, leaning back, directed her voice through an open door. "Father! Someone to see you." The sound of clattering saucepans and a Yiddisher curse heralded the emergence of a big man wearing a striped apron. His face possessed a rough, unfinished quality—raw and pitted skin and nubbly features. Rheinhardt noticed that his exposed arms were insulated by a natural sleeve of wiry black hair. It was difficult to believe that he was the pretty girl's father.

"Inspector Rheinhardt. Security office. I'd like to ask you a few questions."

Zucker nodded. "This way, please."

Rheinhardt followed him through the kitchen (in which a cook appeared to be tossing pancakes solely for the amusement of a prepubescent boy) and out into a little cobbled garden.

"Take a seat, Inspector," said Zucker, gesturing toward a bench. "It's quiet out here. At least we'll be able to hear ourselves speak. Can I get you anything? Tea? Coffee? We have some delicious *reis trauttmansdorff*."

"That's very kind of you to offer, Herr Zucker. But no, thank you."

The two men sat down on the bench.

"What can I do for you, then?" said Zucker, taking a packet of cigarettes and a box of matches from his apron pocket.

"I would like to ask you a few questions about some of your customers." Zucker offered Rheinhardt a cigarette, which the inspector declined, before lighting one for himself. "I take it," Rheinhardt continued, "that you are aware of what happened in Josefstadt last week."

"The murder?"

"Indeed."

"Well, of course. It's been all over the papers. The customers don't stop talking about it."

"One of your customers—a young Hasid, I believe—was overheard saying that his master, a preacher called Barash, had prophesied the monk's death."

"Yes, that's true. I was there at the time. But—with respect—you shouldn't be taking very much notice of such things."

"Oh, why not?"

"The Hasidim aren't like the rest of us. They believe all sorts of nonsense. They interpret dreams, commune with the dead, and think that God reveals himself in magic numbers! And as for prophecies . . . Well, they're always saying this thing or that thing is going to happen. They make so many predictions! I mean, it stands to reason they've got to be right about something—eventually! Coincidence, Inspector. That's all it is. Coincidence."

"Did the young Hasid say specifically that the monk would be murdered?"

"No, I don't think so."

"Please, try to remember exactly what he said."

"Well, that's not so easy. As usual, there was a lot of noise, and I was very busy."

"Was your daughter present?"

"No. That's why I was busy."

"Even so, perhaps you could try to remember what was said?"

Zucker paused and thought for a moment.

"They were arguing about religion. A young Hasid, and some workmen. They usually keep themselves to themselves, the Hasidim. But when they do get into arguments with my regulars"—Zucker pretended to cover his ears—"it's worse than a yeshiva."

"A what?"

"A school where they study holy books. There's an old saying: two rabbis, three arguments. And you know, it's not far wrong."

"You were saying . . . ," Rheinhardt prompted the proprietor. "About the young Hasid?"

"Oh yes . . . Actually, I think the workmen were just teasing. But the Hasid was getting more and more agitated, and to prove some point he mentioned his leader's prophecy. To be honest, I can't remember very much more than that." Zucker waved his cigarette in the air, creating a vortex of ash. "Now, are you sure I can't interest you in my *reis trauttmansdorff*? I promise you, once you've tasted it, you'll be back for more."

"You said that these Hasidim are always making prophecies. What other things have you heard?"

Zucker grinned. "Everything from horse race winners to the coming of the Messiah! Now, for the last time, Inspector: my *reis trauttmansdorff*? Are you going to try it or not?"

22

NAGEL'S GENERAL STORE WAS situated in a narrow alleyway that connected two roads on opposite sides of the old ghetto buildings. It was paved with yellowish flagstones—many of them cracked and loose—and the air was suffused with a pungent, penetrating dampness. The alley was so narrow, and so inauspiciously positioned, that it received direct sunlight only for a few hours a day in the summer months. For the rest of the year it existed in a perpetual twilight that intensified to become a precocious night by mid-afternoon. This gloom was relieved by a single naked gas jet, mounted on one of the walls.

The general store was sandwiched between two other shops. A secondhand book dealer's, occupied by an old man whose moldering stock added another harmonic of decay to the musty mélange that tainted the air, and a cardboard vendor's, run by a cadaverous Pole who spoke only Yiddish.

In the window of the general store were various items intended to attract the attention of passersby. However, such light as there was passed through the grimy little panes of glass enfolded the goods in a greenish murk and made the boxes, candles, tins, string, and bottles look like the kind of detritus that collects on the bed of a slow-flowing river.

Nahum sat behind the counter, toying with the weights and his scale. He was arranging the small weights on one side, to counterbalance a large weight on the other. The scale seesawed indecisively on its fulcrum—falling neither one way nor the other. Through the ceiling came the sound of Nahum's father coughing, a horrible bark that crackled with phlegm the color of pus. Nahum knew this because he had inspected the contents of his father's spittoon and noticed the change. The old man's chest problem had obviously gotten much worse. They had scraped together a little money to pay for a doctor, but all he had said was that it would be better for Hayyim if they moved out of their rooms above the shop and away from the damp alleyway. But how were they going to do that?

The stockroom—really a cupboard—was empty, and there were still some of the suppliers who hadn't been paid. Nahum tapped the smaller weights, and watched them descend, slow to a halt, and rise up again. The shop had never made much of a profit, but now it was running at a loss.

Rebbe Barash had promised change. He had held Hayyim's hand and promised the old man that life would be better, very soon. But if things went on like this, it would be too late.

From outside, Nahum recognized the heavy tread of hobnailed boots on the flagstones. The door flew open, and the little bell chimed. Two thickset men stepped into the shop. Their broad shoulders and lumpy features became all that Nahum could see. One had a distinctive scar that cut through his left eyebrow and continued as a white weal down his cheek. The other had the broken nose and grazed knuckles of a pugilist.

"You came only last week," said Nahum.

"Open the cash box," said the man with the scar.

"But we've hardly sold anything . . ."

The man swung his fist over the counter and knocked Nahum's hat off.

"Next time it'll be your head."

Nahum, with trembling fingers, took the cash box from under the counter and, taking the key from his pocket, opened it up. Inside was change amounting to no more than three kronen.

"Where's the rest? I wasn't born yesterday, you know."

"There isn't any more!"

The man grabbed Nahum by the collar and pulled him over the counter. He pressed his face up close.

"Go and get it."

"There isn't any more!"

The man lifted Nahum off his feet and threw him against the shelves. A bottle fell off and smashed on the floor.

"Nahum . . . Nahum?" It was the old man.

Nahum looked up and shouted, "It's all right, Father. . . . It was nothing . . . an accident."

"Be careful, why don't you?" the old man croaked.

"I will, Father."

The two men looked at each other and smirked.

"Please," said Nahum, lowering his voice. "I beg you. He's very ill."

The man with the scar scooped the coins out of the cash box and put them into his pocket.

"Listen. You get us the rest of the money by next time, or we'll give you a beating to remember. Do you understand?"

They stormed out of the shop, accompanied by the innocent tinkling of the bell. Nahum collapsed onto his stool and wiped the perspiration from his brow.

23

Rheinhardt had been smoking cigars all the way from Josef-stadt to Hietzing. As a result, when he opened the carriage door, he emerged from the confined space like Mephistopheles, surrounded by a roiling yellow cloud. He placed a foot on the step and jumped to the ground, his coat catching the air and rising up like a black wing. The young constable who greeted Rheinhardt was somewhat over-awed by the inspector's theatrical *débouché*. The constable was already in an excited state, and his nervous energy found easy expression in garrulous speech.

"The man who found the body, sir—Herr Quint—he's in the church with my colleague. He was walking home after spending an evening with friends—Well, that's what he said, but I think it more likely that he'd been enjoying the company of a *lady*. He discovered the body and then ran over to the hotel." The constable pointed across the road. "The night porter called the station. We're in Dom-mayergasse—not far, just around the corner—and we got here within minutes. Would you like to see the body, sir? Horrible it is, horrible, the sort of thing that'll give you nightmares—and so soon after the other one. A priest, wasn't it? I never thought we'd see the likes of this up here, not in Hietzing. This way, sir, this way."

Rheinhardt grabbed the constable's arm.

"Just one moment."

The constable, sensing the detective inspector's disapproval, froze. "Very good, sir."

Dawn was breaking, and a thin mist hung in the air. They were standing on a large cobbled concourse where several roads met. The buildings in the vicinity were rather grand. One had a double-domed turret, the smaller dome sitting on top of the larger, while another possessed a fine stone balcony. But the most commanding architectural landmark was a parish church—white, baroque, with a tall spire adorned with finials and crosses.

"Maria Geburt?" Rheinhardt asked.

"Yes," said the constable. "The empress Maria Theresa used to attend services there." He then pressed his lips together tightly to ensure that no further irrelevancies could escape.

Above the large wooden door was a triple lancet window decorated with quatrefoil tracery. On either side, saintly figures stood on square columns beneath ornate canopies. Extending out from the side of the church was an aerial corridor linking the place of worship to a row of eighteenth-century buildings. It formed an arch over a passage through which similar houses could be seen. The terrace continued to where Rheinhardt was standing, but was interrupted by an entrance, above which was written *Volksschule der Stadt Wien*.

Another school, thought Rheinhardt.

"It's by the side of the church, sir."

"What?"

"The body."

"Yes, of course. You'd better show me."

They walked across the concourse, and the mutilated remains came into view.

The victim was dressed in a smoking jacket, casual linen trousers, and a pair of slippers. He was wearing an expensive wristwatch, and on his right hand was a gold ring set with diamonds. A pool of blood had collected around his shoulders. Rheinhardt reconstructed events in his mind: the vessels severing, the hot fluid spurting out, the hiss and splash of grisly rain . . .

"Where's his head?" asked Rheinhardt.

"Over there," said the constable, holding a finger out but shying away in the opposite direction.

Rheinhardt felt a tingling sensation rise up his spine, accompanied by a strong impression of déjà vu. He was looking at a pillar of stone, on top of which was a figure of the Virgin, her head circled by a halo of stars. It was a plague column, though smaller than the one in front of the Maria Treue Kirche.

"Next to the monument, sir," the constable added.

Rheinhardt pulled a box of cigars from his pocket and lit a slim panatela.

"Wait here," said Rheinhardt. He could see that the young man was not keen to join him. "If anyone comes along, don't let them walk anywhere near the body. Make them walk on the other side of the road."

"Yes, sir," said the constable, clicking his heels.

A breeze corralled wispy threads of mist around the hem of the Virgin's robe. She gazed expectantly up into the gray sky, her head tilted to one side. The effect was peculiarly dreamlike, and for a moment the detective inspector wondered whether he was still lying in his bed, and whether, in a few more seconds, he would wake up, throw his arms around his wife's soft belly, and bury his nose in the sweet-smelling dishevelment of her hair. However, the scene did not dissolve and deliver him to his bed, but instead became more intense and more insistently real.

The shadows at the foot of the monument seemed to shift with Rheinhardt's approach, breaking up and coalescing into new forms. This process of clarification eventually revealed the dead man's head. He was probably in his fifties, and his expression was strangely peaceful: eyes closed, mouth slightly open. Rheinhardt managed to block out the dreadful glistening interior of the man's neck, the sickening flounce of stretched skin, but his stomach still contracted, and he had to fight the urge to retch. He puffed on his cigar to steady his nerves.

The monument's column twisted organically like a deformed tree, its trunk swelling and bulging with uneven excrescences. Cherub heads, with little wings sprouting out like oversize ears, adhered to the lumpy surface. They increased in number as the column spiraled upward, and at its summit the stone blistered with a chaotic outcrop of faces—some ecstatic, some anguished, others upside down. The entire edifice was supported by a cross-shaped pedestal, each arm of which was occupied by a large angel. Their expressions were inscrutable, having been worn down to vacant smoothness by the weather. One was kneeling in the throes of religious rapture—or grief—while another seemed to be flexing its wings, preparing to take off.

Rheinhardt moved away from the plague column and dropped what was left of his cigar into a drain. He heard the sound of hooves and the jangling of a bridle. Looking up, he saw the glow of carriage lamps in the haze. The vehicle halted next to him, and his assistant, Haussmann, jumped out, landing with effortless grace and stirring something close to envy in the portly inspector.

"What kept you?" said Rheinhardt.

Haussmann's brow wrinkled. "I came as soon I could, sir. The driver didn't arrive until—"

"Never mind," said Rheinhardt, swatting the air.

Haussmann glanced toward the church, where the constable stood by a conspicuous mound.

"Is that the body, sir?"

"Yes. You'll find the head by the plague column."

"Like Josefstadt?"

"Identical."

"Who is it, sir?"

"I don't know. He's rich, though. He's wearing some very expensive jewelry. I'm going to talk to the witness. Start with a plan of the location and instruct the photographer when he arrives."

Rheinhardt set off for the church but stopped when he felt the ground sucking at his feet. He looked down at his shoes and noticed that they were filthy. The cobbles were covered in mud. He squatted and tested its consistency, pressing his fingers into the mush. The clods were thick and sticky, like clay. He remembered doing the same thing outside the Maria Treue Kirche. Once again, there were no tracks to suggest that mud had fallen off the wheels of a carriage. He took a handkerchief from his pocket and wiped his hands clean.

What could it mean? So much mud . . .

His handkerchief now looked as if it had been smeared with excrement. He put it back into his pocket, guiltily, knowing that his wife would surely discover it in the laundry and scold him.

"Haussmann?" he called out. "Be sure to get some samples of this mud."

"Yes, sir."

Rheinhardt stood up, privately lamenting the stiffness of his joints, and marched to the church door.

The interior was gloomy, illuminated by a single tree of candles. Nevertheless, the light found the reflective surfaces of a fabulously ornate altar that was decorated with gilded statues and flanked by marble columns. A man was sitting in one of the front pews, talking in a low voice to a constable. When Rheinhardt entered, they both stood up. The constable gripped the hilt of his sabre.

"It's all right, Constable. You won't be needing that! I'm Detective Inspector Rheinhardt, from the security office." He advanced, showing the policeman his identification. "Perhaps you would be so kind as to join your colleague outside while I interview Herr Quint."

"I'm sorry, sir. I thought you—"

"It doesn't matter."

The constable bade Herr Quint farewell and made his way down the aisle. The noise of the closing door resonated loudly in the empty church.

"Please sit," said Rheinhardt.

Herr Quint was in his late thirties, but he looked much older. He was a rather shabby man, his hair mussed, his necktie loose, and his wing collars projecting at different angles. His frock coat was greasy, and when he sighed, the air became tainted with the smell of stale cigar smoke and alcohol.

"Terrible, terrible," Quint muttered. Then, as if responding to a challenge, he added, "I'm not leaving here until it is properly light outside. Whoever did it must be a madman—completely insane! None of us are safe!"

He clasped his hands together, and his exaggerated expression reminded Rheinhardt of a melodramatic actor. The impression was reinforced by Quint's accent, which was, unexpectedly, very refined.

"You may stay here as long as you wish," said Rheinhardt. "This is a church."

Quint muttered something to himself and finally responded, "Indeed. A church."

Rheinhardt took out his notebook.

"Do you live in Hietzing, Herr Quint?"

"I rent an apartment in the twelfth district. Längenfeldgasse."

"That is some distance. Almost Margareten."

"It's not that far, Inspector . . ."

"And the number?"

"Forty-four."

"What were you doing in Hietzing?"

"Seeing friends. Well, I say friends . . . associates, really."

"Associates?"

"Yes."

Rheinhardt looked at Herr Quint more closely. Although his frock coat was in a parlous state, it was well tailored and lined with silk. He had only recently fallen upon hard times. The reason was not difficult to deduce.

"Would I be correct in assuming that your associates are members of the gaming fraternity?"

Herr Quint's lips widened and turned downward, suggesting painful resignation.

"I was rather unlucky and had to leave the table early."

"Where do your associates meet, Herr Quint?"

"Oh, *that* can't be very important, can it, Inspector? I mean, after all, there has been a murder!"

"The address, Herr Quint?"

"Lainzerstrasse 23."

"Who lives there?"

"Widhoezl. I don't know his Christian name. I've only ever called him Widhoezl, and he's only ever called me Quint."

"You left the table early. Did you intend to walk home?"

"Yes. There weren't any cabs, of course. Besides, I don't have a single heller left." He turned out his pockets by way of demonstrating this and then stuffed them back in again.

"How much did you lose, Herr Quint?"

"I'm not sure exactly, but I can assure you that it won't happen again."

Herr Quint attempted to recover some of his dignity by tightening his necktie and sitting up straight.

"How did you discover the body?"

"I was walking behind the church—"

"Behind? You mean on this side?" said Rheinhardt, pointing across the nave. "Where the terrace of houses is?"

"Yes."

"What were you doing down there? I would have thought you would have been following the main road."

Herr Quint sighed. "Oh, this is most embarrassing . . ."

"Go on."

"My bladder was very full, and I needed to relieve myself."

"So you went behind the church?"

"Yes."

"And?"

"I was very tired. The night had been long and rather taxing. I suffer from nervous exhaustion, you see, and had allowed myself to become somewhat overexcited. Subsequently I decided I should rest a little. I sat in a doorway and . . . er . . ."

"Fell asleep?"

"Yes."

"Then what happened?"

"I was woken up . . . by a noise."

"What kind of noise?"

"A sort of whirring sound—a clicking, whirring sound, like a giant insect."

"A giant insect?"

"It frightened me. I was confused, having just woken up. To be quite candid, Inspector, I'd forgotten how I'd gotten there."

"Did you hear anything else?"

"I'm not sure."

"A carriage? Footsteps?"

"A carriage . . . possibly . . . I can't be sure. I was disorientated, Inspector. Whatever you may think, I am not a man who is accustomed to waking up on other people's doorsteps. I remained in this confused state for some time. Eventually my head cleared and I became calmer. I got up and walked around the church, and there he was! I couldn't believe it." Quint shuddered and wrung his hands. "I ran to the hotel across the road, and the night porter telephoned the police station. When the constables arrived, I was escorted back here. That is all I can tell you."

Rheinhardt removed his hat and scratched his head.

"Thank you, Herr Quint. Let me know when you are ready to leave, and I will get one of the constables to escort you home."

24

PROFESSOR MATHIAS STOOD BETWEEN two mortuary tables. On one was the headless body, on the other the abomination of its disconnected head. He looked from one to the other. "Yes." The syllable was prolonged, and its satisfied descent suggested sudden insight.

"What?" asked Rheinhardt.

"The head definitely belongs to the body," replied the old professor.

Rheinhardt sighed loudly, betraying his irritation.

Mathias turned toward the inspector, and his eyes—enlarged behind the thick glass of his spectacles—delivered a tacit but powerful reproach.

"A rather important fact, I feel," said the pathologist, pronouncing each syllable with precise and equal emphasis.

"But one that has already been established, Herr Professor!"

"Has it? Have you made a close examination of his trapezius, his levator scapulae, his arytenoid cartilage? I think not."

"Why would anybody trouble to decapitate two people, mix up the parts, leave one chimera where it can be found, and conceal the other?"

"It's no more absurd than bothering to decapitate anyone in the first place. After all, there are much more convenient ways of ending a life. Who is he, by the way?"

"We don't know yet."

"The wristwatch looks expensive."

"That's what I thought."

Professor Mathias crouched down and rested his hands on his thighs. He stared at the man's head, peering into the neck. Then, turning slowly—while maintaining his stance—he stared into the great, gaping hole between the man's shoulders. He repeated this maneuver several times, while humming to himself. The tune wandered around a tonal hinterland before finally settling in a key that was rather too high for Professor Mathias. The upper notes broke up and became nothing more than hoarse croaking.

"Well, Rheinhardt?"

"I believe you are trying to sing *Lachen und Weinen* by Schubert."

"Trying?"

"Your rendition of the opening phrase took certain liberties with the concept of key."

Mathias shrugged. Then he raised his arm and stretched out his fingers in a manner reminiscent of a stage hypnotist. The tips of his fingers almost made contact with the interior of the dead man's neck. Looking down his arm as if he were aiming a pistol, he closed one eye and began to rotate his wrist—first clockwise, then counterclockwise. As he did this, he muttered anatomical terms to himself: "Thyroid cartilage, cricothyroid muscle, fifth vertebra . . ."

Rheinhardt gazed across the morgue to the bank of square metal doors behind which, he knew, the dead had been stacked. He imagined their supine bodies, their bloodless lips and ice-block feet, the enfolding darkness, and the reek of decay. He imagined their brains dissolving, the last physical traces of recollection losing their integrity, and each skull filling with an insensate chemical sludge: memories of love and friendship, clear skies and the sound of rain, music, tears, and laughter—all reduced to nothing. *The fate of all of us,* he thought. Even his daughters, within whom the life force seemed so strong, and whose ebullience and flashing smiles seemed powered by an inexhaustible source of energy, they too would one day surrender their memories to an inexorable process of disintegration. At that moment the terrible sadness of the human condition was converted into a heavy weight that fell squarely on Rheinhardt's shoulders. He became dimly aware of a querulous voice. Its reedy wheedling coaxed him out of his grim meditation like a snake charmer's pipe.

"Wake up, Rheinhardt!"

"I'm sorry. I was thinking . . ."

The professor gave him an equivocal look, seasoned with just enough skepticism to suggest an unspoken (but intentional) slur.

"I said the method employed is identical."

"What?"

"The monk you brought in two weeks ago. Exactly the same—the displacements suggest that the head was twisted off the body. Clockwise cranial rotation."

Mathias rotated his hand to demonstrate the direction.

"How many men would it take to do this?"

"Difficult to say . . ."

"Could you hazard a guess?"

"I would prefer not to."

Rheinhardt sighed again, a great expulsion of air that declared his patience was at an end.

"Oh, very well," said the pathologist, grumbling and wiping his hands on his apron, even though they were perfectly clean. "Come closer, will you? That's it. Bend down so you can take a good look. Good. Now . . . see here." Mathias urged Rheinhardt to peer into the dead man's neck. Under the bright electric light every detail was revealed with sickening clarity. Rheinhardt realized that—until that moment—he had never fully acknowledged what his eyes were seeing. An instinctive revulsion had made him gloss over the arabesques and flourishes of human flesh. He had only registered an impression of gory redness and felt with it a sympathetic horror, a vague tingling of imaginary pain. Now that he was faced with the stark reality, he realized that the interior of the human neck did not correspond with the sketchy representation that had hitherto occupied his mind, that of a hollow tube down which food and air could pass. In fact, the neck was complex, and dense with glistening slabs of meat.

"Look at these muscles. See how thick they are . . . and look at this tissue here." Mathias pulled at a flap of rubbery white gristle. "See how elastic it is? Have you ever seen a fat man hang? No? Well, the neck often stretches. It doesn't tear." Mathias released the elongated sinew, and it snapped back, wetly. "What are you doing, Rheinhardt? Don't look away. I'm trying to explain! Now . . . if I were to pick up that saw and cut through the neck to create a clean transverse section, what would it look like? I'll tell you: the flat end of a substantial ham. Now, let us return to your question, which might be expressed in another form: How many men would it take to tear a large joint of meat apart?"

"It would take quite a few, wouldn't it?"

Mathias gave his tacit assent by raising an eyebrow.

"And it would take time," Rheinhardt added.

"Of course."

"Yet the Piarist monk and this man were both killed in conspicuous locations, on open concourses next to street lamps! They must have been able to achieve these decapitations very quickly. Otherwise they would have risked being caught."

"Then you are looking for two exceptionally strong men . . . or a gang of some kind. Although . . ." Mathias's fingers circumnavigated the ragged perimeter of the giant wound, occasionally lifting the repugnant skirt of skin. "I can't help thinking about that poor chap I told you about, the one who got killed by a bear when I was doing national service. If this man's clothes were torn, and there were scratches . . ."

"You'd say he'd been mauled by a wild animal."

"Precisely."

Rheinhardt frowned. "But his clothes haven't been torn."

"No."

"And an angry bear running loose in Vienna would surely have come to someone's attention by now."

"Indeed," said Mathias. The two men looked at each other, neither of them very sure what the other was thinking. Mathias broke the silence. "It was only an observation, Rheinhardt! I wasn't suggesting that you should go to the zoo to look for suspects!"

The pathologist rolled the head over and riffled through the hair, as if looking for nits. He discovered a laceration on the crown.

"Again—just like the other one, just like the monk. He was struck on the back of the head."

"What with?"

"Something blunt. That's all I can say." Professor Mathias righted the head and stroked the wrinkled brow. He opened both of the eyes, and then closed them again. " 'There is a gentle sleep,' " he whispered, " 'Where sweet peace dwells, Where quiet rest heals the weary soul's sorrow.' "

"You have me there," said Rheinhardt.

" 'Secret Grief,' by Ernst Koch."

25

THE PRIVATE DINING ROOM in which Councillor Schmidt sat—one among many—was where he usually met with his mistress; however, he also used it for other "business" purposes. Schmidt could depend on the landlord, Herr Linser, to be discreet. When it had been proposed by the transport committee that the block of dilapidated eighteenth-century houses, in which the dining room was located, should be demolished to make way for a new streetcar line, Schmidt had argued that the route extension was not really necessary. In due course an alternative had been approved. And when two health and safety officers had paid the establishment an impromptu visit, and had subsequently forwarded a damning report to the relevant bureau in the town hall, Schmidt had made sure that the report was unavailable when the municipal hygiene group met to discuss what action should be taken.

Shortly after, Schmidt had suggested to Herr Linser that, if he so wished, he might choose to express his gratitude in the form of a monthly 10 percent levy, paid in cash and delivered by hand to an associate of Schmidt's named Knabl. When Herr Linser first balked at this suggestion, Schmidt reminded him that reports that had been mislaid could also be found again. Herr Linser apologized for his bad manners, begged to be excused, and promised the councillor that he would never take his patronage for granted again.

Sitting opposite Schmidt were two of his most trusted "business associates," Haas and Oeggl. Both of them were wearing badly fitting suits in which they looked distinctly uncomfortable—Haas in particular, who kept on running his finger around the inside of his shirt collar as if it were too small and were stopping him from breathing.

"More wine, gentlemen?" asked Schmidt.

Haas and Oeggl both nodded, and Schmidt replenished their glasses. Then he emptied onto the table the contents of an envelope that they had given him earlier. It contained a wad of dirty banknotes and an assortment of silver and bronze coins.

"Is that all?" said Schmidt.

"They said they didn't have any more," said Haas, wiping his mouth on his sleeve.

"Well, they're lying—obviously."

"We done everything we could," said Oeggl. His speech was slurred, although not because of the wine. He always spoke like that.

"Come now," said Schmidt, lighting a cigar. "I'm sure two experienced gentlemen like yourselves could be a great deal more persuasive if you put your minds to it."

"Well, we could," said Haas. "But . . ."

"But what?"

"It's risky. Sometimes it's difficult to judge. You know? How far you can go?"

Haas rubbed the scar on his cheek. It looked a little inflamed.

"Oh, don't you worry about that," said Schmidt benevolently. "Do whatever you think is necessary. If something untoward occurs—well, I won't blame you. Accidents happen."

"With respect, your honor," said Oeggl, "if accidents happen, then the police get involved."

Schmidt shook his head.

"How many times must I repeat myself? That really isn't a problem. I'm on exceptionally familiar terms with the boys at the Grosse Sperlgasse station. They won't ask any questions, I can assure you.

So . . . next time, do whatever it takes. Indeed, I would go as far as to say that perhaps the time has come to make an example of someone." Schmidt picked up the coins and let them drop onto the table. "I mean to say, this will hardly keep us in the style to which we have become accustomed, eh, gentlemen? Do whatever is necessary!"

Part Two

The Tree of Life

26

ANNA KATZER WAS WEARING a white blouse with cuffs made of Valenciennes lace and a purple crêpe de chine skirt. Purple was *her* color. Men always noticed her more when she was wearing purple. The effect was very reliable, so much so that Anna was inclined to invest the color with magical powers. It was of some significance, therefore, that Anna had chosen to wear her favored hue for her guest: Gabriel Kusevitsky.

As soon as Gabriel entered the parlor, it was evident that the color had worked its spell. The young doctor was clearly overwhelmed. He made a discreetly flattering remark, but his wide-eyed expression declared the true extent of his appreciation.

Anna remembered what Olga had said about the Kusevitsky brothers: intellectuals, too preoccupied with their work to be interested in the society of fashionable young ladies. *Well,* she thought, *it seems that this Kusevitsky brother is not yet completely lost to the brotherhood of coffeehouse philosophers.*

Anna had invited Gabriel to tea immediately after their first meeting. The invitation had been subsequently repeated, and accepted, on three further occasions. Olga had advised Anna against appearing overly anxious for his company. *Men,* she had said, *are inclined to desire more strongly that which is withheld.* However, on reflection Anna had chosen to ignore her friend's counsel. Gabriel Kusevitsky was an earnest fellow, and would probably find the stratagems of courtship—the games and ploys—confusing, childish, and tedious. She would wear purple, and do nothing more.

Once again, Anna talked about her charity work. She noticed how intently Gabriel listened. He sat very still, as she thought a psychiatrist should, but occasionally raised a finger to his lips. His hands were delicate, a little like those of a boy. Another woman might have described those hands as fragile or effeminate, but Anna considered them sensitive. Anna spoke more seriously than usual. She made fewer flippant remarks and was altogether less girlish. Without Olga there, it was easier to present herself as a more substantial person. In many respects she felt more comfortable in this new guise. As she spoke, somewhere at the back of her mind a certain sentiment was finding quiet expression: *a doctor's wife should conduct herself with dignity.* It was shocking that she should be thinking such a thing, at such an early stage of acquaintance. But she had always imagined that she would marry a doctor. Rather a doctor any day than one of the young businessmen her father was always asking to lunch.

After the tea had been drunk and the cakes consumed, Anna asked Gabriel what he intended to do after completing his research.

"I will apply for a clinical post—within my discipline—at the General Hospital or one of the private institutions. However, I have always harbored a wish to make a contribution greater than that which can be accomplished through the practice of medicine alone."

"Isn't it enough to heal the sick? I can't think of anything more worthwhile or personally satisfying."

"Medicine is a great force for good, but it cannot cure all ills."

"All ills?" Anna repeated.

Gabriel paused and considered his companion. He seemed to be making some kind of assessment. He seemed to be searching out an essential part of her person, a secret corner. His eyes narrowed behind his thick spectacle lenses, and Anna felt a little unnerved.

"There is much wrong in the world," he said softly. Then, after a long pause, he added, "And I want to do something about it."

"Do you have political ambitions?"

"Yes, of a kind."

"The town hall? Parliament?"

The young doctor smiled. "You wanted me to interpret one of your dreams, but now you seem to be more interested in mine."

Anna blushed but quickly regained her composure.

"Yes," she said, flashing her eyes at Gabriel. "I am interested in your dreams."

This time it was the doctor's turn to blush. The frankness of her honest affection was unexpected. Even more so was the soft touch of her hand as it landed gently on his own.

27

THE ADJUTANT ENTERED SCHMIDT'S office.

"Councillor." He bowed and clicked his heels. "Hofrat Holz-knecht would like to see you at once."

Schmidt looked up from his papers.

"I'll be along in a few minutes."

"I believe Hofrat Holzknecht wishes to see you this instant, Councillor."

Schmidt reprimanded himself for his ill-considered response. A politician wishing to ascend the internal hierarchy of the town hall should not keep a person like Holzknecht waiting.

"Of course," said Schmidt. "Forgive me. I was preoccupied with this new housing bill."

He tidied his papers, stood, and followed the adjutant out onto the landing. As they made their way toward Holzknecht's domain on the second floor, Schmidt wondered why he had been so peremptorily summoned. It crossed his mind that he might have been a little careless lately. Perhaps one of his associates had been indiscreet? It would be most inopportune if some of his business dealings came to light at this particular point in time. He was having so many brilliant ideas. He was a man at the height of his powers! It would be tragic—not just for him but for all of Vienna—if he were unable to oversee his various schemes and bring them to a satisfactory conclusion.

They arrived at Holzknecht's bureau, which occupied a whole suite. The adjutant led Schmidt through two small antechambers to Holzknecht, who was seated behind a desk beneath a portrait of the emperor and several photographs of the mayor performing civic duties.

"Councillor Schmidt," announced the adjutant.

"Ah, there you are, Schmidt." Holzknecht did not stand. "Have you heard?" Before Schmidt could answer, the Hofrat dismissed his adjutant by glancing at the door.

Schmidt took a seat in front of Holzknecht's desk.

"About Eberle's proposal for the new housing bill?"

"No, no, no . . . about your colleague Councillor Faust!"

"Faust?"

"Yes, Faust. He's been murdered."

"What?"

"I know. I could hardly believe it myself."

Schmidt did not react. He sat perfectly still, as if stunned. Finally he asked, "When did it happen?"

"On Saturday morning. He was decapitated—like that monk, Stanislav. It's extraordinary. And what a coincidence! Remember we were all together when your nephew found the article in the newspaper. Who would have thought . . . poor Faust . . . that he would be the next victim? It's chilling, isn't it?"

"Do the police have"—Schmidt did not want to betray his excitement and made an effort to keep his voice steady—"any idea who is responsible for these atrocities?"

"No."

"Was he robbed?"

"Not that I know of."

"Then why was he murdered?"

"God knows!"

"Decapitation . . . ," said Schmidt pensively. "It must have been the same person."

"Or persons . . . This morning I spoke to the security office commissioner on the telephone. The state censor intervened with respect to the reports of Brother Stanislav's murder. The monk's head was in fact *torn* from his body. The same thing . . ." The old man balked at the thought. "The same thing happened to poor Faust. It would take more than one man to perform such a heinous deed."

"What a terrible way to die."

"Indeed. Let us pray that he was oblivious when the time came." Schmidt crossed his legs and let his fingers interlock.

"It seems almost ritualistic, don't you think?"

Holzknecht was too distressed to detect Schmidt's meaning, and the councillor thought it prudent not to press the point. He would have many other opportunities in due course. The two men spoke for a while until the conversation became nothing more than disconnected statements of horror and disbelief. Eventually Schmidt said, "You must excuse me. There is some work I must complete for the mayor's transport committee by this evening."

Holzknecht rose from his desk and accompanied Schmidt to the door. Before opening it, he said, "Of course, this means that you now have a very good chance of being appointed to the mayor's special advisory panel."

"With respect, Hofrat Holzknecht," said Schmidt, "I cannot think of such things at present."

"Forgive me . . . ," said the old man. "You were close colleagues, and no doubt close friends. However, I just wanted you to know that I've always regarded you as a man of talent, Schmidt. Perhaps your time has come."

The councillor assumed a rueful expression and walked through the two antechambers with his head lowered. When he reached the corridor, he was smiling.

28

THE CHANCELLOR'S EXPRESSION WAS serious, and his eyes glinted coldly behind his spectacles.

"Herr Doctor, I regret to say that the matter of young Baron von Kortig's death and your obstruction of Father Benedikt has come to the attention of a journalist."

Liebermann raised his eyebrows. "May I ask, sir, how it was that a journalist came to be so well informed?"

"I have no idea; however, it should not surprise us to learn that journalists are always trying to find things out. That is, after all, what they do."

"With respect, Professor Gandler, I have never known such a relatively minor matter to attract the interest of the press before."

"I can assure you, Herr Doctor, that matters of faith are never minor." The chancellor's expression became even more grave. After what seemed like an exceptionally long pause he continued, "I am obliged to ask you a sensitive question, Herr Doctor. When we last spoke, did you omit any important detail from your account of what happened that night?"

Liebermann wondered what the chancellor might be alluding to.

"I don't think so. The baron was dying. Father Benedikt wanted to give him the last rites, and I explained that I did not think this was in the patient's interests. The priest objected . . . he asked my name, and he left. That, essentially, is all there is to tell."

"Unfortunately, Herr Doctor, the journalist has written a rather different story. An allegation is made, concerning the employment of force."

Liebermann was speechless. He touched his chest, as if to say, *By me?* The chancellor confirmed this with a solemn nod.

"Oh, that is utterly absurd!" Liebermann cried. "I have never heard anything so ridiculous.... Besides, there were witnesses present."

"Indeed." The word was not encouraging, quite the opposite. "Think back, Herr Doctor," continued Professor Gandler. "When the priest tried to enter the ward, what did you do?"

"I told him he couldn't go through."

"Yes, but what did you actually do?"

"I may have..." Liebermann lowered his voice. "I may have put my arm across the doorway."

"In other words, you forcibly barred his admittance."

Liebermann raised his hands in frustration. "Well, you could say that. But it would be a gross misrepresentation of the facts."

"Would it really?"

"Yes. To say that I forcibly barred his admittance makes it sound like some kind of assault took place. I merely rested my hand against the doorjamb."

Professor Gandler scowled and repositioned some papers on his desk. "Had you apologized to the committee when I advised you to, Herr Doctor, this problem might have been swiftly and quietly resolved. Instead, you chose to disregard my advice. This article will attract unwanted publicity, the kind that could potentially damage our fine reputation." The chancellor tapped his fingers on the surface of his desk. "A written apology might still stop things from going any further..."

Liebermann shook his head. "I'm sorry, Professor Gandler..."

"Once again, I would urge you to reconsider. This situation could easily escalate, and if it does, you will be sorry."

Liebermann ignored the chancellor's thinly disguised threat. "Where did this article appear, Professor Gandler?"

The chancellor opened his drawer and pulled out a folded newspaper. He tossed it across the desk, and it landed so that the masthead was exposed. It read: *Das Vaterland*. At once Liebermann understood what was really going on. He looked up at the chancellor, and for a moment was consoled by a glimmer of sympathy.

29

THE TWO MEN HAD finished their music-making and taken their customary places in Liebermann's smoking room. Somewhat unusually, though, it was Rheinhardt who spoke first. "You seem a little preoccupied, Max."

"Yes," Liebermann replied. "I do have a lot on my mind. Something happened at the hospital a few weeks ago that has had unforeseen consequences, and I now find myself in an invidious position."

He told his friend about the death of the young Baron von Kortig, his—Liebermann's—alleged forceful obstruction of Father Benedikt, and of his unhappy interviews with the chancellor. Throughout, Rheinhardt's solicitous expression was constant. Occasionally he muttered "outrageous," "appalling," or "intolerable." When Liebermann had finished, the detective inspector blew out a great cloud of cigar smoke and asked, "What do you think will happen?"

"I have no idea. But I simply refuse to make an apology. This would be tantamount to an admission of improper behavior."

"Indeed. As far as I can see, you acted irreproachably—thinking first and foremost of your patient. The old baron should have been grateful that his son's dying moments were spent in the care of such a scrupulous physician." Rheinhardt sipped his brandy and added, "Who do you think contacted the journalist?"

"I don't know. It could have been anyone: Father Benedikt, the old Baron von Kortig, one of the committee members . . . even the nurse or the aspirant."

"Someone is clearly trying to turn an inconsequential incident into a scandal—and, sadly, their motivation is all too transparent."

"Yes. I tried to resist the obvious conclusion, but the article in *Das Vaterland* soon brought an end to my doubts. The author repeatedly stressed that fewer and fewer doctors in Vienna understand the importance of the *Christian* sacraments."

They spoke for a little while longer about Liebermann's situation, until the young doctor seemed suddenly to grow impatient and tire of the subject. He made a gesture with his hand as if to brush the matter away. After a short pause, Liebermann said in a more animated voice, "I stopped for coffee at the Café Museum this afternoon and saw the late editions."

Rheinhardt nodded his head solemnly.

"Burke Faust," Liebermann added.

"*Councillor* Burke Faust," said Rheinhardt, emphasizing the man's title. "His remains were discovered next to the plague column by the church of Maria Geburt in Hietzing. Death was caused by decapitation, and the method employed was exactly the same as before. His head had been *torn* from his body. He was dressed in the kind of clothes a gentleman usually wears in his study: a smoking jacket, loose trousers, and a pair of slippers. It was obvious that he hadn't been walking the streets dressed like that. He must have been knocked unconscious before being transported to the plague column. Professor Mathias found evidence of a blow delivered to the back of the head, and later we learned that his Hietzing villa had been broken into."

"Did you find any signs of a struggle?"

"No."

"The obituaries in the late editions suggested that he was a rising star at the town hall."

"He certainly was. In fact, he was the prime candidate for a plum job in the mayor's office. Some believed he might, in due course, have been selected as a future mayoral candidate. As you would expect, Faust's political instincts were not dissimilar to Lueger's, although Faust was thought by many to be more extreme."

"As exemplified by his recent article in which he referred to Jews as a plague."

"Good heavens," said Rheinhardt. "Have you read it?"

"No," said Liebermann.

"Then how—"

"I assumed, under the circumstances, that such an article *must* exist."

Rheinhardt frowned and continued, "When we were interviewing Faust's colleagues at the town hall, one of them mentioned that the councillor had written a piece for *Die Reichpost*, and that it had impressed the mayor. It's full of the usual rhetoric but is distinguished by Faust's espousal of a carefully constructed three-phase plan for eliminating Jews entirely from public life—*and* the professions."

"And who did he think the good people of Vienna would consult when they became ill?"

"Faust was exercised largely by the problem of how elimination of the Jews from the professions might be accomplished, rather than by its actual consequences."

Liebermann poured more brandy and stared into the fire.

"Was he married?"

"No. He lived alone."

"What about his staff?"

"They live in an apartment building near the train station. He would have had no one to call upon for assistance when he was attacked."

Liebermann turned his brandy and contemplated the flames through the repeated motif of the cut glass.

"Apart from the obvious commonality of the plague columns, were there any other similarities between our two murder scenes?"

"Yes," said Rheinhardt, extending the syllable and sounding somewhat hesitant. "Once again there was a great deal of mud in the vicinity of the body, and once again it seemed to have been purposely put there rather than dislodged from a vehicle. There were no tracks, other than those on the main road."

"Did you have the mud analyzed?"

"I did, and it proved to be entirely unremarkable. You might collect it anywhere on the banks of the Danube or up in the woods." Rheinhardt twisted one of the horns of his mustache, and added, "Oh, I almost forgot to say, there was another similarity. Maria Geburt, like Maria Treue Kirche, has a school close by."

Liebermann continued to turn his glass, seemingly entranced by the patterns of light.

"Who discovered the body?"

"A hapless fellow called Octavian Quint. He'd lost all of his money playing cards and had been ejected from the table. On his way home he went to relieve himself behind the church and fell asleep in a doorway. He claims to have been awakened by a noise that he described as a whirring, clicking sound . . . like a *giant insect*."

The young doctor stopped looking into his brandy glass, and his head slowly rotated to reveal, degree by degree, an expression of such profound skepticism that it might just as easily have been provoked by an insult.

"A giant insect?"

"That's what he said," Rheinhardt replied gruffly. "And whatever it was, I'm sure it frightened him."

"Had the man been drinking?"

"Almost certainly."

Liebermann gestured as if to say, *Well, there you are, then.*

"How many plague columns are there in Vienna?" asked Lieber-mann.

"The Graben, Saint Ulrich's, the Rochuskapelle Pensinger-strasse—a considerable number."

"Too many to be kept under observation?"

"The Karlskirche, Dornbach." Rheinhardt was raising his fingers. "Yes, far too many."

"What about if you restricted observation to those plague columns close to schools?"

"That is a possibility."

The young doctor took another cigar, lit it, and sank back into his chair. In only a few seconds he had produced a dense, fragrant haze. He was evidently deep in thought. Rheinhardt made a fanciful connection between the smoke and his friend's intense mental activity, imagining the billowing clouds to be the product of an overheated brain. A log on the fire hissed, crackled, and threw up a fountain of sparks. The pyrotechnics roused Liebermann, who pulled himself up to speak.

"These two murders," he began, "are characterized by peculiarities that indicate the workings of an idiosyncratic but *purposeful* mind. There is a scheme here, obviously: two rabid anti-Semites who have recently likened Jews to a scourge are found dead, justly punished for their invective." The young doctor grinned, to show that the sentiment was not his own. "Found dead at the foot of the Treue Kirche and Maria Geburt plague columns. They have been decapitated, a method of execution that is associated with the demise of kings. Thus, we are to understand that men of influence, the *heads* of religious and civic life, are being warned against the promulgation of hateful ideologies. The proximity of the schools reinforces this message. Prejudice can easily be transmitted from generation to generation—thus those who occupy positions of power are doubly cautioned against the abuse of authority. So far the symbolism presents us with few interpretative difficulties; however, there are other features that remain utterly incomprehensible. Why were the victims decapitated in such an impractical way? And what does the mud represent? Filth, excrement, moral turpitude? To these questions I have no ready answer."

Liebermann stubbed out his cigar and immediately lit another. Rheinhardt patiently waited for his friend to continue.

"Earlier, I said that the peculiarities of these murders indicate the workings of an idiosyncratic mind: obsessionality, symbolism, the construction of dramatic tableaux. These are all 'signatures' that we have learned to associate with a particular kind of criminal, the lone fanatic whose delusional system, unchallenged, thrives in isolation, its internal structure becoming increasingly intricate and mythic, and promoting in the process a form of messianic narcissism. Nevertheless, these murders could not have been perpetrated by one man alone."

"Professor Mathias was of the opinion that it would require the efforts of at least two exceptionally strong men to remove a human head by ripping it from the body in this way."

"Indeed. Now, it is commonplace for individuals to become delusional, and delusional beliefs might easily guide a campaign of retributive violence. But what we seem to have here is a delusional individual who has persuaded others of the legitimacy of his vision."

"Ahh . . . ," said Rheinhardt, suddenly sitting up straight and waving his index finger in the air. "I believe you have said something there that might prove to be very significant."

"Oh?"

"Clearly, the perpetrators of these two murders are Jews." Rheinhardt paused to allow Liebermann to disagree. The young doctor said nothing. "And you will remember that on a previous occasion you suggested that the hereditary leaders of the Hasidim often wield great power over their people, and that their sects are relatively self-contained."

Liebermann thought for a moment. Suddenly he smiled and said, "So I did!"

"Well, then, it seems to me that you have already proposed an ideal environment in which the phenomenon you seek to explain might occur. If my memory serves me correctly, you said that a rebbe might claim to receive instructions from God, and that his devotees—in the absence of any other counsel—would very likely obey his orders without question."

"Yes," said Liebermann, impressed by his own perspicacity. "I did say that, didn't I?"

"There is a rebbe among the Hasidim of Leopoldstadt called Barash, who is said to have predicted the death of Brother Stanislav."

"Did he prophesy that the monk was going to be decapitated?"

"We're not sure. One of his sect became involved in a religious argument and was overheard making the claim."

"Where did this happen?"

"In a coffeehouse. Zuckers. I wonder, would you be willing to interview Barash, Max?"

"Of course. But if we are correct, and it transpires that these murders are the work of a Jewish cabal, can you imagine how the Christian Socials and the clerics will react! Think of the political capital they made out of that miserable wretch Hilsner!" Liebermann flicked his glass, and the crystal emitted a soft chime. "Which makes me wonder . . . what if? What if these murders are not what they appear to be? What if they are a means of turning public opinion against an all too obviously guilty party?"

Rheinhardt poured himself another large brandy.

In his mind, he saw an angry horde crossing the Danube canal and marching into Leopoldstadt. He saw men in caftans being dragged from their houses, and he saw blood on the cobbled streets. He tried to think of something else, but the images were vivid and persistent.

30

PROFESSOR PRIEL TROTTED DOWN the stairs of the university and paused on the pavement to extricate his watch from his vest pocket. He noted the time, and set off in a southerly direction. If he hurried, he would be able to deliver the envelope that he carried in his pocket to Frau Meyer and be back in good time to give his afternoon tutorial. The envelope contained a donation from the Rothenstein Education Fellowship, and its purpose was to provide Frau Meyer with sufficient funds to equip her new school on Alois Gasse with some basic classroom furniture. The donation would probably be reported in the newspapers, and once again the public would be informed of Rothenstein's outstanding generosity. Priel, of course, would not be mentioned. He never was.

Another man might have felt envious or resentful, but Priel was remarkably sanguine concerning his situation. Indeed, he rather liked being an éminence grise: advising, making suggestions, his judgment trusted. He associated himself with the Talmudic legend of the *lamed vavniks*, the righteous men. Living in the world there are, at any given time, thirty-six righteous men whose good deeds stop the world from ending. They accomplish their work in secret and are never rewarded. When one dies, another is born. And so it goes on, from generation to generation, thirty-six anonymous Jews standing unthanked between civilization and ruin.

Priel thought about Frau Meyer. A widow, dedicated to improving the lot of the latest wave of immigrant children who had arrived in Leopoldstadt. He would give her the envelope, and she would smile, clasp his hand, and express profound gratitude. And he would then reply, as he always did, *It isn't me whom you should be thanking.*

Rothenstein was always too busy hobnobbing with royalty to decide who should—or shouldn't—be the recipient of his largesse. And Rothenstein's wife, Priel's sister, was completely self-obsessed. The fate of the poor meant nothing to her as compared with the unmitigated disaster of wearing the wrong kind of dress at a palace function. Priel's two nieces and his nephew were equally indifferent. Brittle, shallow, and spoiled, their German was embarrassingly inflected to sound like the imperial dialect known as *Schönbrunnerdeutsch.* Over the years Priel had been given more and more responsibility for the distribution of Rothenstein's bounty. Occasionally, when Priel presented Rothenstein with documents to sign, the great banker would ask a few bland questions. But if Priel attempted to give him a proper answer, Rothenstein would soon look bored and end the conversation by saying, "I'm sure everything is in order. I have every confidence in you, Josef." Like the rest of his family, Rothenstein enjoyed the gala balls and the public recognition much more than the process of determining which causes were the most deserving.

Priel passed the town hall and glanced up at its Gothic façade: the huge central tower, the elevated loggia with its curved balconies and delicate tracery.

Thirty-six righteous men . . .

They wouldn't be found in there. Of that he was quite certain.

Priel accelerated his sprightly step. He was looking forward to seeing Frau Meyer again. She was an intelligent woman who appreciated philosophy and good music. The last time they'd met she had asked him what he thought of Nietzsche's *The Case of Wagner.* The discussion that followed had been most stimulating. Moreover, she had kept her figure.

Having warned his students and the Kusevitsky brothers that

great thinkers should be wary of the snare of marriage, he reprimanded himself.

Hypocrite!

He might not be a righteous man, exactly, but he was nevertheless
a man of honor. He had an example to set. And as much as he would
enjoy the company of Frau Meyer at the opera, it was probably better that he continued to go alone. He would give her the envelope,
have a cup of tea, and leave.

31

NAHUM NAGEL PLACED THE small weights on one side of his scale and a large weight on the other. The equipoise was so perfect that even his breath caused the left side to dip lower than the right. His friend Yudl Berger was sitting on the other side of the shop counter on a three-legged stool.

"My cousin knows about these things," said Yudl, winding around his fingers the knotted tassles that hung from his waist. "And in his opinion Faust would have caused us a lot of grief, had he lived. He wanted to introduce special taxes and special police."

Upstairs, Nahum's father began coughing. It sounded like someone sawing wood, a horrible double rasp. Yudl glanced upward. "Has he seen a doctor?"

"Zingler came a few weeks ago. He said we should consider moving so as to get away from the damp." Nahum made a hopeless gesture with his hands. "How could we possibly manage that?"

Yudl nodded sympathetically but returned to his original theme. "You know Pinhas the draper? He was delivering some curtains up to the big hotel in Hietzing, where the body was found. He actually saw it, by the plague column." Yudl raised his eyebrows and in a melodramatic stage whisper added, "Mud everywhere."

Nahum looked up from his weights. "You don't really believe . . ."

"Doubrovsky knows the shoeblack who sits outside the theatre in Josefstadt. When the police were getting ready to leave, several of them walked up to have their shoes cleaned. The shoeblack said they were filthy. Covered in thick mud. Like clay. Josefstadt *and* Hietzing."

Nahum shook his head. He was evidently unconvinced.

"Our rebbe Barash says that things are going to change," Yudl continued. "For the better."

"Ach! He said the same thing to my father, and look at us!"

The look in Nahum's eyes was desperate, his voice angry.

"He was right about the priest, wasn't he?" Yudl responded, defending their spiritual master. "He said the priest would never make trouble here again—and he won't, that's for sure! And did you hear what he said to old man Robak? He promised him justice, vengeance. Two weeks before!"

The expression of sulky resentment on Nahum's face was replaced by curiosity.

"Who told you that?"

"My wife. Old Robak's eldest daughter is a friend of my wife's aunt."

Nahum tapped the pyramid of small weights on the scale. He wanted to believe, but his faith in the zaddik had been weakened. It was only a matter of time before the two men came again, making impossible demands. He and his father were close to ruin.

"Mud," he said pensively. "In both places?"

"Yes," said Yudl. "It can mean only one thing."

32

LIEBERMANN MADE HIS WAY to the old ghetto district and Rebbe Barash's residence. He was received by a sullen maid who ushered him into a sparsely furnished parlor: two armchairs, a stove, and an old sideboard. The walls were a dreary buff color, as were the curtains and the faded rug. Indeed, the whole room seemed to have been drained of vitality: everything in it was of an anemic, indefinite hue.

The young doctor sat down and waited. Time passed, and he occupied himself by performing some of the Klammer Method exercises. First wrist rotations, and then, holding his hands out in front of his body, he repeatedly touched the proximal phalanx of his little fingers with the tips of his thumbs. This movement, Professor Klammer suggested, was invaluable for development of the abductor pollicis brevis, opponens pollicis, and flexor pollicis brevis muscles. Liebermann continued his regimen until he reached exercise eleven, at which point the door opened and the zaddik entered.

In his general appearance, Barash conformed to Liebermann's expectations, a Hasidic jew with a shaven head, skullcap, coiled sideburns, and heavy frock coat. He was, however, astonishingly large, a man whose dimensions demanded nothing less than comparison with features of the natural world. He was positively mountainous, possessing broad, peaked shoulders, and a face that resembled a serendipitously anthropomorphic arrangement of rocks. His scowl was evocative of the darkness that precedes a thunderstorm.

Barash sat directly opposite Liebermann, resting his big sculpted hands on the arms of his chair.

"My name is Dr. Max Liebermann. I am an associate of Detective Inspector Oskar Rheinhardt of the security office." Liebermann produced his official papers, but the zaddik showed no interest. "You were informed in advance of my visit?"

The zaddik nodded.

After some preliminary remarks, it was clear to Liebermann that Barash did not want to prolong their meeting with inconsequential courtesies. Indeed, after only a few polite exchanges Barash said curtly, "Herr Doctor, your business?"

"Rebbe Barash," said Liebermann, "were you acquainted with Chaim Robak?"

"Yes," Barash replied. "He used to attend one of my study groups."

"A good student?"

"Exceptional."

After a little prompting, Barash talked freely about his former pupil. He remembered a virtuous young man—quiet, bookish, but not shy, a young man with many friends, respectful of his father, and loved by his sisters. Barash delivered his obituary in a steady monotone, his features set fast. Nevertheless, his eyes betrayed him, revealing genuine sorrow in their moist, reflective glaze.

"Who do you believe was responsible for his murder?" Liebermann asked.

"You know what happened *that* day, the day his body was found?"

"Yes."

"Well, then," said the zaddik. "It must have been one of the agitators."

"Where were you when the trouble started?"

"I was right here, sitting in this very room, reading. I could hear them, though. They had gathered for their rally in the market square. At first, I thought it would be wise to stay inside; however, the noise—the shouting and shrieking—became very loud, and I decided that I should go out after all. I thought I might be able to assist if anyone got hurt. I told my wife to go down into the cellar with the children. They were very frightened."

"What did you see?"

"People running around—confused, trying to get away from the fracas. When I got to the market square, there was fighting, but it wasn't long before the police arrived and the crowd dispersed. In actuality, there wasn't much I could do. A few young men had been hurt and were sitting on the cobbles, holding bloodied handkerchiefs to their faces. But no one had been seriously injured."

"Did you see the monk, Stanislav?"

"Yes, I did. As a matter of fact, we came face-to-face. He was marching away from the square, surrounded by henchmen. We almost bumped into each other."

"Did he say anything to you?"

"No. He didn't notice me. He seemed eager to make a quick departure."

Liebermann paused.

"Rebbe Barash, has anyone told you about the articles that Brother Stanislav wrote for the Catholic newspaper *Das Vaterland*?"

"No."

"In one of them he likened Jews to a plague."

Liebermann watched Barash for a reaction, but the zaddik merely shrugged. His expression was impassive. Liebermann continued, "Does the name Burke Faust mean anything to you?"

"He was a councillor—murdered last week, I believe."

"Do you know how he was murdered?"

"Decapitated, same as the monk."

"He was also the author of an article in which Jews were likened to a plague."

"I have heard, from people better informed about such matters than myself, that he was a bad man."

Liebermann tilted his head against his clenched fist, unfurled his index finger, and tapped his temple.

"Do you believe in prophecy, Rebbe Barash?"

"Yes, I do."

"Is it a gift that you possess?"

"I am the spiritual leader of my community," Barash replied obtusely.

"It is rumored that you predicted the death of Brother Stanislav."

"Who told you this?"

"Inspector Rheinhardt. He has friends in Leopoldstadt. Well, is it true? Did you predict the death of Brother Stanislav?"

"Yes," said Barash, his hooded eyelids lowering a fraction. "I did."

"How was that possible?"

"It was written . . . on his face."

"I beg your pardon?"

"It was written on his face," Barash repeated. The zaddik sighed and continued. "We—that is to say, my congregation and I—venerate the teachings of Isaac Luria."

"Who?"

Barash's scowl intensified.

"Isaac Luria. A great holy man who lived in Palestine hundreds of years ago. He practiced metoposcopy, the art of reading lines on the human face. It is very similar to palmistry, a sister discipline that has proved more popular since Luria's time." Liebermann bristled. "Is it such a peculiar notion, Herr Doctor? Many educated medical men—like yourself—accept physiognomy, do they not?"

"They do. But I am not one of them. I am not persuaded that a man's character is revealed by the shape of his nose."

"You might, however, agree that men frequently acquire the faces they deserve. By that I mean that men often make choices, and these choices have consequences with respect to their appearance. For example, a man overly fond of schnapps will look very different from his abstemious neighbor." Liebermann thought the argument was specious, but he conceded the point and gestured for Barash to continue. "Lines on the forehead often suggest letters of the Hebrew alphabet, and these can be interpreted."

Liebermann was unable to conceal his incredulity. "So, you saw letters on the monk's forehead, and it was written there, in Hebrew, that he would die?"

"Let us say," Barash replied with mysterious precision, "that what I saw was enough for me to know that he would not live for more than thirty days." Before Liebermann could formulate his next question, Barash added, "You are a doctor who specializes in treating diseases of the mind?"

Barash gave no sign that he was exercising his metoposcopic powers. Liebermann assumed that it was merely a good guess.

"Yes, I am."

"Then you and I are not so very different. It is said that every evening Luria would look closely at his disciples' faces until he could discern scriptural verses on their foreheads. He would explain the meaning of these verses and instruct his disciples to reflect on them before going to sleep. On waking, his disciples recorded their dreams, which were later taken to the master for interpretation. Through cycles of close observation, explanation, and dream interpretation, Luria helped his disciples to understand themselves better and resolve their spiritual dilemmas. I try to extend the same service to my students. Now, isn't this—or at least something very similar—what you do for your patients? Surely, a good psychiatrist observes his patients closely, tries to read their faces, and offers them interpretations. And when a patient tells you about his dreams, do you not listen very carefully? For you know as well as I that the secret life of the soul is revealed in dreams."

Liebermann was tempted to ask Barash if he had read any Freud. But he decided against it.

"Did you know that Burke Faust was going to die?"

"No, of course not. How could I? I hadn't seen his face." The zaddik stroked his beard and added calmly, "Herr Doctor, am I a suspect?"

"You will appreciate," said Liebermann, "that as far as the police are concerned, the accuracy of your prophecy is rather worrying."

The zaddik shifted in his chair.

"You are not a believer, are you?"

"A believer?"

"You do not practice your faith."

"No. I don't."

Barash broke eye contact, and his line of vision found Liebermann's forehead. His dilated pupils began to oscillate. The experience was unnerving.

"Where does your family come from, Herr Doctor?"

"My mother's family are mostly German. But my father's family . . . I think his side were Czech."

"You sound doubtful. Are your origins of such little consequence?"

"We are Viennese now," said Liebermann plainly.

"Perhaps," said Barash, "if you had troubled to take a greater interest in your own origins, in the traditions and history of your people, then you would not be wasting your efforts talking to me now. You would have at least some inkling of what these murders might mean."

"Rebbe Barash, if you know something more, then you must say. This is a police matter."

Barash laughed, a mirthless convulsion.

"No, it is not a *police matter*. It is a matter between us and them, and whether you like it or not, Herr Doctor, as far as *they* are concerned you are one of us. Allow me to give you some advice. Your forefathers would have worshipped in the Old-New Synagogue in

Prague, the most important temple outside of Jerusalem. Go there, Herr Doctor, and pray. Pray for enlightenment. Go to the cemetery and pray for your ancestors to be merciful. Perhaps they will pity you and guide you back to your faith, and then—only then—will you understand, *fully* understand, what is happening. You think me misguided, don't you? A superstitious fool, no different, really, from the madmen whom you attend at the hospital. I am deluded, whereas you . . . you are a *rational* man! But, Herr Doctor, your arrogance, your conceit, blinds you!"

Liebermann pinched his lower lip. After a lengthy pause he said, "Rebbe Barash, you put me in a difficult position. Am I to understand that you know more about these murders than you are evidently prepared to say? Us and them? Who are you referring to? The agitators, the Christian Socials, the nationalists? I must warn you, unless you are more candid, I will be obliged to submit a report in which—"

"Do as you please!" Barash cried, thumping the chair arm with his massive fist. "Tell the police what you like. Arrest me! Try me! I have nothing to fear. I am innocent. If you want answers, look to Prague. I'll say no more."

The zaddik stood up and walked to the door. He opened it and waited for Liebermann to stand. He was breathing heavily.

The young doctor rose, adjusted his cuffs, and shook the creases from his trousers.

"I seem to have caused you some distress, Rebbe Barash," he said softly. "Please accept my apology."

Before leaving, the young doctor glanced at the zaddik's hands. He imagined them on either side of a human head, turning it around and around, the cracking of vertebrae and the severing of arteries.

33

We interrupted our circumnavigation of the ring at Karls-platz, where we found a bench on which to sit and admire the Karlskirche. I was reminded of a fact originally learned at school: during the plague of 1713, Emperor Karl VI vowed that if the population of the city survived, he would build a church dedicated to Saint Charles Borromeo, a former arch-bishop of Milan and the patron saint of the plague. What an odd notion, to have a patron saint of plagues. I wonder if the Catholic Church has considered appointing a patron saint of gallstones or—even better—syphilis. Is it any wonder that Vi-enna leads the world in medicine? It seems to me that the Vi-ennese have always been preoccupied by death and diseases.

I shared this speculation with Miss Lydgate, who asked how long it had taken to build the Karlskirche. "Twenty-five years," I was able to tell her. She scrutinized the church for some time before saying, "The Italianate dome owes a great debt to Brunelleschi, don't you think? The lantern, for exam-ple?" Needless to say, I had to confess that I didn't know whom she was referring to. "Filippo Brunelleschi," she replied, "the architect who designed the dome of Santa Maria del Fiore in Florence. The largest dome in the world."

As is her habit, she enthused about her topic and men-tioned in passing a treatise, "On the Tranquility of the Soul,"

written by one of Brunelleschi's disciples. It was of some interest to me because the subject matter of this work was the treatment of depression. Two men, both depressed, are conversing
beneath Brunelleschi's newly constructed dome. One of them
lists a number of traditional remedies for low spirits: wine,
music, the company of women, and exercise. But to these he
adds a new remedy: the contemplation of giant hoists of the
kind that Brunelleschi had devised to raise his creation.

I was obviously amused by this idea. Miss Lydgate, however,
was not altogether impressed by my reaction. She explained
that this "treatment" was not really as absurd as it might at first
seem, particularly if one considered it in its proper context.
The dome of Santa Maria del Fiore was nothing less than a
miracle to the people of Renaissance Florence. Therefore machines that made such buildings possible were viewed as
equally miraculous, symbolic of human ingenuity. To contemplate Brunelleschi's hoist, in that age, was to realize the unlim-
ited potential of the human mind, an undeniably uplifting
consideration.

She then described to me Brunelleschi's mechanical mar-
vel: a large frame that supported a number of vertical spindles,
each rotating the other by means of variously sized cogged
wheels. Miss Lydgate reserved her most profligate praise for
Brunelleschi's revolutionary gear mechanism, the operation
of which involved a large screw with a helical thread. This
gear mechanism was, I gather, of some considerable significance, but I am not altogether sure why. Miss Lydgate's account was complex and difficult to understand without the
aid of a diagram. In truth, I fear that her erudition was rather
lost on me. I am bound to confess too that my intellectual
powers had gradually deserted me as I became absorbed by the
unique coloring of her eyes.

Over the years, marble and masonry weighing millions of pounds—I forget the exact figure—were lifted hundreds of feet by Brunelleschi's hoist with astonishing efficiency. The mechanism was set in motion by a single ox. I inquired of Miss Lydgate how it was that she had come to know so much about a subject that must—in all fairness—be described as obscure. She replied that her father was greatly interested in the Renaissance and had taken her to Florence when she was only thirteen. While there, he had made it his business to gather information about the dome of Santa Maria del Fiore and its construction. On his return to London he had composed a pamphlet on Brunelleschi's hoist for the edification of his pupils (how delighted they must have been).

I formed the impression that Samuel Lydgate had used his daughter as an amanuensis, and that she had spent most of her time during this Italian <u>adventure</u> traipsing around old buildings and holed up in dusty archives. This, I could see, she regarded as entirely normal! The sun was setting, and its red light found corresponding tones in her hair. She was talking about a geometric feature of Brunelleschi's dome called the <u>quinto acuto</u>, or pointed fifth. I have a dim recollection of certain words: "radius," "curvature," "intersecting arches." But what I remember most is a feeling of quiet desperation. I wanted so much to reach out and link my fingers with hers. But instead, I found myself agreeing with her on some point that I had barely been able to follow.

On returning home I attacked the Chopin Studies: a definite improvement. Perhaps the Klammer Method is working. On the other hand, venting one's frustrations at the keyboard typically produces a more impressive performance. And I am at present nothing if not frustrated.

34

GABRIEL KUSEVITSKY OPENED THE door of his apartment and found his brother Asher lying on the sofa, a pen in one hand and a glass of wine in the other. On his lap was a notebook. The pages were covered in Asher's jagged script and splotches of ink. Distributed around the sofa were balls of scrunched-up paper, unsuccessful drafts that had been ripped out. Although it was still light outside, the curtains had been drawn and a paraffin lamp burned on the table. The air was stale with cigarette smoke.

Asher looked up. His eyes were bloodshot from lack of sleep.

"Where have you been?"

Gabriel started to respond, stopped himself, and then smiled nervously. He dropped his umbrella into the stand and said, "I went to see Anna."

"But you saw her only a few days ago."

"Yes, that's true, but..." Gabriel's sentence trailed off. He shrugged, and moved toward his bedroom door.

"Gabriel?" Gabriel stopped and looked back at his brother. "Gabriel, it wasn't easy for Professor Priel to get you that scholarship. The case for such a research project had to be made. There were many applicants, all of them good."

"Yes, I know."

"You have work to do."

"I know. You're right. Of course you're right." Gabriel walked over to the sofa and rested a hand on his brother's shoulder. "How is the new play coming along?"

Asher made a sweeping gesture with his hand, drawing Gabriel's attention to the scrunched-up sheets of paper.

"Slowly."

"Have you been out today?"

"No."

"Have you eaten?"

"No."

"Do you want me to get you something?"

"I'm not hungry." Asher looked up at his brother. "Did you really go to see Anna again?"

"Yes."

"You must be very fond of her."

Gabriel nodded. "I am."

"I'm happy for you. But you must not let Professor Priel down, and you must not neglect your work."

Gabriel put his hand into his pocket and pulled out a book with a battered cloth cover.

"Look at this."

"What is it?"

"Hildebrandt's treatise on dreams. It's a first edition—1875, Leipzig. I bought it for next to nothing from an old man selling books from a stall. He had no idea what it was."

Asher took the volume from his brother and flicked through the pages.

"Would I understand it?"

"Yes, it isn't very technical. Professor Freud quotes Hildebrandt, an observation Hildebrandt made concerning memory and dreams . . . that dreams often reproduce remote or even forgotten events from our earliest years." Asher closed the book. "Do you still get such dreams?"

"Sometimes."

"I still get the hunting dream."

"I know. You had it again the night before last. You were making noises in your sleep."

Gabriel's expression became intense.

"We were lion cubs this time, running across a frozen waste."

"Did we get caught?"

"I could hear the Cossack behind us. The drumming of hooves. The swish of his blade. Then I woke up."

"We escaped, then." Asher passed the book back to his brother. "Go to bed. I want to finish this act tonight."

35

Councillor Schmidt offered Bishop Waldheim more tea and a plate of *steirische schneeballen*—strips of dough molded into "snowballs," fried until golden brown, and generously dusted with powdered sugar. The bishop accepted, and after biting through the crisp exterior of the pastry emitted a low growl to express his satisfaction. They had just finished interviewing Nurse Heuber.

"Not as forthcoming as we had hoped," said the bishop.

"No," said Schmidt.

"She was obviously quite anxious."

"That's it, you see. . . . I think these people need to know that they have nothing to fear, that they have our full support."

"Well, that goes without saying, doesn't it?"

"Perhaps not, Bishop. Perhaps not." Schmidt sampled a snowball and was impressed by his cook's achievement. The brittle surface offered just enough resistance, and the soft interior was redolent of vanilla and rum. "I may be a little more direct with the next witness," Schmidt added. He looked toward the bishop for approval, his eyebrows raised slightly, expectant.

"Do whatever you think best," said the bishop, collecting up the snowball remnants on his plate and pressing them between his unusually rosy lips.

When they had finished their tea, Schmidt summoned his butler and asked for Edlinger to be shown in. When the young man appeared, the councillor came around the table and shook his hand.

"Edlinger, dear boy, delighted you could come. We are most grateful."

Schmidt introduced Bishop Waldheim, and the young man—impressed by his office—bowed ostentatiously low. The bishop, however, responded only by raising his hand and tracing a vague cruciform benediction in the air. Schmidt offered Edlinger a seat and then returned to his place beside the bishop.

"So, Edlinger," said Schmidt. "I understand that you are a friend of my nephew Fabian."

"Yes, we are well acquainted."

"Indeed, he speaks very highly of you."

Edlinger looked a little embarrassed, painfully aware that Fabian's esteem had not been earned by acts of Christian charity.

"Well . . . ," said the young man, shrugging and hoping that his inarticulacy would pass for modesty.

Schmidt produced a benign, indulgent smile.

"You are an aspirant?"

"Yes."

"And where do you want to practice, once you are qualified?"

"At the General Hospital."

"And why not? It is, after all, the finest medical institution in the world. Do you have a special interest?"

"Liver disease."

"Liver disease, eh? Well, I suppose Professor Hollar is your man. If you could get a position working under a specialist with his reputation, well, that would be a tremendous advantage, wouldn't it?"

"Yes," said Edlinger, somewhat confused. "It would."

"A man like him has more private referrals than he can possibly see. He's always passing wealthy patients on to his juniors. Yes, you couldn't hope for a better start to a career in medicine."

Again, Schmidt smiled.

Edlinger glanced nervously at the bishop.

"Well," Schmidt continued, "I must apologize for involving you in a disciplinary matter, but you were present on the evening when the young Baron von Kortig died. You are, therefore, a key witness, and we would very much value your assistance. There are certain details that need to be—as it were—*clarified*."

"Clarified?"

Schmidt picked up a piece of yellow paper. "I have here a letter, written by Father Benedikt to the old Baron von Kortig. In it he describes what transpired when he arrived to administer the last rites to the young baron." Schmidt summarized the priest's account. "Clearly, this is a very serious incident. The young baron was heinously denied the consolation of his faith, on his deathbed." The bishop rumbled like distant thunder. "Incidents like this have the potential to destroy public trust in the medical profession, and bring the great institution of the General Hospital into disrepute."

"Quite so," said the bishop.

Edlinger bit his lower lip and stroked his dueling scar.

"Would you say," Schmidt continued, "that Herr Dr. Liebermann's manner—on *that* evening—could be described as aggressive?"

"Aggressive . . . ," Edlinger pondered. "I can remember feeling that Herr Dr. Liebermann should have shown Father Benedikt more respect. And I can remember appealing to him. . . . I said something like, 'What right do we as medical men have to interfere with a priest's obligation to administer a sacrament?' "

"But would you say he was aggressive?"

"I'm not sure. Disrespectful, dismissive, perhaps."

"He did obstruct Father Benedikt. Physically . . ."

"Yes, he did."

"What would have happened, one wonders, if Father Benedikt had been more insistent? What if Father Benedikt had tried to get past him? Do you think Dr. Liebermann would have resisted, exercising even greater force?"

"He was quite adamant that Father Benedikt should not pass."

"Disgraceful," muttered the bishop.

"Was Father Benedikt at any point threatened?" Schmidt continued.

"He was not threatened with violence, no."

"Though I suspect he must·have *felt* threatened. Dr. Liebermann barred his entrance to the ward. Obstruction is a kind of violence. This was surely *threatening* behavior?"

Edlinger looked to the bishop, who was nodding sagely, and back to Schmidt.

"Well, I suppose it is possible that Father Benedikt felt threatened. He didn't look very comfortable or happy with the situation."

"Indeed. So if you were asked—let us say during the course of a hospital committee inquiry—if Dr. Liebermann's manner was *threatening*, you would have to answer yes."

Edlinger's brow furrowed. "I . . ." He hesitated and scratched his head.

"Edlinger, I cannot help noticing that you have a dueling scar. What is your fraternity?"

"Alemania."

"Ah yes," said Schmidt, as if he were enjoying the aromatic waft of a fine coffee. "Alemania," he repeated. "Did you know that I am very well acquainted with Professor Hollar? Did Fabian mention that? We sometimes share a box at the opera. A young man like you needs to consider his prospects, his future. Medicine is a very competitive profession. And there's a lot you could do—right now—to expedite your advancement at the hospital."

Edlinger's eyes widened. "I would say that Dr. Liebermann's attitude was disrespectful . . ." Schmidt and Bishop Waldheim were both nodding. "And threatening. Yes, most definitely. *Threatening.*"

Schmidt sighed with relief, and the bishop smiled.

36

MORDECAI BEN JUDAH LEVI, a distinguished scholar from another Hasidic sect, had written to Barash requesting a favor. In his letter he had explained that he was currently drafting an exegetical work and wished to discuss a particular point of law with special reference to the teachings of Isaac Luria. The zaddik had promptly consented, and his guest had arrived the following evening with a satchel crammed with books and annotated papers. It transpired that the question posed by Levi was not as testing as Barash had expected. Indeed, he was immediately able to provide an exact answer, allowing the two men to indulge in a more far-reaching conversation, a conversation that repeatedly strayed away from the ordinary and embraced the arcane.

"Are you familiar with the principal means by which demons propagate?" asked the zaddik's guest.

The curtains were drawn, and the only light in the room came from a single sputtering candle on the sideboard. A harsh wind had blown in from the east, carrying with it an icy memory of its Carpathian origins. It was curiously expressive, finding in every flue and vent an excuse to wail inconsolably. This disembodied moaning was most appropriate to their subject.

"I have not made a very detailed study of this area," said Barash modestly.

"Onanism," said the guest. "It is without doubt the principal means of demonic generation. Lilith, the queen of demons, and the familiars in her retinue excite concupiscent desire in men so that they are wont to engage in solitary acts of debauch. The demons do this so that they can make bodies for themselves from the lost seed." The guest tilted his head, and appeared to be listening intently to the lamentations of the wind. "No man can be complacent, even the virtuous man whose desires are satisfied within the sacred and lawful union of marriage. Lilith is ever eager to trespass in Eve's dominion. Thus, the Zohar recommends we perform a rite that keeps the demon temptress from the marriage bed. When the husband enters the bedroom, he should think only of holy things and recite the prayer of protection."

The zaddik's guest intoned a verse:

> Veiled in velvet—are you here?
> Loosened, loosened be your spell
> Go not in and go not out
> Let there be none of you and nothing of your part
> Turn back, turn back, the ocean rages
> Its waves are calling you
> But I cleave the holy part,
> I am wrapped in the sanctity of the King.

"Then," he continued, "the wise husband must wind cloth around his own head, and his wife's head, and sprinkle fresh water on the connubial sheets."

Barash was impressed by his guest's encyclopedic knowledge of the Zohar, and of so many other holy tomes. He was not only familiar with *The Book of Creation*, *The Book Bahir*, and *The Book of Visions* but also numerous lesser works: *The Treatise on the Emanations on the Left* by Rabbi Isaac ben Jacob ha-Cohen and *De Arte Kabbalistica* by Johannes Reuchlin.

Barash was flattered that a scholar as renowned as Levi had chosen to consult him. However, as their conversation progressed, he became increasingly uneasy. The point of law that his guest had wished to discuss was easily dispensed with, and he had begun to suspect that the question had been merely a pretext. The scholar seemed to be testing Barash, exploring the extent of his knowledge—and, by implication, his power.

They spoke for some time about demonic entities—their provenance and exorcism, and rites for protecting the dead. Eventually, however, their talk subsided and the room was filled with only the sound of banging shutters and the mournful cry of the wind. The zaddik's guest closed his eyes; he might have been sleeping were it not for the slow rise and fall of his right index finger. In due course, the scholar spoke. "The monk and the councillor." The words seemed to sustain an unnatural presence, like the protracted reverberation that follows the striking of a bell. "We have heard rumors. Your prophecy, scattered earth . . ."

So, thought Barash. *Now we have it at last.*

"And I hear that your students have been telling, once again, the old stories. The old stories of the Prague ghetto." The wind created a full-throated, almost human cry of desperation, and the scholar opened his eyes. They glinted in the darkness like mica. "My people want to know what is happening."

"Then tell them. Give them answers."

"What answers?"

"The answers that you know to be true, in your heart."

A sudden draft extinguished the candle, and they were plunged into total darkness. Barash could hear the scholar breathing: fast and shallow.

"Did you make it?" Levi asked, his voice no more than a whisper.

"No."

"Then who? Who among us today has the strength?"

"I don't know," Barash replied. "But surely, whoever it is, he will soon reveal himself."

37

Today I saw Clara, the woman I once loved. Or perhaps I should say the woman whom I thought I once loved. The woman who by now would have been my wife, had I not broken off our engagement. It is a strange consideration. Marriage. She looked stunning, coming out of the Imperial in the company of a handsome lieutenant. I had heard rumors, of course. They say she met him at a sanatorium in the Tyrol where her father had sent her to convalesce. I had always derived consolation from this news. It served to assuage my guilt. I couldn't be held responsible for ruining her life. Indeed, she might find true love with her lieutenant, and be patently much happier than she ever would have been with me. I wished her well, because if she found happiness in the arms of her handsome lieutenant, then my judgment would be vindicated. There, you see? It was for the best, after all.

So why is it, I wonder, that when I saw them together today I felt so ungenerous, so empty of goodwill? They stepped out of the Imperial, and the lieutenant hailed a cab. Clara was smiling. She was wearing a long fur coat with a matching hat and looked like a Russian princess. A cab pulled up, and the lieutenant helped her inside. As she ascended the step, he held her gloved fingers in one hand, and pressed the small of her back with the other. It was casual contact, accomplished with careless, practiced ease. He was used to touching her, and she was used to being touched. As the cab rolled off, I saw them kiss. A merging of shadows in the frame of a small window, glanced a moment before the curtain swished across to protect her honor.

It left me feeling excluded and horribly alone: standing on a corner, a revenant, or less—a voyeur—blinking into a gritty, chill wind. I remembered kissing her: the desire, the wanting. She was, and remains, a very beautiful woman. She was not right for me, and I was not right for her. I know that. I knew that then and I know that now. Even so, when I go to bed this evening, I will be going to bed alone. What have I replaced marriage with? An obsession. A fetish. The pursuit of a woman whose inaccessibility is equaled only by that of the stars. I am no different from some of Krafft-Ebing's cases. Excepting, perhaps, that their erotic lives are more satisfactory than mine! At least they have real outlets, whereas I appear to have none at all.

Amelia Lydgate was my patient. Her hysterical symptoms arose from a sexual trauma, the unwelcome advances of a man in whose household and care her parents had thought she would be safe. Miss Lydgate has now placed her trust in me. If I attempt to become intimate with her, will this not re-create elements of the very situation that made her ill? I wonder, what correspondent memories would a passionate embrace arouse in her mind? Schelling, stealing into her room at night and attempting to force himself upon her? The mattress tilting as he crawled over the bed, the suffocating weight of his body? How can I make my feelings known to such a woman, knowing as I do what she has experienced?

38

Rabbi Seligman awoke and saw his wife's face looming over him. He had dozed off while reading in an armchair next to the fire.

"Wake up!" She shook his shoulder. "Wake up. Kusiel is here."

"Kusiel?"

"Yes, Kusiel. He says it's urgent."

The rabbi got up from the chair and shuffled out into the hall, where he found the old caretaker.

"It's happening again," said Kusiel. "You must come."

Seligman signaled that Kusiel should lower his voice. Taking his coat from the hall stand, he called out to his wife, saying that he wouldn't be long. The two men stepped out into the night and walked the short distance to the synagogue. The Alois Gasse Temple was dark, except for the eternal light that danced in front of the golden edifice of the ark. Kusiel lit a paraffin lamp.

"It's been terrible. It's like something's being tortured up there."

The old man rolled his eyes.

Seligman listened. All that he could hear was his own pulse hammering in his ears.

"I can't hear anything."

"Wait . . . and you will."

The silence unfurled like a bolt of cloth, accumulating in suffocating, heavy folds. It was unyielding and contained within its emptiness a foretaste of oblivion.

"Perhaps you have been working too hard," said Seligman. "You might have fallen asleep and had a dream."

"There is something here, Rabbi. Something unnatural."

Kusiel's expression was resolute.

Time passed, and Seligman allowed himself to feel less anxious. Perhaps the old man really had imagined the noises after all. The hammering in Seligman's ears slowed. He was just about to say *I'm going home* when there was a sound that trapped the words in his throat: a deep, loud groaning. The quality of the vocalization suggested not so much torment—as Kusiel's reference to torture had suggested—but rather rage or anger. There was something brutal about its depth and fury, like the bellow of a taunted bull.

The whites of Kusiel's rheumy eyes glinted in the darkness.

"It's upstairs, Rabbi. Come. You must confront it."

Seligman's legs were weak with fear. Was it possible? Had some demonic entity found a home in his synagogue? No! He was letting the old caretaker's credulous talk get to him. There would be a rational explanation. He took the paraffin lamp from Kusiel and climbed the stairs to the balcony.

When they reached their destination, there was a loud thud: the floorboards shook.

"It's coming from behind there," said Kusiel, pointing to an old door.

The two men looked at each other, amazement mirrored in both their faces.

"Impossible," whispered Seligman.

"It hasn't been opened in years," said the old man. "Your predecessor lost the key."

"Was there anything in there?"

"No. It's just an empty attic space."

Lumbering steps and another bellow: impatient stamping. The cacophony conjured a picture of something mythic and bovine in the rabbi's mind. Seligman moved closer to the door. He reached out and clasped the handle, but as he did so, whatever was on the other side crashed against the woodwork. Seligman released his grip as if he had been electrified, and sprang back. He steadied himself by grasping the balcony rail, his legs shaking.

"I am g-going," he stammered.

"Shouldn't you do something first?" pleaded Kusiel.

"No," said Rabbi Seligman. "I'm calling the police!"

39

LIEBERMANN SPENT THE ENTIRE morning seeing patients. He was on his way back to his office with a number of case files under his arm when his friend and colleague Stefan Kanner stopped him in the corridor.

"Ah, Maxim, I'd buy you lunch, but I very much doubt you'll be free to accept my kind offer."

"Why do you say that?"

"There's someone waiting for you."

"Who?"

"A policeman," said Kanner, adopting a comic expression. "But you can still get away, of course. We can leave by the back entrance, have a leisurely schnitzel in Josefstadt, and be at the Westbahnhof by two. You'll be in good time for the Munich train, and I'd recommend changing at Paris for London. They'll never find you!"

Liebermann smiled and walked on.

When he arrived at his office, a constable was waiting outside. The young man looked very conspicuous in the bare hospital corridor.

"Dr. Liebermann?"

"Yes."

"Constable Mader, sir. I was sent here by Detective Inspector Rheinhardt of the security office."

Liebermann assumed that the constable was the bringer of bad news.

"Has there been another murder?"

"No."

"What, then?"

"Inspector Rheinhardt would like you to join him in Leopold-stadt."

"But why? What's happened?"

"Nothing's happened, as such . . ." The constable took off his spiked helmet and brushed his hair back. "More like . . . something's been found."

"What's been found?"

"Well, it's . . ." The constable shrugged, apparently lost for words. "I think you'd better see for yourself, sir."

Two carriages were already parked outside the Alois Gasse Temple and a policeman was standing by the entrance. A group of onlookers had gathered on the sidewalk close by.

"Make way, please," Constable Mader called out. "Make way for the doctor."

"Has someone been hurt?" asked one of the crowd.

"He says someone's been hurt," cried another.

"Move back."

"Let them through."

"He's brought a doctor."

The bodies peeled away, creating a narrow channel. Liebermann felt like Moses parting the Red Sea, an ironic "identification" given his near-constitutional skepticism. He ascended the stone stairs and, passing through a small vestibule, entered the main sanctuary. He stopped for a moment and viewed his surroundings. He was reminded of his childhood, going to the Stadttempel with his father and being bored to tears by the interminable prayers. He looked at the ark—with its gilded, intricate carvings—and experienced the same simmering resentment that he'd known as a child. Barash's words sounded in his mind, distant but precisely remembered: *Perhaps if you had troubled to take a greater interest in your own origins, in the traditions and history of your people, then you would not be wasting your efforts talking to me now. You would have at least some inkling of what these murders might mean.*

Nonsense, thought Liebermann. *Utter nonsense.*

Still, Liebermann could credit the zaddik with being right about one thing: he *did* think Barash was a lunatic, and had said so in the report he had prepared for Rheinhardt. The zaddik's account of metoposcopy was equal in absurdity to anything he had heard issuing from the mouth of a patient with dementia praecox.

Constable Mader coughed to attract Liebermann's attention and gestured toward a staircase.

"Inspector Rheinhardt is waiting upstairs."

"Of course," said Liebermann, a little embarrassed that his abstractedness might have been mistaken for reverence.

They began to climb the wooden steps but had to stop to let a photographer pass on his way down.

"Extraordinary," muttered the photographer. "Quite extraordinary."

A youthful assistant followed, carrying a tripod on his shoulders. Liebermann thought that the boy's expression looked somewhat confused, but also a little fearful.

The stairs delivered Liebermann and Constable Mader to a balcony.

A door stood ajar, and through the opening Liebermann could see Rheinhardt and Haussmann. The younger man was kneeling on the floor, collecting samples of dust, while the older was twirling his mustache and looking up at the ceiling. When Rheinhardt heard Liebermann arrive, he turned, acknowledging his friend's presence by raising his eyebrows. Like that of the photographer's assistant, his expression was troubled.

Liebermann stepped across the threshold and found himself, if not in another world, then certainly in another century.

The room was windowless except for a small dirt-streaked skylight, and the walls were entirely lined with shelves. Each of these shelves was crammed with a gallimaufry of items: stoppered bottles, dishes, leather-bound books, scrolls, statuettes, rubber tubes, retorts, and several examples of obsolete scientific equipment. It was almost too much to take in. Among the general clutter, Liebermann saw an eighteenth-century shagreen single-draw telescope, a rusting astrolabe, and what appeared to be a very primitive electric battery. Paper labels had been gummed to the bottles and inscribed in Greek, Latin, and Hebrew. Liebermann walked the length of the nearest wall, pausing to inspect some of the labels, and deciphering the writing where possible.

Phosphorus, antimony, cinnabar, sulfur, oil of vitriol . . .

A workbench was littered with astrological charts and mathematical tables. An ancient calculating cylinder (made from three interlocked metal rings) and a pair of compasses had been employed as paperweights to keep a length of rolled parchment flat. It looked like an old horoscope. Against a background of fading concentric wheels and nebulous patches of moldy discoloration were planetary symbols, newly executed in bright red ink.

The floor had been decorated with a large esoteric design. It consisted of ten painted circles arranged in an approximate diamond shape and connected to one another by thick lines. Some of the circles were more interconnected than others. Thus, the central circle possessed eight lines of connection, whereas those occupying the extremities of the diamond had only three. Every circle and every thick line was marked with a letter (or several letters) from the Hebrew alphabet.

Liebermann's attention was captured by a row of large glass jars on the opposite side of the room. Floating in a pale yellow liquid were several body parts—eyes, heart, fingers, and spleen—and included in this macabre collection was a small creature in a state of advanced decomposition. Liebermann drew closer. The skull and rib cage were visible beneath remnants of decaying flesh, and thin threads of hair floated up from the exposed beige-ivory crown. Lower down, the spine sank into a pocket of tarnished silver scales that tapered before expanding outward again as a ribbed fish tail. It was utterly grotesque. The young doctor snorted in disgust.

"Take a look in those barrels."

It was Rheinhardt. He was pointing to the other end of the room.

The barrels were very big, the size used by breweries to transport large quantities of beer. As Liebermann removed one of the lids, a mature loamy fragrance, almost fecal, rose up from inside. The barrel was full of mud: moist, dark earth.

"Mud?" said Liebermann.

"Yes, mud."

"You think there is some connection?"

"There must be, surely."

Liebermann replaced the lid.

"Do you know anything about this synagogue?" asked Rheinhardt.

"No," Liebermann replied. The tone of his voice was slightly offended.

"The rabbi—Rabbi Seligman—has explained to me that this room has been locked for more than ten years. The key was lost. A few weeks ago the caretaker said that he could hear noises coming from inside. Unusual noises. In fact"—Rheinhardt paused and looked round the room—"he thought they were produced supernaturally. In due course the rabbi too heard the noises and called the police."

"How did *you* get the door open?" Liebermann asked.

Rheinhardt pulled a bunch of skeleton keys from his pocket and rattled them in the air.

"Rabbi Seligman believes that this room has been used by a kabbalist, which I gather is some kind of Jewish sorcerer. Have you any idea what he's talking about?"

"Yes," replied Liebermann, "but only vaguely. Kabbalah is a form of Jewish mysticism, a hybrid of alchemy, astrology, and other vatic arts."

"How on earth did this fellow manage to get all these things in here without being noticed?"

"Not by magic, I can assure you! The staff of the security office can't be the only people in the world who know about skeleton keys."

"The lock was stiff. It didn't feel like it had been recently opened."

"Then he must have lowered things through the skylight." Liebermann looked up. "It would be a tight squeeze, but I think it's possible."

"Those barrels look too large to me."

"All right, maybe the barrels have always been here."

"And what if they haven't?"

"Then the barrels would have been made up in this room, from parts that were small enough to be lowered through the skylight."

"Wouldn't that be very noisy?"

"You said the caretaker *did* hear noises."

Rheinhardt made a sweeping gesture. "There's so much, though. How could one man . . . ?"

"He probably had an apprentice, like the one in Goethe's poem!"

"Max, be serious."

"I *am* being serious," said Liebermann. "However, I see very little purpose in trying to establish their exact methods right now! Suffice it to say that we are supposed to consider the existence of this 'laboratory' magical. The pressing questions are, first, why would anyone trouble to construct a kabbalist's lair? And second, do these barrels of mud link the former occupant—or occupants—of this room with the murders of Faust and Brother Stanislav? I have as yet no answer to the first, but I am already inclined to agree with you as regards the second."

Haussmann had finished collecting samples and was packing envelopes and boxes into a leather case. When he had finished, he stood up and took another look at the disintegrating mermaid.

"Herr Doctor . . . what is this? I mean, it looks real."

"Well, it *is* real in a sense," said Liebermann. "It is probably made from the skeleton of a small monkey, human hair, and an exotic fish. In the eighteenth century there was much interest in fantastic creatures, and many strange and wonderful things began to appear in private collections. These *exhibits* were usually put together by impecunious medical students who were able to make a modest income by selling their handiwork to gullible members of the aristocracy."

"It's definitely a fake, then?"

Liebermann rolled his eyes. "Yes, Haussmann, it's a fake!"

Rheinhardt joined his assistant and ran his finger around the rim of the jar. "Dust," he said. "Thick dust! The caretaker started hearing noises in here about two weeks ago. These jars have been untouched for much longer than two weeks."

Liebermann sidled up to Rheinhardt and said quietly, "Has it occurred to you that Rabbi Seligman and the caretaker might be unreliable witnesses? They could have done all this themselves—very easily—and then called the police."

"Rabbi Seligman and the caretaker seemed genuinely shocked when I arrived. Moreover, there are many valuable objects in this room. If I am not mistaken, some of these books"—Rheinhardt tapped the nearest spines—"were printed in the sixteenth century, and Rabbi Seligman is not a wealthy man."

"Sixteenth century, you say?"

"Indeed."

"Why would anyone want the people of Vienna to believe that a magician—a Jewish magus—was casting spells in Leopoldstadt?"

"To produce wonderment?"

"Or fear?" Liebermann asked.

"Or contempt. Christians have always been suspicious of Jewish rituals."

"You are thinking of the blood libel."

"And Hilsner, who supposedly killed a Christian virgin for her blood," Rheinhardt replied.

Liebermann took a scuffed leather volume from the shelf and allowed the pages to fall open. The paper was thick and maculated, and exuded a ripe mildewy fragrance. The text was in Latin. He flicked to the title page and read: *De Arte Kabbalistica* by Johannes Reuchlin.

40

"Furthermore," said Professor Freud, reading from his manuscript, "it is clear that the behavior of a child who indulges in thumb-sucking is determined by a search for some pleasure that has already been experienced and is now remembered. In the simplest case he proceeds to find this satisfaction by sucking rhythmically at some part of the skin or mucous membrane. It is also easy to guess the occasion on which the child had his first experiences of the pleasure that he is now striving to renew." Freud paused to draw on his cigar. "It was the child's first and most vital activity, his sucking at his mother's breast, or at substitutes for it, that must have familiarized him with this pleasure. The child's lips, in our view, behave like an erotogenic zone, and no doubt stimulation by the warm flow of milk is the cause of the pleasurable sensation." Again Freud paused to draw on his cigar. He turned back a few pages to check something and then continued. "If the erotogenic significance of the labial region persists, then these same children when they grow up will have a powerful motive for drinking." Freud pushed the cigar back between his lips, and his pout shrunk to form a tense annulus.

"And smoking," Liebermann ventured.

"Of course—didn't I just say that?"

"You said, 'a powerful motive for drinking.' "

"*And smoking.*" The professor was insistent. "A telling failure to apprehend, don't you think? You, a smoker, are resisting the deeper significance of your habit."

Freud drew lustily on his cigar, producing a volcanic eruption of

950630612000407066007474944

billowing cloud. Liebermann was fairly sure that it was Freud who had not finished his intended sentence (demonstrating resistances of his own) rather than he, Liebermann, who had unwittingly blocked the words from his own mind. However, Liebermann did not challenge Freud's interpretation but simply bowed his head in deference to the great man's perspicacity. Freud, pleased with both his observation and the compliance of his pupil, continued to read from his new work. On finishing the chapter, the two men discussed autoeroticism before turning to the lighter subject of the summer program at the opera, which had just been announced.

Most of the medical men in Freud's circle were aware that their mentor was not particularly musical, a conspicuous deficiency in a city where even the cab drivers could whistle whole arias from memory. Therefore, Liebermann was not surprised to hear Freud express an opinion concerning Mozart's *The Magic Flute* that Liebermann found so lacking in judgment as to be almost offensive.

"I went to see it last year. Director Mahler was conducting . . . ," said Freud, lighting yet another cigar. "It left me feeling rather disappointed. Some of the tunes are nice enough, but the whole thing rather drags, without any real *individual* melodies. I found the action ridiculous, the libretto insane, and it is simply not to be compared with *Don Giovanni*."

"Indeed, they are quite different works—and must be considered accordingly; however, I believe *The Magic Flute* to be the more intriguing work, being closer in construction to a dream, and therefore more deserving of study and interpretation."

"A dream? How so?"

"With respect, Professor, the *insane* libretto—as you so call it—is like the disconnected elements that compose the *manifest content* of a dream. It consists of symbols and distortions that disguise an underlying and perfectly coherent *latent content*, and it is the study of this latent content that permits us to understand the *true* subject matter

of the opera—namely, the resolution of conflict arising between mas-
culine and feminine principles. It is also supposed to contain—in
coded form—much of the secret lore of the Freemasons."

Freud suddenly became extremely interested. He was always fascinated by riddles and conundrums. Liebermann explained the symbolic elements of *The Magic Flute*, and the old man was obviously
very impressed. He was particularly attentive when Liebermann
gave an account of how Masonic purification rituals had been incor-
porated into the libretto to serve various dramatic purposes. It was
clear from Freud's responses that he knew a great deal more about secret societies than Liebermann had expected. Indeed, the professor
was knowledgeable not only about the Masons but about many similar groups. They were all, according to Freud, part of an occult tradition greatly influenced by the writings of Hermes Trismegistus, an
Egyptian priest and a contemporary of Moses.

The young doctor looked at Freud's desktop, which was crowded
with his collection of ancient statuettes and figurines. Among them
Liebermann recognized Isis and Osiris, several Sphinxes, and a terra-
cotta woman with a fan, which he had become curiously fond of.
They were all steeped in a layer of cigar smoke that rolled over the
edge of the desk and cascaded gently down to the floor like a slow-
motion waterfall.

"Of course," said Freud, "there is some debate over the existence
of Hermes Trismegistus. Some scholars believe that the famous *Cor-
pus Hermeticum* was in fact the work of later authors; however, one
cannot be certain. Other facts would contradict this assertion. I believe, for example, that Trismegistus is mentioned in the holy book of
the Muslims, where he appears in the person of Idris."

The professor kissed his cigar and expelled the smoke through his
nostrils.

"I wonder," said Liebermann, "does your interest in antiquities,
mythology, and old systems of thought extend to the kabbalah?"

Freud turned his gaze directly on his disciple. His expression was difficult to read, but contained within it the slightest suggestion of suspicion and unease.

"Did you ever see Jellinek talk?" asked Freud.

Liebermann looked puzzled.

"No," Freud continued. "Of course not. You're too young. Adolf Jellinek. He was a preacher, here in Vienna, and very popular too. He gave some talks that I was lucky enough to attend ten or perhaps even fifteen years ago. He had translated some of the medieval kabbalists into German. It was all very interesting."

"Then you know something about it? The kabbalah?"

"Yes." The syllable dipped in the middle and was produced with evident reluctance.

"May I?" Liebermann gestured toward some notepaper. Freud handed him a sheet. The young doctor took a pencil from his pocket and proceeded to sketch an arrangement of interconnected circles. It was the design that he had seen on the attic floor of the Alois Gasse Temple.

"Do you know what this is?" Liebermann handed the illustration to Freud.

The professor stubbed his cigar out and contemplated the image.

"Yes. It is called the Tree of Life. It is a diagram of how the universe was created and describes the dispersal of primal energies. It encapsulates the kabbalistic worldview."

Freud rose from his desk and approached a small chest next to the stove. He took a key from his pocket and turned it in the lock. When he returned, he was carrying several books. He piled them on the desk and invited Liebermann to examine them. One of the volumes was extremely old and was bound in crumbling leather. Freud opened it and carefully turned the fragile pages until he came to an illustration of a bearded man in medieval dress, sitting on a chair in a cell. The man's right hand grasped the lowest strut of the Tree of Life.

"What is this book?" asked Liebermann.

"A Latin translation of *The Gates of Light*—a very influential work. It was originally written by Joseph Gikatilla in the thirteenth century. The other books are German translations by Adolf Jellinek and his associates. Except this one here, which is a French translation of *The Book of Splendour.*"

Liebermann was surprised that Freud had so many volumes of Jewish mysticism in his possession. The old man had always been scathing about religion and was famously ambivalent about his own racial identity. Indeed, he had once said to Liebermann that he was concerned that so many of his followers were Jewish. *I don't want psychoanalysis to turn into a national affair,* he had said.

Only moments earlier the idea that Freud might be a clandestine kabbalist, poring over arcane holy books in the dead of night, would have seemed absurd. Yet the evidence suggested otherwise.

"Are you, then . . . ," said Liebermann hesitantly, "a believer in . . ."

"No, no," said Freud, shaking his head and waving his hand. "I abandoned the illusory consolation of faith many years ago. I no longer need to defend myself against unpalatable truths—the insignificance of humankind and the inevitability of my own demise. However, I have found a close reading of these books to be very instructive. In *The Book of Splendour,* for example, I first encountered the notion that the mind can be understood using the same exegetical techniques employed to study scripture. Kabbalistic writings also contain some extremely interesting accounts of human sexuality and the interpretation of dreams. . . ."

Freud smiled, but he was clearly a little embarrassed. He seemed to be confessing that the inspiration for psychoanalysis had come from reading works of Jewish mysticism. Immediately, Liebermann understood why Freud was so ambivalent about Jews and Judaism, and why he kept his kabbalistic books locked in a chest out of view.

Liebermann rested a finger on the drawing of the Tree of Life. Once again, the zaddik's words returned to haunt him: *Perhaps if you had troubled to take a greater interest in your own origins, in the traditions and history of your people, then you would not be wasting your efforts talking to me now. You would have at least some inkling of what these murders might mean.*

The zaddik's scolding no longer sounded ridiculous, and Liebermann found himself wondering how Freud would react if he asked to borrow his Latin translation of *The Gates of Light*.

41

LIEBERMANN AND HIS FATHER, Mendel, were sitting in the Imperial. The pianist was playing Chopin's *Mazurka Number One in F sharp minor*; however, his abrupt changes of tempo and volume made the piece sound like cheap café music. This was entirely intentional, as the pianist had learned that the patrons of the Imperial preferred their Chopin this way.

"Do you remember Blomberg?" said Mendel.

"The gentleman I met at the lodge?"

"Yes. He spoke to Rothenstein about the new department store. I would never have done such a thing myself. It was disrespectful, really. I mean . . . a man like Rothenstein!" Mendel shook his head and took a mouthful of *apfelstrudel*. "Rothenstein wasn't interested, of course, but he said that he knew a man who would be, and he put Blomberg in touch with Marek Bohm, another gentleman of considerable means and an associate of the banker. Well, to cut a long story short, it looks like the capital can be raised. Blomberg is going to go ahead with his plan for a second department store." Mendel slurped his coffee and dabbed his lips with a napkin. "I'm definitely going to go in with him," he continued. "Blomberg's a decent enough fellow, and his other store is doing very well indeed. It's too good an opportunity to miss. What did you think of him? Blomberg?"

"I didn't really speak to him for very long."

Mendel frowned. "Even so, you must have formed an impression?"

"He seemed very energetic."

"Oh, he's hardworking, that's for sure."

"And agreeable."

"If you have to work with someone over a long period of time, character becomes important, let me tell you. I remember, many years ago—before you were born, in fact—I tried to set up some dyeing works with a man named Plischke, and every meeting we had was like a funeral. In the end I couldn't take it anymore. What's the matter with your *mohnstrudel*? You've hardly touched it!"

"Nothing—it's very good." To prove the point, Liebermann sliced a large chunk off of the pastry and put it into his mouth. "Delicious."

Mendel shrugged.

"Anyway, I've decided to go to Prague. I'm going to visit some of the factories and have some meetings: Doubek, Krakowski—some of the shop owners. I also intend to see your uncle Alexander." At the mention of his younger brother's name, Mendel grimaced and emitted a low grumbling sound. "He's always been good at finding us new associates out there, but when it comes to overseeing the day-to-day running of the business, he can be quite careless. He never double-checks his figures and doesn't see Slavik as often as he should. I've got to make sure he understands the situation. The books *must* add up. We can't have someone like Herr Bohm raising doubts about our competence."

Uncle Alexander had been a distant and exotic presence throughout Liebermann's life. He used to stay for weekends in Vienna when Liebermann was a child, but these rare visitations had become even less frequent as Liebermann had grown up. By the time Liebermann had reached adolescence, Uncle Alexander's brief sojourns had stopped altogether. This was probably because his uncle and his father didn't get on. They were very different people—opposites, in fact. Mendel was resolute, ambitious, determined, whereas Alexander was languid, easygoing, and rather too fond of the bachelor's cheery existence to take the family business very seriously. This difference of outlook, Liebermann supposed, must have been the cause of many arguments. Liebermann remembered a handsome well-dressed man, with bright eyes and a mischievous smile. He had always been very fond of Alexander and guiltily recalled how, when very small, he had wished that his uncle could take the place of his father.

"Why don't you come along?" said Mendel, swallowing his last piece of *apfelstrudel*. He brushed his beard to make sure that no errant crumbs had found tenancy among his wiry curls.

"To Prague?"

Mention of Prague had made Liebermann feel uneasy. He remembered the zaddik: *Go there, Herr Doctor, and pray. . . .* It felt as if some strange power were attempting to draw him to the Bohemian capital, the city of his ancestors. It was a feeling that he—as a rational man—found distinctly uncomfortable.

"Yes," said Mendel. "You might learn something . . . about negotiating. You never know. It might come in useful one day."

Mendel still hoped that his son would take over the family textile business. It was a futile hope, but one that he could not relinquish in spite of his son's obvious lack of interest.

"I can't, Father. My patients, the hospital . . ."

Mendel sighed. "I thought you'd say that." The old man pushed his plate forward and beckoned a waiter. "The bill, please?"

Mendel knew as well as his son that there was nothing else to say. They would leave the Imperial and go their separate ways.

42

THERE WERE MANY WÄRMESTUBEN in Vienna, "warming-up rooms" where people in need, regardless of their circumstances or origin, could find shelter from the cold and receive a free meal. None were asked to prove their indigence or to produce licenses for police inspection. Anna and Olga were proud of the Spittelberg *wärmestube*, which they had worked hard to establish after securing large donations from Baron Königswarter and Baron Epstein. The opening ceremony had proved to be a rather glamorous occasion (some believed distastefully so) in the presence of the emperor's daughter, Archduchess Marie Valerie, who had attended in her official capacity as the principal patron of Vienna's *wärmestuben* association.

Anna and Olga were now standing by a giant tureen of bubbling soup. It was Anna who ladled the thick yellow liquid into a tin bowl, which was then picked up by Olga and handed to whichever unfortunate had arrived at the head of the line. A third person doled out bread and spoons. This process was mechanically repeated until everyone in the line had been served.

The Spittelberg *wärmestube* was larger than most, possessing a dining area in which sturdy wooden benches were arranged in parallel rows. All the seating seemed to be occupied, and Anna had to squeeze people together to make more room. Even though the *wärmestube* was full, it was remarkably quiet. All those who had assembled there—including the children—were too exhausted, miserable, and cold to make noise or conversation. The aroma of the fragrant soup, which smelled strongly of onions and garlic, was not redolent enough to swamp the disagreeable olfactory undertow of unwashed clothes and fetid breath. Some of the people in the *wärmestube* had traveled to Vienna over immense distances. Only that week, one man claimed to have come, mostly on foot, all the way from Odessa.

There was a loud clattering sound, followed by the hum of anxious voices. An empty tin bowl rolled across the floor, spiraling in smaller and smaller circles until it came to a clamorous halt. It belonged to a young woman who had passed out. One of her neighbors had managed to catch her as she slumped forward, preventing her limp body from toppling off the bench.

Anna and Olga rushed over to assist.

"I thought she was ill," Anna whispered to her companion. "When she was collecting her soup, I noticed she was wincing, as if in pain, and when she walked away, she was dragging her feet, like an old woman."

"Michael, Egon," Olga snapped. "Come over here." Two helpers made their way down an aisle. "Take this young lady next door and lay her down on the rest bed. Then one of you must hurry and find a doctor."

Within minutes Michael returned, accompanied by a venerable gentleman with white hair, half-moon glasses, and a pointed beard. He introduced himself as Dr. Janosi. Anna and Olga left him alone with his patient. When he finally emerged from the room, almost an hour later, he was escorted to a private room on the first floor, which was normally used for meetings.

"I'm afraid she is very unwell," said the doctor, "and will have to be taken to a hospital."

"What is the matter with her?" asked Anna.

"She has an injury."

"What kind of injury?"

"Ladies," said the doctor, "I managed to rouse the young woman with some smelling salts. She is originally from Galicia. She was—until a few days ago—a resident in a house of disrepute, here in Spittelberg."

"She is a prostitute?"

The doctor nodded.

"And her injury, Herr Doctor?" Olga pressed.

Dr. Janosi looked over his half-moon spectacles.

"I do not think it is appropriate to say. It is neither seemly nor fitting for young ladies such as yourselves, from good, respectable families, to hear such things."

"Herr Doctor," said Olga firmly, "we are grateful for your consideration; however, I can assure you that Fräulein Katzer and I are experienced fund-raisers for charity, and our work has necessitated frequent contact with the lowest and most unfortunate elements of society. We are modern women and do not balk at the harsh realities of existence."

"But, ladies . . ."

"Herr Doctor." Olga raised herself up to deliver her final, imperious command: "You will please speak plainly."

"Very well," said the doctor. "She is suffering from blood loss due to an *internal* injury."

"Internal?" Olga repeated. "Then she was . . . *overcome*?"

The doctor grimaced. In his day, a young lady would never have said such a thing.

"Her German was very bad," said the doctor, "but as far as I could tell, she has—until this evening—been receiving men in the house of a procurer, a villain called Sachs. She had decided, however, to move out of his establishment and had told him of her intention to do so. He said that she could not leave her *situation*. They argued; Sachs became violent and began to abuse her. He *overcame* her . . . but such is the depth of his depravity . . ." The doctor's sentence trailed off, and he looked away.

"Dr. Janosi?" Anna inquired, persisting.

"He held her down and inserted the wooden handle of a floor brush into her person. It was the vigorous movements of this implement that caused the bleeding. I am sorry—it is a dreadful affair. Such brutality should not go unpunished."

"Will she live?" asked Anna.

"If we can get her to a hospital soon," said the doctor, "there is a chance."

43

The note had been slipped under Liebermann's door while he had been attending Professor Heideck's morning ward round. He knew immediately that it was another summons from the chancellor.

When Liebermann arrived at the chancellor's office, Professor Gandler received him with a sullen stare and a few costive words of greeting. Liebermann sat down and waited politely for Gandler to speak. The silence that followed was deeply uncomfortable. The chancellor shifted in his chair and managed to say only "Herr Dr. Liebermann . . ."

"Am I to understand," ventured the young doctor, "that there have been some developments?"

"Yes," said the chancellor, as if addressing himself in a moment of abstraction. "Developments. There have been some developments."

Liebermann raised his eyebrows, willing Gandler to continue.

"When we last met, Herr Doctor, you will recall that I expressed grave concerns as to what consequences might follow from the publication of the article in *Das Vaterland*—that is to say, the article in which references were made to your alleged misconduct on the night when the young Baron von Kortig died. It gives me no pleasure to inform you that my misgivings have since been proved uncannily prescient. The issue of your alleged misconduct has come to the attention of several members of parliament. These gentlemen belong to the Christian Social party and take a keen interest in *religious* issues. Questions have been asked, explanations demanded, and I am of the opinion that this matter will shortly receive much greater attention in the wider press."

"But that is outrageous!" Liebermann cried.

"I would find it easier to offer you sympathy, Herr Doctor, had you not shown such disregard for my previous advice, which—I can assure you—was given in good faith. I told you that this business had the potential to escalate. You were warned, Herr Doctor."

"Be that as it may," said Liebermann, "your advice, however intended, does not alter the fact that I behaved as I did to best serve the interests of my patient, and with respect to the practice of medicine, I have still done no wrong."

Professor Gandler's upper lip curled to form a haughty sneer.

"I cannot believe your naïveté, Herr Doctor. Nor can I believe your selfishness. For the sake of making some self-indulgent, self-regarding, self-important moral stand, you have succeeded in exposing the hospital to the most serious public criticism. Yet you are still vain enough, in the light of what has so far transpired, to maintain your belligerent attitude. I would suggest, Herr Doctor, that a little humility might now be in order! Do you not see what is happening here? What some sections of the press will make of all this? Do you not see how the hospital will be portrayed as a haven for atheists and religious agitators? And can you not imagine what effect such a scandal will have on the number of charitable donations we receive!"

"It was never my intention to bring the hospital into disrepute, Herr Professor. As you know, I merely sought to honor my principal obligation, which was to my patient, and to him alone."

The chancellor shook his head. "Such worthy sentiments would be all well and good, Herr Doctor, if we lived in some perfect platonic world. But we don't. We live in a real and very complex world in which decisions have numerous consequences, all of which have to be taken into account. To do some good in this world—and by that I mean substantial, practical good—requires an individual to rise above simplistic juvenile idealism."

Liebermann was surprised by the chancellor's vehemence. Moreover, his insult was finely honed. It was penetrating and hurtful, Liebermann realized, because it was also insightful. There was some truth in what Professor Gandler had said.

"What do you want me to do?"

"Nothing," said the chancellor. "It's too late for an apology now. However, given the current situation, I have decided that it is in the best interests of all concerned if you are relieved of your clinical duties pending a special meeting of the hospital committee."

"What do you mean, 'relieved'?"

"You must not have any further contact with your patients."

"But that's impossible. Some of them are very ill."

"Then they will have to be reassigned to another physician."

Liebermann raised his hands in the air, a futile mute beseeching.

"What is the purpose of this suspension? What does it achieve?"

"The hospital must show that we are taking the matter of your alleged misconduct seriously. If we permit you to continue your clinical duties, then there is nothing to stop you from repeating the offense. Such a possibility cannot be countenanced."

"Professor Gandler," said Liebermann, attempting unsuccessfully to maintain a steady voice, "the circumstances surrounding the young Baron von Kortig's death were somewhat unusual. I do not expect to encounter such a situation again in the foreseeable future. Surely it would be better if I were relieved only of ward duties. I could then continue to see individual cases."

The chancellor was shaking his head before Liebermann had finished his sentence.

"No, that wouldn't be wise. I'm sure you can busy yourself in other ways. Spend some time in the library, write up a few old cases, plan some research . . ."

"When is this special meeting of the hospital committee planned?"

"We don't have a date yet, but as soon as everyone is agreed, I'll let you know. You will be expected to attend."

"I thought you said it was too late for an apology."

"It is."

"Then why must I attend?"

"To justify your actions so that the committee can make a decision concerning your position here at the hospital. I fear, however, that little can be done now. Unless something very remarkable happens, I believe that you will be dismissed. I did warn you, Herr Doctor. I did warn you."

44

LIEBERMANN WAS ALREADY SITTING in the little coffeehouse by the Anatomical Institute when Rheinhardt came through the door. The inspector hung his coat on the stand and made his way over to Liebermann's table. A waiter who had been lurking in the shadows emerged to take Rheinhardt's order.

"A *türkische*, please," said Rheinhardt. "With plenty of sugar."

Liebermann, finely attuned to the nuances of his friend's behavior, registered that Rheinhardt had neglected to order a pastry. This he took to be a very bad sign indeed. Only something of the utmost importance would make Rheinhardt forget his partiality for the chef's exotically spiced *topfenstrudel*.

"Well," said Liebermann, "I must suppose that you have called this impromptu meeting because a very considerable problem has arisen with respect to the investigation."

Rheinhardt shook his head. "No, Max, on this occasion you are quite mistaken." The inspector pulled a chair from under the table and sat down heavily. "This morning," he continued, "I was approached by Hohenwart. . . ."

"Hohenwart?"

"Alfred Hohenwart: one of my colleagues at Schottenring. He is aware of *our* association." Rheinhardt's finger oscillated in the air, linking himself and Liebermann. "Hohenwart investigates individuals and groups who seek to cause social division by religious agitation. Yesterday he received a dossier from a member of parliament that included letters from the old Baron von Kortig, a statement from a medical aspirant named Edlinger, and a draft copy of a scurrilous article soon to be published in the satirical magazine *Kikeriki*. Needless to say, the article is purported to be an account of events surrounding the death of the young Baron von Kortig, and describes—in very colorful terms—your dispute with the priest. The honorable gentleman suggested that it might be prudent for Hohenwart to make you, Herr Doctor, the subject of a comprehensive inquiry."

Liebermann opened his mouth and waited for a suitable expletive to give expression to his feelings, but all that he could manage was a horrified gasp.

"I know," Rheinhardt continued. "It is truly appalling. I explained to Hohenwart what *really* happened, and he agreed that there was insufficient cause to mount an inquiry; however, this is, of course, a very disturbing development. You will understand now why I wanted to see you as a matter of some urgency."

"The chancellor warned me that things might escalate, that my situation could become worse, but I never envisaged this!"

Liebermann told Rheinhardt about his recent encounter with Professor Gandler and explained how there was a good chance that he might lose his position altogether.

The waiter arrived with Rheinhardt's *türkische*. The inspector tasted it, grimaced, and spooned some extra sugar into the cup.

"Things stand to get very ugly indeed," said Rheinhardt. "Particularly if the newspapers get involved. You'll be hounded by journalists. Given that you've been relieved of clinical responsibilities, I'd recommend that you keep a low profile. Why don't you get away for a few weeks?"

"Where?"

"I don't know. It doesn't have to be very far, just somewhere they can't find you. In the meantime, I can have a word with the editor of *Kikeriki*. Perhaps I can apply a little pressure and get him to withdraw the article. I'll also request a meeting with the censor, who might be persuaded to intercept similar articles. After all, I very much doubt whether the emperor would approve." Rheinhardt sipped his coffee and added, "I wonder who's behind all this."

"It can't be just one person. You will recall that Councillor Faust wanted to eliminate Jews from professional life. There must still be others in the town hall who share his views, and creating a climate of hostility toward Jewish doctors would certainly help prepare the way." Liebermann took a box of small cigars from his pocket and offered one to Rheinhardt. "How ironic . . . that I—a man without any religious convictions whatsoever—should find myself described as a religious agitator!"

Rheinhardt took a cigar.

"This chap Edlinger—I gather he described your behavior as threatening." Rheinhardt struck a match, lit his friend's cigar and then his own. "Why should he have done that? Is it possible that he had reason to hold a grudge against you?"

"I hardly know him," Liebermann replied. "He *did* object to the position I took when I was arguing with the priest, so it could be that Edlinger is a devout Catholic, but I don't think so. Edlinger isn't really the type. He's a rakish fellow with a dueling scar. No, I suspect that his animosity stems from a simple but universal human failing. Psychoanalysis informs us that we often harbor resentment toward those to whom we owe a debt, and Edlinger is—without doubt—very much in my debt. He shouldn't have given the young Baron von Kortig morphine, nor should he have administered such a large dose. In fact, it was probably the morphine that accelerated the young baron's demise. I could have mentioned this to Professor Friedländer, but I didn't."

"Why not?"

Liebermann produced a twisted smile. "Doing so might have damaged Edlinger's prospects. I thought it unnecessary."

"The scoundrel," said Rheinhardt. "You should definitely report him now."

"I'm not sure that would be wise, Oskar. He could deny that he administered morphine—or such a large dose, at any rate—and that would cast me in a very unfavorable light."

"Wasn't there a nurse present?"

"Yes, Nurse Heuber. But she was wearing a crucifix, and it was she who went to fetch Father Benedikt. I don't think I can count on her for support." Liebermann drew on his cigar and blew out a jet of blue smoke. "Do you really think that I should leave Vienna?"

"Yes. Let me know where you're staying, and I can send you a telegram when it's safe to come back."

"Then perhaps I will go to . . ." Liebermann hesitated before saying, "Prague." The city was now inextricably linked with the zaddik's injunction. Once again, he felt as if he were being drawn there by fate. "My father asked me to accompany him to Prague on a business trip. He leaves tomorrow morning."

As he said these words, Liebermann felt as if he were making a concession not only to his father but, irrationally, to the zaddik as well. Still, it was the obvious solution to his predicament. He told himself that he should take advantage of the opportunity.

"Don't tell anyone at the hospital where you're going. Just leave a telephone number—your mother's, perhaps, and then she can contact you if the hospital committee is about to convene. I'll see what I can do. . . ."

Liebermann rested a hand on his friend's arm and tightened his grip.

"Thank you, Oskar."

The inspector, embarrassed by Liebermann's gratitude, made some dismissive noises and said, "Cake. We haven't had cake."

Rheinhardt called the waiter over and ordered two *topfenstrudels*.

"How is the investigation proceeding?" Liebermann asked.

"Do you really want to talk about that now?"

"Of course I do."

Rheinhardt shrugged. "Well, if you insist. Haussmann has been watching Barash's residence but has had nothing remarkable to report, although Barash has been receiving a large number of visitors—other Hasidim, from different sects."

"How did Haussmann know that they were from different sects?"

"They wear different hats, apparently. Haussmann also formed the impression that most of these visitors were community leaders—zaddiks, like Barash."

"What do you make of that?"

"It could, I suppose, be something to do with our discovery at the Alois Gasse Temple."

"Very likely, I imagine. Presumably you have someone posted there?"

"Yes, a constable from Grosse Sperlgasse, but the kabbalist has not returned to resume his activities." Rheinhardt raised his cigar and inspected the twisting column of smoke that rose from its burning tip. "Whoever created the kabbalist's lair wanted it to be discovered. They made loud enough noises to ensure that the room would be opened. Clearly they wanted us to make a connection between the lair and the murders, the barrels of mud serving to remind us of the deposits found close to the bodies of Brother Stanislav and Councillor Faust."

"Have you compared the samples?"

"Yes. The laboratory results showed they were identical." Rheinhardt puffed at his cigar and added, "Incidentally we went up onto the roof of the Alois Gasse Temple. It is certainly possible that many of the items we found could have been lowered through the skylight. The houses on that side of the street are dilapidated, and several of the rooms are unoccupied. A dedicated team working from a top-floor hideout could have accomplished the operation quite easily."

The waiter arrived with the two strudels.

Rheinhardt broke the flaky pastry with his fork, and the sweet curd filling spilled out, exuding a distinctive aroma of cinnamon, vanilla, and something less easily identified, an unknown ingredient that evoked images of a caravanserai and sand dunes.

"Exquisite," said Rheinhardt, his spirits rising with his appetite. "I wish I knew the chef's secret."

Liebermann stirred the froth around in his coffee and said, "I've been doing a bit of research into the kabbalah myself."

"Really?" said Rheinhardt somewhat vaguely, his attention having been captured almost entirely by his pastry.

"Yes. That floor design, the one consisting of interconnected circles. It's called the Tree of Life, and it represents creation and the subsequent dispersal of vital energies through the universe. Kabbalistic scholars believe that a thorough understanding of its principles can give a man godlike powers."

"Is that so?" said Rheinhardt.

Liebermann picked up his fork. He knew that he could not compete with Rheinhardt's *topfenstrudel*. He would have to wait for the inspector to finish.

Part Three

Prague

45

THE WHISTLE BLEW AND the train began to roll out of the Nord-bahnhof. Leaning his head against the window, Liebermann looked out at the receding platform—at luggage porters, army officers, smartly dressed women and children, the tide of humanity flowing backward as the locomotive engine gathered speed. The last person Liebermann glimpsed on the platform was an elderly gentleman holding up a white handkerchief, fixed in the attitude of his final parting gesture. It was a sad image that kindled a sympathetic pang of grief in Liebermann's chest. He did not want to be leaving Vienna. The train chugged through Brigittenau, crossed the Danube over an iron bridge, and thundered off through a thinly populated suburb out into open countryside.

"So," said Mendel. "What made you change your mind?"

"It's a long and rather complicated story."

"Well, we won't be arriving in Prague until midday, Maxim. You've plenty of time to explain yourself."

Liebermann sighed and told his father about the young Baron von Kortig, Liebermann's interviews with the chancellor, the article in *Das Vaterland*, his suspension from clinical practice, the allegation of religious agitation, and the forthcoming committee meeting at which, in all probability, his career as a doctor would be blighted. Mendel sat through the account in silence, but his expression showed that his feelings were complex, vacillating between conflicting states of horror and hope. He was furious that his son had become the victim of anti-Semitism, but at the same time he was aware that the demise of his son's medical career would force him to consider alternatives, one of which would surely be to enter the family business. Never before had Mendel's foremost wish come so close to fulfillment.

"Well, that's very bad. Very bad indeed," Mendel muttered. "Do you need a lawyer? I'd pay, of course."

"I don't think that would help, Father."

"Perhaps not." Mendel took off his hat and laid it on his lap. "Despicable, the way they treat us. Despicable." He looked down and toyed with the hat's label. "I know how much medicine means to you, Maxim. But if you do lose your position, and can't find another post . . ." Somehow the offer of employment seemed to be more tactful if implied, rather than spoken.

Ordinarily, Liebermann would have responded with a verbal parry, or a defensive change in posture. But now he was feeling tired and drained. He had succumbed to an insidious, enervating pessimism. He nodded and said, "It might well come to that, Father."

Mendel had not expected the concession to come so easily, and he looked up, surprised.

"It's not such a bad life," said Mendel cheerily. "Business!"

Liebermann managed to smile, but the pretense was unsustainable, and an expression of blank despondency quickly reasserted itself.

Father and son fell silent. The rocking motion of the train was conducive to private meditation, and some thirty minutes passed before Mendel stirred again. He opened his bag and pulled out a ledger book.

"Here. Take a look at this."

Liebermann crossed the compartment and sat next to his father.

"Now," said Mendel, stroking the cloth cover, "here we have the principal financial record book of the textile company. It contains details of transactions, assets, and liabilities." Liebermann tried to listen, to understand what his father was saying, but the language of commerce was totally foreign to him. It failed to find any purchase in his mind, becoming a meaningless, disconnected babble: "expenditure," "solvency," "returns," "profit," "imports," "loss," "receipts," "equity." Indeed, Liebermann marveled at his own inability to learn anything. Something deep inside him refused to cooperate. He recognized it as a form of resistance, the strength of which was almost pathological.

The journey felt interminable, and when the train finally pulled into Prague, although Mendel's spirits were unusually high, his son's were correspondingly low.

They hailed a cab and traveled first to the Old Town Square, where Mendel had arranged to collect a garnet necklace, a present for his wife. While Liebermann was waiting for his father's return, he stepped down from the carriage and found himself standing next to a massive astrological clock. The upper disc, being the timepiece, was ringed with golden numerals. The lower disc, which appeared to be a calendar, was richly illustrated with seasonal tableaux and the signs of the zodiac. Set among the allegorical figures that adorned the clock was a skeleton: death, carrying his hourglass.

Across the square, Liebermann observed an imposing Gothic structure, which he knew to be the Church of Our Lady Before Týn. Its two towers, of unequal height, were festooned with sharp pinnacles. It looked nothing like the baroque churches of Vienna, with their ebullient ornate façades, which always reminded Liebermann of confectionery. The Church of Our Lady Before Týn was a much darker piece of architecture—brooding, even sinister. The black, bristling spires were menacing, the home of some horrifying storybook evil.

Liebermann shivered in the breeze, chilled more by his fanciful imaginings than by the cold. He got back into the cab.

Mendel returned, carrying a jewelry case. He opened it up and took out a necklace of bloodred garnets, suspended in a delicate web of silver chains.

"It's beautiful," said Liebermann.

His father allowed himself a smile. "A surprise. She'll like it."

Their hotel, the Ambassador, was on Wenceslas Square. After depositing their luggage with porters, they proceeded to the restaurant, where Mendel had agreed to meet his brother Alexander. The restaurant had a large plush interior in which a piano trio played music that—unusual for him—Liebermann did not recognize. He suspected that the composer might be Dussek.

As soon as they were seated, Mendel began looking at his watch and huffing impatiently.

"Father, he isn't late yet," said Liebermann.

"Yes," said Mendel. "But he will be. He always is."

The restaurant clock struck one, and Alexander did not arrive. Mendel grunted and seemed to derive satisfaction from the fact that his brother was now genuinely late. Another twenty minutes passed before Uncle Alexander made his entrance. He glided through the double doors, a tall, distinguished-looking man with long hair swept back from his forehead. Hanging loosely over his shoulders was a long camel-hair coat, and in his hand he carried an ebony cane with a silver handle. He moved with a distinctive fluid ease.

"Mendel, how good to see you," said Alexander. The two brothers embraced, Mendel exhibiting a certain awkwardness when they touched. "And Maxim. Maxim, my boy." Liebermann felt a surge of affection for his uncle. Alexander kissed Liebermann and hugged him close. "Maxim," he repeated. "How you've changed."

They sat down, and Alexander immediately began asking questions. How was Rebecca? And Leah, and baby Daniel? Hannah and, of course, Leah's husband, Josef? Mendel reciprocated by inquiring about Alexander's health.

"Old age . . . ," said Alexander, making a helpless gesture with his hands. "There's no future in it."

He delivered his bon mot in an indolent drawl, one word slurring into the next. He then spoke a little about his knee, which was arthritic and quite painful. For the two brothers, orthopedic problems supplied a rare topic of mutual interest. In the absence of more conventional commonalities, this was the closest they came to enjoying an effortless dialogue.

The waiter arrived, and Alexander insisted that they try the liver dumplings, followed by duck roasted with chestnuts and served with red cabbage. Apparently the chef was a master of traditional Czech cuisine.

Alexander then turned to Liebermann. He made some small talk about the pleasures of living in Prague and enthused about the city's cultural institutions. Like his nephew, Alexander was a very competent pianist. Indeed, one of Liebermann's earliest memories was of sitting on his uncle's lap while he played bravura arrangements of Strauss waltzes.

"You should go to the philharmonic while you're here," said Alexander. "An excellent orchestra, and the chamber groups are very good too. I can recommend the Czech Quartet. Their second violin, Suk, is a pupil of Dvořák and—I believe—is married to the great man's daughter. Suk's piano works are exquisite. The *Polonaise-Fantasy*, the *Village Serenade*, and the *Bagatelle*—lyrical but distinctive. The music shop in the old town stocks his piano scores. I'll give you the address." He took a pencil from his pocket and wrote the details on one of his visiting cards.

On no fewer than three occasions, Mendel attempted to raise the subject of work, but every time, Alexander managed to steer the conversation in alternative directions: theatre, politics, Czech wines, and the relative virtues of Budweiser and pilsner beers. Eventually Mendel, who Liebermann could see was becoming impatient, barked, "Alexander! I'm supposed to be meeting Doubek at three. We must talk about the factories!"

Alexander looked surprised, even a little hurt.

"Of course, of course . . . the factories. I was just getting to them."

He said this with appeasing gentility, but his mellifluous tones were tainted with a hint of condescension. It was clear that Alexander thought his brother was being inexcusably bad-tempered.

The food was served, and there then followed a conversation that Liebermann found excruciatingly dull. He took some consolation from the fact that his uncle seemed to be suffering just as much as he was. The remainder of their meal was dominated by talk of productivity and pay.

After they had eaten, they removed to a private lounge on the first floor of the Ambassador and waited for Doubek, a factory manager. Doubek was punctual, and the meeting seemed to go well. Indeed, at its conclusion, the jolly Czech produced a bottle of Borovička—a juniper-flavored spirit—and proposed a toast to lasting friendship and prosperity. Their second meeting was a short distance from the hotel at the offices of an accountant named Slavik. Unfortunately Slavik was unable to answer many of Mendel's questions, and the atmosphere soon became tense and edgy. Occasionally the accountant would glance at Alexander, his eyes appealing for help; however, all that Alexander could offer in return was a pained grimace. When the meeting was over, Mendel's silence and sullen expression declared his displeasure.

"You'd prefer it if I dismissed Slavik," said Alexander, "wouldn't you?"

"Yes," said Mendel bluntly.

"Is that really necessary? I know he wasn't very impressive today, but I think that's because of his wife. She hasn't been well lately—a chest infection. He's been distracted."

"Are we a charity now?"

"No, but ..." Alexander sighed and shook his head. "We play cards together." Mendel turned on his brother, his eyes incandescent with anger. "All right, all right," Alexander resumed. "I'll deal with it."

Liebermann and his uncle exchanged a confidential glance. Alexander looked a little discountenanced, but this did not stop him from winking. He had never taken his brother's temper very seriously.

46

IT WAS EARLY EVENING, and they had just finished another substantial meal in the hotel restaurant.

"Well," said Mendel, draining his coffee cup, "I think we should all retire early. Tomorrow will be another busy day."

Alexander rubbed his knee.

"My leg's a bit stiff. It happens if I've been sitting still for too long I think I'll go for a walk and a smoke before going home. How about you, Maxim? Do you feel like a walk?"

Liebermann looked across to his father. The old man shrugged, as if to say, *Do as you please.* Liebermann and his uncle bid Mendel good night, collected their coats, and left the hotel. They strolled through the Staré Město, veering east through quaint narrow streets toward the Vltava. Liebermann had to get used to his uncle's unhurried gait. Alexander took his time, occasionally stopping to examine the contents of a shop window or an interesting stucco decoration above a door. He was also in the habit of raising his hat and smiling at every pretty woman who passed. This was achieved with the natural, unconscious charm of a seasoned roué.

When they reached the Bethlehem Chapel, Alexander said, "I was surprised when Mendel told me that you would be coming along. I always understood that you weren't interested in the family business."

"I'm not."

"Then why are you here?"

"The fact is, Uncle, I've got myself into a bit of trouble."

"Trouble, eh?" Alexander looked mildly amused rather than concerned.

For the second time that day Liebermann described the von Kortig affair and the events leading to his suspension.

"Well, that's truly dreadful," said Alexander. "And I imagine that after today, the prospect of joining the family business is even less appealing. However, if you are forced out of medicine, you wouldn't have to stay in Vienna. You could always come here and work with me. I suspect that you would find working in the Prague office less onerous."

Alexander produced a complicit smile.

"Thank you, Uncle," said Liebermann. "That's very kind of you. I'll bear that in mind."

"Yes, you do that."

The twilight was deepening as they approached the Charles Bridge, and ahead the Gothic portal loomed into view: a tower of dark brick surmounted by a massive wedge-shaped spire, out of which sprouted numerous gold-tipped pinnacles. The two men walked under the central arch into a preternatural night and then out onto the bridge itself.

The prospect that came into view inspired wonder. It possessed a strange phantasmagorical beauty. An amphitheatre of hills provided a backdrop, the northeastern summits of which were dominated by Prague Castle and the spiky silhouette of Saint Vitus Cathedral. Red roofs appeared among the greenery of the lower slopes, which cascaded down to the left bank of the river. The low walls on either side of the bridge were punctuated by large statues of religious figures and converged in the hazy distance, where two more Gothic towers marked its end.

Liebermann and his uncle advanced until they were about

halfway across. They had arrived at the feet of a bronze saint, green with age, his head surrounded by a halo of gold stars. In his hands he held a palm branch, also of gold, and a giant crucifix.

"Who is this?" asked Liebermann.

"Saint John of Nepomuk. The Bohemians have made a cult of him." Alexander pointed to a relief tableau. "This shows his body being thrown off the Charles Bridge after he had been tortured to death."

Liebermann noticed that the saint's patina had been worn away by the touch of countless pilgrims. The little upside-down figure had been polished to a striking brightness.

Alexander took out a silver cigarette case and a box of matches. He offered a cigarette to Liebermann, who took it, and soon they were both leaning over the parapet, smoking. High, wispy clouds were reflected in the steely flow of the Vltava, and an eerie ancient melody, plucked from a stringed instrument by an invisible musician, floated on the air. The first star ignited above the castle.

"I was sorry to hear that you broke off your engagement with Clara Weiss," said Alexander. He did not turn to look at his nephew but stared fixedly at the lone sentinel, burning in the sky.

"It was difficult. A hard thing to do."

"I can imagine."

"I upset a lot of people. The Weisses, Mother and Father—and Clara, of course. She had to go to a sanatorium, you know. To recover." Liebermann drew on his cigarette and directed a stream of smoke upward. "Still . . . she's with somebody else now. And I understand she's happy."

"And what about you?"

"Am I happy?"

"No. Have you found somebody else?"

Liebermann's answer was hesitant.

"There's this . . . this Englishwoman."

"English, eh? I had an English mistress once." Alexander's expression softened, and he fell into a dreamy state of abstraction. After a few moments he blinked as if waking from a trance and said, "Forgive me, Maxim. Do go on . . . please."

"I have strong feelings for her. But the circumstances of our meeting were rather unusual. You see, she was a patient whom I treated at the hospital."

"These things happen. I have a doctor friend who is always having assignations with his patients. Even the ones who are married!"

Liebermann shrugged. "It hasn't happened to *me* before."

"There's always a first time, my boy."

"She is a woman whose appeal I find difficult to describe. Indeed, the majority of men might find her manner somewhat peculiar."

"Well, she's English. Is she beautiful?"

"Yes. Very. But she is strangely dispassionate."

"Cold?"

"She can be."

"Ah, then you have found yourself a *cruel mistress. A Belle Dame sans Merci.*"

"Not at all. She is kind and compassionate. It is just that she . . ." Liebermann searched for the right words. "Is uncommonly rational. I've never met anyone like her before. She is quite unique."

"Have you become intimate?" Alexander's emphasis left no doubt as to his meaning.

"No."

"But you *desire* her?"

"Yes."

"Then why haven't—"

"The moment is never right. Besides, I am not in any way confident that a physical demonstration of my affection would be welcome."

"Why do you say that?"

"She has had . . . an unfortunate experience. With a man."

"I see," said Alexander, perceiving his nephew's discomfort. "Do you love her, Maxim?"

Liebermann made a helpless gesture with his hands.

"I don't know what I can expect from such a woman. I can as much imagine her managing a home as I can imagine myself managing a factory! And as for children—"

"Maxim," Alexander cut in. "Excluding a man's mother, there are three women in every man's life. His wife, his mistress, and the *unattainable object of desire*. His wife becomes commonplace, his mistress a frivolous expenditure, but the unattainable object of desire remains alluring in perpetuity. She is the guardian of his vital powers. Her currency never depreciates. She is never cheapened or diminished by consummation, and her stock rises as we grow old. Even when our flesh becomes arid and we succumb to the depredations of time, she reminds us of what it was like to be young. This Englishwoman, if I am not mistaken, is your unattainable object of desire. Let her serve her purpose, because in all likelihood she has no other." Alexander dropped his cigarette into the water below. "A handsome fellow like you should be enjoying life, not fretting over a frigid English girl."

The sudden bluntness startled Liebermann. He turned to look at his uncle, who reached out an affectionate hand and squeezed Liebermann's arm.

"You probably think me an old fool—or, even worse, an old cynic. But I have always been fond of you, Maxim, and I do not like to see you unhappy."

Liebermann acknowledged his uncle with a smile. He stepped back from the wall and looked toward the Gothic bridge tower, which was now looking distinctly sinister in the fading light. Beyond was a pleasing cluster of umbrous domes, onion steeples, and triangular pediments.

"That dome," said Liebermann, pointing to the largest, "owes a great debt to Brunelleschi."

"What?"

"Brunelleschi, an Italian architect. It was he who set the precedent for putting lanterns on top of domes."

Alexander tilted his head quizzically, but decided that his nephew's non sequitur did not merit further inquiry.

"Come," he said. "Let's get a nightcap."

They walked back through the Staré Město and stopped at a beer hall near the House of the Two Golden Bears, a Renaissance edifice with eponymous ursine relief work. The landlord of the beer hall was obviously well acquainted with Alexander. When Alexander introduced Liebermann as his nephew, the landlord shook his hand and insisted they have a few Gambrinus—on the house. When they had finished their beers, Liebermann was alarmed to hear his uncle ordering a bottle of liqueur.

"Becherovka," said Alexander. "It's made with herbs. I often take it as a tonic."

The amber liquid tasted bittersweet.

When they left the beer hall two hours later, it was nighttime, and Liebermann was conscious of the fact that he had drunk far too much. Indeed, his legs had become unreliable and he had acquired a style of speech similar to his uncle's.

"Well, good night, Maxim." His uncle kissed him on the cheek. "And cheer up, eh? Life is too short to be taken seriously. I'll see you in the morning. Sleep well." He winked and chuckled. "Sleep well."

Alexander turned and walked off, whistling a melody from an Offenbach operetta.

When Liebermann got back to his room, he undid his necktie, took off his shoes, and flopped back onto the bed. He thought about the hospital committee, what life would be like if he came to work with his uncle in Prague, and his recent conversation with Alexander on the Charles Bridge.

The unattainable object of desire . . .

Perhaps his uncle was right. Perhaps he had become fixated on Miss Lydgate simply because she was, in so many ways, inaccessible. And such was the human mind, with its childish inclinations, that what was held beyond reach was always what was perceived as most desirable. Liebermann rubbed his chin, which was scabrous with stubble. His thoughts became disconnected, and he sank into a fitful sleep.

Liebermann woke with a start.

A gentle rapping, knuckles on wood.

He got up, steadied himself by touching the bedpost, and made his way to the door. His head felt full of glue. A young woman was standing outside. She pushed through the opening and stood proudly in the center of the room.

"Fräulein," said Liebermann, brushing his hair from his eyes. "I think you've made a mistake."

"My name is Anezka." She took off her hat and threw it onto a chair, then narrowed her shoulders and let her unbuttoned coat fall to the floor. She was wearing a tight silk dress, the intrepid neckline of which descended steeply, revealing a plenitude of bulging flesh. "Herr Dr. Liebermann?"

"Yes."

"Then there has been no mistake. I am a present."

"A present?"

"Yes, from your uncle."

She rushed up to Liebermann and pushed the door closed. Then, taking him by the hand, she pulled him to the bed and playfully pushed him so that he was seated on the edge.

"I'm really not sure about this," said Liebermann.

"The gentleman said you might be a bit shy. But he said I should persevere."

Taking Liebermann's hands in hers, Anezka placed them on her hips. Her corset creaked as she bowed to kiss the top of his head.

"Well," she said, "do you think I am pretty?"

"Yes," Liebermann said. "I think you are very pretty."

He knew that he should ask her to leave; however, the machinery of articulation failed to engage. He looked up, into the woman's black eyes, and they seemed to expand until there was nothing but an infinite, starless void. His will to resist evaporated. The hot breath on his neck made him sigh with pleasure. He allowed his body to go limp, and he fell back onto the mattress, confident that he was surrendering his body to the ministrations of a skilled professional.

47

Anna Katzer and Olga Mandl stepped down from the carriage on Burggasse and walked arm in arm up the cobbled incline of an adjoining street. The houses they passed were dilapidated, and the air smelled vaguely of refuse. From somewhere beyond the end of the street a bugle sounded, establishing the proximity of the barracks. They arrived at their destination, a decrepit hovel, and paused to examine the filthy exterior. Pieces of stucco had fallen off the façade, revealing the underlying brickwork, and the windows were streaked with bird droppings.

A door was thrown open on the opposite side of the road, and a plump red-faced woman stepped out. She frowned at the two well-dressed young women and proceeded to shake some bed linen.

Anna lifted the cast-iron knocker and rapped loudly. Nothing stirred in the house, so she tried again.

"Excuse me," Anna called over to the red-faced woman. "Do you know if Herr Sachs is in?"

The red-faced woman shrugged and continued with her work. Anna turned and struck the door with her fist.

"Herr Sachs, are you in? Herr Sachs?" She tilted her head and addressed her companion. "Did you hear something?"

"Yes," said Olga, "I think I did."

"Herr Sachs? Open the door!"

They waited, and their patience was rewarded by the hollow thump of footsteps descending wooden stairs. A bolt was drawn aside, and the door creaked open. The man standing in front of them had evidently just gotten out of bed. His hair was mussed, and he seemed slightly disorientated. He was wearing a stained dressing gown and had not bothered to put on his slippers. Anna glanced down and was repulsed by his corneous clawlike yellow toenails. On the exposed carpet of matted hair that covered his chest sat a circular pendant that contained a Star of David. He rubbed one of his half-closed eyes with a grazed knuckle and, when he had finished, blinked blearily at the two women.

"Herr Sachs?" Anna inquired.

"Who are you?" he replied, the words forming from the gravelly sounds that he made as he cleared his throat.

"My name is Anna Katzer, and this is my associate and friend Olga Mandl. Are you Herr Sachs? Jeheil Sachs?"

"What if I am?" the man said. The fogginess of sleep suddenly dissipated from his expression. He studied Anna and Olga more closely, his gaze wandering disrespectfully from head to toe, his mouth twisting into a lecherous grin. "What if I am?" he repeated, and added in a softer tone, "Ladies . . ."

Anna and Olga bristled simultaneously.

"It is our understanding," said Olga, "that you are acquainted with a Galician woman named Kadia Pinski." Sachs stiffened. "Well?" Olga persisted. "Is it true?"

Sachs nodded. "Yes, I know her. Why? And where is she?"

"In the hospital," said Anna.

Sachs's tongue moistened his cracked lower lip.

"What is your relationship with Fräulein Pinski?"

"That's none of your business," Sachs snorted. Then he added in a more conciliatory tone, "All right. If you must know, I help her out a little. Financially. I've introduced her to a few soldiers who've given her a good time. Hospital, eh? What happened to her?"

"You know very well what happened to her!" said Anna, her voice brittle with anger. "What you did was despicable!"

When Sachs tried to close the door, Anna threw her weight against it, keeping it open.

"We know what you did!"

"I don't know what you're talking about."

"Have you no conscience, no self-respect?" said Anna. "To profit from the misery and hardship of your own people."

"You can't prove anything," said Sachs. "I helped the girl out, that's all. If she's gotten herself into some sort of trouble, it has nothing to do with me." Sachs looked across the street at the plump woman, who had stopped doing her chores and was watching the altercation. "Hey!" he shouted, making a shooing-away gesture with his hand. "This is a private conversation!" Sachs spat onto the cobbles and swore under his breath.

"We have a doctor's report, Herr Sachs," said Olga.

"Good," said the procurer. "Do you think I care? If she's accused me of anything, then it's my word against hers. Do you think she's the first drunken whore to get herself into trouble and make up a story?"

"Justice will be done, Herr Sachs," said Anna. "Believe me. We will see to it that justice is done."

Sachs suddenly lost his temper.

"Go away! The pair of you! Meddling bitches. I've had enough! Go back to your fancy apartments and perfumes and fine wines, eh? I'm going back to bed!"

Sachs pushed Anna out of the way and pulled the door shut.

"Are you all right?" said Olga, placing an arm around Anna's shoulder.

Anna didn't notice her friend's ministrations. She clenched her fist and banged it against the door.

"We'll be back, Herr Sachs," she shouted. "I promise you, we'll be back."

48

WHEN LIEBERMANN ENTERED THE restaurant, he saw that his father and uncle were already seated for breakfast.

"Good morning, Maxim," said Alexander. "Did you sleep well?"

"No," said Liebermann. "I didn't. The room was rather hot."

"What are you talking about, hot?" said Mendel. "It was freezing last night."

"The young don't feel the cold like us," said Alexander innocently. "It doesn't get into their bones."

Liebermann sat down and tried to disguise a yawn.

"And what time did you get back last night?" Mendel growled at his son.

"Not too late," Liebermann replied.

"We stopped off for a nightcap," said Alexander. "That's all."

A waiter appeared with a cart.

"Coffee, sir?"

"Please," Mendel replied. The waiter filled their cups with coffee and then served freshly baked *honzova buchta*—fruit buns. When broken, they steamed slightly and exuded a sweet, wholesome smell that made Liebermann's stomach gurgle. They tasted heavenly, combining the simple virtues of a staple food with the piquant pleasures of an indulgence. Mendel read the newspapers, and Alexander talked to his nephew about various aspects of piano technique. Liebermann recommended the Klammer Method, and turned his thumbs under his hands to demonstrate their flexibility. Given what had transpired the previous evening, it was a remarkably controlled performance, by both parties.

After breakfast, the three men headed north, to Josefov, where they met with several shop owners. Mendel's business with them was thankfully brief, and at its conclusion he declared that they had an hour or so to spare.

"I know a splendid coffeehouse near the cemetery," said Alexander.

"The old Jewish cemetery?" asked Liebermann.

"The proprietor's wife makes extremely good chocolate éclairs," Alexander continued, failing to acknowledge his nephew's question.

Liebermann recalled the zaddik's exhortation: *Go to the cemetery and pray for your ancestors to be merciful.*

"I've heard it's very beautiful—the old cemetery," Liebermann pressed.

"Yes, it is, if you like that sort of thing. Myself, I find it rather gloomy."

"If we're passing," Liebermann continued, "could we go inside? I'd like to see it."

Alexander looked over at his brother.

"I don't see why not," said Mendel. "We have the time."

Liebermann detected suspicion in the network of creases around his father's eyes.

"And if we're quick," said Alexander, "we won't have to forgo the pleasure of Frau Ruzicka's delightful pastries."

The old Jewish cemetery was built on what appeared to be a small hillock and was completely surrounded by a perimeter wall.

"Are any of our family buried here?" Liebermann asked his father.

"Probably. Your great-grandfather was a Praguer—although he's buried in the new cemetery, of course. I think they stopped burying people here more than a hundred years ago."

"What was his occupation, my great-grandfather?"

"He was a tailor."

"Do you remember him?"

"No. He died long before Alexander and I were born."

They climbed up a steep path and were soon surrounded by headstones. These were of varying sizes and were packed closely together. Some were leaning over, others had fallen flat, and all were covered in Hebrew inscriptions. Nearly five hundred winters had taken their toll, rendering the older monuments illegible. The lettering had filled with moss, creating strange emerald patterns against the gray stone. Although chaotic and decayed, the necropolis possessed a sombre majesty. Even Liebermann, who was generally inured to such things, felt something akin to reverence.

Liebermann and his uncle walked along the path, leaving Mendel behind. The old man seemed to be tarrying on purpose. Glancing over his shoulder, Liebermann saw his father standing very still in the dappled shadows beneath a lime tree. He guessed that Mendel wanted to be alone in order to say a prayer.

The route that Liebermann and his uncle had chosen ascended until they were level with the first-floor windows of the buildings beyond the perimeter wall. The path took them on a meandering course that squeezed between the serried graves. Liebermann noticed that several of the dead had been honored in the traditional Jewish way: pebbles had been placed on the headstones as a mark of esteem. One of the headstones was particularly conspicuous in this respect. The tributes and folded messages of supplication were so abundant that many had fallen and scattered on the ground.

"Who is buried here?" asked Liebermann.

"Oh, I think this is the grave of Rabbi Loew. He was a holy man . . . and a sort of Hebrew magician. A kabbalist."

Liebermann turned sharply to address his uncle.

"Do you know much about him?"

"Not a great deal. The local Hasidim have lots of legends about his good works. He was supposed to have performed miracles and to have protected the ghetto in times of persecution. He used to preach at the Old-New Synagogue. They still have his chair there."

Your forefathers would have worshipped in the Old-New Synagogue.

"Where is it?"

"The Old-New Synagogue?"

"Yes."

"Just over there." Alexander raised his arm and pointed. "On Maiselova."

Mendel was approaching.

"Well," he called out, "just enough time for a coffee, and then we must see Broz and Holub."

"Father," said Liebermann, "forgive me . . . but I'd like to see the Old-New Synagogue."

"What?"

"Would you mind?"

Mendel came to a halt and looked somewhat puzzled. "Can't you go later? Since when have you been interested in synagogues?"

"I would very much like to go *now*," Liebermann answered. The tone of his voice was firm.

"You spend half the night drinking with your uncle—and don't deny it." Mendel lifted a finger to silence Alexander's anticipated objection. "And then you want to go to the synagogue!" Mendel looked up at the sky as if beseeching God for assistance. "Sometimes . . ."

Liebermann had already started to retreat.

"I'll see you back at the hotel, Father."

"Why can't you see the synagogue and catch us up at the coffee-house? It won't take you long."

"No. I'd prefer to take my time, if you don't mind. Good-bye, Father . . . Uncle Alexander."

Liebermann bowed and hurried off.

Mendel turned to his brother, shaking his head.

"I don't understand him. Do you?"

Alexander leaned both hands on his cane and replied, "No. I thought I did. But, on reflection, I realize I was quite mistaken."

49

COUNCILLOR SCHMIDT WAS SITTING at his preferred table in the Café Eiles. He had just finished eating a potato goulash with frankfurter sausages and had begun to study the newspapers. Leafing through the *Wiener Tagblatt*, he came across a salacious headline: ONGOING SCANDAL SURROUNDS SCHNITZLER'S BOOK *REIGEN*.

> Two months ago the Viennese publishing company released the first edition of Arthur Schnitzler's book *Reigen*. This scandalous book harms the feeling of honor of every Viennese. The "Reigen" consist of ten dialogues about sex. After each act a partner is exchanged. There has never been such a pornographic work.

Schmidt tutted to himself and shook his head. *Jews. Obsessed with smut.* He read on:

> In 1901, Arthur Schnitzler's book *Lieutenant Gustl* also brought controversy with the public. The result was that Arthur Schnitzler was relieved of his title as an officer.

"Quite right!" Schmidt said aloud.

At an adjacent table a lawyer wearing a green bow tie looked up from his soup to see if he was being addressed.

Turning to the political pages, Schmidt came across a small piece on forthcoming appointments at the town hall. He read, with pride, that the candidates for the mayor's special advisory committee included Councillor Julius Schmidt, "a resourceful and popular advocate of small businesses and the rights of hardworking families."

I'm going to get the job.

The thought sent an electric charge of excitement through his body. With Faust eliminated from the new short list, the only other serious contender was Armannperg, and Armannperg was too old. He—Julius Schmidt—would get the coveted position, cultivate support among the most elevated members of the party, and be ready to run for mayor when the time came—and surely, given Lueger's failing health, he would not have to wait very long.

But even as he imagined himself ensconced in the mayor's office, he was troubled by an irritating secondary consideration. Lueger's failing health was *rumored*, not fact. There were whisperings, overheard conversations, raised eyebrows, if the mayor was not looking his best. But Schmidt had to admit that, for an ailing man, Karl Lueger was alarmingly spry and energetic. He could be mayor for some time to come. Certainly long enough for several of the ambitious young pretenders at the town hall to establish themselves as credible alternatives.

Lueger could never be usurped. A political challenge was out of the question.

Always someone in the way . . .

The pundit writing in the *Tagblatt* had correctly identified one of Schmidt's strengths. He was indeed a *resourceful* politician and rather good at finding solutions—often unconventional ones—to difficult and seemingly intractable problems. He drummed the table with his fingers and considered his options.

When the waiter came to collect Schmidt's empty plate, the councillor ordered an *einspänner* coffee and a large *reisauflauf mit äpfeln.* He read the flattering line about his resourcefulness and popularity again, and then picked up a copy of the *Illustrierte Kronen-Zeitung.*

Inside, he found a report on the discovery of a magical laboratory above a synagogue in Leopoldstadt. The article was accompanied by an illustration of a Jewish magus—a kabbalist—conducting rites in a room filled with the trappings of alchemy and astrology. The magus was dressed in long ceremonial robes embroidered with the Star of David. He was standing in a pentacle, his hands raised as if he were commanding some supernatural being to appear. His features were executed crudely in an unflattering caricature: thick eyebrows, coiled sideburns, a massive nose, and a flowing black beard. On his head the magus wore an oversize beaver hat.

Schmidt glanced through the article.

Alois Gasse . . . locked room . . .

A superstitious race . . .

Ritualistic practices . . . common among Jews.

The waiter returned and deposited the contents of his silver tray onto the table: a black coffee, served in a tall glass and topped with whipped cream, and a steaming slab of rice soufflé, sitting in a wide, deep red pool of raspberry syrup. Schmidt became curiously absorbed by his pudding.

"Uncle?"

Schmidt looked up, surprised to see his nephew standing next to him. The councillor had been mesmerized by the redness of the syrup, and a chain of associations had formed in his mind: *raspberry syrup, blood, blood libel . . .*

"Ah," said Schmidt. "Fabian!" He tapped the open newspaper and pretended he had been looking at the illustration rather than at his *reisauflauf.* "Have you seen this?"

Fabian sat down next to his uncle and started to read the article.

"I don't understand," said the councillor's nephew. "What does it mean?"

"What does it mean?" Schmidt chuckled. "A busy afternoon, that's what it means. A lot more could be made of this." Fabian returned a puzzled stare. "Oh, never mind. How's your friend Edlinger? Did he get on with Professor Hollar?"

LIEBERMANN LEANED BACK AND looked upward. The steep brick gable of the Old-New Synagogue appeared black against the bright blue sky. It was a striking piece of architectural design. The sloping edges of the gable were serrated with sharp, pointed teeth, giving it a curiously sinister appearance. There was something about its primitive execution that conveyed an impression of great age and mystery.

Your forefathers would have worshipped in the Old-New Synagogue in Prague.... Go there, Herr Doctor, and pray.

Liebermann moved on and, turning along a side street, found the entrance: stairs descended to a vestibule and a closed door, the tympanum of which was decorated with intricate carvings of vine leaves and twisted branches. Liebermann opened the door and stepped inside.

His first impression was of a relatively narrow space, but with a high ceiling. Small windows admitted very little light, and most of the illumination came from bronze chandeliers. A continuous wooden bench skirted the walls. The center of the temple was occupied by a wrought-iron Gothic grille behind which stood the cantor's platform and lectern. Liebermann advanced, his footsteps finding a resonant reply in the farthest corners of the building.

Two massive octagonal pillars rose up to a ceiling of ribbed vaults, and between these hung a red standard decorated with a yellow Star of David. Against the far wall, an eternal light drew Liebermann's attention to a wooden ark. It looked so ancient that it might have been carried out of Egypt by the Israelites.

Go there, Herr Doctor, and pray.

Superstition!

He had no intention of praying.

Liebermann remembered something his father had told him: The ark is always positioned on a wall that faces Jerusalem.

Jews are always looking backward! thought Liebermann.

He was a man of science, a man who embraced modernity. He was a citizen of the most sophisticated city in Europe! Yet the young doctor felt a curious stirring in the depths of his being. His conversation with Gabriel Kusevitsky came back to him: *cultural unconscious, endopsychic myths.* Was it really possible? Could people of the same race share ancestral memories that found expression in the symbolic language of dreams? And were those ancestral memories also the cause of the peculiar emotion that was now tightening his chest? It was like an experience of déjà vu, but much stronger than he had ever known before.

The door opened and a man entered. He was an orthodox Jew wearing a leather vest and a collarless shirt. He was carrying what appeared to be a box of tools. On seeing Liebermann, the man smiled. He put his toolbox down on the floor, produced a skullcap from his pocket, and offered it to Liebermann.

"Oh, I'm sorry," said Liebermann. "Of course . . ." He took the skullcap and placed it on his head with conspicuous care. It was not something he was accustomed to doing. "Thank you," he muttered. The man simply continued smiling. "I'm a stranger here," Liebermann added defensively. "Do you speak German?"

"Yes, I do," said the man. His accent was slight.

"A very beautiful temple," said Liebermann. "How old is it?"

"More than six hundred years old."

Liebermann glanced at the man's toolbox.

"Are you the caretaker?"

"I am indeed."

"Such an old building . . . I suppose your work is never done."

"Never. Broken door hinges, loose tiles, woodworm—there's always something."

"Why is it called the Old-New Synagogue? Why not just the Old Synagogue, or the Maiselova Temple?"

"It was called the New Synagogue originally—*New* because it replaced a much older house of prayer. Over time, more synagogues were built, all of which were *newer* than the New Synagogue. So to avoid confusion people started to call the New Synagogue the Old-New Synagogue, and the name stuck!" The caretaker paused and stared at his companion. "So, where are you from? Vienna?"

"Yes."

"I thought so," said the caretaker. "A lawyer?"

"No—a doctor."

"Well, it had to be one or the other!" Liebermann was amused by the caretaker's perspicacity. "It's your coat, sir," the caretaker added. "Only a professional man would wear a coat like that."

Liebermann asked the caretaker a few more questions concerning the temple's history and found him to be very knowledgeable. He was a good-humored man and evidently enjoyed acting as a guide, but Liebermann suspected that his eagerness to please was not entirely innocent. The fluency of his patter suggested frequent rehearsal and the expectation of a reward for a job well done.

"Notice the vaulting, Herr Doctor. It has five ribs instead of the usual four. This was to avoid anything that might resemble a cross. The red banner was a gift from Ferdinand the Third. He gave it to the Jews as a token of gratitude. The Jews helped him fight off the Swedes in 1648—the Battle of Prague. Without the Jews, the Swedes would have marched right into the Staré Město, and all would have been lost."

The caretaker beckoned, and Liebermann followed. They walked toward the ark.

"And this," said the caretaker, pointing at a high-backed chair, "is Rabbi Loew's chair."

Liebermann became aware of his heart beating more swiftly and made efforts to conceal his excitement.

"Ah yes," said Liebermann, feigning nonchalance. "Rabbi Loew. I've heard of him. He was a great magician, wasn't he?"

"Well, a wise man, and a learned scholar."

"A kabbalist?"

"The most powerful ever—so they say."

"When did he live?"

"About four hundred years ago. He was chief rabbi and head of the rabbinical court of the holy community. A terrible time it was for Jews, because of the fanaticism of the Catholic priests. The clergy were constantly making unfounded accusations of ritual murder. Subsequently, the goyim were suspicious of the Jews, who were wrongly arrested, abused, and mistreated."

"I was told that Rabbi Loew performed miracles—to protect his people."

"There are many stories," said the caretaker, maintaining his smile but now turning oddly silent. Liebermann put his hand into his pocket and jingled some loose change. It was subtly done and had the desired effect. "Yes, many stories . . ." The caretaker continued as though there had been no pause. "But he is most famous for making a golem."

"A what?"

"A golem. An artificial being. He collected mud from the banks of the Vltava and made it into the shape of a man, which he then brought to life after consulting the *Sefer Yetzirah*, the book of creation. The golem had supernatural strength and protected the ghetto Jews for many years. Although in one version of the story, the golem is supposed to have become uncontrollable and destructive."

"Like in 'The Sorcerer's Apprentice'?"

"Yes. Rabbi Loew had to use his most potent spells to stop the golem. Otherwise—such was the creature's might—he would have destroyed half the ghetto. They say the golem is still here, laid out in the attic. When the Jews were no longer threatened, Rabbi Loew ordered the golem to take its bed upstairs. He made the golem sleep and covered the body with prayer shawls and holy books. Rabbi Loew forbade anyone to go up there again. He said that he was worried about someone causing a fire, but the real reason was the golem. Few people have been up there since Rabbi Loew's time, but all have come down again gibbering like idiots."

"Do you have a key to the attic?"

The caretaker laughed.

"It's a story, Herr Doctor, only a story—although, to be honest, I wouldn't want to go against the will of Rabbi Loew. Would you?"

"Mud. He made the creature out of mud? You're quite certain of that?"

"Yes. As God made Adam. From the earth."

Liebermann took off his skullcap and handed it back to the caretaker along with a silver coin.

"Thank you," he said. "You have been most helpful"

Pray for enlightenment. Go to the cemetery and pray for your ancestors to be merciful. Perhaps they will pity you and guide you back to your faith, and then—only then—will you understand, fully understand, what is happening.

Liebermann had not prayed for enlightenment, but he had drawn a little closer to his roots, and Barash had proved himself to be an impressive prophet: either that, or a zealot capable of monstrous violence.

51

"HE WAS A DISGUSTING man," said Anna. "A vile creature."

Gabriel Kusevitsky could see that Anna was distressed; however, he did not offer her solicitous platitudes. Instead, he watched her closely and listened. There was something about his posture that betrayed his medical training, a certain detachment and ease in the presence of anguish. But his composure was never in any danger of being misconstrued as boredom or lack of interest, for Kusevitsky's eyes—dark, perceptive, and penetrating—showed intense mental engagement.

"What he did was unforgivable," Anna continued. "That poor girl. That poor, poor girl. How she must have suffered." For a moment Anna's gaze became glassy with incipient tears, but she set her jaw and did not let herself cry. "Olga and I reported the incident to the police, but they weren't very helpful. We were told that Kadia would have to make a statement herself. But this isn't possible. Kadia is as frightened of constables as she is of Sachs. She has no papers and thinks she will be thrown into prison. Moreover, she is still in terrible pain—her internal injuries were appalling. We felt so frustrated, *so* angry that we decided to pay Herr Sachs a visit ourselves. He'll soon run out of money, and when he does, he'll be scouring the streets looking for another girl like Kadia—a *replacement*—and, believe me, he'll have no difficulty finding one. All he's got to do is wait outside any of the *wärmestuben*. There are so many girls like her. We thought that if he knew Kadia was being looked after—and that we were trying to get the police involved—he might think again.

We were wrong, of course. He didn't take our threats seriously. He was confident that the police wouldn't care very much about Kadia's fate, whatever evidence we produced. And now I suspect the villain may be right. I could see what the police were thinking: 'If a woman chooses to live such a life, then what does she expect?' But it is the police's indifference, their lack of compassion, that permits wicked men like Sachs to evade justice. It is so very wrong."

"You shouldn't have gone to see Sachs on your own, you know," said Kusevitsky.

"I don't think we were in any real danger," Anna replied. "I am not a psychiatrist, Gabriel, but I believe that men who abuse women are, without exception, cowards. He wouldn't dare harm us; although that isn't quite true. He did . . ." Anna looked at the floor guiltily. "Push me."

"He did what?"

"I was holding the door open, and he shoved me out of the way in order to close it."

"The swine!"

"It was nothing. Honestly."

"Where does he live? I've a good mind to—"

"No, Gabriel."

"Asher is an excellent swordsman."

"We must be patient and hope that in due course our efforts with the police will be rewarded. Olga and I can be very persistent."

Kusevitsky recovered his professional calm.

"Where is Fräulein Pinski now?"

"Actually we managed to get her admitted into your hospital."

"Really?"

"Dr. Janosi is a friend of Professor Kraus's."

"I will visit her."

"That is kind of you. But you must not ask Kadia about her

dreams." Anna smiled sadly. "We must suppose she only ever has nightmares."

"And when she is recovered from her injuries? Where will she go?"

"I have no idea."

"I will mention her case to Professor Priel. He might be able to provide her with pecuniary assistance from one of the Rothenstein contingency funds. It won't be much, but it should be enough to keep her in lodgings until she finds respectable employment."

Anna reached out and covered Gabriel's hand with her own.

"Thank you, Gabriel."

Kusevitsky, somewhat embarrassed, withdrew and stood up. He paced over to the window.

"Jeheil Sachs," he muttered.

"What a pig," said Anna. "Wallowing in his own filth."

"No, not a pig—more a parasite. A parasite living off the misfortune of others. These procurers . . . they shame us all. They are a scourge. A plague!"

Anna reached out. "Come. Sit down."

She had never seen Gabriel looking quite so troubled.

Kusevitsky crossed the room and sat down beside her. She took his face in her hands, kissed him, and stroked his forehead.

"It's all right," Anna said. He was hot, and his eyes were glazed—like a child with a fever.

52

From the journal of *Dr. Max Liebermann*

I spent the remainder of the afternoon browsing in the second-hand bookshops of the Jewish quarter. The booksellers—shriveled old men with white beards, all of whom were almost blind from reading too much—were as erudite (and eccentric) as university professors.

The legend is an old one. Golem stories have been told for centuries. Even Jacob Grimm mentions the Polish Jews making a man from clay and mud; however, since the sixteenth century, the golem has become particularly associated with the name of Rabbi Loew. Orthodox Jews have many tales about the Maharal of Prague, which typically involve him outwitting a vindictive Christian adversary (most notably an evil priest called Thaddeus). In most of these, his supernatural assistant, the golem, ensures that the enemies of Jewry are punished.

Mankind has always been preoccupied with the idea of aping the creator, stealing fire from the gods. In literature the tradition extends from ancient times to the present. (I am reminded of Mary Shelley's Frankenstein, a work that I have discussed with Miss Lydgate.) It is a didactic tradition that alerts mankind to the dangers of hubris. A golem can be created, but not necessarily controlled. When men act like gods, danger follows.

Prague is a dark place, a city that has always welcomed astrologers, kabbalists, and animators. One has only to stroll around the Staré Město and Malá Strana, looking up at the relief door signs—numbers, stars, devils, compasses, and occult symbols—to see evidence of Prague's magical past. There is even a narrow lane called the Street of the Alchemists up by the castle.

But now, it seems, the golem is no longer confined to the Prague ghetto: neither the <u>physical</u> ghetto nor the <u>imaginary</u> ghetto of Hasidic folktales. It has broken free of its own myth and now haunts the broad avenues of Vienna. Prague! I have already been here too long. These archaic places, which make an appeal to the deepest levels of the unconscious, corrode reason. I find it all too easy now to imagine a monstrous hulk lurking in the shadows, the magic holding its form against the laws of nature, the spell occasionally weakening, and the supernatural flesh transmuting back into mud. The great expenditure of energy as it rips the head off its victim producing a momentary dissolution—clods on cobbles—and then the creature rising, its bulky body impossibly fleet, returning to the kabbalist's lair above the Alois Gasse Temple.

Yes, it comes all too easily, as though the wellspring of dreams has been unstopped. The images spout up and spill into the real world. I can't stop thinking about the conversation that I had with Kusevitsky: dreams, myths—a <u>racial</u> unconscious. Professor Freud: "When the work of interpretation has been completed, we perceive that a dream is the fulfillment of a wish." But not just any wish—a <u>forbidden</u> wish, a wish unacceptable to the censoring agency of the mind.

A golem is the embodiment of a forbidden wish, a wish to unleash unconscionable violence on the enemy—an abrogation of civilized values and the triumph of the primitive unconscious. A people who have endured persecution for millennia would have necessarily repressed the urge to strike back at their tormentors. Such a reservoir of anger and resentment must be fathomless. Regiments unite behind a standard and nations behind a flag. Who are they, I wonder, who are now uniting behind the figure of this terrifying mythic avenger?

53

THE CHANCELLOR WAS FROWNING.

"You wish to discuss a staff member. Herr Dr. Liebermann, is it?"

"That is correct," said Rheinhardt.

"Has he committed an offense?"

"No," said Rheinhardt. "Dr. Liebermann has not committed an offense; however, he is known to us at the security office."

"Well, to be frank," Gandler cut in, shaking his head, "that doesn't surprise me."

"Herr Professor," said Rheinhardt, "Dr. Liebermann is not a suspect. He is a consultant."

"A consultant?"

"He is a very gifted psychiatrist, who has been of great service to my department."

"Well, I am delighted to hear that," said Professor Gandler. "However, I'm afraid he is away at present and can be contacted only through his family."

"I know," said Rheinhardt. "It was I who suggested that he should leave Vienna."

Professor Gandler's expression became clouded with puzzlement.

"I understand," Rheinhardt continued, "that Dr. Liebermann has been suspended from clinical duties pending a meeting of the hospital committee. I am fully aware of the circumstances surrounding this decision, and the concerns you expressed about the hospital demonstrating that it takes accusations of religious agitation seriously. Moreover, I believe that you suspended Dr. Liebermann in anticipation of the imminent publication of unfavorable articles, the most damaging of which was expected to appear in *Kikeriki*."

"Then you are very well informed, Inspector."

"Well, Professor, I have good news for you. The offending article will not be appearing in the satirical magazine after all. And in the interests of social harmony, and the reputation of the world's finest hospital, the censor has agreed that any similar articles that come to his attention will be suppressed in the usual manner. It is only after the hospital committee has convened, and Dr. Liebermann's fate has been decided, that the prohibition will be lifted."

"I see," said Professor Gandler, his face showing no obvious sign of relief.

"Given that the position is now quite changed, I was wondering . . ." Rheinhardt smiled. "Would you be prepared to reconsider Dr. Liebermann's situation?"

"What do you mean, exactly?"

"The hospital will not receive adverse publicity. You personally will not be accused of complacency. Therefore, surely Dr. Liebermann can be reinstated."

"As I explained to Dr. Liebermann, I cannot have him working on wards where he would be free to repeat his . . . misdemeanor. Dr. Liebermann is unapologetic and unrepentant."

"Come now, Professor. The good doctor is not a fool. If the same situation were to arise again, he would be more circumspect. Besides, he's a psychiatrist. The chances of him being called again to attend a dying man are rather slim, are they not?"

"Even so, Inspector, I have responsibilities. I must respect public *sensitivities*. I cannot appear—in any way—to be condoning behavior likely to cause upset."

"All right. Then keep him off the wards. He could still see individual patients. Why not?"

"He suggested something very similar himself."

"What could be better, eh? A traditional Austrian compromise."

The chancellor rearranged some papers on his desk. The action was unconscious, like a nervous tic.

"Why are you trying to help this young man, Inspector?"

"Because he's useful to the security office," said Rheinhardt, feigning bluff pragmatism. "He's very good at what he does."

"That may be true, Inspector. But he's also very stubborn and arrogant. I advised him not to make a moral stand against the hospital committee right from the beginning. He refused to listen. If he loses his job, well, that'll be his own fault."

"Yes," said Rheinhardt. He decided to be honest. "He can be a frustrating fellow, if not downright irritating at times; however, he is also a man of singular courage and conviction. And these, in my humble estimation, are not trivial qualities." The chancellor made an arch with his fingers and looked closely at Rheinhardt. "Courage and conviction," Rheinhardt repeated. "Qualities I hope that we *all* possess, at least in some measure."

It was a carefully worded sentence that found its mark. When Rheinhardt saw doubt creeping into the chancellor's expression, he applauded himself for being something of a psychiatrist too.

54

"I KNOW YOU DON'T want to dismiss Slavik," said Mendel, "but the man is incompetent. If you were more willing to check his figures yourself, then perhaps things would be different."

"I could try," Alexander replied.

"That's it, you see. I don't believe you would, Alexander. Come now, I'm your brother. I know you better than anybody."

Alexander bit into his fruit bun and shrugged.

Liebermann sighed.

His father had woken up in a combative mood.

"Blomberg will be meeting with Bohm again next week, and if I'm not mistaken, he'll demand to see our books. If he doesn't have confidence in us, he won't invest—and that will be the end of it. No department store."

"All right, all right," said Alexander, raising his hands as though he were being held up at gunpoint. "I understand."

"Good," said Mendel. "Max has met Blomberg, haven't you, Max?"

"Indeed," said Liebermann.

"And you liked him, didn't you?"

"Yes, he was very agreeable." Liebermann managed a vacuous smile.

The reception clerk arrived with a silver tray and addressed the general area of the table, "Herr Dr. Liebermann?"

"Yes?"

"A telegram, sir."

Liebermann took the envelope off the silver tray and read the communication inside.

SUCCESSFUL CONFERENCES WITH EDITOR OF KIKERIKI, CENSOR, AND GANDLER. OFFENDING ARTICLE WITHDRAWN. PERMISSION TO RE-SUME SOME CLINICAL DUTIES GRANTED, BUT NOT ON WARDS. SHALL EXPECT YOUR RETURN SHORTLY.

RHEINHARDT

55

Liebermann crossed the busy road and entered the little park in front of the Votivkirche. Seen from the front, the church was an assembly of steeples, pointed windows, and arches that drew the eye upward, to a blue sky quartered by two crocket-covered spires. The exuberance of the architecture suited Liebermann's mood. He was glad to be back in Vienna and eager to see Rheinhardt. There was much to discuss.

As he walked, he thought he could see his friend sitting on a bench in the distance. He quickened his pace but came to an abrupt halt when an organ-grinder's monkey leaped out onto the path in front of him. It chirruped and raised an empty tin cup. The organ-grinder, who was dressed in a bowler hat and shabby tailcoat, was standing behind a barrel organ of medium size, its lacquered box supported by a long retractable metal spike. A strap around the man's neck helped him to balance the instrument with one hand, leaving the other free to turn the crank handle. The doors at the front of the device had been left open, displaying the pipes and a rotating drum. As a result of his efforts, the sound of the Maximilianplatz traffic was drowned out by one of Schubert's German Dances.

Liebermann bent forward and dropped a few coins into the monkey's cup. Immediately, the creature scampered up the organ-grinder's legs and then to his shoulders, where it lifted the man's hat to express gratitude. Liebermann smiled and continued toward the church.

He found Rheinhardt enjoying the rays of an unusually bright sun, his head thrown back to catch the warmth and light.

"Oskar!"

The inspector stirred. "Max!"

Rheinhardt stood, and the young doctor gripped his friend's arm.

"Oskar, I don't know how to thank you."

"Oh, it was nothing really," said Rheinhardt. He gestured that they should sit, and produced a brown paper bag from his pocket. "Pumpkin seed?"

Liebermann shook his head.

"I am deeply indebted," Liebermann continued. "Accompanying my father on his business trip to Prague was unspeakably boring. You have no idea."

"Ah, but I do," said Rheinhardt. "A detective inspector in this bureaucratic empire is no stranger to tedium. You forget how many forms I am obliged to complete! Now." Rheinhardt sat up straight. "Why did you want to see me? Am I justified in assuming that it was not merely to thank me in person?"

"That is correct."

"You have discovered something?"

"I have."

"Pertaining to the investigation?"

"Yes."

"In Prague?"

"Indeed."

"Then perhaps you would be so kind as to tell me?"

"Forgive me, Oskar. On this occasion I am not being coy. Merely considering how best to explain myself."

Rheinhardt poured some pumpkin seeds into the palm of his hand.

"Thankfully," sighed the inspector, "I don't have to be back at

Schottenring for another hour, by which time I sincerely hope you will have decided upon a satisfactory turn of phrase."

Liebermann took a deep breath.

"When I interviewed Barash," he began hesitantly, "he said some things to me that I did not include in my report."

"Oh?"

"I didn't think they were of any consequence at the time. They were rather personal. He accused me of failing to respect my origins, which are Czech on my father's side, and he urged me to visit the Jewish cemetery and the Old-New Synagogue in Prague. He suggested that if I embraced my Jewish heritage, I would gain insights into the murders of Brother Stanislav and Councillor Faust. Needless to say, I interpreted these exhortations as further evidence of his derangement—no better or worse than his confidence in metoposcopy! However, when circumstances conspired to transport me not only to the Czech capital but also to the locality of both the cemetery and the synagogue, I must admit that curiosity got the better of me."

Liebermann paused, allowing two ladies with wide-brimmed hats to pass out of earshot.

"In the Jewish cemetery, I came across the tomb of a famous sixteenth-century scholar, Rabbi Loew. He is reputed to have been one of the greatest kabbalists of all time. He preached at the Old-New Synagogue, and he has become a kind of folk hero among the Hasidim. Of the many tales told of his miraculous ministry, there is one that seems to have become a favorite. It is said that when the ghetto Jews were being persecuted, Rabbi Loew used his magical powers to create an artificial being of great power to protect them. The being he created was called a golem, and it was made from mud."

Rheinhardt dropped the bag of pumpkin seeds onto his lap. A few spilled across the path.

"Mud?"

"Yes."

Rheinhardt's eyebrows rose, and his mouth contracted into a tight circle.

"I am not suggesting," Liebermann continued, "that a golem created in Alois Gasse killed Stanislav and Faust. But this is clearly what we—or at least those who are familiar with the legends of the Prague ghetto—are being invited to believe. A kabbalist's lair containing barrels of mud . . . mud strewn around the bodies of anti-Semites . . . These similarities cannot be coincidental. Moreover, the golem legend also explains one of the most puzzling features of the Josefstadt and Hietzing murders: Why did the perpetrators choose such an inconvenient method of decapitation? Well, now we have a very plausible hypothesis. The heads of the victims were torn from their bodies to suggest the exercise of supernatural strength."

"Extraordinary," said Rheinhardt.

"The legends of the Prague ghetto are not well known beyond the city, but they are told by Hasidim everywhere. Subsequently I suspect that they are the only inhabitants of Vienna who would appreciate the significance of the Alois Gasse lair, the mud, and the brutal decapitations."

"What are we to conclude, then? That Barash killed Brother Stanislav and Councillor Faust?"

Liebermann looked up at the Votivkirche spires.

"Barash's sect is not the only one to be found in Leopoldstadt. And if he is guilty, I wonder why he chose to implicate himself further by demonstrating that he was in possession of relevant knowledge. The golem legend *does* make the murders more intelligible."

"You have already questioned his sanity," said Rheinhardt bluntly. "Perhaps he was just behaving irrationally; however, his familiarity with the golem legend doesn't necessarily implicate him further. If, as you say, the golem is a staple of the Hasidic storytelling tradition, then Barash would have, quite naturally, connected the murders of Brother Stanislav and Councillor Faust with Rabbi Loew's monster. He was simply pointing this out to you, albeit in an oblique way."

Liebermann shook his head. "Barash told me to go to Prague before the discovery of the Alois Gasse lair. And none of the newspaper reports have, to my knowledge, said anything about the mud discovered close to the bodies. In addition, Barash was quite definite when he said that if I visited the Jewish ghetto in Prague I would better understand the nature of the murders."

"All right, then. For the sake of argument let us entertain the notion that Barash is guilty. What is his purpose?"

"To foment some kind of religious revival, perhaps? I believe that Hasidism, and particularly Lurianic Hasidism, is a messianic belief system."

"And are you still of the opinion," Rheinhardt continued, "that the decapitations were a joint enterprise, requiring the combined effort of more than one man?"

"Barash is a big fellow, but I cannot believe that he is strong enough to make short work of tearing a man's head off."

"Then we must assume that he was assisted by his disciples."

Rheinhardt detected a pumpkin seed nestling in the folds of his trousers and promptly put it into his mouth.

"I am reminded," said Liebermann, "of the condition known as 'folie à deux.' The term is employed to describe the curious phenomenon of two individuals sharing the same—usually paranoid—delusion. Although contagious insanity, as it was once called, typically affects two people, it can extend from the original pair to three, four, or even five persons. The infectious delusion tends to arise in a man of strong character, and is subsequently imposed on weaker and more impressionable associates. Thus, it is also sometimes designated *folie imposée*."

"Perhaps you should interview Barash again?"

"Yes, I think that is a good idea."

The organ-grinder's monkey scampered across the grass and began to make a meal of Rheinhardt's spilled pumpkin seeds.

"This is a grave business," said Rheinhardt. "We must now suppose that the perpetrators, even if they are not Barash and his disciples, are more than likely to be Hasidic Jews."

"You are worried about how the Christian Socials will respond?"

Rheinhardt nodded.

"Saladin!" It was the organ-grinder, chasing his pet. "Saladin!"

The man came toward them, the lacquered box swinging from the straps around his neck.

"Saladin, you scoundrel! Leave the gentlemen alone."

The monkey scooped up the last of the pumpkin seeds and ran back to his master.

That evening, Liebermann played a selection of Chopin Studies, including the testing *Number Twelve in C minor*. He was pleased with his performance, particularly the ease with which his left hand now provided the thunderous accompaniment to the dramatic chords in the right. The Klammer Method was yielding quite exceptional results. Closing the volume, he discovered beneath it a copy of the *Opus 45 C sharp minor Prelude*. He had intended to stop practicing, but the prospect of Chopin's enigmatic masterpiece prevented him from leaving the music room. Liebermann placed his hands on the keyboard and produced a sequence of descending harmonies that found a melancholy resting place in the resonant lower octaves of the Bösendorfer. A bel canto melody gradually emerged, but in due course surrendered its authority to an arpeggiated bass.

Liebermann began thinking about Prague—not the Jewish cemetery, the Old-New Synagogue, Rabbi Loew, or the golem, but instead his hotel room—and the pretty prostitute, Anezka.

What I did was shameful.

The arpeggiated bass executed a series of dreamy, remote modulations.

And such folly . . .

That he, a doctor, should have taken such a risk. It was a depressing thought, but now, for all he knew, he might be destined to suffer the same fate as the young Baron von Kortig.

Alexander!

He felt angry at his libertine uncle. But his ire could not be sustained. How could he blame Alexander? His uncle had only meant to cheer him up. It was his own fault, and his fault alone.

Liebermann came to the cadenza, and the sense of key dissolved in a cascade of tritones. This untethering of tonality reflected Liebermann's mental state. He felt emotionally lost, without direction.

The bel canto melody returned, and the prelude coasted to its sombre close. For a few moments, Liebermann remained still, his head bowed, listening to the fading notes. Then he closed the lid, and retired to his bedroom.

After his ablutions, he changed into his nightshirt and tried to go to sleep. The attempt was futile, as his memory kept on tormenting him with spectral impressions of accommodating flesh, black eyes, and red lips.

It must have been past two in the morning when the telephone rang.

"Max?"

"Oskar?"

"There's been another murder."

"A decapitation?"

"Yes."

"Where?"

"Saint Ulrich's—Spittelberg."

"Do you want me to—"

"Come. Yes, if you don't mind. I'll send a police vehicle."

"Who is it? Do you know?"

Rheinhardt paused before giving his answer. "A man named Jeheil Sachs."

"Jeheil Sachs . . ."

"Yes. A Jew. Now, I wonder where that leaves us?"

Part Four

The Vienna Golem

56

LIEBERMANN AND RHEINHARDT STOOD beside the headless body. The dead man was obviously impoverished. Liebermann noticed that the leather sole of one of his shoes was worn through and the cuffs of his coat were frayed. Scattered around the corpse were clods of mud, plainly visible in the yellow light that fell from a gas lamp mounted on the church wall.

The two men were situated in a narrow alley that followed the east-facing side of the Ulrichskirche. The featureless stucco of the nave ascended toward a ribbon of starry sky. On the other side of the alley was a large and uninspiring building with regularly spaced windows, all of them black and lifeless. The effect was claustrophobic. Liebermann felt hemmed in.

Rivulets of blood flowed between the cobbles. They formed an inverted delta, the apex of which marked the convergence of the glistening streams. The victim's head lay beyond, having been encouraged to roll some distance from the body by the alley's incline.

Close by, the police photographer and his assistant were setting up their equipment.

Liebermann crouched down to examine what remained of the dead man's neck.

"I can't see very much," he muttered.

Rheinhardt produced a flashlight. Pushing the metal bar forward, he released a pulse of illumination that revealed the lurid interior of the stump: fractured bone, muscle tissue, and pale vessels hanging loosely in space. The ferrous smell of fresh blood was almost over-whelming.

"Again," said the young doctor.

The inspector obliged, and another pulse of light coaxed the nightmarish vision back again. It seemed to emerge slowly out of the darkness, a macabre blossoming like the unfolding petals of a strange carnal flower.

"Just like the others," said Liebermann. "The cervical structures have been identically displaced."

"Now," said Rheinhardt, "look at this."

The beam of light played on the slick cobblestones. Something glinted, and Liebermann leaned closer. It was a Star of David on a chain.

Standing up, Liebermann surveyed his surroundings. His expression changed suddenly from mild disgust to perplexity.

"What is it?" Rheinhardt inquired.

"There's no plague column."

"Yes, there is. You approached the Ulrichskirche from Neustift-gasse. There's a plague column up there." Rheinhardt jerked his thumb back. "At the back of the church."

"I'd like to take a look."

"Of course."

Leaving Rheinhardt to speak with the photographer, Liebermann soon found himself standing on a wide, empty thoroughfare. Across the road were tall five-story apartment blocks. Several of the upper windows were illuminated: together with a well-placed street lamp they provided Liebermann with enough light to make his inspection.

The plague column, a vertical scrum of saints and putti, was situated directly behind the church. It was much more like the famous plague column on the Graben than the one he had seen outside the Maria Treu Kirche, being vaguely organic—like the twisted bole of a tree—and designed to convey an impression of frenetic activity.

Approximately halfway up, a figure projecting out of the tumbling horde was made even more conspicuous by a radiant sun. At the summit, Liebermann saw a Christlike figure clutching a massive golden cross, and another bearded ancient holding a golden orb. They were separated by an eagle that seemed to hover between them with no obvious means of support.

On either side of the monument were statues of saints, their names engraved in the stone pedestals on which they stood. Saint Barbara, represented like an operatic diva, threw her head back and clasped a chalice to her breast. Her robes had fallen off her shoulder to reveal an impressively lithe figure. She looked commandingly beautiful, and her dishabille imbued her with a subtle erotic charm. Saint Rosalia struck a more modest pose, the copious folds of her abundant gown gathered in one hand, a personification of maidenly virtues.

Rheinhardt appeared from behind the church and joined Liebermann by the column. He offered his friend a Trabuco cheroot, which the young doctor accepted.

"Do you know anything about these saints?" Liebermann asked.

"Saint Barbara was a renowned beauty and, I believe, is the patron saint of artillerymen. As for Saint Rosalia"—Rheinhardt lit Liebermann's cigar, then his own—"I'm afraid my memory fails me. Although she may have halted a plague once, which is probably why she is here."

Liebermann nodded and exhaled a stream of smoke.

"How did you discover the victim's identity?"

"He was carrying some papers. In fact, he lives just around the corner. I'll be going to take a look at his house once we've finished here. Would you care to join me?"

"I can't," said Liebermann, shaking his head. "Patients."

"Of course."

"Who found the body?"

"A fellow called Bietak, a hotel porter. He was on his way home after work."

"Did he see anything unusual? Hear anything?"

"No."

Rheinhardt stepped off the pavement and looked up and down the silent street.

"Well, what do you think?" he asked. "I thought the golem was supposed to protect Jews."

"It doesn't make sense," said Liebermann, his voice strained by disbelief. "It doesn't make any sense at all!"

57

RHEINHARDT KNOCKED AT THE door. There was no response.

He observed across the street a plump red face looking out of one of the windows. The pressure of the woman's nose on the glass had turned it upward, revealing two circular nostrils. Seen through the frost of her condensed breath, she appeared distinctly porcine. She did not avert her gaze when detected but continued to watch with a fixed stare.

Rheinhardt indicated that he wished to speak with her. She blinked at him and then withdrew behind the drapes; however, she did not come to the door immediately.

Because it was still early, Rheinhardt assumed that the plump woman was making herself presentable, if such a thing were possible. He then chastised himself for entertaining this uncharitable thought. After all, his own figure left much to be desired. In due course there was the sound of a metal bolt being drawn, and the door creaked open.

The woman stood squarely, in an attitude of defiance, with ruddy arms folded across a bust of considerable bulk.

"Yes?"

"Good morning. My name is Rheinhardt. Detective Inspector Oskar Rheinhardt." He produced his identification. The woman squinted, her eyes shrinking in the morning light. "May I ask you a few questions?"

"Questions? What questions?"

"Well, perhaps we could start with your name?"

"Tilde Warmisch."

"Very good. Now, Frau Warmisch, that house over there." Rheinhardt pointed at the filthy exterior opposite. "Do you know who lives there?"

"Yes. Herr Sachs."

"Jeheil Sachs?"

"I don't know about his first name. I just know him as Sachs, the Jew."

"When was the last time you saw Herr Sachs?"

"Does he owe money? That wouldn't surprise me. Let me think." Frau Warmisch sucked on her lower lip. "Yesterday . . . at about six o'clock."

"What does Herr Sachs do?"

"Do you mean work?"

"Yes. His occupation."

Frau Warmisch sneered. "He doesn't do anything. He lives off women."

"He lives off women?" Rheinhardt repeated.

"This is Spittelberg, Inspector. You know what goes on here."

"He's a procurer?"

"Call it what you like." The woman made a snorting sound—as evocative of the farmyard as her round face—in lieu of laughter. "Pretty girls, some of them, and his own kind too. Yes, always his own kind. What's he done wrong?"

"Would I be correct in surmising that you are not overly fond of Herr Sachs?"

"Yes, you would be. He isn't much liked around here."

"Why?"

"He's ill-mannered. Rude, dirty, and he . . ." Frau Warmisch trailed off.

"Yes? What were you going to say?"

"You won't tell him I told you?"

"That, I can promise you with complete confidence."

"He mistreats his women," she went on. "In the summer, with the windows open, you can hear everything. But the noise the last one made was terrible." She shook her head, and the wattle of flesh that hung beneath her neck swung like a pendulum. "I almost called the police myself. And I haven't seen her since. Did the ladies send you?"

"What ladies?"

"The two smart young ladies."

"No. They didn't. To whom are you referring?"

"They came to see Sachs about a week ago. They were accusing him of something. I think it must have been to do with the last one—you know, his doxy, his girl. They said that they'd got a doctor's report, and that justice would be done. One of them was furious—banged on his door and shouted about coming back."

"Had you ever seen them before?"

"No. We don't get their sort in Spittelberg, Inspector."

"Could you describe them to me?"

"Well-to-do, smart. One had black hair, the other brown. Their dresses were made of silk. Quite pretty . . ."

"How tall were they?"

"Not very. They were quite small, really—smaller than me."

"Indeed," said Rheinhardt. He cringed internally, embarrassed by his careless use of language. Frau Warmisch, however, was not offended. "Any other details?" Rheinhardt asked, eager to move the conversation on.

"I think they were Jews too," said Frau Warmisch. "They were telling him off for using Jewish women. They said something about how bad it was for him to be making money from his own people."

Rheinhardt took out his notebook and made some jottings. When he was satisfied that he had learned all that he could, he thanked Frau Warmisch, bowed, and began to walk back toward the main road.

"Inspector?"

Rheinhardt turned.

"Don't you want to know their names?"

"I beg your pardon?"

"The names of the fine ladies."

"You *know* them?"

"Yes. I heard them introduce themselves. Anna Katzer and Olga Mandl."

Rheinhardt took out his notebook again and began writing.

"It's a cold morning, Inspector," the woman added. "Are you sure you don't want to come in for a few minutes? Just to warm up."

Rheinhardt detected a certain lascivious cast in Frau Warmisch's expression. She was leaning against the doorjamb and had raised her gown a little to reveal a chunky, swollen ankle.

"Most kind," Rheinhardt replied. "But no, thank you." He hurried off, his mind filled with nightmarish images of porcine congress.

58

FRAU ARABELLE POPPMEIER ENTERED the consulting room and hesitated by the door. She had mousy blond hair, bright eyes, and although not beautiful, she might have merited that accolade with the very slightest alteration of her features. Liebermann stood, walked around his desk, and rested his hands on a high-backed chair. It was obvious, from the looseness of her sunny yellow dress and her bulging abdomen, that Frau Poppmeier was pregnant. She saw how Liebermann's gaze had momentarily lowered, and smiled coyly.

"Please, do come in."

Exhibiting the ponderous gait typical of gravid women, she walked to the chair and took Liebermann's offered hand. With this small assistance, she was able to achieve a graceful descent in spite of her condition.

"One moment," said Liebermann. Snatching a pillow from the rest bed, he lodged it between the base of her spine and the back of the chair. "There, that should be more comfortable."

"Thank you, Doctor," she said.

Liebermann sat behind his desk and opened a file of blank pages.

"So, Frau Poppmeier, how can I help?"

"Well, it isn't my problem, exactly. But then again, I suppose it is my problem—insofar as any problem that affects one's nearest and dearest also affects oneself. It's my husband, Ivo. He hasn't been very well lately. He's still working, but—"

"What is your husband's occupation?" Liebermann interjected.

"He's a salesman for a firm of jewelry designers and manufacturers. They have offices on the Graben."

Liebermann began to take notes. "And where do you live?"

"On Krongasse."

"In the fifth district?"

"Yes. Not far from the Naschmarkt. We've been very happy there. It's a little cramped, I suppose. . . . We already have a daughter, Leonie. She's four now. But when the little one arrives"—Frau Poppmeier laid a hand on her belly and smiled—"we will probably have to move. I'd like to get an apartment somewhere around here, but Ivo says we can't afford it. So perhaps it will have to be Landstrasse. It's not that he isn't doing well. In fact, he's been promised a promotion next year. But one can't help worrying, what with this *problem* of his." Her lips became a horizontal, bloodless line. "He isn't himself."

"How do you mean—not himself?"

"He's been sickly . . . less vigorous."

Liebermann asked a few more questions but found that Frau Poppmeier's answers were imprecise. She seemed embarrassed. A touch of color occasionally rose to her cheeks. Liebermann assumed that her husband's *problem* was most probably sexual. The physical changes that altered a woman's body during pregnancy increased libido in some men while reducing it in others. She had mentioned her husband being less *vigorous*, which sounded like a euphemism; however, it was most unusual for a woman to present on her husband's behalf. This tended to happen only when the husband had become overly fond of drink. Liebermann decided that it would be in everyone's interest to expedite matters by being direct.

"Frau Poppmeier, if your husband is suffering from a problem that is affecting your marital relations—"

"Oh, good heavens, no," she quickly interrupted. Glancing down at her bulge, she added, "Ivo has *always* been able to function as a man. Our relations have become less intimate of late, but that is only because he is concerned for my and the little one's safety."

Raising the topic of sex had not caused Frau Poppmeier any awkwardness. What, then, was she so embarrassed about?

"Frau Poppmeier, you have suggested that your husband is out of sorts, unwell, not himself, but could you please try to be a little more specific?"

The young woman sighed, and began to enumerate her husband's symptoms: indigestion, nausea, constipation, changes of appetite . . .

Liebermann looked up from his notes.

"Frau Poppmeier, I think there must be some mistake. This is the department of psychological medicine. It sounds like your husband requires the services of a specialist in gastric disorders, not a psychiatrist."

"We've already seen one. Herr Dr. Felbiger."

"Felbiger?"

"Yes. It was he who suggested we come to see you."

Liebermann scratched his head. "Are these symptoms making your husband depressed?"

"Not really . . ." Frau Poppmeier shifted on her chair and grimaced. "This is rather difficult, Herr Doctor. My husband's nausea tends to happen only in the morning. . . . He retches but only occasionally vomits. I said that his appetite has changed, but really it would be more accurate to say that he has developed odd food cravings. Fads. And he complains of pressure in his pelvis, tightness of the abdomen, and . . ." She paused and adjusted the drop of her skirt.

"Yes?" Liebermann prompted.

"Quickening sensations."

Liebermann put his pen down. Frau Poppmeier looked perfectly sane, but what if she wasn't? What if everything she had said was an elaborate delusional fantasy? It certainly sounded that way. The young woman detected the change in his expression: the narrowing of his eyes, the setting of his jaw, both suggesting suspicion and doubt.

"Herr Doctor," Frau Poppmeier continued, "I think you must be well aware of what these symptoms mean."

Liebermann involuntarily glanced at the woman's belly.

"What did Dr. Felbiger say?"

"What you are probably thinking but cannot say for fear of sounding foolish. My predicament exactly!" She threw her hands up in a desperate appeal to the heavens. "But yes, you are quite right. My husband appears to have gotten himself pregnant."

59

"Does the name Jeheil Sachs mean anything to you?" asked Rheinhardt.

Anna Katzer was wearing a crisp white blouse and a pink skirt. She straightened her back, frowned, and said, "Yes, unfortunately it does."

Rheinhardt flicked his notebook open.

"How did you become acquainted?"

Anna's frown became more pronounced.

"I wouldn't call Herr Sachs an acquaintance, Inspector."

"Why not? Didn't you pay him a visit last week?"

Anna was evidently surprised. "Who told you that? He hasn't made a complaint, has he?"

"No," said Rheinhardt calmly. "No, he hasn't."

Anna scowled.

"Well, Fräulein Katzer?" Rheinhardt asked. "Why did you go to see Herr Sachs?"

"Inspector, do you know the new *wärmestube* in Spittelberg?"

"Yes."

"On Wednesday, a Galician woman named Kadia Pinski fainted there. A doctor was called, and he discovered that she had been badly injured. She was a prostitute, and the man she named as her attacker was also her procurer—Jeheil Sachs." Anna paused and secured one of her hairpins. "Apparently Fräulein Pinski had wanted to end her association with Herr Sachs, and he had responded by violating her person in the cruelest way imaginable. You see, Inspector . . ." She touched her neck and looked away. "Fräulein Pinski's injuries were *internal*, and had been inflicted with the handle of a brush." Rheinhardt winced. "Had she not received medical attention, she most probably would have died."

"Where is she now?"

"Recovering in the hospital. We were able to make arrangements for her care."

"We?"

"Myself and my dear friend Olga Mandl. As you can imagine, Inspector, we were horrified—and we resolved to pay Herr Sachs a visit in order to issue him with a warning, before he assaulted some other poor wretch."

"Why didn't you call the police?"

"We did, but Fräulein Pinski was too frightened to make a statement. Besides, as I am sure you are aware, Inspector, the police are disinclined to assist women of her nationality and profession."

Anna looked directly at Rheinhardt. She was tacitly challenging him to deny her allegation. He couldn't: What she had said was perfectly true. Rheinhardt sighed, the exhalation carrying his next question. "What did you say to Herr Sachs?"

"I can't remember exactly," Anna replied. "We told him that we knew what he had done, that we had a doctor's report, that we would be taking things further . . ."

"And how did he react?"

"At first he wasn't very much bothered. He was clearly confident that the police wouldn't be interested. He admitted introducing Fräulein Pinski to some soldiers, so that she could have, as he called it, 'a good time,' but denied everything else. He became angry only when we refused to leave."

"What did he do?"

"He shouted and pushed me out of the way."

Rheinhardt tilted his head quizzically.

"I was holding his door open," Anna explained. "He had to get me out of the way to close it."

Rheinhardt made some notes.

"It was a foolish thing that you did, you and your friend—going into Spittelberg to rile a man like Sachs. You could have been hurt as a consequence. What did you hope to achieve?"

"We thought we might scare him," said Anna.

Rheinhardt had to make a conscious effort not to laugh out loud.

"Inspector," Anna asked, "why are you here, asking me these questions? Is Herr Sachs involved in one of your cases?"

"Yes," said Rheinhardt. "You could say that." He squeezed one of the horns of his mustache between his thumb and forefinger, twisting it to sharpen the point. "Apart from the police—and the doctors who are taking care of Fräulein Pinski—have you spoken to anyone else about Sachs?"

"My parents and . . ."

Rheinhardt detected a certain hesitancy.

"Yes?"

"Another friend."

Her voice had softened.

"What is your friend's name?"

"Gabriel. Gabriel Kusevitsky."

Rheinhardt looked up. "And where might I find this gentleman?"

60

HERR POPPMEIER WAS A dapper man in his early thirties. His hair was a fair reddish-brown color and was parted in the center. He looked quite young for his age, almost cherubic, and his mustache—which was also fair and meticulously combed—did little to mitigate a first impression of immaturity. His clothes were finely tailored, and his tiepin (a flamboyant coral reef of colored stones) looked conspicuously expensive. He was in the habit of constantly making small adjustments to his cuffs, and his use of cologne was so liberal that he had been preceded by a cloud of blossomy fragrances long before his actual arrival.

"Were you a happy child?" Liebermann asked.

"Happy enough. . . . I got on well with my mother and father."

"And your brothers and sisters?"

"I don't have any."

"An only child . . ."

"Yes. I'm sure my mother and father wanted more children, but there must have been a problem. I used to see my cousins occasionally—but not very often." He blinked and pushed out his lower lip. "Is this relevant?"

The tone of the question was confused rather than belligerent.

"What were they like, your mother and father?"

"They were very loving, but also rather anxious. I suppose this was because I was their only child. They tended to mollycoddle me. If I so much as sneezed, they would keep me home from school. Of course, I was delighted with their behavior at the time, but I grew to regret it in adult life."

"Did you enjoy school?"

"Not much. I've never been very academic, and the school I went to was a grim place: whitewashed walls and hard benches that made your bones ache. The teachers were awful, strict disciplinarians— and petty. They used to cover the windows in the summer so that we wouldn't be distracted, and we had only one break, ten minutes, standing like miserable wretches in a stuffy hall."

"If your parents were so concerned about your welfare, why didn't they send you to a better school?"

"There wasn't a better school. It was supposed to be the best in our neighborhood."

Liebermann nodded sympathetically. He asked Herr Poppmeier more questions about his childhood, and formed a picture in his mind of a rather lonely, unhappy boy, somewhat stifled by his overprotective parents.

"You said that your mother and father wanted more children . . ."

"Yes."

"How do you know that?"

"My mother and father used to tell me that I was going to have a little brother or sister . . . but he or she never arrived. I imagine that my mother was getting"—he hesitated and winced—"pregnant." Then, knitting his brow, he persevered with his unfinished sentence: "And while in the first flush of excitement, they would share their good news with me. But my mother must have miscarried."

"Were you disappointed, when the promised brother or sister did not arrive?"

"Not desperately. I was accustomed to having the exclusive attention of my parents. I'm not sure that I was eager to share them with anyone else."

"Can you remember your mother and father becoming sad?"

"Yes, I can. But in due course these episodes of sadness became less frequent. They must have stopped trying."

Liebermann summarized his thoughts with great economy, writing only *Self-blame?* in his notes.

After discussing Herr Poppmeier's childhood, Liebermann then asked him about his work. He immediately appeared more comfortable.

"I'm a salesman, for Prock and Hornbostel. I take samples of our jewelry around Vienna, but I am also required to travel quite a lot: Pressburg, Linz, Budapest. I once had to go as far as Trieste. We cater for all tastes—and classes." Herr Poppmeier then went into an extensive and detailed description of the contents of the Prock and Hornbostel catalogue. His intonation immediately changed, acquiring the persuasive strains and cadences of a seasoned salesman. "The Belvedere range has been crafted to the highest possible standards; the brooch with pendant is quite exquisite: beaten gold leaves, inlays of pearl and shell, with a suspended tear of topaz and diamond."

Liebermann thought that it would be prudent to interrupt. "Thank you, Herr Poppmeier. That is all very interesting, very interesting indeed." He leaned forward to arrest the salesman's pitch. "May I ask, when was it that you first became aware of your symptoms?"

Herr Poppmeier's expression darkened. Clearly his well-rehearsed patter had brought him some small relief—temporary deliverance— from the shameful strangeness of his condition.

"About three weeks ago. . . . I think I experienced the initial bout of morning sickness around the time when Arabelle's pregnancy started to show. When she started wearing maternity dresses."

"Did you get any of these symptoms when your wife was pregnant before?"

"No. I was perfectly healthy."

Liebermann paused to make some notes, but before he had finished, Herr Poppmeier said, "She was pregnant another time . . . just over a year ago. Sadly, we lost the child. The labor was complicated. Arabelle almost died. The child was stillborn."

"I'm sorry. That must have been dreadful."

"Yes, it was. And I was away when Arabelle went into labor. On one of my trips . . . I got a telegram."

"Where were you?"

"Lin—" The syllable slipped out before he corrected himself. "No, Steyr."

Liebermann made a note of the blunder. The arrival of momentous news was indelibly associated with the circumstances of the recipient. The brain absorbed everything, suspending the tragic communication in a preservative of easily accessible sense memories. Why would Poppmeier have made such a slip?

"Herr Doctor?"

Liebermann looked up.

"Will I have to stay here . . . in the hospital?"

"For a short period, for observation, yes—after which it might be possible to treat you as an outpatient. Let's see."

"What is the matter with me?"

"That is what we must find out."

"These symptoms . . . I know what they are, obviously." Again, Poppmeier winced, and a hectic rash appeared on his neck. He loosened the stud holding his collar. "I was once told that you psychiatrists treat people by learning the meaning of symptoms. Well, you don't have to be a psychiatrist to understand the meaning of *my* symptoms. I know what they mean already, and they still won't go away."

"You are quite right, symptoms often remit when patients discover their significance; however, there are meanings—and then there are *hidden* meanings. It is the latter that are most important."

"I don't understand. Hidden?"

"Hidden in your own mind."

"But if they are hidden, how can we find them? And where are they hidden?"

Liebermann smiled. "Tell me, Herr Poppmeier, what did you dream last night?"

61

Councillor Schmidt was sitting in his room at the town hall, smoking a cigar and thinking about his mistress. She had started to make unreasonable demands. From his experience, all women were the same in this respect. They became over-curious, meddlesome. They always wanted more. Private dining rooms, trinkets, and bouquets were no longer sufficient to keep them happy. They became morose, subdued in the bedroom, and maddeningly inquisitive.

Where are you going tomorrow night? Is it an official engagement? Will there be any society ladies present?

And so on . . .

He treated these questions as he might the singing of a canary, being barely conscious of the incessant warbling until its cessation.

Inquisitive mistresses were a liability. He did not want *them*, or *anyone*, to know his whereabouts. His plans (and he now had many of them) could be endangered by loose talk. The less people knew, the better.

Schmidt leaned back and rested his feet on his desk. The cigar tasted good. It was expensive and had been given to him, with other incentives, by a business associate in return for a small favor. The associate's lawyer had needed to study a certain title deed in the town hall archive. A promise of future preferment was all it had taken to persuade the archivist to hand him the desired document.

The tobacco was pungent, but teased the palate with a fruity sweetness. Schmidt dislodged some ash and continued thinking about his mistress.

Yes, it's been diverting enough—especially at the beginning, when she was more vivacious, lively, and appreciative. But the dalliance has probably run its course now. Time to move on.

There was a knock on the door.

Schmidt quickly shifted his feet off the desk, spread some papers, and picked up his pen. Adopting the vexed attitude of someone in the middle of a taxing piece of work, he called out, "Enter."

The door opened, and his nephew appeared.

"Oh, it's you." Schmidt relaxed and tossed his pen across the desk.

He saw that his nephew was clutching his mail. It was Fabian who opened and read all his official correspondence. The majority of which consisted of requests for assistance, support, advice, good causes—the sort of thing he could let Fabian attend to. The mayor's motto was "We must help the little man." A laudable sentiment, but in practice remarkably time-consuming and very unprofitable.

"Come in, dear boy," said Schmidt. "What have you got for me?"

"Uncle Julius," said Fabian, "you'll never believe what's happened. There's been another murder—a decapitation again, just like Brother Stanislav and poor Faust."

"Where?"

"The Ulrichskirche. I tried to walk through Ulrichsplatz this morning and was stopped. There were policemen and a journalist. They said it happened in the small hours."

"And the victim?"

"A Jew, a penniless Jew."

"A Jew, eh? Perhaps someone with a bit of backbone has finally decided to retaliate, an eye for an eye. What do you think? One of the dueling fraternities? When I was your age, I can remember Strength and Unity was full of high-spirited fellows." Schmidt stubbed out his cigar. "The reports in the newspapers have been so tame—so assiduous in their efforts to avoid stating the obvious—that it wouldn't surprise me. The censor is supposed to protect the public interest, not a parasitic minority."

Fabian handed Schmidt the wad of papers. "Your mail, Uncle."

"Anything I need to look at?"

"Not really. Oh, no . . . there was something." Fabian licked his finger and, leaning forward, rifled through the papers. "Yes—this, from Professor Gandler at the hospital. You must reply today if possible."

Schmidt took the letter from the pile and began to read.

62

THE STOVE HAD BEEN lit, but the room still felt cold. As before, Liebermann found the dull, lifeless décor of Barash's parlor enervating. It seemed to sap his strength.

"I followed your advice," said Liebermann. "I have just returned from Prague."

Barash tilted his head to one side and raised his chin.

"You surprise me, Herr Doctor."

"I visited the Jewish cemetery and the Old-New Synagogue, just as you recommended."

"Then I hope you benefited from the experience."

"The cemetery and the synagogue have a very particular atmosphere, a poignancy that is difficult to describe."

"Again, you surprise me. I had thought you would be inured to such *influences*." The zaddik toyed with the tassels hanging from beneath his frock coat. "So, Herr Doctor, do you *understand* now?"

From outside came the sound of a man whistling. The melody was full of the complex embellishments that typified the music of Eastern Jewry, exotic intervals and imitative sobs and sighs. Liebermann waited for the melody to fade.

"I discovered the grave of Rabbi Loew and learned of his remarkable ministry, how he protected his people in difficult times."

"Your journey was not wasted," said Barash concisely.

A lengthy silence followed.

"May I ask..." Liebermann was hesitant. "How does one go about making a golem?"

Barash's expression altered. It might have been a smile, but if so the small, flickering light of good humor did little to relieve the darkness in his eyes. The overhang of his brow ensured that his face could never be wholly free of disapprobation.

"The procedure is described in many places," the zaddik replied. "However, the clearest instructions can be found in the commentary of Eleazar of Worms on *The Book of Creation*." Liebermann's face showed no sign of recognition. "Eleazar ben Judah of Worms," Barash continued, "was a thirteenth-century German kabbalist and liturgical poet. His instructions for the making of a golem have been revised and presented as a separate work. It is called *pe'ullath ha-yetsirah*, which means 'the practical application of *The Book of Creation*.' Eleazar tells us that two or three adepts should take part in the ritual. Untilled earth is kneaded in running water and molded into human form. The transformation—from inanimate to living matter—is achieved through the recitation of letters taken from the *Sefer Yetzirah*. Other methods have been described, but it is Eleazar's method that commands the greatest respect among students of kabbalah."

"Not difficult, then? Simply a matter of following instructions."

Barash glowered. His expression was as oppressive, and baleful, as the gloom preceding a deluge.

"The ritual is highly dangerous. It must be observed precisely or catastrophic consequences will follow. An error in the ritual would not damage the golem, but it would very likely destroy the creator. He would be returned to his primal element. He would be sucked back into the earth."

These words were spoken with such fierce conviction that they produced a complementary image in Liebermann's mind: a wide-open mouth, screaming and sinking, being filled with loam. It was a disturbing image, and it sent a shiver down Liebermann's spine.

"Rebbe Barash, have you ever tried to make a golem?"

"No!" cried Barash. "I would not be so reckless, so presumptuous, so foolhardy!" The denial was emphatic. "I have the power—" The zaddik quickly corrected himself: "I *do not* have the power."

Liebermann noted the slip. Professor Freud asserted that people often betrayed themselves—their true beliefs, wishes, and intentions—by making verbal blunders. *What*, Liebermann wondered, *does this slip mean?* Did Barash believe that he was capable of performing Eleazar's ritual? Did he believe that he had already succeeded? Or was it merely a symptom of the man's megalomania—an unconscious fantasy of omnipotence?

"I assume you've heard about the discovery in Alois Gasse?"

Barash's massive hands came together, the fingers interlocking.

"It was inevitable that *he* would reveal himself."

"He?"

"The creator of the Vienna golem."

Liebermann suspended his disbelief and continued the conversation as if he accepted that such a creature could exist.

"Who is he, this creator?"

"I don't know. He wishes to remain unknown. Or perhaps he must remain unknown as a condition of his being in the world, like the righteous—the *lamed vavniks*—the thirty-six hidden saints whose presence here on earth prevents humanity from descending into barbarism. We might pass him on the street, seeing only a humble peddler, but believe me, he is a *great* soul." Barash shrugged, his mountainous shoulders rising and falling like a geological upheaval. "A great soul," he repeated. "Perhaps the revenant may even be Loew himself come back to us."

"How could that be?"

"*The magid of Safed* teaches us that the soul is eternal, participating in long chains of transmigration, back to the very beginning." Barash closed his eyes for a moment, and then opened them again slowly. "They say that Rabbi Loew's golem still sleeps in the Old-New Synagogue, waiting for a time when he is needed again; however, I understand this to be figurative, a promise on which we can build our hopes. When the forces of darkness gather, and our people are in danger, a great soul will come into the world to assist us."

"Do we live in *such* bad times?" Liebermann asked.

"We do, Herr Doctor. And the tragedy is that *you* and the legions of dispossessed like you do not realize it."

Barash was quite mad, but he had an annoying habit of saying things that were perceptive. Liebermann's predicament at the hospital was almost entirely due to his refusal to take anti-Semitism seriously. Discomfited by Barash's pointed remark, Liebermann became interrogative.

"Rebbe Barash, what were you doing last night?"

"I was praying."

"All night?"

"Yes."

"Why?"

"I often pray into the night. It is peaceful . . . and I feel closer to God."

Liebermann continued to ask questions, but Barash's answers revealed nothing of consequence. In due course Liebermann said, "There has been another murder."

Barash responded calmly. "Like the others?"

"Yes. The victim's head was torn from his body and his remains were left outside a church."

"Then it has struck again."

"The murder was the same in all respects," continued Liebermann, "with one exception." He paused dramatically.

"Which was?"

"The victim was not an enemy of Jewry."

"Are you sure, Herr Doctor?"

"Quite sure."

"But how can you possibly say?"

"He was Jewish."

The zaddik appeared genuinely surprised. His thick eyebrows rose up, and his lips parted.

"That is not possible." He spoke hoarsely, his basso profundo momentarily robbed of its savory depth. Liebermann played a five-finger exercise on the chair arm. The soft percussion of his fingertips on the wood filled the hiatus, until Barash added more steadily, "No. You must be mistaken."

Liebermann's fingers stopped moving. "All of the evidence suggests the contrary. Whoever—whatever—killed Brother Stanislav and Councillor Faust also killed Jeheil Sachs."

Barash shook his head, slow and bovine. His coiled sideburns continued bouncing after the movement was completed. "No. You are mistaken. Another party is responsible." His expression communicated that he saw no point in discussing the matter any further.

Liebermann was dissatisfied. Apart from the zaddik's slip of the tongue, the interview had not been very revealing. Feeling frustrated, Liebermann asked, "Did you sleep at all last night, Rebbe Barash?"

"Yes. I retired at about four or five this morning."

"Last time we spoke, our conversation touched upon the subject of dreams. May I ask, when you slept, did you dream?"

"I did."

"What about?"

The zaddik's eyebrows joined, and his brow became a network of deep creases, "I cannot tell you about my dreams," he said disdainfully. "They are sacred, and it is most impertinent of you to make such an inquiry. When you ask a man about his dreams, you ask him to expose his soul. You eavesdrop on a conversation between man and God."

Barash stood up.

"Herr Doctor, I am afraid I have other business. I have attempted to answer your questions in good faith, but it is clear to me that you still believe that I am in some way connected with the deaths of the monk Stanislav and Councillor Faust. Once again, I must protest and declare my innocence. If I am to be arrested, then please proceed. Tell your associates at the security office that I am ready. However, if it is not your intention to arrest me, then I would ask you to leave me in peace."

Barash crossed the room and opened the door. Liebermann followed.

The young doctor thanked the zaddik for his assistance; but Barash did not respond. He stood in the doorway, perfectly still, his gigantic frame swaying slightly. It was an unnatural stillness, and it reminded Liebermann of the *absences* that he had observed in certain hysterical and neurological cases. Liebermann then noticed that the zaddik's gaze was focused on Liebermann's forehead. Quite suddenly Barash blinked as if waking from a deep sleep and grumbled an apology.

"I am sorry, Herr Doctor. I am tired. Perhaps you could see yourself out."

Liebermann did not move. "What did you see?"

Barash extended his hand and touched the doorjamb in order to steady himself. "Great danger," he whispered.

"Am I going to die?" Liebermann asked.

"We are all of us going to die, Herr Doctor," said Barash obtusely.

"Am I going to die in the next thirty days?" Liebermann persisted. "Is that what you saw?"

The zaddik's face was inscrutable. "Be very careful."

Liebermann wasn't sure whether Barash was showing compassion or issuing a threat.

63

THE DANUBE CANAL WAS bathed in late afternoon sunshine. A shimmer of light played on the gray-green water as Liebermann crossed the Maria-Theresien Bridge and headed off toward the Börse. He did not hail a cab. He wanted to walk, to clear his head and dispel the oppressive atmosphere of the zaddik's parlor. It clung to him like the scent of mildew, and filled his mind with images of dust, decay, and interment. As he proceeded through the backstreets, Liebermann decided that he needed a very strong coffee. The Café Central—the favored haunt of writers, poets, and freethinkers—was just beyond the misshapen old town square, and the prospect of its splendid interior and decadent patrons was irresistible.

Liebermann crossed the open concourse, glancing in passing at the central fountain with its vigilant circle of bronze nymphs, and entered a shadowy street on the other side. Soon he was standing outside his destination, a little flushed but feeling better for having physically exerted himself. He opened the door and entered.

Inside, sturdy columns with ornate capitals rose up to a high vaulted ceiling. The pianist was playing a Brahms waltz, and the cavernous space was resonant with loud conversation and laughter. In the far corner a gaggle of art students (one still wearing his paint-spattered smock) was watching a billiard game.

Liebermann searched for somewhere to sit. He ventured farther into the coffeehouse, passing an inebriated cavalryman and squeezing between tables. Amid the general hubbub, he caught snatches of political debate, jokes, and immoderate language. After completing an unsuccessful circuit, he stopped and surveyed his surroundings. It was hopeless: the place was full. He would have to go somewhere else. But just as he was about to depart, he noticed a man, some distance away, rising from his chair and waving. It was Gabriel Kusevitsky, the young doctor whom he had met at his father's lodge.

"Excuse me, sir." A waiter with a full tray was trying to pass.

"I'm sorry," said Liebermann, veering off in the direction of Kusevitsky's table.

Kusevitsky stood to greet him.

"Liebermann, how good to see you. Would you like to join us?" He gestured toward his companions. The first was a youth whose physical features duplicated Kusevitsky's. The second needed no introduction. "My brother, Asher Kusevitsky, and Arthur Schnitzler." Liebermann bowed. "Herr Dr. Max Liebermann." Kusevitsky added, "Another devotee of Professor Freud."

Schnitzler was wearing a large pale hat with a wide brim, tilted at a perilously steep angle. His velvet jacket and embroidered shirt were rather dandified, as was his somewhat overwhelming and sweet-smelling cologne. His substantial mustache was combed out sideways, and his triangular beard was trimmed to a sharp point.

Liebermann sat down.

Schnitzler was in the middle of a story and evidently intended to finish it. "I made a few timid efforts to gain recognition for *The Adventure of His Life*. First I sent it to Siegwart Friedmann, who ignored it, then to Tewele, who as a friend of the family at least felt he had to say a few pleasant words about it. Director Lautenburg had already had a copy of the script sent to him from Vienna by Eirich. I had heard nothing from him, but when Lothar arrived, a meeting was arranged with Lautenburg at a restaurant—Krziwanek—and Lothar soon found a way to shift the conversation tactfully to my comedy. At first Lautenburg didn't seem to remember it. I reminded him of a few scenes. Suddenly he knew what we were talking about, gave me a polite, pitying look, shook his head, and said just one word: Terrible."

Schnitzler grinned.

"What a fool!" said Asher.

"That's not all," Schnitzler continued. "A few minutes later, as if to console me, he added, 'Your first effort, I presume?' Because I couldn't even offer him this as an excuse, he apparently gave me up as a hopeless case, and we talked of other things."

"Well," said Asher, "I'll bear that in mind." He tapped the side of his nose, an odd gesture that suggested some kind of private understanding had been reached.

After a short pause, the conversation became more inclusive, turning to recent theatrical productions, and Liebermann was invited to give his opinion; however, he was painfully aware that he had not been to the theatre very much of late and had little of consequence to say.

Liebermann recalled reading something about Schnitzler only the previous week in the *Wiener Tagblatt*. His latest publication, the text of a dramatic work called *Riegen*, had been dubbed pornography. Liebermann had not read *Riegen*, but he had seen one of Schnitzler's plays, *Paracelsus*, at the Court Theatre, and had once come across an interesting academic paper by Schnitzler (who was also a doctor) on the treatment of functional aphonia using hypnotic suggestion.

As the conversation progressed, Liebermann gleaned that Asher Kusevitsky was a burgeoning playwright and was in some way connected with Schnitzler's circle. The famous author was nodding vigorously; however, Liebermann noticed that he was somewhat distracted. He kept looking over at a pretty young woman seated at an adjacent table. She was smoking a thin black cigarette and sipping red wine. Asher Kusevitsky, in the throes of an impassioned speech about the hammy excesses of an actor called Obermoser, was oblivious to his companion's lapses of concentration.

A waiter arrived, and Liebermann ordered a large, very strong *schwarzer*.

When the conversation started up again, an invisible curtain seemed to have been drawn across the table, separating Gabriel Kusevitsky and Liebermann on one side from Asher Kusevitsky and Schnitzler on the other. The two literary gentlemen clearly had some business to discuss.

"So," said Liebermann, addressing Kusevitsky, "how is your research progressing?"

"Very well," Kusevitsky replied, straightening his stylish purple necktie. He was looking much smarter. Liebermann observed a small pearl in the tie knot. "I have already collected a considerable amount of fascinating material. I am now utterly convinced of Nietzsche's assertion that in dreams some primeval relic of humanity is at work."

"Have you reported your preliminary findings to Professor Freud?"

"Of course, and he was delighted with my results." Kusevitsky smiled, though the contraction and release of facial muscles was so brief that it was more like a twitch. "Through such research, Professor Freud believes that psychoanalysis may claim an elevated position among the historical sciences, superseding even archaeology. The mental antiquities that lie buried in the deepest stratum of the mind will be aeons older than anything excavated in Egypt."

The waiter returned with Liebermann's coffee.

A fragment of Asher's conversation intruded: ". . . A secondary purpose of *The Dybbuk* . . . to raise Jewish consciousness." The sentence was drowned by applause as the pianist began a sentimental Ländler. It obviously had special significance to some of the regulars.

Kusevitsky described several dreams in which he identified the presence of universal symbols: kings, queens, sages and devils, towers, skeletons, and stars. All of them were supposed to have a specific meaning, each being an inherited residue resulting from generations of repeated human experience.

Liebermann remained unconvinced. He could accept that dreams contained symbols. That much was incontrovertible. But the idea that dreams could be understood in terms of fixed representations and that these representations were invariant from generation to generation seemed faintly preposterous. Adopting such a view made psychoanalysis seem indistinguishable from fortune-telling. A doctor became no different from the charlatan mystics on the Prater, reading off the meaning of dreams as if they were nothing more than the psychological equivalent of a pack of tarot cards.

"I wonder," said Liebermann, his eyes sparkling with mischief, "what you will make of this, then, Kusevitsky—a dream reported to me by one of my patients." He paused in order to recollect his own dream of Miss Lydgate in the tropical garden. "Let us, for reasons of confidentiality, call my patient Herr D, a professional gentleman in his twenties suffering from . . ." Again Liebermann paused before adding, "Obsessional indecision and doubting."

Kusevitsky gave his tacit consent.

"The dream," Liebermann continued, "was as follows: Herr D found himself in a vast garden of exotic flowers and high trees. A woman, with whom he had become acquainted through his work and whom I shall call Fräulein Lisa, appeared beside him, naked. She then spoke to him, saying something like, 'I won't lie below you. I am your equal.' Consequently they began to argue. During the course of this argument, Fräulein Lisa pronounced the name of Herr D's father, who then appeared, sitting on a throne."

While Liebermann was recounting the dream, he was unnerved by changes in Kusevitsky's expression. The young man's eyes were opening wider and wider. His initial interest had undergone a strange metamorphosis, becoming, with its final transition, something closer to shock or fear.

Liebermann pressed on. "The old gentleman said to his son, 'It isn't good for you to be alone.' Herr D pointed toward where he thought Fräulein Lisa was still standing, but she had in fact vanished. There. What do you make of that?"

"Extraordinary!" said Kusevitsky, his voice sounding slightly strangulated. "Quite, quite extraordinary! I *must* see this patient."

"I'm afraid you can't."

"Surely *you* would have no objection? And it would not be *so* onerous for him to sit with me for an hour or two. Could he not be persuaded if told, for example, that he would be helping to advance scientific knowledge? You did say he was a professional gentleman."

"I'm afraid that's not possible, Kusevitsky. He has left the country."

"Do you have his address?"

"I can look, but why?"

"He is Jewish, of course—this patient."

"Yes, he is, but he's not very religious."

"Even better. I don't suppose you'd know whether or not he was familiar with Hebrew creation myths?"

"Well, because you ask," said Liebermann tentatively, "I think I can say with some confidence that the answer to that question would be no."

"In which case, Herr D's dream is a remarkable example of an archaic remnant. Its elements correspond exactly with the legend of Lilith, as recounted in *The Alphabet of Ben Sira*. Herr D is Adam, his father is God, and Fräulein Lisa is Lilith."

"And who, may I ask, is Lilith?"

"Adam's first wife."

"I thought he was married to Eve."

"He was. But according to many Jewish sources, Adam had another wife before her: Lilith. She was a fiery and rebellious woman, refusing to obey her husband and God. Her fate was to become the queen of demons. She was much feared in ancient times, and is still feared today by the Hasidim. Some believe she makes infernal offspring by stealing wasted seed, a belief that might explain the origin of the taboo against masturbation." Kusevitsky sat back in his chair, recovering from his excitement. "Extraordinary. Quite extraordinary. Please promise me that you'll look for Herr D's address. I would be most indebted."

"Of course," said Liebermann. "I'll do my best."

Liebermann was perplexed. He could not—*would not*—accept that his dream had been shaped by a racial memory, a narrative template buried deep in his own unconscious. The only other explanation was *cryptomnesia*, the spontaneous recall of something forgotten without any memory of having learned it. But this was hardly a compelling alternative. Where would he have encountered the Lilith legend before? And why should it have been so powerfully repressed? Kusevitsky, now less agitated, extracted a further assurance from Liebermann that he would look for Herr D's address; they exchanged visiting cards, and the subject was allowed to drop from their conversation.

"And how are things at the General Hospital?" asked Kusevitsky.

Liebermann sighed. "Actually at present not very good. I've run into some difficulties."

Once again, he was obliged to provide a summary of the events surrounding the death of the young Baron von Kortig.

"My dear fellow, I am so sorry," said Kusevitsky. "If there's anything I can do?"

Liebermann shook his head. "No, but thank you for your kind offer."

He became aware that the conversation on the other side of the table had stopped. Asher Kusevitsky and Schnitzler had been listening.

"They won't be happy," said Asher bitterly, "until they've got us out of the theatres, out of the hospitals, and, in the end, out of Vienna altogether! That's what they really want. They want a purge. They treat us like a plague. . . ."

"Mmmm . . ." Schnitzler hummed, the note rising and falling. "Very interesting. Very interesting indeed." He did not look sympathetic, like Gabriel, or angered, like Asher—merely curious. In fact, Liebermann thought he saw the author's lips twisting to form a sardonic smile. "A story with definite potential," Schnitzler added. "Yes, definite potential. Now, if you wouldn't mind, Liebermann, could you tell it again, starting from the very beginning."

64

HERR POPPMEIER WAS LYING on a rest bed, his hands behind his head, looking up at the ceiling. His youthful face had assumed an expression of perplexity. Liebermann, who was seated out of his patient's view, was waiting for the salesman to resume speaking. The session had not been very productive. In fact, none of Herr Poppmeier's sessions had been very productive. When asked to freely vocalize whatever came into his mind, without censorship or restraint, his chain of associations invariably led back to items included in the Prock and Hornbostel catalogue. In due course, Poppmeier said, "I had another dream last night. Do you want me to tell you about it?"

"Yes, of course," said Liebermann, eager for something substantial to work on.

"It's not the first time either. I've had it before."

"A recurring dream . . ."

"Yes." Poppmeier crossed his legs. "Do you have a cigarette?"

"I'm afraid not."

"I'd love a cigarette right now."

Interesting, thought Liebermann.

"Arabelle wants me to give up smoking," Poppmeier continued. "She doesn't like the smell of tobacco. I've tried, but it's extremely difficult. I get so irritable, and then feel guilty afterward. I can be quite disagreeable."

The salesman seemed unaware that he had strayed off the subject. Liebermann made a note: *Delay—resistance?*

"Herr Poppmeier," said Liebermann, "you were going to tell me about your recurring dream?"

"Oh yes, so I was." The salesman bit his lower lip. "It's like this . . ." He drummed his fingers on the mattress. "I'm staying in a hotel, a very pleasant hotel with red carpets and gilt mirrors and busy waiters and miniature palm trees, a little like the Kaiser in Steyr, and—this is most peculiar, even embarrassing—I am a priest." Popp-meier laughed nervously. "I am sitting in the foyer, listening to a string trio, when I am approached by the concierge and asked to give the last rites to a dying child."

Mention of the last rites made Liebermann sit up.

"Go on . . ."

"I am escorted to a room that is full of my jewelry samples—rings, pendants, brooches. The rings are from the Prestige range and feature some very attractive stones imported from Bohemia. The pendants are heart-shaped, silver—with two opals set in a decoration of per-pendicular silver bars. The brooches—"

"Herr Poppmeier," Liebermann cut in. "Your dream?"

"Oh yes . . . There is a child in a bed, being cared for by a pretty nurse. For some reason, which I cannot justify, I refuse to perform the sacrament and leave."

Poppmeier resumed chewing his lower lip.

"Is that it?"

"Yes. An absurd dream, but always remarkably vivid."

"When did it first occur?"

"Difficult to say."

"Do you think you've been having it for years? Months?"

"Not years, exactly—but for quite a long time."

"A year, then?"

"About that, yes."

Liebermann flicked through his notes and found the entry he was looking for: *Frau Poppmeier: Gravida 3/Para II. Intrapartum death—1902 (early?)*.

Poppmeier's wife had been pregnant twice before her current pregnancy and the second pregnancy had ended in the tragedy of a stillbirth. The timing was exact.

65

"YES," SAID ASHER KUSEVITSKY, addressing Professor Priel. "Schnitzler had some interesting things to say about Lautenburg. The man's a fool, just as I thought. I won't be sending him any of my scripts in the future."

The walls of Professor Priel's parlor were covered in examples of modern art. They were mostly allegorical works, in which personifications of philosophy, poetry, or music were rendered in a style that owed a considerable debt to Klimt. The figures, usually women, stared out full-face against a background of strong tonal contrasts. In addition, there were numerous contemporary portraits, some of which were quite disturbing. Sketches and watercolors of troubled individuals—emaciated, gaunt, their skin discolored, suggestive of putrescence. The models might have been recruited from a mortuary.

All the art that Professor Priel possessed had been made by impoverished young men who had benefited from a Rothenstein creative bursary. Although he wasn't particularly fond of the portraits, he recognized that they were original and most probably indicative of a significant trend. He had not, however, purchased them as an investment. He had bought them to bolster the confidence of the young artists. They were always delighted to see their work hanging on his walls.

The only non-modern piece in Professor Priel's collection was a plaster cast reproduction of Michelangelo's *Moses*. It occupied a central position on the sideboard. Even though it was only a fraction of the size of the original, the copy was still powerfully evocative:

Moses the lawgiver, seated like a Titan or a great warrior, his muscled arm resting on the commandment tablets, his long beard a wild tangle of writhing serpentine spirals.

A servant arrived with tea for the professor's guests and a glass of magnetized water for the professor. A daily circuit of the Ringstrasse and a glass of magnetized water was—so he believed—the key to a long and healthy life.

"Gabriel," Asher continued, "tell Professor Priel about Liebermann and the von Kortig business." He then turned to face Priel. "Listen to this. It's quite scandalous."

Gabriel Kusevitsky repeated Liebermann's story.

When he had finished, Professor Priel was silent, his head slowly shaking from side to side.

"It's political, of course, and what worries me is where it could lead," said Asher. He spoke quickly, making expressive gestures with his hands. "I mean to say, if Liebermann is dismissed—and they get away with it—who will be next? Where will it end? *Lieutenant Gustl* has already cost Schnitzler his rank in the reservists, and I don't believe for one minute that it was because he broke the code of honor by writing it, as the authorities insist. It cost him his rank because he is a Jew. One can see where this is going. There are passages in *The Dybbuk* where I am critical of the church. If things continue like this, I wouldn't be at all surprised if an official turns up and closes down the theatre."

"Liebermann," said the professor. "What's his first name?"

"Max," said Gabriel. "Professor Freud speaks very highly of him. I've read a few of his case studies and was most impressed by his paper on paranoia erotica. It would be a great shame if his career was blighted because of political opportunism."

"Oh, then I *really must* do something," said Professor Priel.

Gabriel sipped his tea and returned the cup to its saucer. On landing, it produced an unusually loud chime.

"Be that as it may," Gabriel continued, "he is not very active in our circle. He has not associated himself with our charitable organizations and causes."

"Is he a member of the lodge?"

"No, I don't think he is. I met him there when Professor Freud gave his last talk, but I had never seen him there before—and have not seen him there since."

"I don't think that should concern us," said the professor. "He is a talented young man with prospects. He needs help, and I may be in a position to provide it. Rothenstein has some exceptional lawyers in his employ. One can't just stand by and watch something like this happening. Asher is quite right. In the end, if something isn't done, we'll all be affected. Never forget what Councillor Faust was proposing in his article. Where can I find him, this Liebermann fellow?"

Gabriel was dressed in the very same jacket that he had been wearing in the Café Central. He reached into his pocket, found Liebermann's card, and gave it to Professor Priel.

"He works at the General Hospital."

"Good. I'll see what I can do."

Priel took a swig of magnetized water. He could feel the energy coursing through his veins, invigorating and refreshing his nerves and muscles. He looked over at the reproduction of Moses. A good man's work was never done.

66

Nᴀʜᴜᴍ Nᴀɢᴇʟ ᴡᴀs sɪᴛᴛɪɴɢ behind the counter of the general store, watching the scales seesaw. He was deep in thought.

Everybody was convinced.

Everybody was expecting salvation.

But was it really going to happen? When the thugs came again, what should he expect? Would the ground tremble as its massive feet stomped down the alleyway? Would the shop door be thrown open, would it duck beneath the lintel and grab the villains? Would it rip off their heads, right there, on the other side of the counter, before his very eyes?

The gossip went round and round in his head, like whispering in a cloister.

Alois Gasse . . . mud . . . Prague . . . golem . . .

Upstairs, his father was coughing. If they didn't move very soon, the old man would die.

Nahum removed one weight and added another. The scale tipped and began, through its slow reciprocal motion, to negotiate a differ-ent resting point. As the dishes rose and fell, it struck Nahum that the process was like a dialogue between two parties: offers made, re-jected, reviewed, and finally accepted. The angle at which the scale bar finally came to rest was, in effect, a compromise.

Nahum's thoughts crystallized.

The universe that God made is imperfect. That is what Isaac Luria taught his disciples. We have no need of complex philosophical arguments to explain why God has let evil into the world. Its presence is a mistake. The vessels broke and must be repaired. Humanity can either assist in the process of healing or compound the disintegration of all things through acts of self-interest and cruelty. Luria places the fate of everything not in the hands of God but in the hands of humanity: the peddler, the kitchen maid, and the street cleaner. Everyone is responsible.

The familiar sound of hobnailed boots resonated in the alley. It grew louder, and the door swung wide open. Haas entered the shop and strolled up to the counter, kicking a tin of olive oil over as he came forward.

"Well," he said. "I believe you owe me some money."

"Where is your friend?" Nahum asked.

"Why? Have you missed him?" Haas laughed.

Nahum stared at the scales.

The zaddik had spoken with conviction.

You have nothing to fear. You have only to call and the golem will come to assist you.

"Give me the cash box!"

Nahum handed Haas the tin. The thug opened it up and looked inside. He turned the empty container upside down and threw it over his shoulder. It clattered across the floor.

"I'm not in the mood for jokes."

Nahum closed his eyes. *Come to me, help me . . .*

And, to his surprise, the prayer was answered.

The golem arrived, but not in the form that he had anticipated. It came not as a supernatural being. It came instead as blind, pitiless rage.

They are evil, and their evil is my responsibility.

Nahum opened his eyes.

"The money," said Haas.

The shopkeeper snatched up the heaviest weight from the counter and swung it against the side of Haas's head. It made a strange, sickening thud. Nahum then allowed his hand to drop.

Haas did not move. He remained standing, swaying slightly, his expression showing nothing more than mild irritation. Blood ran down his cheek in a straight line until it was diverted along the arc of his scar. His eyes rolled and he fell backward, crashing to the ground.

Nahum stepped out from behind the counter and began to go through the thug's pockets. He found a wallet bulging with notes, enough to pay for dry rooms and a specialist in lung diseases.

Haas was still breathing.

"Father?" Nahum called out.

"Yes?" the old man croaked.

"Get your coat. We're leaving."

67

Professor Kraus entered Gabriel Kusevitsky's room without knocking.

"There's a policeman outside," said the professor. "He wants to speak to you."

"Me?" said Kusevitsky, rising unsteadily from his chair.

"Yes, you. What on earth have you done, Kusevitsky?"

"Why, nothing, sir. Well, nothing wrong, at least."

"This is a private hospital," said the professor. "We can't have the police snooping around the wards. It won't do."

"Indeed, sir, but I can assure you—"

The professor cut in, "Just make sure he doesn't come back, eh? You young fellows are all the same. Dueling, drinking, parties, and ridiculous pranks. You're not a student anymore, Kusevitsky."

"With respect, sir, I have never—"

"And incidentally," the professor pressed on, "that necktie is far too loud. It lacks gravitas. And if there's one thing a patient expects from his physician, it is gravitas."

"Very good, sir," said Kusevitsky. "I will wear only a black necktie in the future."

"His name's Rheinhardt."

"Sir?"

"The policeman. I managed to hide him away in the common room."

"Thank you, Professor Kraus. I will see him immediately and make sure that when he leaves he does so via the kitchen entrance."

The professor made some grunting noises and left. His footsteps (loud, regular, and implacable) resounded down the corridor.

Gabriel Kusevitsky sighed, tidied his notes, and made his way to the common room, where a portly gentleman in plain clothes was waiting. He had been expecting a constable with spiked helmet and sabre. The man stood up, bowed, and said, "Herr Dr. Kusevitsky? I am Detective Inspector Oskar Rheinhardt of the security office. Forgive me for interrupting your day."

His civility was a pleasant change after Professor Kraus's insults.

The two men sat down at a table covered with medical journals.

"Does the name Jeheil Sachs mean anything to you?" asked Rheinhardt.

"Yes. He's a procurer. Why?"

"What else do you know of him?"

"Well, he lives in Spittelberg and recently assaulted a poor young woman, Fräulein Pinski, who was admitted into this hospital." Kusevitsky produced a flickering smile, a fast series of facial contractions. "I think there must have been some mistake or misunderstanding, Inspector. She is not in my care. You really need to speak to Professor Kraus and Dr. Goldberger."

"No," said Rheinhardt. "There has been no mistake."

"But I know nothing of this woman's circumstances. Other than that she was a prostitute, of course."

"Tell me," Rheinhardt continued, resting his elbows on the table and locking his fingers. "How did you get to hear about Herr Sachs?"

"One of my friends—Fräulein Katzer—she does charity work in Spittelberg and told me what had happened, about the assault."

"Fräulein Katzer . . . Is she just a friend? Or are you romantically associated?"

Kusevitsky's cheeks flushed. "We are associated, yes," said the young man stiffly.

"And when she told you what Sachs had done to Fräulein Pinski, what was your reaction?"

"I was angry. Very angry. It was a brutal and ugly attack."

"Fräulein Katzer went to see Herr Sachs with . . ." Rheinhardt consulted his notebook. "Fräulein Mandl. Why didn't you go with her?"

"I learned of her visit only after she'd already gone. It was a foolish thing to do."

Rheinhardt twisted his mustache. "Where were you on Thursday night?"

"At home, with my brother, Asher."

"Doing what, exactly?"

"What possible use would such information be to you, Inspector?" Rheinhardt allowed the ensuing silence to build. "Very well," said Gabriel, shrugging. "I was writing up some preliminary results of a study I am conducting into the nature of dreams."

"Ah, dreams," said Rheinhardt. "A very interesting topic. You must be a devotee of Professor Freud."

Kusevitsky was surprised. "Yes, as it happens, I am. Are you familiar with Professor Freud's works?"

"I have read *The Psychopathology of Everyday Life* and some of *The Interpretation of Dreams*. I enjoyed the former but struggled to finish the latter. The technical passages at the end were somewhat obscure." Rheinhardt glanced nonchalantly at one the medical journals. "What time did you retire?"

"On Thursday night? Quite late. The early hours of the morning, I imagine."

"Yes, but what time?"

"I can't remember. But it must have been around one or two."

Rheinhardt made a note.

"Inspector?" The young man was looking at him intently. "Your questions and manner lead me to conclude that something has happened to Herr Sachs. Has he, by any chance, been murdered?"

Rheinhardt reached into his pocket and took out a folded copy of the *Illustrierte Kronen-Zeitung*. On the cover was a crude drawing of a plague column and a headless corpse lying—its position inaccurate—on the pavement next to it.

"You haven't seen this, then?"

Kusevitsky took the newspaper and examined the image.

"Did he deserve to die?" Rheinhardt asked.

"That is not a question I have the moral authority to answer," the young doctor replied calmly.

68

THEY HAD JUST COMPLETED the *Schöne Müllerin* song cycle and
were very satisfied with their performance. Rheinhardt's voice had
sounded particularly good, discovering in each perfectly constructed
phrase new registers of bittersweet feeling.

The images still lingered: murmuring brooks, water mills, broad
skies—a landscape of innocent pleasures. And, for any self-
respecting German romantic, the natural setting for tales of unrequited love and suicidal despair.

"One more," said Liebermann, rummaging in his piano stool for a
suitable song to end with.

"Yes, but only one more," said Rheinhardt. "My voice is going."

"Nonsense," said Liebermann. "You're in excellent form. Ah, how
about this?"

He placed some more Schubert on the music stand: *Gretchen am
Spinnrade*. Gretchen at the Spinning Wheel.

It was not an obvious choice, the sentiment of the poetry being,
strictly speaking, more appropriate for a female singer. Nevertheless,
Liebermann found that he was seized by a curious desire to hear
Schubert's beautiful lyric melody. *Gretchen am Spinnrade* was a miracle
of precocity. It had been completed before the composer had reached
twenty, and most music aficionados agreed that even if Schubert had
lived to a hundred he would not have been able to improve a single
note.

Rheinhardt shrugged. "Very well."

Liebermann's hands dropped to the keyboard, producing on contact the fluid semiquavers that evoked with astonishing fidelity the turning of Gretchen's spinning wheel. So powerful was this impression that the listener could all but hear her foot pumping the treadle. The semiquavers were relentless, their melancholy revolutions suggesting not only poignant yearning but tired resignation. Schubert's account of Gretchen's wheel had, perhaps, more in common with the medieval *Rota Fortuna* than with a machine for making yarn. Human beings might rail against fate, but ultimately each individual had to accept his or her destiny. There was no other choice. Gretchen's wheel reproduced in the listener's mind an intimation of universal circularities: orbiting worlds and the motion of stars. Never, thought Liebermann, had a composer responded so comprehensively to a given text, finding within the poetry meanings that might even have escaped its author, no less a genius than the godlike Goethe.

Rheinhardt's baritone was rich and dark:

> *"Meine Ruh ist hin,"*
> My peace is gone,
> *"Mein Herz ist schwer,"*
> My heart is heavy,
> *"Ich finde sie nimmer, Und nimmermehr."*
> I shall never, ever find peace again.

Why, Liebermann wondered, *did I want to hear this song again, this song of yearning and fate?*

A series of ghostly images flickered in front of his eyes.

Uncle Alexander on the Charles Bridge: *This Englishwoman, if I am not mistaken, is your unattainable object of desire.*

Miss Lydgate in front of the Karlskirche: *Brunelleschi's revolutionary gear mechanism employed a large screw with a helical thread.*

The chancellor: *Had you apologized to the committee when I advised you to, Herr Doctor, this problem might have been swiftly and quietly resolved.*

Barash: *We are all of us going to die, Herr Doctor.*

These images were connected in some way and were struggling to tell him something, but he couldn't say what, exactly. Their deeper meaning, like the latent content of dreams, was elusive. Nevertheless, he was acutely aware of the great *Rota Fortuna* turning, bringing him closer and closer to an uncertain fate. Ordinarily, Liebermann was not superstitious. But he could not dismiss a nagging presentiment of peril that had made its home in the pit of his stomach.

The spinning wheel figure was interrupted at the song's emotional climax, and Rheinhardt's voice rang out above inconclusive, questioning harmonies. A brief pause. Then, hesitatingly at first, the revolving figure began again, proceeding inexorably to the final bar: a tonic minor chord, held into silence.

Liebermann closed the music book, and he and Rheinhardt retired, without exchanging a single word, to the smoking room.

A full ten minutes passed before Liebermann said, "So, what have you learned about Jeheil Sachs? The newspaper articles said very little about him—other than that he was Jewish, of course."

Rheinhardt nodded.

"He was a small-time procurer whose business was conducted in a tiny hovel in Spittelberg. He solicited for a young Galician woman named Kadia Pinski. She had become dissatisfied with her sorry existence and wanted to make a new life for herself. Sachs assaulted her. It was a brutal assault, in which he violated her person with the handle of a brush." The expression of disgust on Rheinhardt's face disambiguated his euphemistic sentence. "She almost died. Fortunately, she was able to get medical help, but only after she had collapsed in the Spittelberg *wärmestube*. The two women who run it, Anna Katzer and Olga Mandl, called for a doctor, and Fräulein Pinski was admitted into a private hospital."

"Does she have friends? Relatives?"

"People who might want to take vengeance on Sachs? No. Not

here in Vienna. She was all alone, easy prey for a procurer: young, destitute, unable to speak German. I daresay that she must have initially thought Sachs was her savior, a charitable coreligionist, offering her food and shelter." Rheinhardt drew on his cigar and expelled a prolific quantity of smoke. "The *wärmestube* fräuleins—Katzer and Mandl—took it upon themselves to visit Sachs in order to issue some sort of legal threat. Pinski was too frightened to make a statement, and besides, the police—I am ashamed to admit—are reluctant to come to the aid of unlicensed prostitutes: especially those of Galician origin. A witness reported that the women and Sachs argued."

"Anna Katzer and Olga Mandl. Those names sound familiar to me."

"They are two socialites who have made it their avocation to raise money for charitable—and mostly Jewish—causes. They are often mentioned in the society columns."

"Yes, that's it. I remember reading something about them in the *Neue Freie Presse*. The archduchess Marie Valerie attended the opening of the Spittelberg *wärmestube*." Liebermann poured some brandy. "Surely you don't suspect . . ." Liebermann allowed the sentence to trail off.

"Sachs's treatment of Pinski was heinous. He was an odious man who would have no doubt continued to exploit young women. They are wealthy. They are well connected. They wanted to stop him."

"Yes, but if murder was their aim, then Sachs could have been dispatched neatly and efficiently with a stiletto. There are, as we know, villains who would willingly provide such a service for a relatively small sum. Why on earth would they choose to link his demise with the deaths of Brother Stanislav and Councillor Faust?"

"We have previously speculated about the operation of a group—a cabal—whose intention all along has been, for whatever reason, to revive the myth of the golem, to inspire belief in its existence. Now, if the golem's purpose is to protect Jews, then one can imagine why such a creature might have been commanded to kill an individual such as Sachs. In his own way, Sachs was as much a threat to the Jewish community as were Brother Stanislav and Councillor Faust. The Church has been warned, politicians have been warned, and now the Jewish community itself has been warned: punishment will be meted out to anyone who harms Jews, even Jews who harm other Jews."

"Well," said Liebermann, "if we posit the existence of a militant secret society, then there is no reason why its generals shouldn't receive intelligence from unlikely agents."

Rheinhardt tapped the ash from his cigar.

"Fräulein Katzer is romantically associated with a young doctor, a gentleman called Kusevitsky."

"Gabriel Kusevitsky?"

"Yes. Do you know him?"

"Indeed. We've met twice: once at my father's lodge—B'nai B'rith—and again in the Café Central only a few days ago. He is an enthusiastic supporter of Professor Freud."

"I interviewed him yesterday."

"And . . . ?"

"I thought him rather odd."

"He's a psychiatrist."

"Indeed." Rheinhardt smiled. "However, I believe his peculiarity exceeded my usual expectations even for a member of your esteemed profession."

"Interesting . . . ," said Liebermann, turning his brandy glass and examining the patterns of light thus created.

"What is?"

"Kusevitsky knows a great deal about Jewish mythology, and he is currently conducting research into universal symbolism in dreams." Rheinhardt looked bemused. "That is to say, symbols that have the same meaning from person to person. They are thought to be residues of collective human experience that pass from one generation to the next via an inherited region of the unconscious. Universal symbols are also thought to appear in folktales. It follows that different races may have different common symbols."

"Now," said Rheinhardt. "That is interesting."

Liebermann remembered Asher Kusevitsky's words: *They want a purge. They treat us like a plague.* . . .

"His brother, Asher Kusevitsky, is a playwright. He was with Gabriel when we met in the Café Central. They were both sitting at Arthur Schnitzler's table. Asher was talking to Schnitzler about his latest play. I formed an impression that Asher is as preoccupied with myths and legends as is Gabriel. He has written a play called *The Dybbuk*, which I believe is an evil spirit in Jewish folklore."

"When we last spoke, you mentioned a medical condition—folie à deux. You described it as contagious insanity. You said that it typically affects two people."

"Indeed, and it is observed most frequently in couples who are related: spouses, for example—or siblings." Rheinhardt raised his eyebrows. "However," Liebermann added, "I must urge caution. We are getting carried away with ourselves. Surely you *must* have noticed Gabriel Kusevitsky's physique. His brother is just the same. Did you shake Gabriel's hand?"

"No."

"He is a weakling. I was worried that I might snap his fingers."

Rheinhardt stubbed out his cigar. "Still, there is something to discover here, perhaps—something worth pursuing. We need to know more about these brothers." The inspector poured himself a brandy. He raised the glass to his lips and signaled his approval. "So—Barash. What did he have to say this time?"

"He told me, in his cryptic way, that I am about to die."

Rheinhardt coughed and spluttered. "What?"

"Another prophecy, I fear," said Liebermann calmly. "He was right about Brother Stanislav, of course. I can only hope that he is wrong about me. I must admit that since our interview I cannot walk down an alley without first glancing over my shoulder."

Liebermann stood by the window, looking out into the night, his breath producing a silver-gray condensate on the cold glass.

The remainder of the evening had been taken up with discussion about his interview with Barash and the zaddik's slip of the tongue. Barash had inadvertently claimed to have the power to make a golem. Could it be interpreted as a kind of confession? Or was it merely a symptom of the man's underlying megalomania? A zaddik, after all, was supposed to communicate with God.

Liebermann had raised many questions and provided too few answers. His conclusions about Barash were equivocal. Before his departure Rheinhardt had asked Liebermann if he wanted protection. The young doctor had declined. He did not want a constable following him everywhere.

In the street below, a peasant cart rolled past, its driver illuminated by a red lantern. The spoked wheels reminded Liebermann of the music that he had played earlier, the repetitive figures that Schubert had employed to represent endless rotation.

The mill wheel, the spinning wheel: turning, turning, turning . . .

Again he found himself thinking about the conversation he had had with Miss Lydgate outside the Karlskirche: gear mechanisms, screws, helical threads.

He went to bed and fell into a fitful, disturbed sleep.

In the morning, Liebermann unlocked his bureau and took out his journal. He would take it with him to the hospital. He needed to work through some of his thoughts.

69

Professor Priel was already seated in the parlor when Anna Katzer entered. She was wearing purple because she suspected that this was to be no ordinary social call. The professor's note had promised *some news pertaining to the matter raised—on your behalf—by the Kusevitsky brothers*. The "matter" that he had alluded to could only be the women's refuge in Leopoldstadt.

The Kusevitskys had introduced Anna Katzer and Olga Mandl to Priel after a theatrical event, and the two women had spoken to him at some length about their plans. He had been very attentive and had asked a number of questions.

Anna's heart was beating fast with excitement. She wished that Olga Mandl were there, but her friend had been unable to come. She was languishing in bed with a very bad cold.

The professor stood to greet her. He was taller than Anna recollected, and spry, with unusually bright eyes.

"Fräulein Katzer!" he declared. "So good to see you again."

Anna offered her hand, and the professor leaned forward, brushing his lips and whiskers against her skin.

"Professor Priel, I am so sorry to have kept you waiting." She was feeling guilty, having taken far too long to decide what she would wear.

"Not at all. I was admiring the landscapes."

"Tea?"

"Thank you. That would be much appreciated."

Anna called the maid and communicated their need for refreshment with a mimetic gesture, a barely noticeable tilt of the wrist.

The professor waited for Anna to sit. Then, adjusting his frock coat, he lowered himself onto the sofa.

"Well, Fräulein Katzer, I have some good news for you. I have spoken to Herr Rothenstein about your plans for the new refuge, and he was extremely impressed." Anna produced a radiant smile and clasped her hands together. "I mentioned Hallgarten's promise of five thousand kronen and suggested to Rothenstein that he might consider donating an equivalent sum; however, Rothenstein declined." Anna's smile died on her face. "He is a generous man," the professor continued. "But also a proud one." He shook his head. "Pride. A human frailty all too common, I am sorry to say, among the captains of commerce and industry."

"But you said you had some good news," Anna sighed.

The professor raised his finger, tacitly requesting her to suspend judgment.

"Herr Rothenstein would not—*could not*—countenance an arrangement that would place him on an equal footing with Hallgarten. He was insistent that he should be named as the principal benefactor. Subsequently, he authorized me to provide you with funds, payable to the Jewish Women's Refuge Trust, of fifteen thousand kronen." Anna's mouth fell open. "Congratulations, Fräulein Katzer. A very deserving cause. I wish you and Fräulein Mandl every success in your enterprise."

Anna was speechless for a few moments before she laughed out loud. "Thank you, Herr Professor. I don't know what to say. Thank you so much."

"Oh, you don't have to thank me," said Priel. "After all, it isn't my money."

"However, it was you, *dear* professor, who brought our project to Herr Rothenstein's attention."

"Yes," said Priel, extending the syllable and allowing its pitch to fall and rise. "But only because of the Kusevitsky brothers. If it wasn't for them . . ." He finished his sentence with a shrug, as if divesting himself of any last vestige of responsibility for having obtained the donation.

The maid arrived with a tray full of tea things and a plate of vanilla biscuits. Anna was too excited to drink tea. In fact, her tea, untouched, went cold as she spoke with compelling sincerity about her intention to make the Leopoldstadt refuge a model institution.

Priel had heard unfavorable reports about Anna and her friend Olga Mandl, how they were superficial, flighty, and more interested in flirting with industrialists than they were in social policy. But it was now clear to the professor that he was in the presence of a genuinely good woman. The smears had obviously been motivated by jealousy, the casual spite that older women reserve for their younger, and more attractive, counterparts. Anna Katzer was not a striking beauty, but there was nevertheless something about the set of her small, delicate features, the overall composition of her face, that was undeniably very pleasing to look at. And the cut of her dress—or was it the striking purple?—suggested more than just a penchant for luxury. It promised sensuality.

The professor was much relieved. She would make an excellent wife for Gabriel Kusevitsky, and her father's dowry would be very substantial. He imagined the young doctor ensconced in a smart Alsergrund apartment, receiving private patients.

Yes, he thought. *A very satisfactory outcome.*

In due course, their exchanges became less mannered. They spoke of mutual acquaintances and, inevitably, of the Kusevitsky brothers. Professor Priel praised the two young men, and Anna detected in his eulogy a warmth of feeling more typical of a parent. She found herself echoing the professor's sentiments. Indeed, she had to stop herself when her enumeration of Gabriel's many virtues threatened to expose the strength of her attachment. But the abrupt caesura and her subsequent embarrassment had already revealed more than she had intended.

"You are fond of Gabriel," said the professor, a faint smile of encouragement playing around his lips.

"Yes, very fond," Anna replied. Her commitment to egalitarian values was evident in her level gaze. She would not betray her sex by showing shame. Her needs were as natural and acceptable as any man's.

"They are remarkable fellows, the Kusevitsky brothers," said the professor. "More remarkable than most people who make their acquaintance ever realize. Has Gabriel spoken to you of his origins, where they come from?"

"He told me that his parents died when he was very young and that he and his brother were raised by an uncle in Vienna."

The professor squeezed his lower lip.

"That is true," he said. "But it is not—as it were—the whole truth. We cannot judge Gabriel unkindly if he has elected to remain silent. His reticence merely reinforces his claim on our high regard. He and his brother are strangers to self-pity. I have never known them to seek sympathy. Yet I am convinced that it is in the interests of those who have suffered to be surrounded by intimates who have at least some inkling of the trials that they have survived." The professor crossed his long legs. "I am not breaking a confidence, you understand? The Kusevitskys have never sworn me to secrecy."

"Trials?" Anna repeated.

"The Kusevitskys," Professor Priel continued, "were born in the eastern Ukraine. Their father was accused of stealing. It was a false accusation, and the inhabitants of the nearest village took the law into their own hands, a common occurrence in those times. A Jewish family could not go to the authorities for help. It was after the Czar had been assassinated, and Jews were being blamed for everything.

The situation worsened, threats were made, and the boys were told to flee to their uncle's house. It was November, and their uncle lived some twenty-five miles away. Can you imagine what it must have been like for them? The freezing cold? The darkness? Two frightened children, running for their lives? Gabriel was five, Asher six. And there were evil forces abroad. Cossacks." Priel shook his head. "One shudders to think of what might have happened, what sport their discovery would have afforded those wicked barbarians. The boys must have been protected by angels, because somehow—it is little short of a miracle—they managed to cross the frozen steppe and reach their destination."

The professor paused. The room had become unnaturally quiet.

"Asher was carrying a note. The boys' parents had expected to die. They begged the uncle to abandon his home and escape with their children to the relative safety of Austria-Hungary. He was a simple, hardworking man—but wily. He knew what lawlessness meant for the Jews. They set off immediately."

Professor Priel leaned back and stroked his beard.

"In due course, they settled in Leopoldstadt and the boys were educated at a humble *bürgerschule*; however, Asher and Gabriel were conspicuously intelligent. A kindly teacher advised the uncle to apply for two charity places at the gymnasium, funded by Rothenstein. I had some modest involvement with the scheme and subsequently made their acquaintance."

"Is their uncle still alive?"

"He died three years ago. Scarlet fever."

"How sad."

"Yes. But he lived long enough to see his nephews become students at the university. He died contented, his labors thus rewarded."

"An extraordinary story," said Anna. "I had no idea. And how terrible that they should have suffered so."

"Indeed. Still, I am of the opinion that some good has come from their tribulations. They have a rare bond, a degree of closeness that I have observed otherwise only in identical twins. Perhaps I am being fanciful, but I believe that this special bond was forged on their miraculous journey. It drew them together. Sometimes they seem to be party to the same thoughts and feelings. Have you noticed how they complete each other's sentences? Or answer a question simultaneously with the very same words? And although they have different specialisms, I cannot rid myself of a curious impression that they are like the scientific and artistic faculties of a single mind."

Anna detected a certain uneasiness in Priel's expression.

"Professor," she ventured hesitantly, "why are you telling me these things?"

He made an appeasing gesture.

"I wanted to give you some advice, which I trust you will accept in good faith. I promise you it is well-intentioned, and it is this: never come between them. Never come between these two brothers. In a way, if you choose to marry Gabriel, you also marry Asher." The professor's expression suddenly lightened. "This friend of yours, Fräulein Olga. She's met Asher, hasn't she?"

Anna's eyes widened.

"Well?" asked the professor. "Did she not like him?"

70

Wheels, gears, pulleys, levers! All have the power to confer mechanical advantage, the factor by which a mechanism multiplies the force put into it. Brunelleschi raised the great dome in Florence with the assistance of an ox—marble and masonry, weighing millions of pounds, lifted hundreds of feet! I wonder whether the golem's strength is attributable to mechanical advantage? With the right apparatus a weakling could tear the head off an elephant! Use of a device is also suggested by the fact that all three decapitations were remarkably uniform: clockwise cranial rotation, matching displacements of cervical structures. An identical force, utilized in exactly the same way, is likely to produce the same results. Would a golem—or a group of human beings attempting to perform a golem's task—produce such consistent results?

Stanislav, Faust, Sachs. Three men, each in his own way a threat to Viennese Jewry, are murdered. Their bodies are found near plague columns. In the case of the first two murders, the plague column embodies the prejudice of the victims (Jews are a plague). In the case of the third murder, the plague column fulfills a somewhat different cautionary purpose. It declares that those who would exploit and harm their own people are vermin.

All three men are decapitated, but in such a way as to suggest the exercise of great force (an illusion probably achieved through the use of a mechanical instrument). Mud distributed around the bodies, and the kabbalist's lair discovered above the Alois Gasse Temple, are clearly intended to revive memories of the Prague golem. But to what end? Why must we believe that Stanislav, Faust, and Sachs were killed by a "fairy-tale" creature? Answer: to make Jews—or their enemies (even consanguineous enemies)—believe in the return of a supernatural retributive agency. But again, why? Answer: to deter anti-Semites from violence. No. There is <u>more</u> to it than that. Much more. Schiller once wrote that deeper meanings can be found in fairy tales than in all the lessons we learn from real life. Fairy tales contain knowledge and lessons distilled from many lives.

I suspect that the <u>key</u> to this mystery is to be found in the fundamental meaning of the golem legend, its essence. What, then, does it teach us? What lies at its heart? Empowerment! *Empowerment!* It is a tale about empowerment. By "enacting" the golem legend, the perpetrators remind us of the need of a beleaguered community to defend itself and of Rabbi Loew's triumph. They are making an appeal, the potency of which might be multiplied tenfold if theories of a collective racial memory have any legitimacy. Their macabre theatricality is less a warning and more a call to arms. And if that is their intention—to radicalize Jewry—then they *must* be stopped. Vienna is already too divided. Rheinhardt should continue to monitor the Hasidim closely. But he should also cast his net wider. Jewish political societies, dueling fraternities such as Kadimah—even B'nai B'rith.

I am reminded of something I overheard Kusevitsky's brother saying in the Café Central. He was referring to

71

THERE WAS A KNOCK on the door. Liebermann stopped writing, closed his journal, and placed it in his desk drawer.

"Come in," he called out.

The door opened slowly, and a gentleman stepped into his office. He was carrying a homburg hat in his hand and wearing a long frock coat. Liebermann recognized him—bald head, long beard, pince-nez—a professor of philosophy whom he often saw around the university. He had also seen him somewhere else, but he couldn't quite remember where.

"Herr Dr. Liebermann?"

"Yes."

"My name is Priel. Professor Josef Priel. Do you have a moment? There is a matter I wish to discuss with you."

"Concerning?"

"Concerning the death of the young Baron von Kortig."

Liebermann assumed that the professor had some involvement with the hospital committee and offered him a chair. Priel bowed and sat down, crossing his long legs.

"I was informed by an associate of yours, Dr. Gabriel Kusevitsky—and his brother, the dramatist, Asher Kusevitsky—that your future here at the hospital is now uncertain on account of your conduct at the time of the young baron's demise. But it is obvious to any right-thinking person that you acted in the best interests of your patient. Therefore one can only suppose that your present predicament owes much to the mischievous interference of politically motivated parties."

"Indeed," said Liebermann. "That is almost certainly so."

"The Kusevitskys mentioned a dossier . . . sent to an investigator at the security office?"

"Yes, by a member of parliament. It contained letters from the old baron, an unfavorable statement by a witness—an aspirant named Edlinger—and the draft of a scurrilous article."

"Extraordinary."

"If it had not been for the intervention of a friend, I might have been made the subject of an official inquiry."

"And charged with religious agitation, no doubt."

"That might have been the outcome, yes."

"A very worrying development," said Priel, tutting. "Very worrying. I understand that you are to appear before a hospital committee soon."

"That is correct."

"And a final decision will be made about your future."

"Yes. Unfortunately, the chancellor is not very optimistic about my prospects."

"The chancellor. Would that be Professor Gandler?"

"Yes."

Priel hummed. When the sonic possibilities of the note had been thoroughly explored, he said, "Gandler will be more concerned about pleasing patrons than about your welfare. He has friends in the town hall, you know."

Liebermann sighed. "I didn't realize."

"And if you are dismissed, what are your plans?"

"It will be difficult for me to get another position here in Vienna."

"There are other hospitals—private establishments—that would not be unsympathetic; the hospital where Gabriel Kusevitsky works, for example."

"I do not know the medical director," said Liebermann meekly. He had not troubled to socialize advantageously, and now he regretted it. His only professorial acquaintance was Freud, a man who possessed little influence outside his own small circle of devotees.

"Introductions could be made," said Priel, disregarding Liebermann's reservation. "However, if your appointment at another institution was arranged, it would solve *your* problem, but it wouldn't solve *the* problem." Priel altered the position of his head, and his pince-nez flashed as they caught the light. "If you are dismissed, and the decision of the committee is not challenged, it will set something of a precedent—don't you see?—a dangerous precedent in these difficult times."

"Challenged?" Liebermann repeated. Not quite sure what the professor was proposing.

"This scandalous affair was never really about your ability to practice medicine. My dear fellow, there is more at stake here than your position." The professor was beginning to sound a little like the chancellor. "We have a *collective* responsibility . . ."

The rest of Priel's sentence was drowned out by a frantic banging on Liebermann's door.

"Yes, please come in." Liebermann called out over the noise.

A nurse appeared. Her face was flushed and she had clearly been running.

"Herr Doctor—Herr Poppmeier . . ."

"Yes? What about him?"

"You must come—immediately."

"Why?" Liebermann's first thought was that his patient might have—quite unexpectedly—attempted suicide. "What's happened?"

"Something unbelievable." The nurse glanced warily at Professor Priel and then back at Liebermann. "Please hurry."

"Has he tried to harm himself?"

"No. He's gone . . ." She raised her hands and stamped her feet. "He's gone into labor!"

"But that's ridiculous!"

"Forgive me, Herr Doctor, but I must insist that you come this instant. Herr Poppmeier *is* having a baby. He really is."

Liebermann stood up.

"I am sorry, Herr Professor, but I must attend to one of my patients who—if I have understood Nurse Stangassinger correctly—is about to transcend the biological limitations of his sex."

The professor smiled, wrinkles fanning out from his eyes.

"I am happy to wait. Not only am I anxious to finish our conversation, but I am now equally anxious to hear the outcome of Herr Poppmeier's miraculous confinement."

72

LIEBERMANN FOLLOWED NURSE STANGASSINGER down the corridor and up a broad flight of stairs. They came to a set of rooms set a short distance apart from one of the psychiatric wards. Herr Poppmeier's screams could be heard long before their arrival.

Nurse Stangassinger opened one of the doors, and Liebermann entered. The traveling salesman was lying on a cart. He was wearing a plain white hospital gown, which rose up to accommodate his swollen belly. The roundness and size of the swelling presented a fair imitation of pregnancy. Poppmeier, evidently in considerable pain, was clutching his distended abdomen. He was flanked by two nurses, one of whom was cooling his brow with a damp sponge.

"Dear God," he cried. "What is happening to me?"

His eyes were bulging, and he appeared to be semi-delirious.

"How long has he been like this?" Liebermann asked.

The nurse with the sponge said, "We don't know. He was in the toilet cubicle most of this afternoon."

"Herr Poppmeier," said Liebermann, "when did your stomach start to enlarge?"

"Oh, the pain," said Poppmeier, writhing. "Please do something, Herr Doctor. Operate. Do anything you can. Get it out of me, for mercy's sake!"

Liebermann grabbed Poppmeier's jaw and held his head still.

"Look at me, Herr Poppmeier. When did your stomach start to swell? It is important. Try to remember."

"I had some pains...earlier this afternoon. I thought it might have been something I'd eaten. I shut myself in the water closet, but to no avail. Evacuations did not solve the problem. In fact, the pain got worse." Poppmeier gritted his teeth. "My stomach began to swell and it started to get hard."

Liebermann raised the gown and laid his hand on the lower region of Poppmeier's abdomen. The skin was tight and translucent. He felt movement—not as sharp as a fetal kick, but movement nevertheless. His patient rolled over, groaning.

"Please keep still," Liebermann growled, hauling Herr Poppmeier back into his original position. He covered the man's navel with the palm of his hand and applied some pressure. "Does that hurt?"

"Yes, yes. It's very tender."

"And here?"

"Yes. There too."

"And what about here?"

"Argh!" Poppmeier cried out. "For heaven's sake, man."

"I'm sorry," said Liebermann. Then he found a stethoscope on a nearby cart and rested the diaphragm on Poppmeier's stomach.

Gurgling sounds: a swashing and murmuring—a strange, primordial effervescence.

Liebermann whispered something to Nurse Stangassinger, who subsequently left the room.

"Well?" said Poppmeier. "Is it trying to get out?"

Liebermann shook his head. "Herr Poppmeier, you are not carrying a baby."

"How can you say that? Look at me!"

"You have swallowed a large amount of air and are suffering from severe abdominal distension."

"What are you talking about? I haven't been swallowing air!"

"It can happen without awareness. Unconsciously."

"But I can feel the thing inside me. I can feel it kicking."

"No, Herr Poppmeier, you are mistaken. You can feel the movement of air. Now, it is very important that you relax."

"I can't relax. I'm having a baby!"

Nurse Stangassinger returned, carrying a syringe.

"Now," said Liebermann gently, "please keep very still. I need to give you an injection, something to relieve your pain."

Poppmeier offered his arm, and Liebermann slid the needle beneath his skin.

Almost immediately, Poppmeier stopped writhing.

"Ahh . . . that's better," he said. "Thank you, Herr Doctor."

"It will make you sleep."

Poppmeier's eyelids began to flutter. But before slipping into oblivion, he belched loudly and whispered, "I do beg your pardon."

Liebermann handed the syringe back to Nurse Stangassinger.

"Keep the patient in here. The swelling will subside in due course."

Nurse Stangassinger's cheeks reddened, a sprinkling of vivid paprika.

"I'm sorry, Herr Doctor. I shouldn't have—"

Liebermann silenced her with a wave of his hand. "Please. There is no need to apologize."

"Herr Doctor?"

Liebermann turned. Another nurse was looking through the half-open door.

"Yes?"

"Frau Poppmeier arrived a few minutes ago. We asked her to wait in the next room. She is quite anxious. Could you speak to her?"

Liebermann sighed. He thanked the nurses for their assistance, bowed, and made his exit.

Arabelle Poppmeier was standing by the window, biting her nails.

"Ah, Herr Dr. Liebermann. Is something wrong?" She came forward a few steps. "The nurses looked worried, and I heard shouting. It sounded like Ivo. Is he all right?"

"There is no cause for concern, I promise you. Your husband is well—and sleeping. Please, do sit down."

Liebermann offered her a chair.

"Why was he shouting? It *was* him, wasn't it?"

"Yes. He was in pain because of abdominal distension probably caused by the swallowing of air. He convinced himself that he was going into labor. Needless to say, he became very distressed and I had to sedate him with chloral hydrate."

"Oh, dear God," said Frau Poppmeier, dabbing at her eyes with a handkerchief. "He has gone quite mad. What am I to do?"

"He has not gone mad," Liebermann said calmly. "He is suffering from an excess of sympathy—for you. Thus, he is attempting to share the burden of your pregnancy. But this decision was not made consciously. It was made in a region of his mind that is ordinarily inaccessible: the unconscious. The unconscious is very resourceful and can communicate symbolically through the body. It creates symptoms, which have meaning—in your husband's case, symptoms that express solidarity with your condition."

"Was this . . ." Frau Poppmeier hesitated. "Was this *attack* caused by Ivo's unconscious?"

"Very probably. It is seeking to reproduce the signs of pregnancy. Subtle changes of respiration might have sufficed to cause the swelling and pain that your husband mistook to be the onset of labor."

"But why is this happening to him? Other men are *sympathetic*— very sympathetic—but they don't become pregnant!"

Her eyes glittered with frustration and anger.

"I don't know why, as yet," Liebermann replied. "But when I do find out, I am confident that he will be cured."

Frau Poppmeier stuffed her handkerchief into her coat pocket.

"May I see him?"

"He won't awaken for another hour or so. And when he does, I'm afraid he won't be very communicative. It might be better for you to go home. He will be in better spirits tomorrow morning."

Frau Poppmeier nodded. Liebermann offered his arm and helped her to stand. She walked to the door.

"Frau Poppmeier, before you leave . . . I am sorry, but I must ask you an indelicate question. It concerns the stillbirth . . . last year."

Frau Poppmeier rested her fingers on the door handle, but she did not turn it.

"When you went into labor," Liebermann continued, "your husband was away from home. Can you remember where?"

"Linz," she replied.

"Linz. You're quite sure it was Linz, and not Steyr?"

"Quite sure."

"Thank you, Frau Poppmeier."

The woman looked at Liebermann quizzically.

"Thank you, Frau Poppmeier," Liebermann repeated, not wishing to explain himself. "We will see you tomorrow morning, I hope."

Liebermann discovered Professor Priel still waiting in his office. He was studying a clothbound book that he had evidently been carrying in his coat pocket. He was holding a stubby pencil in his hand and writing comments in the margin.

"Professor Priel, I am so very sorry."

The professor looked up and smiled. "Sorry? Why sorry?"

"For keeping you so long."

The professor laughed.

"Have you been long? I hadn't noticed. I've been rather absorbed by this little critique here of Ernst Mach's positivist philosophy." He scribbled down some final thoughts and closed the book. "So, did your patient defy the immutable laws of biology and science?"

"No. His symptoms—although dramatic—were nothing more than hysteriform phenomena."

"What a shame. I had hoped that Nurse Stangassinger's excitement presaged a more interesting report. Now, where were we?"

"Collective responsibility?"

"Indeed. However, before returning to that very important topic, may I ask you a few questions concerning the pending hospital committee meeting, and in particular the evidence against you?"

"If you wish."

"Have you seen the aspirant's . . . What was his name?"

"Edlinger."

"Have you seen Edlinger's statement?"

"No."

"Do you know what Edlinger alleges?"

"I believe he alleged that I used force to stop the priest from seeing the young Baron von Kortig."

"And did you?"

"Of course not. I put my hand across a doorway. If Father Benedikt had come forward, I would have let him through. I had no intention of wrestling a priest to the ground! I have a duty to my patients, but there are limits to what even I am prepared to do for them."

"Have you seen Edlinger since that evening?"

"No. He was transferred to another department shortly afterward."

"Were there any other witnesses?"

"A nurse."

"Could she be called upon to give a more truthful account?"

"It was she who called the priest in the first place."

"Ahh . . . I see," said the professor. After a lengthy pause, he took out his pocket watch, and his expression showed surprise.

"Forgive me, Herr Doctor. I must be brief." He dropped the watch into his fob pocket. "You are without doubt being exploited by individuals with political objectives. If you are dismissed and the hospital committee is not challenged, others will suffer in due course. My brother-in-law is a very powerful man: Rothenstein, the banker."

Liebermann suddenly remembered where else he had seen Priel. Not only strolling around the university, but also talking to the wealthy banker at his father's lodge.

"Rothenstein is a very charitable man," Priel continued. "He is always keen to support good causes. If you require funds to mount a legal challenge, they will be made available to you. Similarly, if you require legal advice, Herr Rothenstein will ensure that the very best lawyers are at your disposal. Moreover, we can introduce you to journalists who would be willing to promote your cause in the liberal press, should the need arise. Mayor Lueger is not the only one who appreciates the importance of newspapers! I trust you will give Herr Rothenstein's offer very serious consideration. I can be contacted at the university." The professor inclined his head. "Good day, Herr Doctor."

Before Liebermann had the chance to say thank you, the professor had gone.

73

Mordecai ben Judah Levi and Barash were seated opposite each other. The scholar, who had previously spoken out confidently, demonstrating his extensive knowledge of kabbalistic arcana, was now less sure of himself. Barash's Spartan parlor, with its various dun and indefinite shades, had absorbed Levi's charisma. He was curiously diminished, and Barash correspondingly enlarged.

Introductory remarks had been superseded by a lengthy silence, which, although discomforting for Levi, did not trouble Barash. He tolerated the hiatus with the infinite patience of a statue. Levi shifted in his seat, coughed into his hand, and ventured a question. "You said he would reveal himself. And the following week: Alois Gasse. How did you know?"

"It was inevitable," said Barash.

Another silence.

"What transpired at the Ulrichskirche . . . ," Levi began again. "It was most unexpected."

"Indeed," Barash replied. "At first, I did not believe such a thing possible. But we live in interesting times, and the victim was, I am informed, a wicked man—a procurer." Barash linked his fingers. "Let us suppose, then, that Jeheil Sachs met his end staring into the eyes of the kabbalist's creation. What can this mean? Just one thing, surely, a signal—and a clear one at that: we must be united, or a great tragedy will befall us."

Levi massaged his forehead. A feeling of pressure had begun to build up behind his eyes accompanied by a dull, aching pulse.

"Unity . . ." Levi's voice faltered. "Unity, so that we are strong?"

"If *he* calls, my people will be ready. I hope that yours too will be sufficiently prepared."

There were voices outside in the street. Shouting, good-humored banter. It sounded distant, almost from another world.

Levi said, "I heard that one of your students, the young shop-keeper who lives with his sick father—"

"The spirit of Prague," Barash interrupted, "has returned to us. Our enemies will not find us so compliant now, so willing to submit."

"Do you approve of what the boy did?"

"We must protect our interests."

"I agree, but I am not convinced that violence is the answer."

"Then why did Rabbi Loew make his golem? An eye for an eye!"

Barash stood up angrily and went to the sideboard. He opened a door and removed a scroll. Returning to his chair, he unrolled the thick parchment paper and laid the exposed page down on the floor. Levi leaned forward to examine it.

The page was a cosmological chart consisting of circles, constella-tions, and planetary symbols. In various places the letters of Hebrew phrases—quotes from religious works—had been converted into numbers. These products were then absorbed into what appeared to be an ongoing calculation, the overall structure of which resembled an inverted pyramid. The pinnacle was blunt and consisted of four digits executed in bright red ink: 1903.

"This year," said Levi. "According to the Gregorian calendar."

"Yes," said Barash. "A new cycle—a new age."

Levi pulled at his beard.

"With respect: a new age, yes. But are you sure that it will favor us, and not our enemies?"

Barash did not distinguish the question with a reply. As far as he was concerned, his gematria was faultless.

74

"Was it absolutely necessary to tell him about me?"

Gabriel Kusevitsky got up and paced around the room. He was extremely agitated.

Stopping abruptly, he turned to address Anna. "I had nothing to do with that dreadful man Sachs."

"The inspector only asked you a few questions."

"Anna, I don't think you understand. I can't have the police arriving at the hospital asking questions! How do you think that looks? Professor Kraus was furious. He was convinced I'd been up to no good."

"Then Professor Kraus must be a rather silly man."

"Professor Kraus is many things, Anna, but *silly* is not one of them."

"Gabriel, what was I supposed to do? Lie?"

"You didn't have to lie. But you could have been a little more thoughtful, a little more circumspect. You didn't have to tell the inspector *everything*."

Anna looked bemused.

"Inspector Rheinhardt asked me who I had spoken to about Sachs. I told him my parents, and you. I am sorry that the inspector's arrival at the hospital caused you some embarrassment. But you seem to forget that Jeheil Sachs was murdered. This is a serious matter."

"Exactly," said Kusevitsky. "And I have been implicated!"

Anna shook her head. "Gabriel, that is an absurd thing to say."

More exchanges followed, and their differences of opinion gradually became entrenched.

A silence ensued that possessed the lethal frigidity of a vacuum: the singular deadness that pervades a room after lovers have quarreled. Anna looked up, and her gaze met Gabriel's; however, there was no softening of his expression, no sign of the expected reconciliatory half smile. In fact, the cast of his face suggested the very opposite. He was not so much looking at her as *studying* her. He had interposed a "professional" distance, and the narrowness of his stare suggested calculation.

"Anna," he said coldly, "perhaps we have made a mistake."

"What do you mean, a mistake?"

"We are both young, and I fear we may have been premature, impulsive"—Gabriel hesitated before adding clumsily—"in our relations." He then nodded as if agreeing with a concordant response that she had not given. "I must admit, my work has suffered. And I must suppose that you too have neglected your causes."

His statement seemed to repel Anna, physically. She rocked backward before slowly recovering her original position. Even though Professor Priel's injunction to respect the Kusevitskys' fraternal bond was sounding in her head—indeed, perhaps because of it—she found herself saying, "This has something to do with your brother, doesn't it? He has never liked me."

Gabriel was about to protest. He raised his arm energetically, but then allowed it to drop. "We have much to do. Not for ourselves, but for the good of *our* people." Anna was unsure whether he was referring to himself and his brother or to himself and her. "It was wrong of me to pursue your affection," Gabriel continued. "The time is not right. I am sorry, Anna. Please forgive me."

"Am I to understand that you wish to end our . . ."—she was suddenly lost for words, and ended the sentence with a sterile noun—"association"?

The young doctor nodded.

Anna was not accustomed to being dismissed in such a peremptory fashion. All her other suitors had been rejected by her. The reverse was unthinkable. Her response, therefore, was rage, followed by a show of defensive indifference. "Very well," she said. "If that is how you feel, you'd better go."

"Anna . . ." Gabriel made a few faltering steps toward her.

"Please," she said. "Do not insult me with an apology."

Kusevitsky bowed and walked stiffly to the door.

"Oh, and incidentally," Anna added, "it was I who pursued your affection, not you who pursued mine."

Kusevitsky accepted this emasculating barb and left the room. Anna listened for the sound of the apartment door, and then allowed herself to burst into tears.

She ran from the parlor, down the hallway, and into her bedroom. Standing by the window, she concealed herself behind the curtain and watched Gabriel's diminutive figure cross the road below. Something caught in her chest, a more pitiful emotion that made itself known through the maelstrom of anger. She noticed something: a man—who must have been standing in a doorway—emerging and walking after Gabriel. It looked as though he had been waiting for the young doctor to come out. Her thoughts were interrupted by a timid knock on the door.

"Fräulein Anna?" It was the maid. "Fräulein Anna? Are you all right?"

"It's for the best," said Asher Kusevitsky, handing his brother the bottle of schnapps. "You did the right thing."

Gabriel took a swig and wiped his lips on his sleeve. His purple necktie was loose. He pulled it off, examined it for a moment, and then tossed it aside.

"We cannot . . . *must* not be distracted," said Asher

"Yes," said Gabriel. "Of course." After a pause, he added, "I dreamed of Mother and Father last night."

"Did you?" said Asher. "How strange. So did I. The old house?"

"Yes."

"*They* came for them . . . carrying torches . . . and I watched the house burn. Mother called out to me." Gabriel bit his lower lip. " '*Leave*,' she said. '*Run.* '"

"It was the same for me too."

"What? She mentioned Vienna?"

Asher shook his head. "No."

"I heard her quite distinctly. She said, 'Run, run. . . . Leave Vienna.' "

The playwright stood up and extended his hand. Gabriel grabbed it and pulled himself up. "We're not going anywhere," said Asher. "No more running   ever again. We have work to do. Work will set you free!" he said, quoting the title of an old novel.

75

AFTER A MEAL AT the little café by the Anatomical Institute—
two fat bratwurst, a pile of sauerkraut, and a dollop of mustard—
Liebermann returned to his room at the hospital. He reviewed his
case notes and then tried to distract himself by reading; however, he
found that he was unable to concentrate. That afternoon he had received two letters. The first was from the chancellor's secretary, requesting his attendance at the next hospital committee meeting, and
the second was from the aspirant, Edlinger:

> WHAT I DID WAS WRONG. MEET ME BY THE NARRENTURM TONIGHT
> AT TEN-THIRTY. WE <u>MUST</u> SPEAK. THERE IS SOMETHING YOU SHOULD
> KNOW.

It read more like a plea for help than a repentant man's promise of
restitution. The inclusion of Edlinger's statement in the dossier sent
to the security office indicated that he had probably been courted by
Christian Social activists; however, he was young—rash—and might
have regretted his decision to become involved in the von Kortig affair. Perhaps his political masters were making demands that he was
now less willing to go along with? Or perhaps they had revealed the
true scope of their ambition, and Edlinger was having scruples?
Edlinger was a hotheaded young man with a reputation for dueling.
Nevertheless, it was rumored that he rarely drew his sword to defend
an ideal. It was almost always because of a lady.

At first Liebermann was disinclined to meet with Edlinger. If the aspirant had gotten himself into trouble, that was *his* problem. He could always relieve his guilty conscience by confessing to a priest! Moreover, Liebermann did not believe that Edlinger could tell him anything that he hadn't already guessed. Yet, as the day progressed, curiosity got the better of him.

At ten-fifteen he placed his journal and the two letters in his bag. He locked his desk, extinguished the gaslight, and left his room.

The General Hospital was not a single building but a group of interconnected structures, with a hinterland of clinics and university institutes to the north. Liebermann made his way through a complex maze of corridors that eventually took him out into an open space surrounded by various outhouses and a high stucco façade.

The night was cold. Overhead, slow-moving clouds were limned with the silver valance of a hidden moon.

Liebermann's breath condensed on the air, and through the dissolving haze he saw the Narrenturm—the fools' tower. Five stories high, its hooplike structure resembled a *guglhupf* cake (a correspondence that had provided students with a serviceable sobriquet for well over a hundred years). Its curved, dilapidated brick wall was featureless except for a uniform girdle of equidistant slit windows. The absence of any ornament suggested penal austerity—incarceration and hard labor. Yet the Narrenturm had once been the most important psychiatric hospital in the world, attracting not only distinguished doctors but also interested members of the public. Its unique design permitted visitors to circumambulate its corridors and view the unfortunate inmates in their cells as if they were animals in a zoo.

In spite of its historical importance, the Narrenturm now stood on a neglected plot of scrubby grass that was littered with the detritus of construction work: wooden planks, steel drums, and broken slates. A washing line had been attached to a crumbling pillar, and undergarments floated above the ground like the pale body parts of dismembered ghosts.

Only a few windows on the stucco façade opposite were illuminated, but Liebermann's eyes swiftly adapted to the darkness and he was able to find a way to the Narrenturm with relative ease. He had been standing there for only a few moments when he heard the sound of a restive horse: the jangle of a bridle and the stamping of hooves.

Perhaps Edlinger had already arrived and was waiting on the other side?

Liebermann walked to the back of the building, but could see very little: a clump of trees, more building materials, and the faint outline of additional outhouses. He tried to check the time on his wristwatch, but the meager light was insufficient.

Again—the jangling bridle.

Peering across the open space, Liebermann thought he detected some movement, a piece of the night—even darker than its background—detached and expanding. The moon emerged momentarily from behind its cloud and clarified the world: an old man, wearing a frock coat and a massive beaver hat, was heading toward him. He was making slow progress, stooped over a walking stick, and he carried a substantial book under his other arm.

"Excuse me . . . is that someone there?" The voice was thin, and the effort of speech seemed to make the old man cough.

Liebermann tutted. *This is most irritating.*

He walked out to meet the old fellow. As he approached, he noticed the coiled sideburns of a Hasidic Jew.

"Do you need some help?"

"Yes," said the old man. His breathing was labored, and he spoke with a pronounced Eastern accent. "I need a doctor . . ."

He coughed again and dropped his book to the ground. As he moved to pick it up, Liebermann stopped him.

"Please, allow me."

Liebermann crouched down, sensed a sudden flurry of activity, and remained conscious just long enough to recognize the magnitude of his stupidity. Then everything turned black.

76

Rabbi Seligman shook his head. "Leave us? Why must you leave us?"

Kusiel shifted uncomfortably. "My sister's ill."

"I didn't even know you had a sister."

"Yes, a sister and two brothers."

"Why can't you go back home, attend to her, do whatever's necessary, and then come back? I'm sure we could find someone to help maintain the synagogue in your absence."

"Thank you, Rabbi. That's very kind of you. But she's very ill."

"Couldn't your brothers look after her?"

"They've moved away. She's on her own."

"In which case, why don't you bring her back here? We could look after her. My wife would be only too pleased to—"

"She wouldn't want to come. She's like that, stuck in her ways."

The rabbi shook his head. "But how will you survive?"

"I've saved a little. And I'll get a job."

"In rural Galicia? At your age?"

Kusiel replied with a shrug as if to say, *Maybe. Why not?*

The rabbi looked at the caretaker anxiously. "How much have you saved?"

"Enough."

"Are you sure? Look . . ." The rabbi squeezed his shoulder. "If you need more . . ."

"No," said Kusiel sharply. "I couldn't."

"All right," Seligman continued. "But if you find yourself in difficulties?"

"I'll write," said Kusiel.

"You promise?"

"Yes."

"I'll sleep more soundly knowing that."

The old man smiled sheepishly and lowered his gaze. There was something about his inability to hold Seligman's look that made the gentle rabbi uncharacteristically suspicious.

"Kusiel," he said, hesitantly, "you're not leaving Alois Gasse because of that . . . *business* in the attic room?"

The caretaker sighed. "No, of course not."

The rabbi nodded. "We'll miss you."

At midnight Kusiel was leaning over a bridge, looking into the murk of the Danube Canal. He found the old key in his pocket and dropped it into the water. It didn't make a sound, and he did not see it disappear. When he put his hand back into his pocket, he closed his fingers around a roll of banknotes. It was more money than he had ever before seen in his life.

77

Liebermann opened his eyes, but he could not see clearly. His vision was blurred. Two strips of luminescence were separated by a vertical band of darkness, and everything expanded and contracted with the agonizing throb in his skull. The pain was so intense, so all-consuming, that he could not think. He was no longer a person. He was a mute sensorium, receiving impressions but unable to reflect on them. Then there was nothing.

When he opened his eyes again, he was vaguely aware that time had passed. His vision was still blurred, but the detonations of pain were not so harrowing. He set about assessing his situation.

He could not move his legs.

He could not move his hands.

Liebermann could move his head from side to side, but it made him feel very nauseous. After some preliminary tests of this type he concluded that he was sitting on a chair and that his legs and hands were tied together. But when he rotated his wrists, he could not feel the bite of rough hemp. There was no chafing. Something, it seemed, had been placed between the bindings and his skin: something soft, like muslin. It struck him as odd.

He closed his eyes, rested them for a few seconds, and opened them again.

The vertical band of darkness directly in front of him began to re-solve itself into a more precise form: a human figure—seated, legs crossed. On a workbench behind the figure were two paraffin lamps, one at each extremity. Liebermann strained to see more clearly. Outlines became more defined, and gradually details appeared—the man's hat, coat, beard, and coiled sideburns.

A Hasid . . .

The same person, most probably, who had knocked him out.

"Where is Barash?" said Liebermann. His voice sounded glutinous, each syllable poorly articulated. His tongue felt enlarged, and he could taste blood in his mouth.

"Who?"

"Your rebbe. Where is he?"

The Hasid did not reply. Instead, his hands went to his right ear and he detached the hanging sideburn. He then repeated the action on the left side. Leaning back, he dropped the gray coils onto the workbench and removed his hat. A bald dome caught the light. Liebermann squinted and craned forward. It was Professor Priel.

Liebermann glanced around the room. There were no windows. The only pieces of furniture were the workbench, the two chairs on which they were sitting, and a potbellied stove. Some machines that would not have looked out of place in a factory were freestanding. There were also some sheets of metal, chains, and panels of wood scattered about the floor. Propped up against the wall was something that Liebermann was not very surprised to see, even though it appeared quite incongruous within its surroundings: a barrel organ.

"Yes," said Priel, observing Liebermann closely. "You were correct. Mechanical advantage. Any technical-school student would be able to explain the principle and build a device to demonstrate it."

"The Vienna golem," said Liebermann, his eyes lingering on the lacquered box.

"Indeed."

Portable and inconspicuous. It was an inspired piece of deception.

"So," said Liebermann, "which plague column have you chosen for me? Lichtental? Dornach?"

"No, Herr Doctor," said Priel. "Your body will not be found at the foot of a plague column. Your body will be found—whole—on the shores of the Danube. You are going to commit suicide." On Priel's lap was Liebermann's journal. "She must be a remarkable person, this Englishwoman of yours, Miss Lydgate, your unattainable object of desire. However, anybody reading these lines would conclude, as I did, that your attachment to her has become quite unhealthy: joyless, obsessional, morbid. I cannot open a newspaper these days without reading of yet another young fellow who has exchanged unrequited anguish for oblivion. It appears to be the fashion. Love is everything, and to live without love is not to live at all. I blame Goethe."

The professor removed his pince-nez and cleaned the lenses with a handkerchief.

"I take it that you haven't spoken to Inspector Rheinhardt about your most recent speculations?" He licked his fingertip and turned some pages. "Yesterday's entry in particular." He put his pince-nez back on and stuffed the handkerchief into his frock coat pocket. "I'm afraid you really were getting far too close to the truth, Herr Doctor. Far too close." The professor tore out the page he was reading, crumpled it up, and threw it onto the floor. Then, perusing another section, he added, "I'll make the ink run in a few places. Tears, you see? A little touch to emphasize your deteriorating mental state. What with the von Kortig affair and this pitiful preoccupation with the young Englishwoman . . ." His sentence trailed off. He was thinking aloud rather than addressing his prisoner.

Liebermann understood now why Priel had wrapped his, Liebermann's, wrists in muslin. It was to protect his skin! There would be no marks, no impressions left by the cords to show that he had been tied up! A flare of outrage, bracing and astringent, dissipated his stupor. He felt obliged to do everything in his power to spoil Priel's carefully constructed plan. He was still very weak from concussion, but, summoning what little reserves of strength he possessed, he pulled his hands hard apart and began to rotate his wrists. Perhaps, if he generated enough friction, he could produce a small amount of grazing, sufficient to give Rheinhardt cause for suspicion. It would be difficult to accomplish as, in order to avoid detection, he would have to keep the rest of his body still, and the task would take time. It was essential, therefore, to keep the professor talking.

"Professor Priel?"

The professor looked up from the journal.

"Was I correct in my assumption?"

"What?"

"Were the murders of Brother Stanislav, Councillor Faust, and the procurer Jeheil Sachs intended to revive memories of the Prague golem, your purpose being to provide the Jews of Vienna with a symbol of empowerment?"

Priel nodded, but his expression declared that he was contemplating a more comprehensive answer. After a brief pause, he added, "I also hoped that some—the Hasidim, for example—would take a more literal view of the evidence. I hoped that they would actually believe that a kabbalist of Rabbi Loew's stature had returned to protect them, which, I gather, has indeed transpired. A people need to be strong in their faith to survive. I have made a good start with the Hasidim. I am confident that the wider community will follow."

"I do not consider the promotion of superstition an achievement, Herr Professor."

Priel shook his head. "The irrational is an essential part of human nature. To overlook the irrational is to overlook the greater part of our constitution. I would have thought that you, a psychiatrist conversant with the works of Professor Freud, would appreciate this important point."

"Professor Freud indeed acknowledges the irrational, as the principal cause of psychopathology."

"That may be so, but Professor Freud's objectives are somewhat different from mine."

"True. Where he seeks to heal divisions in the psyche, you seek to open them up in society."

As Liebermann spoke, he found that his wrists were moving more easily. Were the bonds loosening?

Priel set his jaw and drummed his fingers on the journal. Eventually he said, "We are a people under threat, Herr Doctor. And the threat is not merely physical but spiritual. And when I use that word—'spiritual'—I am referring not only to the numinous. I am referring to something broader of which religion is but a part, albeit an important one. I am referring to our sense of who we are, which is preserved in our music, our poetry, our stories, and our dreams. They want to take those things away from us—"

"They?"

"The priests, the Christian Socials, the Pan-Germans, and we are complicit in our demise. We assimilate, convert, and become embarrassed by the appearance of a caftan on the Ringstrasse! They divide us. They weaken us at a time when we must be strong. And unlike you, they respect the power of symbols and the irrational wellsprings of human imagination. They have their crosses, their Norse gods, and rune signs to rally behind, while we are left with nothing. While we forget, they remember. While we ignore our archaic heritage, they are celebrating theirs."

"You talk like a prophet, Herr Professor."

Priel shook his head. "You don't have to be a prophet to foresee what is coming."

"Another term for Mayor Lueger, and things will continue just as they are."

"I don't think so, Herr Doctor. I really don't think so."

The professor's movements suggested he was about to stand.

"How did you know about my journal?" Liebermann asked.

Priel sat back in his chair. "I was bored and looked through your drawers when you were called out of your office. A private journal—unattended. It was simply too tempting."

"You didn't know about it beforehand?"

"How could I have known?"

The bonds were loosening! Liebermann pulled his thumbs in and twisted his hands. The Klammer Method was proving more useful than he had ever imagined.

"Well, someone might have told you."

"Who?"

"Gabriel Kusevitsky."

Priel became impatient and stood up. "And now . . ."

"The kabbalist's lair? Was Rabbi Seligman your accomplice?"

"No."

"Then who?"

"The caretaker."

"How did you persuade him to cooperate?"

"I bribed him."

"Did he understand your purpose?"

"He's a simple man, but intelligent enough not to ask questions."

"But he must have—"

"Please, Herr Doctor!" Priel interrupted, raising a finger to his mouth.

"You have already killed one Jew," said Liebermann. "And now you are about to kill another. Perhaps you should study the golem legend more closely? Isn't it true that, ultimately, the Prague golem could not be controlled, even by Rabbi Loew? Isn't it true that it ran amok, destroying parts of the Prague ghetto? Yes, the golem legend is about empowerment, but it is also about the judicious use of power. It is also about being wary of unleashing forces that we may not be able to contain. It is a metaphor. You have released the irrational—the golem within—with inevitable consequences: You are killing your own people, not protecting them."

The professor ran his hand over his pate. His expression was suddenly shadowed by the presence of doubts.

"I..." He hesitated and started his sentence again. "Men like Sachs... they are evil."

"And what about me? Am I evil too?"

"No, Herr Doctor. You are not evil. Merely..." Priel paused to select an apposite term. "Unfortunate. Please understand, I do not *want* to kill you." The professor shook his head violently. "If there were another way..." His voice sounded strained. "But there *is* no other way. What I must do... it is far too important. I must proceed. Don't you see that?"

"When violence is employed to serve an ideal, it invariably negates that ideal. No truly good cause was ever furthered by the use of violence."

"Enough, Herr Doctor!" the professor snapped. "I will not be lectured by you! Do you think the Jews of the Ukraine would agree with you? Do you think they would approve of your *philosophy*, which is nothing but a hollow luxury! Do you know what's happening out there? Do you? It's started all over again, just like before! The horror! The carnage! Villages burned to the ground! Cossack atrocities that beggar belief: cats sown into the bellies of pregnant women!"

"And as before, the Jews will flee—and find safety, here in Vienna!"

"In Mayor Lueger's Vienna?" Priel sneered. "Where Schneider can propose that a special police force supervise the Jews at Easter to prevent ritual murders? Where funds are made available to distribute anti-Semitic literature in elementary schools? And where a Jewish doctor cannot care for a dying patient without being accused of religious agitation!"

Priel tossed Liebermann's journal onto the workbench and opened a drawer. He took out a bottle and a large sponge. As soon as he had removed the glass stopper from the bottle, the room filled with the distinctive sweet smell of chloroform. Liebermann pulled his thumbs in tighter.

Almost, almost . . .

Priel poured some chloroform onto the sponge and turned to Liebermann.

"I am sorry, Herr Doctor." His anger had dissipated, and he appeared to be genuinely saddened by the task he was about to perform. "But I must do this. I really must. Please do not struggle. As you know, the chloroform will be much more effective if you take deep breaths, and I promise to administer the chloroform again, before . . ." He sighed. "Before we reach our destination. Do not be fearful. You will feel no pain or discomfort. I will make every effort to ensure that you do not regain consciousness."

The professor reached out and placed the sponge over Liebermann's nose and mouth. Liebermann complied, taking a deep breath. Chloroform, administered in this fashion, could take up to thirty minutes to produce narcosis. He calculated that he could afford to feign acquiescence.

"Good," said the professor. "Good. Close your eyes, eh? It will be better . . . easier."

Liebermann spoke sotto voce into the sponge. The muffled sound was incomprehensible.

"What?" Again, Liebermann mumbled a string of unstressed syllables, and the professor drew closer. "What did you say?"

Priel put down the bottle and removed the sponge.

Liebermann's hands slipped from the bindings. The muslin dropped to the floor. Professor Priel's eyes widened quizzically.

A heartbeat—time suspended—and a curious magnification of otherwise insignificant details: the pores on Professor Priel's nose, the metal on his breath.

Liebermann swung his arms forward like a man diving. His hands met behind Priel's head. Gripping the length of rope tightly, Liebermann pulled it around Professor Priel's neck, crossing the ends to create a noose. Instinctively, the professor tried to free himself. He struggled to insinuate his fingers between the constricting hemp and his throat. Liebermann responded by tugging harder. The professor began to emit guttural choking sounds, and his complexion darkened. He pulled back, dragging Liebermann's chair with him. The young doctor maintained his grip, but the chair toppled over, dragging Professor Priel down with it. They faced each other, lying side by side on the floor. Priel's eyes were bulging, and his face was distorted. He began to thrash around, and Liebermann, already weakened by concussion and chloroform, felt his fingers slipping.

I have to hold on.

Priel clawed at Liebermann's face. His nails found flesh, and Liebermann felt searing pain as his cheek was stripped of skin. The professor's fingers, crooked into bony talons, then sought out Liebermann's eyes. The young doctor jerked back and pulled harder. It was an extraordinary effort, and it made Priel repeat his original bid for survival. Once again, the professor tried to get his fingers beneath the rope, tried to pry it away from his throat—and once again he did not succeed. Desperate, Professor Priel pushed the heel of his palm against Liebermann's chin and landed an ineffectual blow on Liebermann's thigh.

The young doctor held fast.

More punches. A weak kick . . .

As before, Liebermann experienced a curious illusion of suspended time, accompanied by the heightened perception of detail. He became acutely aware of Priel's eyes. The fear had gone, and in its place something much more difficult to define had appeared: an eloquent sorrow—disappointment? It might even have been pity. The professor's eyelids descended, and the flow of time resumed. His body went limp.

Suspecting a ruse, Liebermann did not let go of the rope. But Priel's final tacit communication had been peculiarly poignant, and Liebermann let the cord become slack. Immediately, Professor Priel began to cough. He rolled over onto his back, groaning and gasping for air.

Liebermann untied his feet and crawled to the workbench. He picked up the bottle of chloroform and knelt next to the professor. He checked the man's pulse and waited for his breathing to become regular. Then he soaked the sponge and pressed it against Priel's face. Liebermann stayed in that position, occasionally pouring more chloroform onto the sponge, until he was satisfied that the professor was unconscious. Then he stood up, righted the chair, and sat down. The fumes had made him feel light-headed, and he reached out to touch the workbench. The solidity of the wood made him feel a little better.

In due course he rose again and crossed to the barrel organ. He opened the doors and examined the interior. No bellows, no pipes—but two leather-covered discs and an array of cogwheels, pulleys, and chains. The discs were parallel and set apart but could be brought closer together, like the plates of a vise. Liebermann turned the crank handle, and the discs began to rotate. In his mind, he could hear Schubert's mesmeric semiquavers, the ghost of Rheinhardt's mellifluous baritone entering at the end of the second bar:

> My peace is gone,
> My heart is heavy;
> I shall never
> Ever find peace again.

The door was locked, and Liebermann had to search through the unconscious professor's pockets for the key. He found it among a bunch of other keys linked together on a ring. The door opened into a dingy lightless corridor that led to a steep stone staircase. At the top of the stairs was another door. This too was locked. He found the correct key, pushed the second door open, and sniffed the night air. It was fresh and cold. He emerged into an alleyway in which a horse and carriage were waiting. Turning around, he locked the door, tested it, and walked toward the tethered animal.

"God bless you, Professor Klammer," he said. "God bless you!"

SOMEWHERE IN THE SCHOTTENRING station a clock struck five.

Rheinhardt was seated behind his desk, writing the concluding sentences of Liebermann's statement. When he had finished, he sat back in his chair, yawned, and offered Liebermann a cigar. Then he poured two glasses of slivovitz.

"The thing that I don't understand," said Rheinhardt, "is this: How is it that you managed to escape those bindings? You said . . ." Rheinhardt consulted the statement. " 'I discovered that the bindings were loosely tied and managed to free my hands.' But that strikes me as rather peculiar, that a man of Professor Priel's intelligence, a thorough man, should make such a fundamental error."

Liebermann sighed. "Well, I don't suppose it was quite as simple as that, but I think that my statement is perfectly adequate for administrative purposes."

"That may be so," said Rheinhardt. "However, you have now succeeded in arousing my curiosity, and if there is an explanation, I would be most interested to hear it."

Liebermann exhaled a cloud of smoke and sampled the slivovitz. "Do you still get this brandy from the Croatian scissors grinder?"

"Yes, I do."

"Why?"

"We have an arrangement. He gives me information and I buy his slivovitz. It's actually from his brother's market stall."

"I see."

Rheinhardt assumed an expression of patient suffering. The pouches of discoloration under his eyes were more marked than usual. He looked a little like a bloodhound.

"The explanation, Max?"

Liebermann took another slug of the slivovitz. "I must begin with Professor Freud."

"Freud? What has he got to do with it?"

"Overdetermination."

"What?"

"I'm sure I must have mentioned the concept before."

"I'm sure you have. Even so, would you care to refresh my memory?"

Liebermann tapped the ash from his cigar.

"A symptom is said to be *overdetermined* if it has more than one cause. The ease with which I was able to escape Professor Priel's bindings can be explained by the happy coincidence of three contributory factors—two of them physical, and a third that was psychodynamic. First, the muslin that Professor Priel had placed between the rope and my wrists—to stop my skin from chafing—allowed me to move my hands. It was a limited degree of movement, but considerably more than would have been possible otherwise. The second contributory factor, or cause, comes in the shape of Professor Willibald Klammer, a hand surgeon who currently resides in Munich."

"Max, you are being purposely obtuse—almost provocative."

Liebermann shrugged and continued. "Professor Klammer is the author of *The Klammer Method*, a system of piano exercises devised to enhance strength and flexibility: finger stretches, wrist rotations, and the like." Liebermann demonstrated. "I am a recent convert, and my Chopin Studies are much improved as a consequence. You should hear my Number Twelve now. The position changes in the left hand are seamless." He reached forward and played a few bars on the inspector's desk. "It would seem that the physical advantages conferred by The Klammer Method are not merely beneficial to students of the keyboard. They are, I have discovered, of equal benefit to would-be escapologists."

"And the third contributory factor?"

"Professor Priel's conscience, or at least that part of his conscience that operates below the threshold of awareness. Although he had identified me as a potential threat to his ambitious plans, he did not count me among the true enemies of Jewry. In truth, he did not want to kill me. Indeed, in order to perform the *unconscionable* act of my murder, he had to repress strong feelings of guilt. Professor Freud has proved that repressed material is rarely dormant. It always continues to exert a subtle influence on behavior, finding expression in slips of the tongue and trifling errors. I believe that Professor Priel did not tie the knots as hard as he might have on account of his unconscious guilt."

Rheinhardt smiled. "Well, Max. That is the most orotund explanation I have ever heard in my life." Rheinhardt opened his drawer and produced a paper bag full of *wiener vanillekipferl* biscuits. "Would you like one of these?"

"No, thank you."

"They're from Demel!"

The inspector looked at Liebermann as if his refusal to accept a biscuit from the imperial and royal confectioners were a sign of madness. He picked out one of the yellow crescents and was about to bite into it when he suddenly stopped.

"What's troubling you?" asked Liebermann.

"The kabbalist's lair," Rheinhardt replied. "How did Professor Priel manage to get all those things up into the attic room of the Alois Gasse Temple without being seen? We haven't really found an answer—which will be a significant omission in my final report."

"He bribed Rabbi Seligman's caretaker."

"How do you know that?"

"I asked Professor Priel and he told me."

Rheinhardt looked impressed. "And do you think this man, the caretaker, was in any way party to the murders?"

"No. His only involvement was with respect to creating the illusion of the kabbalist's workplace. Well, at least that is what I concluded from the way in which Priel spoke of their relationship."

Rheinhardt bit into his biscuit, and a shower of crumbs rained down on Liebermann's statement.

There was a knock on the door, and Rheinhardt called out, "Enter." Haussmann appeared with Professor Priel's barrel organ hanging from his shoulders.

"I'm sorry to interrupt, sir. But what should I do with this?"

Liebermann stood up, crossed to Haussmann, and inspected the painted exterior of the instrument.

"Ingenious." Liebermann opened the doors to reveal the leather-covered discs he had observed earlier and, winding the crank handle, watched them turn for the second time. In motion, the mechanism produced a sound reminiscent of a giant cicada.

"These upholstered plates are adjustable and close against the sides of the victim's face. A complex system of cogs and pulleys creates mechanical advantage, the factor by which a machine amplifies the force put into it. By means of a simple principle of engineering, Professor Priel became endowed with the strength of a golem." The young doctor pushed back a slat of wood on the upper surface of the box, creating a semicircular indentation. "This aperture is for the neck. After Professor Priel had concussed his victims, he rested the barrel organ on the ground, doors open, so that the head he intended to remove was covered. During decapitation, jets of blood issued from the major vessels, jets that would possibly have reached the professor had they not been contained within the barrel organ's casing. Once his monstrous work was done, Priel was at liberty to return to his carriage in the person of a poor itinerant organ-grinder, a *type* with whom we are all so familiar in Vienna. His presence would have aroused little suspicion, even in the early hours of the morning."

Liebermann reached into the barrel organ and wiped his finger across one of the wheels. He then raised his hand to display a red-black residue.

"Do you think he made this device himself?" asked Rheinhardt.

"Very probably. The means by which mechanical advantage can be achieved must be detailed in even the most rudimentary textbooks of engineering."

"Put it over there," said Rheinhardt to his assistant, indicating the far corner of the room. "And then I'm afraid I must ask you to go to Leopoldstadt."

"Why, sir?" asked Haussmann.

"To arrest Rabbi Seligman's caretaker." Rheinhardt turned to address Liebermann. "I will have to speak to Commissioner Brügel about the management of Professor Priel's trial. His intention to radicalize the Jews of Vienna must never be reported. I am thankful that Priel chose Sachs as his last victim. At least this will make it easier for us to ascribe his behavior to lunacy, and disguise his political objectives." Rheinhardt swallowed and added, "Although, of course, that may not be *so* far from the truth. His plan was absurd, wasn't it? Are stories and symbols so very potent? Could they really be used to unite and mobilize a whole people?"

"The Pan-Germans make much of their folklore . . ."

"Yes, but *really*, Max." Rheinhardt pushed the remains of his biscuit between his lips. While chewing he added, "Priel *must* be unbalanced—surely?"

Liebermann walked to the window. The sky was beginning to

lighten. He caught his reflection in the glass and touched the scabs on his cheek.

"Look at me!" he exclaimed. "I've got to go before the hospital committee in a few days. I look as though I've been brawling in a beer cellar!"

79

HERR POPPMEIER WAS SUPINE, looking up at the ceiling with a vacant expression on his face.

"You will recall that we were discussing your wife's second pregnancy." Liebermann spoke softly. "You said that you had traveled to Steyr on a work assignment, and it was while you were there that you received the telegram containing news of the stillbirth. But I could not help noticing, Herr Poppmeier, a small speech error that you made. When I asked you where you were when the telegram arrived, you started to say Linz, but you corrected yourself and said Steyr instead. This is very strange, because people tend to remember exactly where they were at the time when they first received momentous news. I am sure, for example, that you could tell me where you were when the empress Elisabeth was assassinated. Think, Herr Poppmeier. Think very carefully. Were you really in Steyr?"

"You know," Herr Poppmeier replied, "now that you mention it, my memories of that trip are a little vague. I've always put it down to shock. The news was so unexpected. Even so, I'm reasonably confident that I was in Steyr."

"No, Herr Poppmeier. You were not in Steyr. Your wife informs me that you were staying in Linz."

"Well, there you are," said Poppmeier. "My mind is playing tricks on me."

"And the question is, why should it be playing tricks on you? I would suggest that your memory has been distorted by a powerful wish. At the time when you received the telegram, you wished that you were not in Linz. You wished that you were in Steyr, and that is still the case."

"Why should I have wanted to be in Steyr? I had no friends there to comfort me, no special affection for the place."

"Then let me express the wish differently. It wasn't that you wanted to be in Steyr. Rather, you wanted to be somewhere else, anywhere else other than Linz. You chose Steyr simply because it was one of your usual destinations."

"Herr Doctor, this isn't helping me very much." Poppmeier scratched his head, and some flakes of dandruff fell onto the pillow. "This is all very confusing."

"Then let us consider again your recurring dream, which will—I believe—clarify matters. The action of the dream takes place in a hotel that you likened to the Kaiser in Steyr. Once again, note the desire to be away from Linz. You appear in the dream as a priest, which reveals the presence of another wish, a wish that you had been celibate."

"Ah yes," said Poppmeier. "I see what you mean. The dream is an expression of regret. If I had been celibate, if I hadn't made my wife pregnant in the first place, then the terrible confinement—and the baby's death—might have been avoided."

Liebermann tapped his pen on the chair arm.

"I favor another interpretation. After receiving news of your wife's fateful confinement, you wished you had been celibate . . ."—Liebermann hesitated before adding—"not back in Vienna, but in Linz."

Poppmeier rocked his head from side to side. "I'm not really following this. It doesn't make any sense."

"In your dream," Liebermann persisted, "you were asked by a pretty nurse to give a dying child the last rites, and you refused. The dying child is, of course, your own stillborn child, and your refusal to administer the last rites represents the understandable difficulty you experienced in accepting what had transpired. Denial. A very common response when—"

"Yes, yes," Poppmeier interrupted. "But what you said before. What did you mean, exactly? That I'd wished I'd been celibate in Linz?"

"You wished that you had not been conducting an assignation, Herr Poppmeier." The jewelry salesman gasped. "I suspect," Liebermann continued, "that the pretty nurse in the dream was your lover. When you read the telegram, you were horrified—not only by the news it contained but by your own iniquity, the extent of your betrayal. While you and your lover had been enjoying illicit pleasures, your wife had been suffering the agonies of a protracted labor, and had almost died attempting to bring your heir into the world. Subsequently, the memory of your dalliance in Linz was repressed. However, nothing in the unconscious is forgotten. The truth always asserts itself, if only when the censorship of the conscious mind is relaxed during sleep."

Liebermann leaned back in his chair and observed the effect of his pronouncements on his patient. Poppmeier's eyes were now glassy and unfocused.

"One must suppose," Liebermann added, "that your guilt was amplified by some residue of childhood. Your promised siblings did not arrive, and you may have concluded at that tender age that their advent was being prevented magically by your own desire to retain the exclusive attention of your mother. It is possible that a trace of this magical thinking still survives. Thus, somewhere in the depths of your mind you harbor a belief that your assignation exercised a malign influence on your wife's confinement."

Liebermann wondered what Herr Poppmeier was thinking, whether repressed memories of Linz were now rising up and breaking into awareness.

"You wanted to make amends. You wanted to atone. And for you, that atonement has taken the form of symptoms. They are a compensation for your prior neglect. They are a means of sharing the burden of your wife's current pregnancy. In effect, they are an apology and a reaffirmation of your love."

"Dear God," said Poppmeier hoarsely. "The train journey, the hotel bedroom . . . the woman. I had given her a ring from the Prestige range as an enticement. A heart-shaped ring—dear God—with an opal set in a decoration of perpendicular bars." Poppmeier's eyes closed tightly. His expression became anguished, and his lower lip trembled like a child's. Tears trickled down his cheeks. "What am I to do, Herr Doctor?" he groaned. "Must I tell Arabelle? Confess?"

Liebermann sighed. "That is for you to decide. Our work is done now. I would be very surprised if your symptoms persist."

The young doctor stood up, squeezed the jewelry salesman's shoulder, and quietly left the room.

80

LIEBERMANN WAS SEATED OUTSIDE a large double door. He had been waiting there for some time. His heart was beating with uncomfortable violence, and his palms were moist with anxiety. The committee room was located on an upper floor of the hospital, far removed from the wards. An unpleasant musty odor tainted the air, redolent of old wardrobes. Hanging from the wall at regular intervals were portraits of distinguished administrators and benefactors. Their expressions were either haughty or censorious. Liebermann stood and examined the likeness of Princess Stixenstein: sharp features, a cruel mouth, and a pale powdered complexion. The observer, gazing up at her disdainful visage, could not help but feel diminished.

From behind the doors came the sound of muffled voices.

Liebermann glanced at his wristwatch.

The hands had barely moved.

How much longer?

It was intolerable. Time seemed to have slowed down. Each extended second, inching forward, made every minute into an eternity.

Suddenly the hush was broken by the sound of footsteps. The double doors were flung open by a clerk who possessed the appearance and manner of a funeral director.

"Herr Dr. Liebermann?"

"Yes?"

"The committee is ready to see you. When you enter the committee room, proceed to the table and stand in front of the chancellor. Do not speak unless you are addressed first. Is that clear? Good. This way, please."

The clerk led Liebermann through an antechamber, and vanished as they entered a big ceremonial hall. At the far end was a long table, behind which sat five figures silhouetted against a row of tall rectangular windows. Liebermann followed the clerk's instructions and stopped in front of the chancellor, who occupied the central position. When their gazes met, Liebermann bowed.

"Thank you for coming, Herr Doctor," said the chancellor. "Before we proceed I would like to introduce you to my fellow committee members." He gestured to his right. "Dr. Eisler and Professor Roga." And then to his left. "Bishop Waldheim and Municipal Councillor Julius Schmidt." None of them responded to the introduction with any of the usual signs of courtesy. They sat impassively, observing Liebermann with granite faces. The chancellor consulted some papers and summarized the allegations made against Liebermann by Father Benedikt and the medical aspirant Edlinger. He then asked the committee members if they had any questions.

Schmidt raised his hand.

"Please proceed," said the chancellor.

"Thank you, Professor Gandler. Thank you." Schmidt leaned forward. "Herr Dr. Liebermann, these are very serious allegations, are they not?"

"Very serious indeed, sir."

"And do you have anything to say in your defense?"

"Although it is true that I prevented Father Benedikt from administering the last rites to the young Baron von Kortig, I did not use violence to achieve that end."

"You barred the priest's way."

"I placed my arm across a doorway, and he stopped."

"The aspirant—Herr Edlinger—who was present at the time is of the opinion that your behavior was threatening."

"That may have been Edlinger's perception. However, it was never my intention to threaten the priest."

"Then why did you do it? Why did you *physically* stop him from entering the ward?"

"I was concerned for the welfare of my patient. I did not—"

"Yes," Schmidt interrupted. "We know the reasons you gave for denying the young Baron von Kortig the consolation of his faith. But that is a different matter. The question I am asking concerns your conduct toward Father Benedikt. I repeat, why did you *physically* stop him from entering the ward?"

"I did not think he had given due consideration to the young baron's state of mind. I hoped that, after a moment's delay, he might review his position."

"Well, if I may say so, Herr Doctor, that strikes me as a remarkably arrogant thing to suggest. How could you possibly know what Father Benedikt had—or hadn't—considered?"

"Come now, Councillor," said Professor Roga. "I think Dr. Liebermann should be allowed to justify himself. That, after all, is why he is here today. You were saying, Herr Doctor, that you were concerned for the welfare of your patient. . . ."

Liebermann looked over to the professor, a dignified gentleman with kind eyes.

"Thank you, sir. The young baron had been given morphine and was oblivious of his condition. If Father Benedikt had begun to administer the last rites, this would have signaled the young baron's imminent demise. I believe that this would have caused him great distress. He was not mentally prepared to die."

"Herr Doctor," said the bishop, "do you think what you did was wrong?"

"I did what I thought was best for my patient," said Liebermann.

"Yes," said the bishop, "but was it wrong to stop Father Benedikt from administering the last rites to a dying *Catholic*?"

"I am a doctor," Liebermann continued. "When I am called to attend a patient, I do not see a Catholic patient, a Jewish patient, or a Muslim patient. I see only an individual in need of care, a fellow citizen of Vienna."

"But we are not all the same, are we?" said the bishop. "We are, in many ways, quite different."

"I do not believe that people are so very different," Liebermann replied. "Particularly when they are dying. In the final moments, we all want peace, not terror."

The bishop frowned. "If you encountered the same situation again, would you repeat your actions?"

"Yes," said Liebermann. "I would."

Eisler coughed into his hand and caught Liebermann's eye.

"Tell me, Herr Doctor, if you were asked to write a letter to the old baron explaining your reasons for denying his son the last rites, would you do so?"

"Yes, of course."

"And if you were also asked to include in that letter an apology— not for what you did but for causing the old baron distress—would you do that too?"

"Indeed."

Eisler and Professor Roga looked at each other and nodded.

"Well, gentlemen," said the chancellor, "I think we are in full possession of the facts. Could those who consider Dr. Liebermann's conduct unbefitting a physician in the employ of the General Hospital please raise their hands?"

The bishop and Schmidt registered their vote.

The chancellor looked to his left, and then to his right.

"Two in favor of Herr Dr. Liebermann's dismissal, and two against. It is therefore incumbent upon me as chancellor to resolve this matter by casting a vote." Professor Gandler sighed. "Herr Dr. Liebermann, I must be frank. I have not been impressed by your arguments.

Moreover, you have risked exposing the hospital to a damaging scandal. In my personal dealings with you I have found you to be rash, proud, and unwilling to accept advice. You cannot disguise poor judgment behind a veil of immature idealism and expect unanimous approval."

"Hear, hear," said Schmidt.

"This hospital needs good doctors," the chancellor continued. "It does not need self-appointed crusaders, an Order of Hippocratic Knights!" The chancellor paused before adding, "However, you acted in accordance with the necessities of your profession..." Gandler grimaced and uttered his final words with obvious discomfort. "And you will be retained."

"Gandler?" Schmidt was looking at the chancellor, bemused.

The chancellor's concluding remark was so unexpected that Liebermann was not confident that he heard it correctly.

"I can stay . . . in my post?"

"Yes," said the chancellor, unsmiling.

The bishop and Schmidt had begun a private conference.

"Thank you, sir."

"You may leave, Herr Doctor."

Liebermann bowed, turned on his heel, and walked briskly toward the antechamber. The sound of discontented voices followed him.

"Really, Gandler," Schmidt was saying. "This is quite unacceptable . . ."

Liebermann passed through the antechamber, and the moribund clerk opened the double doors to allow him back into the hall. As soon as they were closed behind him, Liebermann made an obscene gesture in the face of Princess Stixenstein, laughed hysterically, and ran toward the stairs. He skidded to a halt when he saw Rheinhardt waiting by the balustrade.

"What are you doing here?" said Liebermann.

"I wanted to be the first to know. Well?"

"I haven't been dismissed. I can stay in my post."

Rheinhardt embraced the young doctor and emitted a deep, resonant chuckle. "Then we must celebrate!"

They walked to the Café Landtmann and sat outside. Rheinhardt ordered mountains of food: *zwiebelrostbraten*, beef tenderloin with crisp onions; *krautrouladen*, cabbage stuffed with mincemeat, parsley, and pepper; *saure nierndln*, soured kidneys; and *warme rahmgurken*, warm cucumbers in cream sauce. He also ordered two bottles of red wine, one of which was consumed in a matter of minutes.

"You know," said Liebermann, "it's most peculiar. I really wasn't expecting the chancellor to vote in my favor. And the municipal councillor, Schmidt, seemed genuinely surprised, shocked almost. I could hear them arguing about it as I left."

"Well," said Rheinhardt, scooping a tangle of onions onto his fork, "perhaps he had good reason."

"What do you mean? Good reason?"

Rheinhardt pulled a face, a slightly pained expression.

"I have a small confession to make."

"What?"

"I wrote a note to the chancellor yesterday . . . and said that the security office intended to commend you to the emperor for an imperial and royal award. I mentioned that you recently helped us to foil a politically sensitive plot to foment racial discord." Rheinhardt shoveled the onions into his mouth. "I indicated that the judgment of the hospital committee would not look very good if they dismissed a doctor so rewarded by the emperor."

"And is it true?" Liebermann asked. "Is the security office really considering putting my name forward?"

"I raised the issue with the commissioner."

"And what did he say?"

"He said he'd think about it."

"Then you lied, Oskar!"

"Well," said the inspector, "that's a matter of opinion." He drained his wineglass and pointed at one of the dishes. "Try those kidneys. They're quite stupendous."

81

I was passing through Judenplatz and stopped to consider the relief depiction of the baptism of Jesus Christ. I can remember my father pointing it out to me as a child and explaining the meaning of the Latin inscription beneath. He doesn't read Latin, so he must have been recollecting what someone else— possibly his father—had told him. The translation he gave, as I remember it, was accurate enough. The inscription says, "By baptism in the River Jordan bodies are cleansed from disease and evil, so all secret sinfulness takes flight. Thus, the flame rising furiously through the whole city in 1421 purged the terrible crimes of the Hebrew dogs. As the world was once purged by the flood, so this time it was by fire." My father explained the nature of the event being commemorated and gave it a name: the first Viennese geserah.

Jews were accused of desecrating churches and of ritual murder. Jewish property was appropriated by the monarchy. The old synagogue—I imagine it must have been like the Old-New Synagogue in Prague—was burned to the ground and Jews were forcibly baptized. Those who refused were put to death in a great fire on the Erdberg. My father said something like, "The city authorities have not seen fit to remove this monument." I am not sure that then I understood what he meant. But it stayed with me because I was aware of his sadness and anger. Although it has taken six hundred years, progress *has* been made. Today, Jews may be insulted and abused, but they will never be consigned to the flames again. We Viennese are far too civilized.

I have arranged to see Miss Lydgate on Tuesday. We are going to a lieder concert—Mathilde Leibnitz with Kronenberg at the keyboard. Gretchen am Spinnrade is on the program. There are three women in every man's life. Wheels turn. Time passes. And she who is unattainable remains forever young, perfected by the inaccuracies of memory and unsatisfied desire.

Acknowledgments and Sources

I WOULD LIKE TO THANK: Hannah Black, Clare Alexander, and Steve Matthews for their valuable comments on the first and subsequent drafts of *Vienna Secrets*, Nick Austin for a thorough copyedit; Rebecca Shapiro, Jennifer Rodriguez, and Bara MacNeill for their assistance in preparing the U.S. edition; Simon Dalgleish for identifying German errors in the text; Luitgard Hammerer for conducting research on my behalf and providing a very good taxi service to Stift Klosterneuburg and the delightful Heurigen of Bisamberg; Penny Faith for casting a Jewish eye over the text; Dr. Julie Fox for describing the clinical signs associated with terminal syphilis; Dr. Yves Steppler, consultant pathologist, for lengthy and detailed discussions on the topics of decapitation and other aspects of pathology of interest to a crime writer; Her Excellency Dr. Gabriele Matzner-Holzer for assistance with establishing some helpful contacts in Vienna; Professor Karl Vocelka (University of Vienna) for providing me with a comprehensive list of the plague columns; and Nicola Fox—for comments, criticism, early proofreading, preliminary editing, and the odd plot contribution.

Das Vaterland was a real Catholic periodical, although I believe it might have been discontinued by 1903. Liebermann's explanation (to his father) of how dreams work can be found in Lecture 14 (Wish Fulfilment) of Freud's *Introductory Lectures on Psycho-Analysis*. The idea of a collective unconscious was current many years before Jung made the idea popular. Freud, and many others, considered the possibility of its existence throughout the nineteenth century (see *The Discovery of the Unconscious: The History and Evolution of Dynamic Psychiatry* by Henri F. Ellenberger). Lurian cosmology is paraphrased and quoted from two scholarly works on Jewish mysticism: *Kabbalah: A Very Short Introduction* by Joseph Dan and *On the Kabbalah and Its Symbolism* by Gershom Scholem. The subjects of demonology and animation are also considered in these works. The rite for keeping Lilith away from the marriage bed is quoted by Scholem in the chapter titled "Tradition and New Creation in the Ritual of the Kabbalists." More specific information about Isaac Luria, his ministry, and the practice of metoposcopy can be found in *Physician of the Soul, Healer of the Cosmos* by Lawrence Fine. Information about B'nai B'rith was based on passages in *Jewish Origins of the Psychoanalytic Movement* by Professor Dennis Klein. The golem legend and its variants are described in *The Prague Golem: Jewish Stories of the Ghetto* (a miscellany including the writings of Chajim Bloch) and *The Golem and the Wondrous Deeds of the Maharal of Prague* by Yudl Rosenberg. The idea that Freud was a closet kabbalist (or at least a secret enthusiast) is explored in *Sigmund Freud and the Jewish Mystical Tradition* by David Bakan. The 1965 edition contains a revised introduction by the author that suggests that Freud owned a collection of Judaica including kabbalistic writings (absent from the official Freud Library catalogue). There were two waves of pogroms in Russia. The first was between 1881 and 1884. The second started in 1903 (the year in which *Vienna Secrets* is set) and went on until 1906. All the atrocities described by Professor Priel are based on authentic accounts. Moreover, all the references to anti-Semitism are historically accurate (see *Karl Lueger: Mayor of Fin de Siècle Vienna* by Richard Geehr). The wall inscription celebrating the Holocaust of 1421 can be found at Judenplatz 2. Anna Katzer and Olga Mandl's description of their women's refuge is based on Bertha Pappenheim's lecture "Welfare for Female Youth at Risk," an excerpt of which can be found in *The Enigma of Anna O: A Biography of Bertha Pappenheim* by Melinda Given Guttmann. Other facts relating to prostitution and the white slave trade are also drawn from the same source. Miss Lydgate's account of the building of Santa Maria del Fiore and "On the Tranquility of the Soul" borrows substantially from *Brunelleschi's Dome* by Ross King. Song translations (including the poem "Silent Grief" by Ernst Koch) were taken from Richard Stokes's *The Book of Lieder*. Freud's speech on thumb-sucking is an almost exact transcription of a passage in his *Three Essays on the Theory of Sexuality*. Freud's views on Mozart's *Magic Flute* can be found in the celebrated Ernest Jones biography. Ivo Poppmeier's condition has been documented by physicians for centuries but is known today as couvade syndrome, a term first coined by Tylor (1865) in an anthropological context. The article that Schmidt reads in the *Wiener Tagblatt*—concerning Arthur Schnitzler—is an almost verbatim transcription from a real article published on January 14, 1903. Schnitzler's anecdote about Director Lautenburg is taken—with slight changes—from his memoir *My Youth in Vienna*.

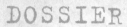

DOSSIER

Vienna Secrets

FRANK TALLIS

MORTALIS

Freud's Secret Books

SIGMUND FREUD WASN'T A very good Jew. He opposed his wife's desire to establish a Jewish home, and his son Martin wrote that the Freud children were raised "without any traces of . . . or instruction in Jewish ritual." None of them, as far as Martin could remember, ever attended synagogue. Even worse, the Freud family celebrated Easter and Christmas! Freud dismissed religion as an illusion, published a critical work on Judaism at a time when thousands of Jews were being transported to concentration camps, and was concerned that psychoanalysis might become a parochial branch of medicine practiced only by Austrian Jews. He didn't want psychoanalysis to become—as he put it—a "Jewish national affair." Indeed, this concern led him to name Carl Gustav Jung (known in psychoanalytic circles as the Teuton) as his successor.

Yet Freud had another, rather different side. He was an active member of a Jewish lodge, B'nai B'rith, played cards with Jews every Saturday night, and loved Jewish jokes. He is remembered today, of course, as a great "Jewish" thinker.

Where then did Freud really stand on the subject of his own religion?

In biographies of Freud, the word ambivalence appears repeatedly in this context. But really, there was nothing truly ambivalent about Freud's position. He thought religion was nonsense but at the same time had many of what Dr. Dennis B. Klein of Kean University has described as Jewish *attachments*. These attachments were encouraged and strengthened by the anti-Semitism that had become so widespread in fin-de-siècle Vienna. Freud once remarked that Jews had "no choice but to band together" for as long as they were being persecuted. Thus, his "Jewishness" was largely expedient rather than natural.

Yet, commentators have often remarked that it is impossible to think of Freud without registering—at some level—that he was a Jew, and psychoanalysis is frequently described as a Jewish phenomenon. The laws of motion would have been the same whatever creed Sir Isaac Newton had professed. If he had been a Hindu, then force would always equal mass times acceleration, and no one would ever have described the second law as an example of "Hindu physics." The same, however, cannot be said of Freud. Even though he rejected Judaism, the fact that he was a Jew still seems relevant to his system of psychology. There is undeniably something about psychoanalysis that "feels" Jewish. This isn't a racist proposition. Many historians of psychoanalysis have made this point, and Freud himself would have agreed, which is why he wanted Jung—the Teuton—to legitimize psychoanalysis for global consumption.

So what are we talking about here? What's so Jewish about psychoanalysis? It's relatively easy to identify resonances between psychoanalytic theory and Jewish stereotypes. Take, for example, the Oedipus complex and the attitude of Jewish mothers toward their sons. The following Jewish joke illustrates the point:

> How do we know that Jesus was Jewish? He lived at home until he was thirty, he went into his father's business, and his mother thought he was God.

The Jewish roots of psychoanalysis may, however, be far deeper. To explain the Jewishness of psychoanalysis, we must get beyond superficial stereotypes and journey into the world of Jewish mysticism.

Although Freud was a rational man, he was fascinated by religions and the myths of antiquity. That is why his consulting room was crammed with ancient figurines and statuettes—little gods and goddesses. He also wrote works on the origins of religious thought, Moses, totemism, the supernatural, and a seventeenth-century case of demonological neurosis. It should come as no surprise, therefore, to discover that such an individual was acquainted with the kabbala—a body of Jewish esoteric teachings dating back to the twelfth century.

When David Bakan's *Sigmund Freud and the Jewish Mystical Tradition* was first published in 1958, the author wrote a preface in which he argued that we cannot fully appreciate the development of psychoanalysis unless we view it against the history of Jewish mystical thought. There are indeed many similarities between kabbalistic writings and psychoanalysis: dream interpretation, symbolism, an interest in sexuality, and close attention to language. Kabbalists study the texts of holy books in much the same way as psychoanalysts study people. In both cases, small things—minute details—matter. Bakan's problem, however, was that there wasn't much direct evidence to support his thesis. That is, until he was contacted by Chaim Bloch, an eminent student of Judaism, kabbalah, and Hasidism, and a one-time acquaintance of Sigmund Freud.

Bloch recalled visiting Freud and, when left alone, taking the opportunity to examine the great man's books. What he saw was quite remarkable. In Freud's library was a large collection of Judaica, now absent from official collections and registers. Among these books were several volumes on kabbalah and a French translation of the Zohar (perhaps the most important work of Jewish mysticism).

In subsequent editions of Bakan's book, he introduced a new preface, and a paragraph that explains the significance of his discovery with particular reference to the Zohar:

It is without question the most important work in the Jewish mystical tradition. A number of features in the Zohar strongly suggest relationship to the psychoanalytic movement—among them the concept of man's bisexuality, and concepts of sexuality in general. There is also in the Zohar the notion that man can be studied by the exegetical techniques associated with the study of Torah; and a theory of the nature of anti-Semitism almost identical with that contained in Freud's Moses and Monotheism. Perhaps even more important, there is an atmospheric similarity—one which cannot indeed, be conveyed in any brief description.

Freud was anxious to be seen as a scientist and spent most his life distancing himself from religion. It is the greatest of ironies then that this supposedly rational, irreligious man might have been influenced by not just spiritual texts but spiritual texts of a mystical nature. If we accept Bloch's testimony, and with it Bakan's thesis, then psychoanalysis might be described as a late kabbalistic school of thought, which makes Freud not a scientist but a closet kabbalist: the last great mage of the Jewish mystical tradition.

I like the idea of Freud poring over his secret collection of magic books. It is a romantic and fitting image. One is reminded of the Talmudic legend of the *lamed vavniks*, the righteous men. At any given time there are thirty-six righteous men living in the world whose good deeds stop the world from ending. They accomplish their work in secret and are never rewarded. When one dies, another is born. And so it goes on from generation to generation: thirty-six anonymous Jews, standing—thanklessly—between civilization and ruin.

Frank Tallis
London, 2009

Sources

Bakan, David. *Sigmund Freud and the Jewish Mystical Tradition (with a new preface by the author)*. New York: Schocken Books, 1965.

Freud, Martin. *Glory Reflected: Sigmund Freud—Man and Father*. London: Angus and Robertson, 1957.

Klein, Dennis B. *Jewish Origins of the Psychoanalytic Movement*. New York: Praeger, 1981.

FRANK TALLIS is a practicing clinical psychologist and an expert in obsessional states. He is the author of *A Death in Vienna*, *Vienna Blood*, and *Fatal Lies*, as well as seven nonfiction books on psychology and two previous novels, *Killing Time* and *Sensing Others*. He is the recipient of a Writers' Award from the Arts Council England and the New London Writers Award from the London Arts Board. *A Death in Vienna* was short-listed for the 2005 Crime Writers' Association Historical Dagger Award. Tallis lives in London.